Susi Osborne lives in Cheshire with her husband and family and their two crazy dogs. It's a bit of a madhouse, but somehow they survive! She worked in a library for many years before moving on to become a classroom assistant in a junior school. She then became the carer for her mum for ten years when she suffered from Alzheimer's. More recently, Susi set up a successful business with her daughter. Vintage Adorables is based in Northwich Antiques and Collectables Centre. She also runs Northwich LitFest, which she started ten years ago.

Other books by Susi Osborne

The Ripples of Life
Grace & Disgrace
Secrets, Lies & Butterflies
Angelica Stone

To Lisa with all best wishes and very many thanks! x

Susi Osborne

Happiness is a Thing With Wings

Susi Osborne

The Book Guild Ltd

First published in Great Britain in 2022 by
The Book Guild Ltd
Unit E2 Airfield Business Park,
Harrison Road, Market Harborough,
Leicestershire. LE16 7UL
Tel: 0116 2792299
www.bookguild.co.uk
Email: info@bookguild.co.uk
Twitter: @bookguild

Typeset in 11pt Baskerville

Printed and bound in the UK by TJ Books LTD, Padstow, Cornwall

ISBN 978 1915122 551

British Library Cataloguing in Publication Data.
A catalogue record for this book is available from the British Library.

To my ever-faithful little dog, Alfie the cavapoochon, who has gazed at me with adoration throughout the entire process of writing this book. He has accidentally managed to delete the odd word here and there and has learned how to close the lid of my laptop when he thinks I should take a break. This book would have been completed much more quickly without his help but the pleasure of his company outweighed all. As a writing partner he is the best!

Chapter One

Okay, so a little gin wouldn't hurt – even if it was only four o'clock in the afternoon. Hendricks – why not? There was probably even a shrivelled piece of cucumber lurking in the fridge somewhere too – she might as well do it in style. She added crushed ice and retreated to the lounge. 'Alexa – play me some music.' And she settled down into her favourite chair, glass in hand. 'Have I Told You Lately That I Love You?' sang Rod Stewart. 'No, Rod, you haven't. You really, really haven't. But feel free to do so at any time.'

She was just having a bad day, that's all it was. The fact that it would soon be her forty-ninth birthday had nothing to do with it at all. In fact, forty-nine was nothing – well not nothing, obviously, but at least she'd still be in her forties. Still relatively young really. What did bother her, though, and even the gin was doing nothing to help, was that this would be the last year she'd be forty anything. In just one more year she'd be... she'd be... FIFTY?! How could that be? She was young! She had her whole life ahead of her! The world was her oyster! Or so it had been. So what had happened to it all? Where had it gone? She'd popped her oyster without even noticing. An oyster-popping life wasted.

Joanna thought back to her childhood. What a blissful time that had been when she hadn't had a care in the world, or so it seemed. But maybe there had been just a few blips in the idyll – like the spats she'd had with her sister about stupid little things like who owned what and why did they have to share. And, even worse, about having to share a bedroom – oh, she had really detested that. Her poor mother, what she'd had to put up with; Joanna smiled as she thought about it now.

A distant memory sprang to her mind. School. Some days she had just not wanted to go, particularly on the days when there was a spelling test. Who knew she was dyslexic? Not then. It had just seemed like all the people on her table were cleverer than her and she'd felt stupid. So one day she'd stood her ground and absolutely refused to go. No way was she moving. She'd sobbed and screamed and stamped her feet and, no matter how hard her mum had tried to persuade, beg, bribe her to go, she was staying put.

But suddenly, and quite out of character, her father had turned into a raging bull. With his cries of 'You WILL go to school!' echoing in Joanna's ears, he'd snatched the clothes prop down from the washing line in the garden and chased her all the way to school with it, sounding like some kind of wailing banshee. Everyone seemed to think it was hilarious. Everyone, that is, except for her. She had felt well and truly mortified.

Joanna wondered what would have happened if she'd still refused to move that day? Her dad had been such a gentle soul, he'd never laid a finger on her. Certainly he would never have done anything with that clothes prop even if she'd stood up to him, of that she was sure, but she'd been too much of a wimp to try. It had taught her a lesson though. She never did refuse to go to school again.

Looking back like this, it seemed life got tougher the older you got. Take puberty, for instance – adolescence. Even the words sounded cringeworthy. Maybe it wouldn't have been quite so bad if she hadn't had a sister. Sorry, Hannah, but there you have it. The thing was, not only had Hannah been younger and prettier, and the obvious choice from the two of them for all the local rampant, hormone-raging males of any value, she was also the sweetest person. Joanna blamed acne for a lot of this. Hannah had never had it, obviously – zits would run a million miles rather than take root upon her glowing complexion. She'd never got puppy fat either, the way Joanna had, nor had she stopped growing when she was five feet tall. No wonder Joanna had always been described as 'the grumpy teenager'; she'd had a lot of teenage angst to put up with whilst Hannah, in her elevated elegance, had smiled beguilingly at all without a care in the world. OMG, no – it hadn't been the best time of her life.

But then Joanna had met David. Not the starry-eyed thing she'd hoped for but the fact that someone had actually liked her without giving a backward glance towards Hannah had been enough for her. David. He'd seemed nice enough – solid, reliable, dependable. It was only later that… hmmm. Anyway, he asked her on a date, first one and then more. He was the first boy she'd ever kissed apart from a disastrous, teeth-clashing, slobbery attempt by Andrew Moore in year nine. Urgh, that didn't even count – made her feel sick just to think about it.

She'd been fifteen when she'd met David. Unsullied by human tongue in passionate embrace, unsullied by anything at all, come to that. Innocence personified, unlike the rest of the girls she knew – apparently. Looking back now, it was obvious the majority would have been lying, trying to make themselves look super-cool. When in reality their fertile bodies had merely been supplying fodder for their overly fertile imaginations. Nevertheless, when David asked her to be his girlfriend it had elevated her to the very top of the class ranking – in ways that mattered anyway. She became 'it'. Some may say she became the 'It Girl' of their year. Having a boyfriend had definitely been the way to gain status back in the day.

Joanna had enjoyed all of this notoriety. She hadn't loved David, didn't even fancy him and in fact he could be quite bossy at times, but it was worth hanging around with him, calling him her boyfriend, just to get her to the top of the popularity stakes in school. And it certainly had done that. Suddenly, instead of being the wilting wallflower with zits all over her face standing alone in a corner, she'd become Miss Popularity Plus and absolutely everyone wanted to hang out with her. Even her zits were doing a runner, knowing they were not welcome on that face anymore.

Through all of this newly found popularity, David hovered; he stuck with Joanna and she with him. It felt comfortable most of the time, like an old pair of slippers almost. Strewth – they'd been seventeen! And much as they indulged in a bit of a grope now and then, there seemed to be no sense of urgency to take things any further – even though their friends were under the impression they were at it like rabbits. That couldn't have been further from the truth. David thought they should save themselves for their wedding night and, to be fair, she didn't really fancy doing it much. And actually, she didn't really fancy him. Hang on a minute… wedding night?

Yes indeed. On her eighteenth birthday, fresh from a slap-up meal at McDonald's, David had got down on one knee and proposed. Well, what could she say? All of their best friends were watching, she could hardly say 'no' could she? And, what was even worse was that, after that day, everyone seemed to turn starry-eyed, even her parents – and even her sister to a certain extent. Everyone, that is, except for her. There was talk of nothing else, just 'the big day'. The dress, the church, the flowers, the reception, it went on and on and on. There was no escape; she would have hurt so many people, they would have lost money, they would have been so angry – she was on a roller coaster of supposed wedding bliss and there was no getting off now.

She wore his ring. People 'ooo-ed' and 'aahh-ed' over its beauty. Personally, she felt she knew how it was for a pig now when it had a ring through its nose. Why hadn't she stopped it all, called it to a halt? Naively, she'd somehow pretended to herself she'd be sparing other people's feelings. In reality, it was because she was a wimp – a wimp who was digging a deeper and deeper hole and climbing all the way into it. A bottomless pit.

There was just one thing about all of this wedding malarkey that Joanna really had looked forward to and that was the hen party. It meant freedom – a whole night of going out and doing what she wanted to do without David watching her every move. Her best friend at the time had been Gemma, still was her best friend in fact, and she had organised a minibus to take them to Jaxx, the trendiest club at the time. Joanna was buzzin'. This was going to be the best night ever. She spent longer deciding what to wear and doing her hair and make-up than she ever would on her wedding day.

Under normal circumstances she wasn't a big drinker back then (oh how times had changed!) but that night was special – it was her hen night for goodness' sake – and everyone was buying her drinks. Amazingly, she managed to keep her head and keep her wits about her, despite the pressure to do otherwise. Admittedly, she got tipsy, but she didn't get plastered – after all, if everyone keeps buying drinks for you it doesn't mean you have to drink them all does it? She could be sensible when she wanted to be, and she was – up to a point. And the point in question came in the form of Gabriel. It was almost as if he'd been sent, like an angel, to rescue her. Except he certainly didn't guide her along the path of righteousness – far from it in fact.

It was weird for Joanna looking back to that night. It was a moment in time that she had kept locked away in the back of her mind. A memory to be taken out occasionally and dusted, just so that it wouldn't disappear forever – it had been too important for that. Even though it had been so long since she'd revisited it, every moment of that night still played out clearly in her mind. His touch, the fragrant scent of him... Pour Homme by Paco Rabanne.

She'd gone hunting around men's toiletries departments sniffing at aftershaves for days afterwards trying to track it down as though somehow, by finding it, Gabriel would reappear. She remembered how his eyes had drawn her in, like a helpless insect all a-flutter drawn into a spider's web. And it hadn't been reluctantly, not at all, it was as though it had been fate – it was meant to be.

When they'd kissed it had unleashed something inside her she never knew existed before, a torrent of passion that left her body screaming for more. Somewhat intoxicated but nevertheless, her friends noticed – how could they not? It didn't take a degree in chemistry and nor would it need a sparky to see the electricity that sizzled between them. Gemma was getting a bit concerned. As the person in charge of the hen night she'd felt a sense of responsibility despite the alcohol. 'Don't forget about David... er, about the wedding, Jo,' she'd whispered in her ear. But it had fallen on deaf ears, obviously. Gemma had reminded her about the room they'd got booked at the Travelodge, about the minibus... but no.

Instead: 'I have a room at the Premier Inn – come with me?' he asked, the ocean-blue pools of his eyes flowing like a tidal wave into hers. Passion flooded through her, a sudden longing – an urgency the likes of which she had never felt before.

'Joanna!' said Gemma, with all the firmness she could muster.

'Yesss,' gasped Joanna, still trying to draw breath.

'Joanna – don't be stupid! You don't even know him,' pleaded Gemma.

But Joanna was full steam ahead, there was no way she was turning back now.

*

'Darling – I'm home!'

'Shit!' Joanna muttered under her breath – what a moment to pick. Just as she'd been about to relive one of the most beautiful moments of her life. And why does he have to call me darling when he so clearly doesn't mean it? So annoying! As you can tell, Joanna really loves her husband. Not.

'You drinking already?' he asked as he came into the lounge, eyes focusing on her glass

'Yep. Do you have a problem with that?'

'Just seems a bit early, that's all.'

Without a further glance in her direction, David picked up the remote and turned on the TV, channel-hopping for a while before settling for *Catchphrase* or some such mindless programme. Not even watching, he picked up the newspaper from where it lay dormant on the coffee table, glanced at the headlines, opened it up and started to read. Predictably, it didn't take long until he was asleep. Head back and lolling to one side, mouth open, snoring. Jeez. She got up and left the room.

Joanna had been enjoying the silence, the peace and quiet, the memories, the gin. No more. In the kitchen she tipped away the remaining dregs from her now-empty glass, chomping on the gin-infused slice of cucumber before she put the glass into the dishwasher – 'Waste not, want not,' her mother had always said. God, how she hated him – how much longer could she go on living like this? It felt almost as if there was a cauldron in her stomach – a permanent pot of anger bubbling up inside.

Double, double toil and trouble;
Fire burn and cauldron bubble.

Sadly, she didn't have a baboon's blood to cool it down. Well… don't even go there, Joanna.

Gin-infused cucumber finally swallowed, she was drawn to the snack cupboard like a magnet. Chocolate, it had to be. You see, this is where she always went wrong, she knew it. Hannah would never do this – that's why she was as slim as an anorexic stick-insect. But then, she had a happy life – she didn't need comfort food. Was that a Bounty lurking at the back there? It was! Hallelujah – she hadn't had one of those for ages. Chocolate… coconut… yum, her mouth salivated prolifically at the prospect. She tore at the wrapper like her life depended on it.

'Mum! I thought you were on a diet.'

Jeez, can you not do anything for pleasure round here? 'I am. I was. I needed it. I've had a bad day. What other explanation do you need? Anyway, what are you doing home already? I thought you were working late tonight.'

Jack grinned at her – he loved winding her up, she was always such an easy target. 'I was meant to be but the rotas got changed. Working late tomorrow now instead. What's for dinner and how long will it be?'

'Erm, whatever you're cooking and whatever time you're cooking it, Jack. Just because I'm a woman it doesn't mean I'm your slave you know – it's my day off today,' she teased.

Still grinning, he kissed her on the cheek. 'Sorry, I didn't mean to rattle your cage. Eat your Bounty, sounds like you need it. I'm just going up to get changed then I'll come down to help.'

'What? I have your full permission to eat it now, do I? You're so generous.'

'Oh I know, Mama – that's why you love me.' And with a cheeky wink of his eye he was gone.

*

Jack. He was the light of her life, that was for sure. Twenty-nine years old and still at home. 'A mummy's boy?' some may ask. But no, not at all. And they wouldn't even ask if they knew him; he was certainly too independent for that. He'd gone away to uni at eighteen – well, to drama school actually, in London. Acting was his passion, although he'd always excelled in dance too – and he had a great singing voice. Quite an all-rounder really.

Joanna had been very proud of him – still was, obviously.

She'd wondered at that time whether he might have been gay. Not that it would have bothered her or anything, in fact she would have been quite pleased. Having never had a daughter it would have been nice to have a gay son to do girly stuff with sometimes. Jack had never given her any real reason to think this, it was just that he'd never mentioned any girlfriends and any of the guys he'd introduced her to had always been obviously that way inclined. But then, she supposed theatrical types did tend to be like that – overly dramatic and full of fun. Just the kind of people whose company she enjoyed really. And who cared who was what anyway these days? She certainly didn't.

Jack had stayed in London for a while after his course had ended. Got himself an agent and bits and pieces of acting work but nothing major. He'd shared a tumbledown, squalor-infested house in Stockwell with three other guys, people he'd never met before who'd been advertising a room to let, and he found himself a job in a bar to pay his share of the rent. It wasn't the best time for him. Tensions ran high in the house. Turned out one of the guys was a dealer – weird people at the door at all hours. As for the other two, they seemed permanently smashed out of their skulls. Not a good place to live, not at all.

Jack hunted around for somewhere else to live, somewhere within his meagre budget, but it seemed to be a physical impossibility. In a cubbyhole under someone's stairs maybe? Or on a friend's sofa? Joanna had been terrified he'd end up sleeping rough on the streets somewhere. In the end he admitted defeat and asked if he could come back home.

Well of course he could – what a silly question! Joanna had been more than happy to have him home again. Not only did it mean she no longer had to worry about him living in those less-than-desirable circumstances in London, but she was really glad to have his company – he was always so full of life. It made such a refreshing change to have him around instead of it being just her and David. Laughter echoed throughout the house again, overriding that heavy, cloying unhappiness she'd felt when it had been just the two of them alone. In fact, 'alone' had been exactly how she'd felt.

Jack managed to get himself a Manchester agent and, amazingly, started getting sent on lots of auditions – vital for any actor, obviously. Little bits of work trickled in – slowly, but nevertheless… He saw a job advertised for a cocktail bartender in Knutsford, which he was overjoyed to get, in addition to one at the local gym. As an actor, it was always difficult to find any jobs that would be willing to be a bit flexible when it came to auditions. However, in both of these places, they appeared to be willing to take a chance on him – thankfully.

'Yeah – it's obvious, they couldn't resist me. It's my amazing good looks and effortless charm that did it. I mean, just look at that face!' schmoozed Jack, gently caressing his jawline with his right hand as he peered into the mirror. 'OMG – what a beautiful specimen I am.'

'Oh, shut up,' laughed Joanna, slapping him playfully on the shoulder. 'You're so full of yourself.'

*

As the weeks passed by, with each slotting happily and with ease into their new routines, life settled down again. Life within the house as a trio rather than a duo, or the uno that it had actually felt like, was so much happier for Joanna, certainly. As for David, he hardly seemed to have noticed. As long as he had his TV and newspaper without interruption, and could drift off to sleep whenever he desired, then life was morosely good.

Jack had certainly settled in well. He was an outgoing, easy-to-get-along-with kind of guy and nothing had changed. And considering acting, bodybuilding and alcohol were his three biggest passions, he was certainly in the best three jobs he could ever have wished for. He soon became Mr Popular Plus. Both at the gym and at the cocktail bar, he was surrounded by young people and it didn't take him long to make new friends. He was certainly a babe magnet. If Joanna had ever had any doubts about his sexuality in the past, that was certainly not the case now.

'Good to see you having fun, but just remember – wear a condom,' Joanna would say, almost every time she saw him disappearing through the door for yet another night out.

'Mother, I'm not a child.'

'Hah – I should hope you're not! I wouldn't be saying that if you were.'

Chapter Two

Hannah, her sister, lived only a short drive away and Joanna went over to see her quite regularly. On rare occasions, like today, she would leave the car behind and jog. But not often, she really wasn't the jogging type – far too lazy for that. However, today's sudden little spurt of energy had really been to assuage the guilt of the gin and of all the chocolate bars she'd consumed these past few weeks. Hmm... really? Just one chocolate bar consumed each day for three weeks equals twenty-one calorie-laden slabs of naughtiness. And, don't forget to add to that two G&Ts a day – at least. Jeez, that's forty-two G&Ts! Even though it was slimline tonic, that's an awful lot of blubber to be jogged off.

Having said that, she'd just worked out that calculation in her head as she was jogging along. That alone must have burnt off a fair few calories. And the fact that the blubber itself was bouncing up and down with each step she took must count for something. She'd be as slim as a stick of celery by the time she got there. Ugh – celery. Greenery of any kind actually – it was far too healthy.

She was wearing her new Lycra outfit. That was one of the main reasons for jogging today, in fact – she'd wanted to show it off. She'd thought having the whole kit and caboodle brand new would be the way forward – make her want to exercise more. A motivational 'new start, new you' kind of thing. She even had new trainers, for goodness' sake – leopard print fronts with luminous pink bits around the sides. Well she couldn't wear plain boring ones that any old trainer-girl would wear now, could she? And as for the outfit – leggings with a matching vest top. Quality it was. Black Lycra. Not the cheapo imitation stuff, none of that, this was the real expensive kind. Designer. And it had luminous pink stars on it – subtle, not chavvy in any way – to match the trainers, obviously.

When she'd seen herself in the mirror in the shop there'd only been one word to describe it – stunning! Now she was not so sure. Her buttocks felt more like two enormous bouncy balls and all she could hear was the sound of her thighs rubbing together. Actually – could that create a fire if it went on for long enough? Like rubbing two sticks together – she'd seen that on *I'm A Celeb*! Maybe not, there's no way her legs could ever be compared to two sticks. But as for her boobs, they were almost taking off, they certainly had two minds of their own – freaky. At 38FF she really needed to buy herself a sports bra before deciding to jog anywhere ever again. This was painful.

Panting, and sweating somewhat profusely, she finally arrived. Propping herself up against the door jamb, she rang the bell. The sound of its jingling heralded her relief. She'd made it – she'd arrived! But then a sudden flurry of worry shot through her. What if her sister wasn't at home? What if she'd gone out? Why hadn't she thought to ring her and check before she'd set off? Joanna slapped her hand against her forehead in frustration – she was such a klutz at times.

She rang the doorbell again starting to panic a little now. It wasn't even as though she could wait round the back – they always kept the side gate bolted against burglars – and intruding sisters. Nothing else for it, if she didn't answer the door in a minute she'd just have to curl up on the doormat and die, she certainly was in no fit state to jog all the way back home again. It might have helped if she'd had her mobile with her but no, as always in times of need, she'd forgotten it. 'Stupid, stupid, stupid!' she cried, slapping her forehead again with each word. One last ring and then the doormat it would have to be.

This time, as if by magic, the door opened and Hannah appeared – a little bit out of breath and looking somewhat frazzled, but obviously not as much so as Joanna.

'Hey you – sorry, I was just in the middle of changing Lottie's nappy.' Her face suddenly registered Joanna's sweaty, dishevelled appearance. 'Whatever happened to you?'

'I jogged here,' gasped Joanna, relief, exhaustion, a feeling of triumph, or a combination of all three suddenly washing over her as she staggered through to the sitting room where she was immediately pounced upon by Woofles, their gorgeous rescue dog.

'Hey Woofles, that's right, give me a wash – I could certainly do with it,' she laughed, as the fussy little fluffball proceeded to lick away all her sweat with his tongue. 'Ooh, you are so gorgeous,' she said, making a big fuss of him, 'I could just take you home with me.'

'Take him – have him, I'd be glad of the peace.'

'Yeah right – imagine your reaction if I did. And even worse – picture David's face if I walked in through the door with him.'

'Hmm, yeah – bad idea, maybe not. Anyway, what's with the jogging again? Where did the inspiration come from this time? And, incidentally – why are you dressed like Bertie Bassett?'

'Cheek! What do you mean, Bertie Bassett?'

'Well, y'know – those Liquorice Allsorts, the round ones with the bright pink sugary bits stuck on.'

'Hannah!'

'Sorry – couldn't help it,' laughed Hannah. 'Why though? What's with all this jogging malarkey again? You're just not a keeping fit kind of person. I have to say though, I love the way you have to have the full outfit – no just pulling on an old pair of tracky pants for you, is there? And as for the trainers…'

'I know – they're crippling me though, my feet will be covered in blisters. Bad idea to buy new trainers and then go running miles in them the very first day you put them on. I need to do something though, Hannah – look at all this blubber I'm piling on. It's all right for you – always were like a beanpole, weren't you? Me – I only have to look at a bar of chocolate and an extra flab roll grows overnight. I might not look quite so bad if I was taller but, at this size, I seem to be turning into a ball – a football actually, rugby balls are a much nicer shape than me.'

Hannah grinned. 'Oh Jo, you do make me laugh. Okay, you're a bit on the chubby side I suppose but that's you, we're all different shapes and sizes. Think how boring the world would be if we all looked the same, just be proud of who you are.'

'I am – most of the time. It just gets to me a bit sometimes, that's all. So I thought, well, why not try and do something about it again?'

'Good on you if you feel like that – but make sure you're doing it for you, though, nobody else. David's not been having a go at you, has he?'

'Well, you know how it is – the odd comment here and there in his rare speaking moments. Always in front of other people, though, just to show me up – in fact usually in front of one of Jack's ever-changing collection of gorgeous, young, slim females. Think he does it to make himself look big but I don't think he's looked in the mirror lately.'

'Ignore him – stupid little man. He doesn't know how lucky he is that you've put up with him for all these years. I don't know how you've done it, to be honest, you're worth so much more.'

'You would say that – you're my sister.'

'But it's true. You could have had anybody and yet you've stuck with that idiot. He doesn't deserve you, truly he doesn't, you could have had a much better life without him.'

'I know. And I don't know why I've stuck with him either. Force of habit I guess. Such a big step to take.'

'It's never too late, Jo – never too late.'

The two of them babbled away like they always did when they were together. There had never been a cross word between them – well, not since they'd been in their teens at any rate. They were not only sisters but the very best of friends as well and supported each other always.

'Anyway, enough of all that – where's Lottie? That's who I came to see really – is she asleep?'

'Yes, I was just getting her changed to put her down for an hour when you were ringing the doorbell – that's why I was a long time coming.'

'Sorry – and here's me with my "poor me" saga instead of asking about the love of your life – well, about the two loves of your life. How is Marcus coping with daddyhood and everything?'

'Yeah, fine.' Unexpectedly a sudden cloud of anguish descended over Hannah's face, replacing the usual glow of happiness which, on other occasions, had always radiated from her whenever Marcus's name was mentioned. 'I'll put the kettle on – not had a drink today yet.'

'Neither have I. Do you have Hendricks? Or any gin will do.'

'I didn't mean alcohol, you klutz, I was going to make some tea. I've got herbal if you'd prefer?'

'No ta, I'll stick with the gin. Have one, it'll do you good.'

'Can't. Breastfeeding.'

'Will you just listen to yourself? You always were such a Snow White. Here – have one,' said Joanna, taking control and heading to the wine cabinet. 'I'm sure one won't affect Lottie, and it'll do you a whole lot of good. I've never seen you look so stressed. Don't worry so much. I remember Mum telling us she actually used to put a bit of brandy in our bottles to make us sleep sometimes and it never did us any harm, did it? Not that I'm suggesting you do that or anything, but your having one small G&T while you tell big sis your problems is not going to harm Lottie. In fact, a de-stressed mummy can only be good for her.'

With a sigh of resignation, Hannah sat back down again and accepted the drink. In fact she took a large gulp of it before Joanna had even started. The latter noticed. Things really must be bad, this was so uncharacteristic of Hannah.

'I'm worried, Jo. Everything's changed. We were so excited that we were actually going to have a baby after all of this time – the stress of all those rounds of IVF, the money, the toll it's taken on us both. It actually brought us even closer together knowing that at last we were going to be a proper family, we loved each other so much. But then Lottie was born, the dream became the reality and suddenly everything changed.

'It's as though Marcus can't bear to share me with anyone else, he wants me there with him all the time, doting on him like I used to, having sex… And I can't, I haven't got the energy for one thing even if I wanted to. He hasn't bonded with Lottie at all, doesn't do anything for her, just leaves it all to me and says he's been working. I can't believe he's acting like this – a baby was the dream for both of us, not just for me. He says he still loves me and even after all this I still love him too but I can't cope and I don't know what to do – I'm scared he's going to leave me, Jo, and I couldn't bear it, I love him, he's my life.

'And, much as I love Lottie, sometimes… and I hate saying this, but sometimes I actually begrudge her being here. I know she can't help it and it's not her fault, it's ours, but I feel like her very existence has created such a huge wedge between us that our marriage won't be able to survive. Marcus will leave and I'll be left in absolute tatters. He's my world, I can't live without him, he's my life. And if he goes and I'm left here on my own with Lottie, how would I feel about her then? I know in my heart of hearts that I'd blame her for evermore. And yes, I know, that's a horrible thing to say.'

Joanna was shocked, finding it hard to grasp. This baby had been so longed for, they'd always been such a loving couple, Marcus being thought of as the perfect man – how could this be?

'Does this make me a bad person?' responded Hannah to her sister's silence.

'Of course you're not a bad person. I'm just shocked, that's all – at Marcus's reaction to fatherhood more than anything. I honestly thought he'd be besotted with her, especially after so many years of struggling to achieve your dream, both so desperate for a baby. All those years of hospitals and tests, egg donors, failed IVF attempts and the money it all cost – as well as the heartache and the anxiety it caused knowing that the years were ticking by. I'll never forget the look on his face the day you came round to tell me you'd had your twelve-week scan and everything was okay – it was like some kind of miracle. I don't think I've ever seen a daddy-to-be look more relieved or happy.'

'I know, I remember, he was absolutely giddy with excitement, wasn't he? We both were. I just don't understand this at all.'

'Look, let me help. Maybe in time he'll settle down a bit. It's hard for anyone at first trying to adjust to being a new parent. I could pop over in the daytime sometimes – take her out for a walk to give you a break. Or perhaps for an evening now and again, so you and Marcus could go out for a meal, have a "date night" or something, spend a bit of quality time together. How about that – would it help at all? Couldn't do any harm, could it – shall we give it a try?'

The vague glimmer of hope registered as a wobbly smile on Hannah's face. 'I'll try anything – thank you. Whatever it takes, I just know I can't lose him.'

'Seriously, call me, I mean that. Any time, day or night, whenever you need me. Give me a ring even if you just need to offload – or I don't mind coming over, it's not as though I'm far away. I know what motherhood is like, that in itself is exhausting, especially at first. But with all of your other worries as well, no wonder you're so stressed. Come here, let me give you a hug, and try not to worry. Hopefully things will work out, it's still early days yet.'

Hannah sobbed as Joanna held her in her arms, releasing some of the tension she'd been holding in for so many days. Letting it go – so glad she had been able to share her problems with her sister, no one else would have understood. And almost as though her baby was still a part of her body and thus was feeling her sadness, a cry came from the bedroom almost echoing her own. Lottie was awake.

'I'll see to her,' said Joanna, 'you sit down.'

'She'll want feeding. Don't think you'll be able to manage that somehow – your equipment will be a bit shrivelled up after thirty years.'

'Ha ha! And unfortunately that's probably not my only bit of equipment that's laid dormant for so long it's shrivelled up.'

'Joanna – too much information!'

'Oh, don't go getting all prudish on me. We aren't all married to a Mr Super Stud you know – sadly the complete opposite in my case. Anyway, enough of me, sit down and have a sip of your drink, I'll go and get madam before she screams the house down. Got a good pair of lungs for one so tiny.'

'Mother's ruin.'

'What?'

'Gin. Isn't that what they call it?'

'Oh shut up.'

Joanna felt so sad for them as she eventually made her way back home. She had intended to jog but her heart just wasn't in it. A walking pace was all she could manage as she mulled things over in her mind. She hated to see Hannah looking so vulnerable. Of the two of them she'd always been the happy and confident one although Joanna could see now that had all stemmed from knowing how much she was loved. In the past Hannah had said how Marcus 'made her feel like a princess every day.' She supposed having someone there to make you feel that special would be enough to make anyone feel confident. She wouldn't know, she hadn't had it.

Until today's revelations, Joanna had always felt quite jealous of Hannah with her perfect marriage to the perfect man. Joanna? Jealous? No. Well maybe just a little bit. For not only had he been the perfect husband, he was... he was actually the fittest man she had ever seen. Oh shut up, Joanna, you can't go getting the hots over your brother-in-law – it's practically incestuous. Hmm, Marcus. He was tall, slim, muscular – chiselled jaw, come-to-bed eyes, mischievous sparkle – the list was never-ending. If only. If only what? If only he hadn't been her sister's husband.

But Marcus, he must be pretty desperate by now since marital duties in the post-baby household had been severely rationed. She remembered Hannah saying in the past what a high sex drive he had and what a massive part of the marriage their sex life had been. She'd felt so envious at the time wondering where she'd gone wrong. Thinking about how she'd only ever been with two men in her entire life. Realising that she'd not actually slept with anyone in that way for years, even though she did share a bed with David every night. She probably wouldn't even know how to do it anymore. Hmm, stop fantasising, Joanna – you're almost fifty for goodness' sake!

*

She had a shower when she got home – a cold one. David was home too by the time she got downstairs.

'Didn't hear you come in.'

'I shouted upstairs to you, darling, but I could hear the shower running so thought I'd leave you in peace.'

Darling. That word again. But at least he was awake.

'Have you seen the newspaper? It's usually here. Can't find it.'

'Sorry, not seen it.'

'What have you done with it – could you look for it?'

'But I was just going to make dinner.'

'I need my newspaper and you've obviously hidden it somewhere. You must know where you put it. Find it NOW – I won't tell you again!'

Oh God, here we go. He could go from zero to off the Richter scale in seconds. 'I haven't even seen your newspaper, I don't know where it is. I've got to make dinner, Jack will be home in a minute.'

'Why do you hide my stuff all the time? I need it and I need it now – you're ALWAYS moving my things! You know I need to read my newspaper when I get home – find it, Joanna, NOW!'

'No. Find it yourself – I'm busy.'

The blue touch paper had been ignited, sparks flew across the room.

'ARE YOU DEFYING ME?' he leapt from his chair to confront her, face pushed angrily into hers. 'Find my newspaper and find it now,' he growled.

Why did she put up with this? What was she even doing here? 'You stupid little man! Find your own sodding newspaper if it's that important.'

His whole stature seemed to puff up with the ugliness of his anger at moments like this – towering over her, almost like an eagle hovering over its prey, he backed her up against the wall.

She refused to be intimidated by him. He was just a pathetic, arrogant bully with an over-inflated ego. 'Jack will be here at any minute,' she said, in a voice so much calmer than she felt. 'Why d...'

'Hello, hello, hello – what's going on here then? Parents caught having a quick snog in the kitchen before dinner? Standards are slipping around here, I must say – I could be scarred for life.'

Jack.

She had to admit, it must have looked a bit like that, seeing them pressed up against the wall with David towering over her. She hadn't heard him come in. It took her a minute or two to pull herself together. 'Sorry, I... oh!' she exclaimed, looking towards the kitchen door in sudden shock.

'Oh yes – this is Pixie, she works with me.'

Joanna had never seen anyone look less like a Pixie, if she was honest – but hey. 'Welcome – pleased to meet you. Sorry about before,' she said, trying to force a smile on her face and gather herself together.

David, of course, was all charm – an instant transformation. 'Pixie, eh? A beautiful name for a beautiful lady,' he said, stepping towards her and kissing her on both cheeks, looking like some dirty old lech.

'Hiya,' she said, looking somewhat embarrassed at the whole scenario.

'Joanna's about to cook. You're welcome to stay and eat with us if you'd like to – although I can't guarantee what it'll taste like, she's not exactly the best of cooks,' David guffawed, rolling his eyes towards the ceiling.

If looks could kill.

Pixie giggled, hand over her mouth, gazing meaningfully at Jack.

'Oh yeah. Right. Yeah. No – it's okay. I just popped back home to get changed and let you know I'm eating out tonight. Pixie's been telling me about this new place that's opened in town – thought we'd give it a go. Sorry Mum,' he said, suddenly noticing the look on her face – a look he couldn't quite fathom, actually.

David, of course, seized the moment. 'She likes him tied to her apron strings of course, that's the problem,' he said, putting his arm around her. 'Isn't that right, darling?'

OMG. She'd throw up in a minute.

Pixie grabbed Jack by the arm. 'Come on then, Jack-yyy. I booked a table – we don't want to be late.'

'Sorry, Mum,' he repeated once more.

*

The next morning normality appeared to have been restored. That was always the problem for Joanna. He could explode without any warning, like there'd been a flick of a switch, and then just a few hours later he'd be back to normal. Crazy – and increasingly difficult to live with. It was like starting out in a marriage with a clean sheet of paper but then, every time there's an explosion, the paper gets screwed up into a ball. You straighten it out but it's crumpled and can never be quite the same again. The thing is, how many times can that same piece of paper get screwed into a ball before there's some serious damage? How long does it take before the paper gets worn into holes and can never be used again?

'For goodness' sake – get a grip,' she said to herself. 'That's far too deep for this time of day. It was an argument over a stupid newspaper, that's all.' But that wasn't all. And she knew it.

*

At work later that day she sat at her desk and pondered over it again. Why did she stay with him? What was the point? In the past she'd always convinced herself she was staying for Jack's sake. That it was better for him to be growing up with two parents rather than one. But she could hardly make that her excuse now, could she? Jack was almost thirty years old with a life of his own; he was perfectly capable of looking after himself – even if he did choose not to sometimes!

She smiled when she thought about her errant son with his seemingly ever-increasing string of girlfriends. He was certainly enjoying himself at the moment, and she was glad that he was. No way did she ever want him to be trapped in a loveless marriage, as she had been. She just hoped when he did find someone he wanted to commit to, that it would be someone nice, and someone that she could get along with too. That was really important to Joanna. She'd heard so many stories from other women about how their daughter-in-law was an absolute psycho who had been hell-bent on destroying their family. There was no way she would ever let that happen to them.

Her thoughts strayed to David. Sad, really, that she'd never felt totally in love with him. Basically, she'd just fallen into a marriage and then stayed there because it had seemed like the easiest thing to do. And yet it had been far from easy. David had always had a temper, she'd known that from the start, but she was used to it and she'd put up with it – stupid really. How much longer was she going to allow herself just to drift along in a loveless marriage? What was the point? You had one life and one life only. Maybe it was the thought of another birthday looming that was making her feel this way. In a couple of months she would be forty-nine. As for the birthday after that – she could hardly bear to think about it. Something had definitely got to change before that point – if not sooner.

Chapter Three

So okay, here was the plan – part one. She was willing to give their marriage one last chance before committing it to the trash can forever. What? Really?! Yes, truly. Very noble of her really, she thought, considering the circumstances. Or very wimpish of her, more like – divorce and pastures new were a much scarier thought than maintaining the status quo.

As it was, the plan had fallen into place itself really. Maybe it was fate. Jack wouldn't be home for dinner that night, he'd texted to tell her earlier. He was going out with Pixie, or Poxie, or whatever the heck her name was. *Let's hope for her own sake it wasn't the latter, thought Joanna with a fleeting wry smile.*

Having worked all day she had just been planning to have something simple to eat this evening, a pre-cooked meal from the freezer or some such, but now the big seduction scene was to be set, she'd have to up her game. Calling in at the supermarket on the way home she bought steak and all the trimmings, plus some beautiful prawns and salad leaves to make a starter. Dessert... dessert... perfect! A scrumptious-looking chocolate cheesecake – who could resist that? As for the wine – Nuit St Georges with the meal, and then a bottle of Moet for the big seduction scene later.

Joanna had to admit to feeling just a little freaked out at the thought of the seduction scene – it had been so long. Could she? Would she be able to? Would *he* be able to? It didn't help that she didn't fancy him, not one little bit, so she'd have to fake it to a certain extent. Maybe he'd grow on her in more ways than one. Unlikely, but she was going to give it her best shot – no one could ever accuse her of not putting any effort into this marriage. But her bits – would they all still be in full working order? Would she have shrivelled up inside like a dried old prune? She popped a tube of K-Y Jelly into her shopping trolley just in case – hiding it carefully beneath the prawns when she reached the checkout.

'Had a busy day?' asked the girl on the checkout. Trust her to pick the queue being served by the chattiest one.

'Quite. Not too bad. You?'

'Been manic here. Don't know why. Not like there's a Bank Holiday or anything coming up, is it? Doing anything special tonight? Special meal is it? Birthday or something?'

'Erm... kind of,' replied Joanna, flustered, hastily packing the items into her carrier bag in an attempt to vacate the premises as quickly as possible. She put her card into the machine and punched in the number.

'Thanks – bye!'

'Excuse me, darlin',' a voice called after her, 'is this yours?'

Joanna turned to see the absolutely hunkiest male specimen she had ever seen in her entire life, holding a tube of K-Y Jelly high in the air, visible for all to see.

Erm, split-second decision. Did she deny all knowledge of it, go home jelly-less, and regret it later when she was unable to oil her shrivelled-up body parts in order to seduce her husband of longstanding whom she didn't love in the hope that it could save their marriage? Yep, it sounded ridiculous even to her but nevertheless...

'Is this yours?' he repeated, still waiting for an answer but enjoying every second of the obvious embarrassment he was causing – her face was scarlet.

All eyes were upon her, conversations had ceased, everyone seemingly awaiting her response. There was really only one thing she could do – one moment of excruciating embarrassment was little price to pay in the grand scheme of things, surely. With as much calmness as she could muster, Joanna walked back to the checkout, smiling seductively at Mr Hunk.

'Thank you – it is,' she said, their eyes meeting as she took it from him.

'Must have slipped out as you picked up your bag,' he said, eyes never faltering.

She swallowed nervously. 'Yes. Well thanks again,' she said, before turning on her heel and almost tripping over her own feet as she hastily made her exit from the shop – she couldn't get away fast enough.

'Stupid, stupid, stupid!' she admonished herself, as she was packing the shopping into the boot of her car. 'Why do you always have to make a fool of yourself? And, as if that's not bad enough, look at you now – getting the hots over a man who's probably young enough to be your son. As if!'

A sudden light tap on her shoulder almost made her jump ten feet into the air, it certainly made her emit a little shriek.

'Sorry, I didn't mean to startle you. I just wanted to apologise for embarrassing you in the shop back there. It was mean of me, I should just have run after you with it instead of shouting out like that and drawing everyone's attention to it. Sorry.'

'Ah, no problem – my own stupid fault for dropping it in the first place. Thanks for returning it to me, it was very kind of you. And I wasn't embarrassed at all – truly.'

'Is that why your face turned fifty shades of red – a bit like it's doing now?' he teased.

'I'm just hot, that's all,' she said, flustered. OMG – this man!

'So I've noticed,' he smiled. A lopsided smile. A seductive smile. *Joanna. Don't even think about it.*

'Cheeky!' It was hard not to smile back.

'Are you married? With someone? I notice you're not wearing a ring.'

'Don't miss much, do you?' she smiled – kind of seductively for Joanna, she'd not had a lot of practice recently. 'Anyway, I don't believe in wearing a ring on the third finger of your left hand just to show whether you're married or not, that's like when a pig gets a ring put through its nose to modify its behaviour.'

He noticed how she'd avoided answering his question but decided not to pursue it – her choice. 'Feisty one, aren't you? Do you fancy hooking up sometime – going for a drink or something maybe?'

What?! Was he asking her on a date? Mr Hunk himself asking her, Joanna Donohue, on an actual date with him when, apart from being the fittest guy she'd ever laid eyes upon, she was probably old enough to have given birth to him. She was in shock. Under normal circumstances she wasn't in the habit of swearing but this moment was anything but normal. 'Fuck!' OMG – had she just said that out loud?

He was almost speechless. This woman was certainly full of surprises. 'Well yes, we can if you want to.'

Her fluster rating was off the scale. 'Nooo! No, I didn't mean that, sorry – the wrong word flew out of my mouth, that's all. I meant to say book – booked up, that's what I meant. Like, I'd love to but I'm already booked up. Sorry – thank you though.'

'But I haven't even said when yet – how can you be booked up if you don't know which day I'm talking about?'

'True. But no, I really don't think I can. Sorry.'

Her embarrassment was palpable – as was her apparent naivety. He really hadn't ever met anyone quite like her before. 'Well look – take my card and then if you do ever change your mind, call me. Okay?'

She took the proffered card from him and glanced at it, trying desperately to appear nonchalant.

'Promise?'

'I will,' she said, gazing boldly into his eyes like this sort of thing happened to her every day, when in reality her legs were shaking so much they would hardly support her.

He turned on his heels and was gone. If she hadn't been left still holding his card she would have begun to think it had all been a dream – a figment of her imagination. But the card was there, gripped tightly in her hand. Jeez. She got into her car and sat down before her legs gave way. 'Gavin James – For all your plumbing and electrical requirements', it read. Well, Mr James, I'm absolutely certain you'd be more than capable of fulfilling all of my plumbing requirements and, at a rough guess, I would imagine that sparks would indeed fly. Joanna! She put the card safely away into her phone case and drove home.

*

Home. After the frisson of excitement she'd just experienced, home seemed like the safest place to be – but a pretty dull place too. *Snap out of it, Joanna!* The plan was about to commence. Remember the plan? It all seemed so long ago now. Nevertheless, part one. She should hurry, there was cooking to be done.

But first of all she needed to get changed into something a little bit more alluring than her office clothes and put on some slap. She was going to be pulling out all the stops tonight and it was important she looked her best, if only for her own self-esteem. The fact that Mr Gavin James had found her attractive in her tatty old work suit and bit of smudged mascara was completely irrelevant.

What to wear? She should have thought about this earlier, she'd had all day to do so but, typically, a last-minute scramble. Clothes flew out of the wardrobe haphazardly in a state of futile rejection.

Too fat, that was her problem – as always. Not enough time today but she'd definitely get back in that tracksuit again tomorrow and go for another jog, even if it did kill her. Ohhh – there must be something that would fit.

Then she found it. There it was lurking away in the back of the wardrobe. Totally unworn and still with its price tag on. *How much?* She must have been feeling extremely miserable on the day she'd bought it; under normal circumstances she would never have dreamed of spending anything like that amount of money on one single item of clothing – not in a million years. She must have been having a 'fat day' and been trying to cheer herself up. Well, if that was the case, that was good – she stood a slight chance of being able to fit into it today then. All that money! No wonder she'd never worn it, she'd have been too frightened – just imagine if she'd spilled something on it!

Anyway, tonight was definitely the night – the perfect dress for the occasion. She glanced over it, amazed it hadn't got creased being stuffed in the wardrobe like that. Quality – obviously. Catching a glimpse of the clock, she ran for a quick shower and then squeezed herself into The Dress. Not the easiest of tasks, and the word 'contortionist', amongst other words far less savoury, were to be heard, but with a few grunts and groans, and sharp intakes of breath, up went the zip – and she was in. Phew!

She plucked up the courage to look at herself in the full-length mirror. Lady in red. Scarlet woman. Red for danger. Whatever. Just look at that cleavage! If that didn't do it for him then nothing would. She could even fancy herself in this. She might have to. At breakneck speed, she put on her make-up – flirty false lashes and her new Mac lipstick. Who was this woman who was staring back at her? Certainly not the same Joanna that she knew, the one she'd seen a reflection of less than an hour ago.

Hair up or down? Down, she thought – she looked more approachable that way, and she certainly wanted to look approachable. She straightened it to get rid of the frizz. There, that'll have to do. She was quite pleased with the result, actually, and took a quick selfie just to prove she could look nice sometimes. In fact, she put it on Facebook and had six 'likes' in a matter of minutes. *And* a 'You look amazing, Joanna!' Her confidence was sky high and flying.

*

Meal prepped and ready to go, table set, champagne on ice and timed to perfection, she heard his key in the lock.

'Darling, I'm home!'

That word again; she'd try not to rise to the bait this time. In fact, hadn't Mr Hunk himself, Gavin, called her that when he'd shouted after her in the supermarket? Yes, but that was different. That was him and just his way. 'Darlin'...' Ohhhh, Gavin. If only. *Not 'if only' anything, Joanna. This is David, your husband. You're attempting to seduce him one last time – remember?* How could she forget?

'In here. I'm in the kitchen.'

'I wondered where you were h... oh!'

'Something wrong?' she asked, glancing up at him from the frying pan, in as much sultry temptress mode as she could muster, given the job in hand.

'You're looking very, err... going out or something?'

'No. Staying in.'

'Don't tell me we've got people coming for dinner again? You know how I hate that, especially when it's people I don't get on with like the last time. Tell them I'm out, I'm going to bed. You can entertain them yourself, you were the one who invited them.'

'Nobody's coming, David, it's just the two of us.'

'So what's the occasion? Not pregnant are you?'

She couldn't even condone that with an answer. What did he think that could have been – another immaculate conception?

Jesus Christ. The second one. This was not getting off to a good start.

'No "occasion", David. Doesn't have to be one, surely, does there? I'm just trying to make a bit of an effort, you have to work at a marriage if you want to keep it fresh, it doesn't just happen. People have "date nights" and all sorts, that's what I'm trying to do. We hardly speak to each other anymore, never mind have a proper conversation. Our marriage has gone stale and will fall apart if we don't do something about it.'

'Oh – stale is it? Charming. Don't be so ridiculous – I'm going upstairs to get changed.'

Quietly seething, Joanna continued with her dinner preparations, trying her utmost to stay calm. Hopefully, some of what she'd said would sink in and he'd come back downstairs dressed for dinner. Optimism overload, she feared.

He was a long time. She gave him a shout, 'David – dinner's ready!'

When he failed to materialise she went in search of him. What she didn't understand was – why was she even remotely surprised? Laid back on the sofa, mouth open, emitting the loudest snores known to humankind and, the biggest crime of all – wearing old grey tracksuit bottoms and a football T-shirt. It was possibly just as well that she'd put down the carving knife before coming to find him.

'David! Dinner!' She flounced out of the room without another word. Again, probably just as well.

*

Conversation around the dinner table was awkward, as it always was when Jack wasn't there to join them. But, at least he'd stayed at the table, not waltzed off into the sitting room with his meal on a tray because 'there was football on.'

Joanna had even googled 'conversation starters' as she knew it would be strained otherwise. Things like 'What are your five most important personal values?' and 'What crazy thing do you want to try someday?' Predictably, they weren't a rip-roaring success but she'd thought it would be preferable to silence. And it kind of was until she asked the fatal question, 'What are your pet hates?'

'Stupid, childish games like this – that's what my pet hates are! Can we stop now, please? I've had enough. How much have you spent on all this lot? And incidentally, how much did you spend on that dress? It doesn't even fit you properly – your top half's hanging out of it and the buttons down the front are stretched so far they look as though they're hanging on for dear life. I'm surprised you can even breathe. You need to lose some weight, Joanna. I mean seriously. I don't know what you were thinking buying all this food, a lettuce leaf would have been too much for you. I thought you were thinking of joining Weight Watchers anyway. What happened to that idea?'

And there was she thinking the Nuit St Georges might have mellowed him a little. Obviously not. She wanted to cry but wouldn't give him the satisfaction. Instead, head held high, she got up from the table and cleared the dinner plates away. She returned with the chocolate cheesecake, half expecting him to have made his escape to the TV. But no, he was amazingly still there. Looking at his phone but still there.

'Dessert?' she asked, through gritted teeth.

To be honest, what she really wanted to do was to push his face right into the fizzing dessert with a splat. But no, she restrained herself, she was a bigger person than that. Well, she obviously was a bigger person – he'd just told her so, hadn't he? Tears prickled at her eyelids. No. She was strong. She would not cry. The blade on this cake knife was very sharp, it glinted at her under the light. No, Joanna!

'No – I'm going to watch the news,' he snapped, picking up his glass and the remainder of the wine in the bottle to take with him. 'Didn't want any more of this, did you?'

Her mouth opened, about to respond but…

'No – thought not,' he said. 'A lot of calories in wine.'

*

And so, table for one it was then. She should be used to that by now. And she was, it's just that this was different. This was meant to be special. She'd put so much effort into tonight – what was the point? And, even worse, there was a grease stain on her new dress. Her beautiful red dress, spoilt, like everything else was. She felt so sad – and angry – but was determined not to cry, she wouldn't give him the satisfaction. Instead, she drowned her sorrows in chocolate cheesecake, practically the whole of it, until she felt sick.

The plan really wasn't coming together, was it? Although it was, in a way. She hadn't exactly been expecting a positive reaction – it was more of a test really, just to prove that things really were the way she'd thought they were, not just something she'd built up inside her own head. In that respect, it had worked out perfectly, so far.

Spurred on by that thought, Joanna cleared everything away and stacked the dishwasher; it would have been too much to face in the morning. She grabbed the champagne and two glasses and made her way upstairs.

'Going to bed,' she called, as she passed the open sitting room door. 'Coming?'

'Later. I want to watch this programme first.'

Great. Stay calm, Joanna – what did you expect? Don't let him wind you up. She went upstairs, took off her make-up and had a quick shower before covering herself in the most expensive-looking body lotion in the cabinet. There were loads to choose from, people kept buying them for her as presents and it wasn't actually something she would normally use. This one smelled gorgeous though and made her skin feel really soft and, to be honest, it needed all the help it could get. Suitably fragrant and feeling quite lush, she put on the slinkiest nightdress she owned – which probably makes it sound a whole lot better than it actually was, the choice wasn't exactly great. But hey, it was certainly better than the comfortable baggy nightshirt she usually slept in.

Finally, she climbed into bed, feeling quite exhausted by this time. No worries, hopefully the champagne would revive her. Ah – the champagne. If she remembered correctly there was a knack to this. It had been a while since she'd opened one herself, it was usually David who opened it if ever they had one. Twist the bottle not the cork, if she remembered correctly. Oh, and maybe put a tea towel over the cork to catch it if it blows off – good thinking. Feeling energised, she leapt off the bed – no tea towel up here, a towel would have to do. Her sudden movement caused the champagne bottle to roll off the bed onto the carpet with a dull thud. Joanna was relieved to see the bottle hadn't broken – lucky escape there, what a mess that would have been.

Back to the task in hand. She wondered how much longer David would be, but decided to open it now, she couldn't wait any longer. Okay, hold the towel over the cork and twist the bottle – simple, or so it should have been. Unfortunately, what she hadn't taken into account was just how much the contents of the bottle had been shaken up when it fell off the bed. Consequently, with a loud pop and a sudden whoosh, the cork exploded from the neck of the bottle, briefly catching the two champagne glasses as it zoomed on its way, full pelt, right into... the middle of David's forehead! It was unfortunate, really, that he'd chosen to enter the room just at that precise moment. Maybe shouting 'One hundred and eighty!' and 'Bull's eye!' were rather inappropriate remarks to make at that point but, to be honest, van Gerwen himself couldn't have done a better job on *Bullseye* and she just couldn't help herself. Meanwhile, of course, champagne was foaming forth at breakneck speed all over their bed and the glasses had been reduced to broken shards embedded in the carpet.

'For God's sake, Joanna, what the hell are you doing?' Clutching his forehead, David was almost rendered speechless. 'Here – give me that, it's spraying everywhere!'

'It's okay, it's okay – I'll sort it,' she said, rushing towards the bathroom sink with the bottle, cutting her foot on the broken glass in the process. 'Ouch!'

'Now what?'

'Ow, my foot – bleeding,' she said, somewhat pathetically, standing on one leg whilst holding the foaming champagne bottle upright in the sink, blood dripping onto the floor.

Jeez. 'Here, give me the bottle, it's okay now. Go and sort your foot out while I pick up the glass. What were you thinking?'

'I just thought it might be nice to have a bit of time to ourselves while Jack's out, that's all – just making an effort,' she said, checking her foot for any remaining little bits of glass before putting on a plaster.

'Well you certainly made something – not sure I'd call it an effort, more like some kind of massacre.' He was actually smiling.

'Ha-ha – sorry. Look at the state of the bed, it's soaking wet!'

'Get some more sheets and I'll give you a hand to change it. How's your foot?'

'Not too bad – could have been a whole lot worse.'

'And you hate blood,' he said, still smiling.

They worked in unison, clearing up the carnage. It seemed quite cosy really – almost like old times. This was all very confusing.

'There. Done. Nothing quite like clean sheets is there? I'll just go down and get two more glasses – we don't want the champagne going flat.'

Joanna climbed into bed, her foot throbbing, but it had almost been worth it – the evening seemed to be turning out better than she'd expected.

He returned with the glasses, well, flutes actually – the expensive champagne flutes they kept for special occasions. He must actually be enjoying the evening more than she'd thought. Weird. She didn't understand him sometimes – well, most of the time to be fair.

'Here's to us,' he said, as they chinked their glasses together.

'Cheers,' she responded, she couldn't bring herself to say more.

But after a couple of minutes of silent sipping and ably assisted by the alcohol, she did venture forth with, 'So you actually enjoyed this evening then? You think it was worth all the effort I put in? You think we should do this kind of thing more often, for the sake of our marriage?'

'I wouldn't go that far,' he said. 'Anyway, there's nothing wrong with our marriage.'

Hmm.

'Don't know about you but I'm ready for bed,' he said, 'it's been a long day.'

'We're in bed.'

'You know what I mean.'

Was this a euphemism? Did he mean what she thought he meant? Were they actually going to…?

'Oh! I just need to go to the bathroom first. I'll only be a minute – don't go anywhere,' she said, in somewhat of a fluster. And there she had been, thinking this moment would never come. Behind the closed door she was actually feeling kind of weird. It had been so long. She felt a bit like a virgin on her wedding night, which was ridiculous – she'd been married to him for thirty years, for goodness' sake. Get a grip, woman. Okay, the K-Y Jelly, that would sort everything out. And it did, more or less, although not entirely in the way she'd intended. Thinking of it reminded her of Gavin – and the encounter on the car park. If only it was him in the next room lying on the bed waiting for her instead of David – she probably wouldn't even need the K-Y in that scenario. *Joanna! That is no way to be thinking. You have a husband – he is waiting for you.*

Suitably lubricated, she left the safety of the bathroom. 'Sorry I took a while,' she said, climbing into the bed next to him, eyes averted – this was embarrassing. He didn't speak. Had he changed his mind? She lay there like a trussed chicken – oven ready. The silence was deafening.

'David?'

The loudest snore ever emitted from a living human creature reverberated around the room. The silence had been preferable. He was asleep. To wake him would have been impossible. She knew it. She'd tried it before.

Chapter Four

Saturday. That meant David would be at home all day. Great. Joanna felt so confused, she really needed to get away. There were far too many thoughts spinning around inside her head at the moment – not all of them good. It was far too confusing. She needed to speak to Hannah, check she was okay, and discuss her own problems with her too.

She could have driven and would have preferred to do so but David's comments about her weight kept echoing in her mind. Not that it should have bothered her whatever he said, he wasn't exactly film star material himself. In fact, she told herself in no uncertain terms that it didn't bother her in the slightest. But she was lying. However, sod him – she wanted to do this for herself. It was her body, her life – she was almost fifty and needed a new start. And, first things first, her body needed a kick-start. She would get fit. There was a whole world out there and she was poised to conquer it. *On with the Lycra and full steam ahead. Such positivity, Joanna!*

Sadly, the enthusiasm was short-lived. The fact that it seemed to take super-human effort to even get into the leggings didn't help. They were so tight! Had they shrunk in the wash? But then the vision of herself stuffing her face with practically the whole of that chocolate cheesecake the night before came into her head. See, it was basically David's fault that she was so fat. If he had only eaten his share of it she wouldn't be in this state now. As for the wine, to say nothing of the champagne, her poor head was almost bouncing off the ceiling. Was she sure she wanted to jog? Ask a silly question, of course she didn't. But she had to do it, she knew she had, it was all part of the new, improved version of Joanna Donohue. She would do it if it killed her.

And it very nearly did. She swore on her life that first hill was steeper than it had been the last time. Hill? Well, hillock. Okay... slope. And the second thing was that because it was the weekend, there were about a zillion people out walking, creating obstacles, in her way, causing her to have to step on the road to get past them. She could have been run over, for goodness' sake! Some people have no manners – would it hurt them to step aside? Surely they must have seen her, she was bright enough – luminous almost.

And that was another thing – bright. Okay, she knew her Lycra outfit and trainers were bright – but they were bright in a good way, not lurid or tacky, not in any way at all. So why then were people staring and pointing – even sniggering in some cases? People with dogs on those ridiculous flexi-lead things, causing a trip hazard. Car horns beeping – she felt like punching them. She was just trying to get fit, that's all, but seriously, people can be so annoying, the next one would get... There it was, another car horn – bloomin' cheek! Her head whizzed round to glare at the driver, which was somewhat unfortunate because...

Unfortunate indeed. Because, in doing so, not only did she lose sight of where she was heading, but she somehow managed to trip over a weirdly invisible thing on the pavement in her cushioned, injury-reducing trainers which, at the speed she was travelling, catapulted her into a concrete lamp post, which seemed to wrestle her to the ground. With a thud. And an 'oww', which sounded sadly pathetic.

A small crowd gathered. She could sense they were there before she even opened her eyes. Which made her not want to open them.

'I think she's unconscious.'

'Perhaps we should ring for an ambulance.'

'She went down with such a bang.'

Another faceless voice suddenly came within range – out of breath and vaguely familiar. 'It is you! I'm so sorry,' he gasped, 'I didn't mean that to happen. It was me – in the car – I was trying to get your attention…'

'What?!' she sat up, suddenly oblivious to the crowd – and to her injuries, apparently.

The crowd dispersed, almost as quickly as it had gathered. 'Lovers' tiff I reckon.' 'You're probably right – best leave them to sort it out. Made a right mess of her face though, hasn't she?' 'Yeah, bet she'll make him pay for that.'

'Gavin?! Where did you appear from?' The feeling of utter, absolute and total embarrassment caused by this whole scenario suddenly outweighed the pain of her injuries one hundred per cent.

He sat down on the footpath next to her, anxiously trying to process what had just happened. 'I can't tell you how sorry I am. I was just driving past and thought I recognised you so I beeped the car horn to get your attention, that's all.'

'That's all? Look at the state of me now! And why is it you always seem to turn up at my most embarrassing moments?' She didn't know whether to be angry with him or just to feel mortified by how she must look.

'Most importantly – are you okay?'

'Okay? Do I look okay?' she snapped back at him, her dignity more bruised than her body.

'You look just perfect. But what I meant was, have you broken anything? You seemed to go down with such a crash.'

Gingerly, she tried moving – thankfully everything seemed to be in full working order, although she felt cut and grazed everywhere. She took a clean tissue from her pocket and wiped her cheek – it was definitely bleeding.

'Here, let me,' he said, taking it from her to dab the wound. 'There, it's fine – just a bad graze really rather than a cut, nothing deep, I think you'll survive. Probably have a black eye when you wake up in the morning though,' he teased.

'My knee hurts too,' she said, in a sad-little-girl kind of voice.

He felt hugely responsible and couldn't let her just hobble away on her own in the state she was in. 'Tell you what – my flat is only down the road, I was just on my way back home, why don't I take you there and you can get cleaned up? I have a first-aid kit to die for awaiting, it contains everything you could possibly need. I can make you a nice cup of tea while you're sorting yourself out.'

Well, Joanna was usually such a sensible person and the idea of going to a flat with a man you've only fleetingly met once before and who, based on today's little episode, could even be stalking her, was about as far removed from sensible as you could ever hope to get.

'Okay,' she said.

There had, nevertheless, been just a tiny bit of logic in her thought process, which was that if she'd asked him to drive her straight home, David's suspicions may well have been aroused. Suspicions about what? Nothing had happened. No, but... Joanna!

*

She didn't know what she'd been expecting, but Joanna was stunned by the appearance of the flat. In fact the term 'flat' did it an injustice, this was an apartment – and a luxury one at that.

'Wow!' she said, 'I am speechless.'

'What? What were you expecting?'

'I don't know, but not this, that's for sure. How long have you lived here?'

'Almost two years now – do you like it?'

'Erm, I think "like" is an understatement!'

'Well, stop standing there open-mouthed – go and sort yourself out before you start dripping blood on everything.'

'Oops, sorry.' She'd been so surprised she'd almost forgotten her injuries.

'The bathroom's just through here,' he said, leading the way. 'I'll get the first-aid kit for you, there's everything you'll need in there.'

'Is this the one to die for? Blimey, I see what you mean,' she said, as he handed it to her.

'It is – but don't go dying on me just yet,' he smiled.

'I'll try my best – but I hate blood.'

'Would you like me to do it for you?' he asked – in a caring way, nothing more.

'No, I'll be fine – honestly. Thank you though.'

'Okay – I'll go and put the kettle on. Give me a shout if you need anything.'

'Thanks.'

No, Joanna, that wasn't what he meant.

*

'All sorted?' he asked, as she came back into the lounge.

'As sorted as I'll ever be,' she said, totally embarrassed by the whole gamut of her appearance from Elastoplast to Lycra and from chavvy trainers to facial scars. Yes, and even she had to admit that, in this setting, her whole jogging outfit which she'd previously thought of as being quite trendy and glam, really had quite a chavvy edge to it.

'Tea? Coffee? Something stronger?'

'Think I'll stick with the tea please, if you don't mind – I need to keep my wits about me.'

'Tea coming right up. You don't need to worry though – I didn't bring you here to have my wicked way with you.'

'I should hope not – I'm probably old enough to be your mother.'

'I'm forty-one so I should hardly think so – unless you're wearing extremely well.'

'Okay, maybe not then,' said Joanna with a slight smile, revealing absolutely nothing.

They sat on separate sofas amid an awkward kind of silence for a minute or two. This whole situation seemed quite surreal – bizarre almost. Thankfully, he broke the ice.

'So, mysterious lady, who are you? I'm curious. I mean you know my name, what I do – well, sort of. You've had a ride in my car, and you even know where I live now. Bit unfair that – don't you think? I don't even know your name! So tell me about you – who are you?'

Joanna smiled, relaxed now in his company. If he was a serial rapist or a crazed stalker-type she didn't think he would behave like this or be so nice to her. Although, come to think about it, she believed that is how they do behave – be nice to you, win you over, gain your confidence and then... Stop it – she was sure he was nothing like that. 100%. Well 99.99% anyway. She could trust him, she was sure of it. And what was more, she really liked him.

'Okay. My name is Joanna Donohue and I'm in my forties – like you!' She didn't have to admit to which end of her forties, obviously. 'I've been married for far too long and have an amazing son, Jack, who used to live in London but has fairly recently moved back home again. I work in a very boring office job which I hate, but at least it pays the bills. Anything else you'd like to know?'

'Yes. You say you're married, but you never mentioned the husband – is he still there?'

'Yup – he's still there.'

Gavin registered surprise at the way she answered. He raised an eyebrow, he was intrigued.

'Sorry, I didn't mean it to sound like that. It's just that I feel I've put up with such a lot for the past goodness knows how many years and I don't know how much longer I can do that – the older I get, the more unbearable it becomes and the more isolated I feel. To be honest, in answer to your question – yes, he is there but, apart from a volcanic eruption now and again, you would hardly notice.

'Sorry, I didn't mean to pour all this out to you when we've only just met – what must you be thinking? Some kind of desperate housewife. Oh, and by the way, I'm definitely not on the lookout for another man, so don't go getting any ideas. Men and relationships are off the agenda for me from now on – think I've been put off for life.' Really, Joanna?

'Pity,' he said. 'Not that I'm implying anything there for myself. I'm a bit like you in that way – some relationships just leave you screwed up.'

Suddenly she felt his pain. She really must stop being so self-centred; other people have problems too, it wasn't all about her.

'So, what about you? I know your name is Gavin James, and I know you're a qualified plumber and electrician. But, try as I might, I can't believe that any money you earn from fixing people's waste pipes or from switching the light back on in their lives would enable you to buy a palace like this. I mean, this place is incredible! Oh, and I also noticed, when I was busily mopping up blood in your bathroom, that you're probably single.'

'Really – how?'

'One toothbrush – it's a dead giveaway. Oops, not that I do that kind of thing on a regular basis or anything, I just thought, when I saw it – that's all.' *Joanna, stop digging a hole.* 'I mean it's nothing to me whether you're with anyone or not – obviously. Like

I said, the last thing I want is another man, I've enough with the one I've got.'

'Okay. Yeah, you're right on both counts. I am a qualified plumber and electrician, it's true. But I'm also a property developer. I just got into it at the right time really and that's what's made me the money over the years. Not only that, but it's something I feel really passionate about and it's something I'm good at too, though I say it myself. I've got eight properties at the moment, all rented out and then another couple that I've done up and sold on. I buy them at auction usually, for a good price, and then I do most of the work on them myself. Some stuff I'm not able to do, obviously, but, being in the trade, I can usually find a mate who can help me out with me doing a job for him in return. It works well. Can be stressful at times and a lot of hard graft but it's definitely worth it. I love what I do, am passionate about it. Sadly most people can't say that about their jobs.'

'That's true. You're so lucky to be doing something you love. It's the dream, isn't it? Most people, like me, just go out to work because they have to, doing something they don't enjoy simply to pay the bills. Ridiculous really, we only have one life, we should make the most of it and do the things that make us happy.'

Gavin smiled at her... indulgently. 'So that's your philosophy of life, is it?'

'I agree, it doesn't seem that way but I am trying to change. Actually, no, more than that, I am *going* to change! Now I see things more clearly, I realise that was my problem: my personal philosophy of life was non-existent. I've spent all these years just wandering about with no clear picture in my mind of what I wanted to do. When things cropped up and choices had to be made I'd just follow what seemed like the easiest route without really thinking where it would lead and whether I would want to be there. I never, ever considered long-term goals and how to achieve them. Tragic, isn't it? All that misspent life.'

She looked so sad, he just wanted to go over and hug her, but he didn't want to scare her away – he kept his distance.

'It is sad, I agree, but it's never too late. You need to think what it is you want to achieve in your life and start taking steps towards making it happen. If you want something badly enough and work hard to reach your goal then anything is possible – I truly believe that, and in fact I'm a prime example.'

He was such an inspiration to talk to and just what she needed right now. 'So did you truly achieve all of this by yourself or were you one of these rich kids with wealthy parents ready to bail you out if things went wrong?'

'Hand on heart, I started without a penny to my name. I grew up on a council estate – not that I'm saying there's anything wrong with council estates in general terms, but in this case it was the roughest of the rough. I think that was good for me in a way though, it made me even more determined that I would escape from the poverty trap and that I would never have to live in a place like that again.

'Actually, it wasn't just the place, it was the people too. I think ASBOs were probably introduced with that estate in mind. My poor mum, she was a nervous wreck – and with good reason, no wonder she was on Valium. My dad had left, you see – gone off with another woman. He went when I was eight, leaving my mum with me to bring up on her own with little or no money. And not only that, but never knowing when the next brick would come flying in through the window, or when some lunatic arsonist would try to set fire to our house. See, I told you it was rough.

'I was an only child and, with my dad no longer there, it left me feeling I had to be the man of the house – I always felt that huge sense of responsibility for my mum. That's why I really knuckled down at school and why I was so chuffed when I managed to get an apprenticeship. It didn't pay me much while I was learning the skills I needed but I just knew that, for me, if I worked hard at it and learned a proper trade, I could eventually set up my own business and grow it as much as I possibly could – it's what I'd dreamed of. University wasn't for me, and we couldn't have afforded it anyway. So I learned my trade, got my skills and my qualification and then I set myself up as a plumber. My mum – she was as proud as punch when I gave her one of my first business cards, I'll never forget it.

'Anyway, I carried on doing that for a while but when out on a job I'd often get asked if I could recommend an electrician for something extra they had that needed doing and I'd think – why not me? So, alongside the day job, I enrolled on a college course, which I'm chuffed to say I completed, and I became a fully qualified electrician.'

'And made your mum even more proud, I'm sure.'

'She really was. I was working and working like crazy and saving every penny I earned but I had one aim and I was determined to achieve it. That aim, as you now know, was to dabble in the property market. I just find it so exciting – finding properties you're interested in and then battling it out at auction, not always successfully, I might add – sometimes it can be really disappointing. But when you manage to get a property you really, really want, that moment when you get the key and go to look inside as the new owner. A neglected building waiting to be restored, needing love and attention to bring it back to life. A blank canvas waiting for your ideas and your skillset to do with it whatever it is you want to do. I tell you, there is no other feeling quite like it in the world.'

'And your mum – is she still living on the estate?'

'What – you think I'd leave her there? No, I managed to get a great little place for her. Falling to bits it was, but I renovated it and did it all up, with her advising all the way along, of course, telling me exactly how she wanted it. She loved the fact that we were working on it together, and so did I. It was the proudest moment of my life the day I was able to help her move in and leave that sink estate behind her forever.'

'Oh Gavin – that is so lovely. What an achievement! No wonder you were proud.' The story had brought tears to Joanna's eyes although she tried not to show it. 'Oh my goodness – is that the time? I've only just noticed! My sister would have been expecting me more than an hour ago – probably thinks I've been abducted by aliens or something, she'll be really worried. Bet she's been trying to ring me and I left my phone at home as well. I must go.'

'Do you make a habit of it?'

'What? Leaving my phone behind?'

'No – being abducted by aliens,' he teased. 'Can I give you a lift?'

'Erm…' She was torn. She knew she'd get an in-depth interrogation from Hannah if she turned up with a strange man in tow. But, on the other hand, she really didn't feel in any fit state to be jogging any more today. 'Well, if you wouldn't mind that would be lovely – thank you.'

Chapter Five

Hannah was indeed concerned. She was standing at her window with baby Lottie in her arms, and therefore in prime position, with a baby to hide behind, when the car drove into the cul-de-sac. She knew virtually every single car that ever ventured into there, probably even knew their registration numbers, she was Neighbourhood Watch personified. But here was one she didn't recognise, driving in right now – and not just any old car, a Merc, if she wasn't mistaken. So, by the pocket-rocket-scientific-genius-of-Hannah logic, this car had definitely got something to do with her missing sister. Hah – she should have been a detective!

So yes, okay, she knew Joanna hadn't been missing for long but Hannah was a stress-head. She'd worry that the paperboy had been mugged if the newspaper was half an hour late arriving in a morning, so a sister being more than an hour late and uncontactable by phone was enough to give her a nervous breakdown. Hide behind Lottie? She didn't think so. Straight out of the front door and up the path to greet the car kerbside was more her style.

The car stopped, the driver's door opened and, somewhat hesitantly, the driver emerged – a handsome and rather muscular young man, the likes of which had never been seen in this cul-de-sac before.

'Hi,' he said, veneers gleaming in the sunlight. At least she presumed they must be veneers, no one could ever hope to achieve such a dentally perfected smile without expensive input.

'Hi,' she was transfixed. She hadn't even bothered to look inside the car to check whether her sister was with him – it could have been anybody, she didn't care.

'Cute kid,' he said, glancing towards Lottie as he whizzed past them to open the passenger door. 'Okay?' he asked as he took Joanna's hand and helped her out of the car. What a gentleman!

'Thanks, Gavin. And thank you so much for today – well, for looking after me anyway,' she smiled.

'Hey – in a way I was duty bound, it was my fault in the first place. But, in the second place, it was my absolute pleasure – truly.'

Joanna gave a shy little giggle. As for Hannah, she didn't think she'd ever been this speechless before in her entire life.

'You didn't give me your number,' said Gavin. 'Will I ever see you again?'

'Probably – I'll text you.'

'Promise?'

'I promise.'

Seeing him about to get back into his car prompted Hannah to snap out of this trance-like state she'd been in and spring back into action.

'Hey, hey, hey, not so fast – I have questions! And "why would you bring my sister here more than an hour late, looking like she just did ten rounds with Mike Tyson?" is only one of them.'

As luck would have it though, for Gavin at least, this sudden sense of urgency and the slight raising of her mummy's voice threw baby Lottie into a meltdown, the likes of which was more than adequate to drown out any form of conversation completely. A good pair of lungs, or so she'd been told – Hannah had been pleased at the time.

'Sorry?' he shouted in response, cupping his ear with his hand, 'I can't hear you. Hopefully see you again – must dash.' And he was gone.

*

Back in the house, of course, there was no escape for Joanna, although neither would she have wanted there to be. She needed to talk this all through with someone and who better than Hannah?

'Hello, gorgeous,' she cooed to baby Lottie, taking her from her mummy for a much-needed cuddle. 'My – you're getting heavy. What is she feeding you on? You'll have to be coming jogging with your Auntie Jo at this rate. Aw – just look at that smile – and it's not even wind is it, my little munchkin? You love your Auntie Jo, don't you – yes you do. It's a good job somebody does, isn't it?'

'Looks like somebody else is a bit smitten too, by the look of things. And *how* old is he? Quite the hunk – I'm jealous. Who is he – what's happening? Come on – spill! And incidentally, what's happened to your face – what have you done?'

'Notice how you want to know about the man before you suddenly remember to ask about me?' she giggled. Happiness was simply radiating from her – Hannah had never seen her look so elated, or certainly not for a very long time.

Joanna regaled her with the full story, from the K-Y in the supermarket to the detailed description of the unbelievably luxurious apartment.

'I don't know how you kept your hands off him – didn't you want to jump him?'

'Hannah! I have a husband – remember?'

'Yeah, right.'

'And he may well have an "other half" somewhere – who knows. We didn't quite get that far. And then I suddenly realised the time and knew you would be worried, wondering where I was.'

'Hah – if only I'd known,' smiled Hannah. 'Oh – so sorry, I've only just remembered,' she said, her facial expression suddenly more sombre. 'David knows you weren't here.'

'What? How?'

'Sorry but I rang your mobile because I was worried when you didn't turn up. David answered – you'd left it at home.'

'On the kitchen table. What did he say?'

'He was just surprised that you hadn't arrived – said you'd left ages ago. Perhaps you'd better give him a call and let him know you're here.'

'I've been here for ages as well – bet he won't believe me. He'll think I've been out galivanting all day.'

'Just tell him the truth. Well, kind of. You were jogging and you fell and hurt yourself. A passer-by took pity on you and invited you into her house to clean yourself up, she made you a cup of tea and you got chatting.'

'She?'

'Well yeah – no point in creating trouble before there even is any. Don't you agree?'

'Suppose. God this all feels very cloak-and-dagger! Like I'm having an affair – and I haven't even done anything.'

'Yet.'

'Shut up.'

*

Hannah gave her a lift home, for which Joanna was hugely grateful. She felt in no fit state to jog all the way back again today after her earlier escapade.

'In here, darling,' David said, as she let herself in through the front door.

Darling. That word again. She let it pass.

'Goodness – you *have* made a mess of your face, haven't you? Probably leave a big scar I should think.'

Great.

'What's for dinner and how long will it be? I invited Pixie to stay. They're upstairs in Jack's room. Think I can guess what they're up to – a little cracker, that Pixie.'

Double great.

*

To say the conversation around the dinner table was a little awkward would have been putting it mildly. For a start David had far too much to drink and went rambling on and on about his past, which was of absolutely no interest to anyone else other than himself. Certainly both she and Jack had heard all of these stories a zillion times over, repeated almost word for word. Even David must be getting bored of them by now – surely.

Pixie-Poxie looked as though she'd rather be anywhere but here, and who could blame her? The only time she showed any sign of life was when she looked at Jack, rolled her eyes, covered her mouth with her hand and giggled – well, sniggered would have described it more accurately. Joanna was liking this girl less and less, although she was trying her best for Jack's sake.

'Would you like some more meat?' asked Joanna with a smile, poised to serve her.

The girl shook her head – presumably that meant 'no thank you'.

'More vegetables then – another potato? You've hardly eaten enough to feed a fly.'

'That's why Pixie's so nice and slim and you're a chubster,' joked David with a huge guffaw, spilling his glass of red wine all over the white tablecloth in the process.

'Oh. Get a cloth, Joanna.'

'Seriously, would you like some more? I'm worried, you've hardly eaten anything.'

'No – we ate before we came,' again that snigger. 'Can we go now, Jack-yy?'

Joanna looked at Jack questioningly, the serving spoon still poised in her hand.

'Sorry, Mum,' he said, guilt etched plainly on his face, but following her out through the door nevertheless, shoulders hunched, like a lamb to the slaughter.

'Joanna, I've told you once – get a cloth! What's the matter with you, are you deaf or something?'

'Can you get one yourself? I'm busy clearing all the food away – she ate nothing, that girl.'

'Are you defying me AGAIN?' he exploded. 'There's wine spilled, it's gone on my shirt, it's everywhere. Get a cloth, woman – and get it now! How many more times do I have to tell you?'

'No, I will not get a cloth for you, David – you're perfectly capable of getting one yourself, I'm not your slave' she said, so much more calmly than she felt.

'WHAT did you say?'

'I said no, David. You spilled it, you get the cloth, you clean it up.' And, with those words still ringing in her ears, she walked out of the room and upstairs to bed.

*

As she lay in bed, Joanna thought back over the events of the day. It had certainly been a strange one. She'd half expected David to follow her up the stairs in a full-blown rage; in fact she was amazed that he hadn't. The worry of course was what exactly he could be capable of doing to her when he flew into a tantrum like that; he was a big, strong man. Not that he'd ever done anything so far, but there was a first time for everything. Which was why, in the past, she'd always walked away from any confrontation, smoothed things over. But for goodness' sake – why should she? She'd had enough. Whether it was the age she was at now that was making her react differently or what – but why should she put up with it? His anger was *his* problem, not hers, it was up to him to learn how to control it instead of expecting her to live on a knife edge, forever trying to restore peace.

Oh God, and then there'd been Poxie. Sorry, Pixie. What was wrong with that girl? She was *supposedly* intelligent – had allegedly been to university – and yet she barely seemed capable of stringing two words together, especially if those two words happened to be 'thank' and 'you'. Certainly it had been difficult to know quite how to react when, in trying to make conversation, Joanna had asked what course she'd taken at uni and the girl had replied 'Communication Studies'. Hah – a lot of good that had done her.

It obviously hadn't come as a surprise to her then when Jack told her, on a different occasion naturally, that Pixie had been kicked off the course. Although actually the reason hadn't been because of her lack of communication skills, amazingly, but because of her behaviour. Warning bells had certainly been ringing in Joanna's ears – why the hell was he with her? The problem was that he was twenty-nine years old – a man. You would think he would have had enough sense at his age to see her for what she was – to notice how she was spinning her web around him like a spider intent on trapping its prey.

The problem was that there were so many girls like this – evil and manipulative. Going all out in that cold and calculating way, using every trick in the book to capture their idea of a perfect man to be their poor, unsuspecting husband. They never went for the rogues, only for the 'nice' guys, the ones they could gain control over. Guys who would listen to their sob stories and who would somehow be sucked in by the pressure of being needed until they realised too late what they had done and were trapped, almost too afraid to leave.

As a mother it was so hard for Joanna just to stand back and watch this happening to Jack but sadly there was nothing she could do about it. He was twenty-nine years of age and had to learn through his own mistakes; she just hoped he would see sense and realise exactly what this girl was like before it was too late. Men could be so dim at times – her own son included.

Hmm – men. Her brain did a sudden somersault – a triple one it felt like, almost taking both her heart and her stomach with it. Gavin. Her thoughts scrambled around desperately. Trying to latch on to some kind of logic. There wasn't any. But who needed it? She hadn't done anything wrong other than a bit of mild flirtation – not even that really. But whatever it was, for the first time in years, her life seemed to have a bit of fun and sparkle in it. Time to fluff out her tutu and dance on? Maybe.

*

She didn't hear him come to bed. Perhaps that was because he hadn't done so. When she woke up the next morning she was surprised to see the space in the bed next to her still empty. Momentarily she felt relief – joy almost. With a big wake-up yawn, she stretched out starfish-style – luxuriating in the wonderment of having the huge bed all to herself. No one else to consider. Bliss.

But then suddenly a slight worry crept into her head and forced her eyes to open. She really didn't want to move but… what if he was dead, choked in his own vomit? He'd certainly drunk far more than he should have done last night, even discounting the glass he'd spilled. Reluctantly, she threw on her dressing gown and went downstairs to check, simultaneously wondering why the heck she was even bothering.

And in fact she needn't have done so. The familiar sound of his loud snores reverberated along the hallway to greet her and led her to him – fast asleep and open mouthed, his body stretched out, still fully clothed, upon the best velvet sofa. Great. Was this the man she really wanted to spend the rest of her life with? She cleared the debris from around him and went back upstairs to shower.

She was at the kitchen table eating breakfast by the time he made an appearance.

'Sorry,' he said.

Blimey – was that the first time in thirty years he had actually said sorry? She was stunned, and looked up in amazement. 'What did you say?' Perhaps she'd misheard.

'I said "sorry". Sorry I messed up last night and sorry I lost my temper – you know what I'm like.'

'Only too well,' she said, giving full concentration to adding more jam to the piece of toast on her plate.

'So, do you forgive me?' he asked plaintively, his hangdog appearance slouched painfully against the frame of the kitchen door.

Well this was a first. Joanna chewed her toast thoughtfully. 'But why should this time be any different from the rest? Why should I believe you?'

'Because I've never said I'm sorry before.'

This was true.

Encouraged by her lack of negative response, he moved slowly into the kitchen and sat at the table to face her. 'I was thinking about what you said – about our marriage going stale. I never really thought about it before but perhaps you're right. We need to make more of an effort, both of us – give it a fresh start. I'm willing to try if you are – what do you think? Sorry,' he said, smiling, and moving his seat back a little bit. 'I probably don't smell too good. Not had a wash or brushed my teeth or anything yet, but I just wanted to get that off my chest.'

Her silence was palpable.

'Well?'

'Oh I don't know, David – this is all so sudden.'

'Sudden? It's what you wanted yourself two days ago.'

A lot can change in two days. 'I'll think about it,' she said, getting to her feet and clearing the table, putting her breakfast dishes into the dishwasher.

'Well bloody hell!' he exploded. 'There's no pleasing you, is there? I've said I'm willing to do what you asked, even though it's a stupid idea, but you're *still* not happy. Well forget it – just forget it. You always think you know best – always have to be the one in control telling everyone what to do. Well fuck you, Joanna – fuck you.'

*

She needed to get out of the house. She felt suffocated by everyone and everything in there at the moment – even by Jack with his Poxie. She needed to breathe. She needed – exercise. It was good for relieving stress – supposedly. Although maybe jogging wouldn't be a good idea – not for the time being anyway. Swimming was out – it would ruin her hair and she'd spent ages straightening it this morning. So what was left? The gym? The very words sent an icy arrow through her heart. The. Gym. It would make her face her fear. It would be good for her. Truly. That's if it didn't kill her first.

She couldn't go to the one where Jack worked for obvious reasons. To do that, not only would the gym kill her but, in addition, he would die of embarrassment. Two dead bodies. That certainly wouldn't be off to a good start for this healthier, fitter, new-look Joanna. However, thinking about it, Jack wasn't actually working there today, he was working at Bojangles, the cocktail bar, she remembered him saying so last night. And his gym always looked a lot more friendly and down to earth than the more upmarket one at the other end of town.

She'd seen the girls going in and out of the latter, they always looked as though they were about to step onto the catwalk for London Fashion Week rather than going to the gym for a sweaty workout. Sweat? Surely their beautiful sweet bodies would be far too superior to admit to producing such a disgusting substance. Unless, of course, it was suddenly found to be the latest magic ingredient to add to moisturiser for a glowing, blemish-free complexion, in which case it would be given an intriguing new name, packaged by Dior and sold at Harvey Nicks.

Joanna swore these tall and skinny fashionistas were about as far removed from her as it was possible to get – in every respect. She knew she'd been fussy herself when choosing her jogging outfit and had bought the most expensive in the shop, but at least that shop had been Sports Direct, not Selfridges. And the trouble was, and what they didn't seem to realise, was that they all looked the same. Tanned to perfection courtesy of St Tropez (the product, not the place), wearing exclusive designer label everything, and flashing the whitest of teeth which could only have been achieved with the aid of veneers. Blonde hair, Botox-ed expressionless faces, lips that resembled those with which a trout is naturally born, and as for the eyebrows, OMG – do they actually think those solid black wedge-shaped things look good? More like two black hairy caterpillars that had been run over by a truck! God – she was a bitch, wasn't she? She'd never quite realised that before.

Chapter Six

After much procrastinating, but deciding she couldn't put it off any longer, Joanna finally arrived at Jack's gym. Well, at the car park actually, having some kind of identity crisis, like 'Who am I? What am I doing here?' As a delaying tactic in order to put a bit of time between her and 'it', she had what she thought was a great idea. She would google to find out what to do on your first visit to a gym. Surprising what you can learn from Google.

1. *Always take a bottle of water and a towel with you.* Great. Fail number one. She hadn't brought either, she'd never thought.
2. *Don't have anything to eat for an hour before exercise.* Oh. That full bar of Cadbury's Dairy Milk Chocolate I ate on the way here to give me some energy – does that count?
3. *On your first visit it's a good idea to go with a friend to help you feel more confident.* Yes, I know I'm a Billy No-mates – no need to rub it in.
4. *Tell them you've never been to a gym before and ask someone to give you a guided tour of the equipment.* Embarrassing… but, okay.
5. *Make sure you wear something comfortable.* Well it was comfortable, but I've eaten so much this week I can hardly breathe in it now.
6. *Enjoy!* Hmm. I'll try my best but I can't promise anything.

Okay, Joanna, enough of the delaying tactics – let's go!

*

The young lady on the reception desk returned her smile as she walked in – at least Joanna hoped she was smiling with her and not at her. On closer inspection the young lady in question could better be described as a girl rather than a lady – she actually looked about twelve years old. Joanna suddenly felt positively ancient. The girl asked her a few questions like 'Have you ever been to a gym before?' Was it that obvious?

'No worries,' said the girl, 'my gran comes here all the time – she loves it, you're never too old to start trying to get into shape, whatever age.'

Well, as if one confidence-destroying insult wasn't enough – two in one sentence? The tiny fragment of ego Joanna had was shrivelling up like a dehydrated plum – she could feel herself gradually transforming into a prune as she stood there, wrinkles slowly creeping in.

'Would you like me to shout someone over to come and show you around – make sure you're okay? Mind the step, by the way, we don't want any nasty accidents, do we?' said the girl, who not only looked twelve years old but who suddenly seemed to have developed an annoyingly condescending voice too.

'I'm sure I can manage, thank you,' replied Joanna, trying to sound like the calm and capable woman she knew that she was, as she promptly fell up the step, landing full length on the floor.

'Do you make a habit of this?' asked a familiar voice as she scrambled to her feet, pride a little bruised but nothing more.

'Are you stalking me, Mr Gavin James?' Try as she might, she couldn't help but put her little flirty face on.

'And why would I want to do that?' he smiled.

'Oh I don't know,' she answered, 'maybe that's how you pick up lady clients who need their plumbing fixing.'

'Cheeky!' he grinned at her. 'Seriously, I'm in here all the time – well, at least a couple of times a week anyway. I didn't realise you came here though.'

'Oh yeah, I'm in here all the time too – surprised you haven't seen me. I do a lot of weight training – can't you tell?'

'Liar.'

'Is it that obvious?'

'Well…' he said. 'I was just about to leave actually – have you finished? Fancy going for a drink or something?'

'Erm, I…' she pondered for maybe half a second. 'Yeah, sure – why not?'

*

'Gav!' called a voice as they made their way across the car park. He turned to look. She stayed put, feeling a little uncomfortable about someone seeing them together even though they'd done absolutely nothing wrong.

Gavin moved towards the voice. 'Hey, mate – how you doin'?'

Without looking back, Joanna walked towards her car, thinking she'd wait inside it until he'd finished chatting. But it was not to be.

'Mum?!' Joanna turned, the voice unmistakable. 'What are you doing here?'

'I could ask you the same question – I thought you weren't working here today.'

'I wasn't, I'm not. Working at Bojangles today but not in until later. Pixie's mum made us this massive breakfast this morning so thought we'd come for a bit of a workout to burn it off before we have to go in. Anyway, what's more to the point – what are you doing here? You've never been to a gym in your life.'

'You don't know everything, Jack, you don't know what I get up to. But so what anyway? I'm just trying to get fit that's all. Do you have a problem with that?'

'No, but…'

'Hang on a minute. So – you're Jack's mum?' asked Gavin, suddenly breaking his hitherto silence.

'Yes.' Where was the harm in that? She could have given birth to him when she was fifteen, it was possible.

'But,' said Jack, looking somewhat confused. 'You mean – you two know each other?'

'Yes.' 'No!' said Gavin and Joanna simultaneously.

'I mean we do know each other – from the gym,' said Gavin, in sudden realisation.

'Jack-yy, are you coming? Hurry up, we've not got very long.'

Well, saved by the bell. Never did Joanna think she'd be pleased to see the Poxie.

*

'Meet you at The Feathers,' said Gavin, as they walked back to their respective cars. 'You know the one I mean?'

'Yeah. The one at the top of the hill.'

'I believe they do good lunches.'

Joanna didn't answer, she was feeling a bit unsure about this whole thing now. Bumping into Jack like that and him seeing them together had been a bit of a reality check. What must he have thought? It must have looked a bit suspicious even though there was nothing actually going on. And, what's more – with one of her son's mates? She was beginning to feel like a child molester!

She got into her car and sat there for a few minutes, hoping he would drive away first. But he didn't move. Obviously waiting for her so he could drive behind her – ever the gentleman. She took out her phone and found the card with his number on it. Taking the coward's way out she texted, '*Sorry but can we do this another time?*' before hurriedly driving away, praying he wouldn't follow. Shit.

She forgot – he'd have her number now, that was not what she'd intended to happen.

Hopefully he'd take his eyes off her car to read the text and that would give her a chance to pull away before he noticed in which direction she was going. All kinds of things were whirling around inside her head at the moment. Feelings of embarrassment, panic, guilt, shame – a plethora of mixed emotions. She needed time to think, time on her own. She couldn't face him right now.

Checking her rear-view mirror constantly, she sped away, turning into roads she'd never travelled down before purely to confuse him should he, perchance, attempt to follow her. She had absolutely no idea where she was but hopefully sat nav would sort her out if she hadn't confused it completely. It seemed to her almost like she'd had some kind of panic attack and the driving was a release. Fight or flight, that was exactly it – the faster she went and the better she felt.

Unexpectedly, she found herself on a dual carriageway, quite a distance from home, and before she knew it she was whizzing past a sign saying Welcome to Wales. This was crazy – had she completely lost the plot? Should she turn back and head for home? That would certainly be the sensible thing to do, she was miles away. But no, a little bit of crazy was what she needed right now; she was sick of being predictable Joanna living life in the slow lane. How about Colwyn Bay? To sit on the sandy beach and gaze out to sea could be just what she needed right now to give her time – time to think. Perfect. She was certainly not living life in the slow lane today, she put her foot down, sped into the fast lane and overtook the car in front – way to go!

Glancing into her rear-view mirror yet again, it was a relief to think she'd managed to get away and leave him behind, even though it would have been nice to be with him in some respects. Poor Gavin. All she could see now though was the car she'd overtaken and even that was fading rapidly into the distance. She blasted out the words to the song on the radio, 'All by myself...' singing at full pelt, her hair blowing freely in the breeze from the open window. She noticed the flashing blue light speeding up behind her. Better pull into the slow lane, there must be an accident somewhere.

Hang on a minute – they were staring at her as they overtook, signalling for her to stop. What did they want her for? She thought they had an accident to get to.

'Could you step out of the car please, madam?'

Oh God. Turned out she'd only been doing 75mph.

*

She was lucky. After much questioning, checking and a strict talking-to, alongside much apologising, explaining and a few feeble, pathetic woman-tears, it turned out there really was an accident – an emergency – and they were called away to it suddenly. They let her off with a warning, a serious one, and told her they hoped they'd never see her again. Phew! Well, that last bit wasn't very nice but she thought she understood what they meant. As for the rest – she felt incredibly lucky. She got back into her car and drove on – at a speed of no more than sixty-five this time, not tempting fate by going even anywhere near the seventy mark. Lesson learned.

*

Colwyn Bay. She'd loved this place as a child. So many happy memories. If she could turn back time and relive them all again knowing the things she knew now – she would live her life so differently. Happily it looked quiet here today, plenty of spaces along the seafront. She pulled into one and parked her car, gazing out to sea. It looked so beautiful. She was glad she'd come here even though it was a bit of a crazy thing to have done. But hey, she was a total fruit loop and she needed some space – who cared?

At least one person would, she was sure. She checked her phone. A text. *'Of course we can – are you ok? x'*

A kiss? That freaked her out a little bit. It was just a kiss though, people do that all the time – even she does it sometimes, it doesn't necessarily mean anything, just being friendly.

'Sorry. I'm fine. It just felt a bit uncomfortable seeing Jack that's all. Another time?'

'Definitely. Are you home now?'

'No.'

'Where are you?'

'At the seaside.'

'WHAT??'

'Don't ask :o) Just needed some space. See you soon.'

'I hope so – take care. x'

Should she or shouldn't she? Sod it.

'x'

*

She got out of the car, surprised to realise how cold it was. In Joanna's dream world of idyllic childhood memories, the sun was always shining at the seaside. Not so. Not today at any rate. Perhaps a vest top and Lycra leggings weren't the most suitable attire. They'd been perfect for her fleeting visit-with-zero-exercise to the gym, but the seafront on a cool breezy day? Maybe not so. However, she was loath to go in search of a shop where she could buy something warmer, especially as she'd come out with very little cash and no debit card.

She checked the car boot for anything resembling a sweater, who knew what could be lurking in there? A tartan blanket – perfect. She wrapped it around herself feeling like Old Mother Hubbard but this was the seaside, nobody knew her, nobody cared – at least she was warm. Splashing out her cash on a doughnut and a hot chocolate from the kiosk further along the promenade, she carried them with her and made her way down onto the beach.

Finding a deserted and amazingly sheltered spot against the sea wall, she settled herself down and munched. Ah – this was the life, she might even get a bit of a tan if she sat here long enough. She gazed out to sea. There was nowhere quite like it when your mind was in turmoil as hers was right now. The soothing sound of the waves lapping gently on the shore, carrying sand and shells and shingle, washing it gently, rhythmically, back and forth, back and forth. Even the cry of the seagulls circling overhead was calming, loud though it was, their sound reminding her of times gone by, childhood days – days when mums and dads were the ones who solved all of the problems and she hadn't had a care in the world.

She'd thought about her mum a lot recently, feeling guilt for not contacting her often enough. They'd never been really close the way a lot of mums and daughters are. Joanna had definitely been a daddy's girl – and so had Hannah really, albeit slightly less so. Sadly their dad had died several years ago now. Joanna still missed him every single day – especially on days like today. He would have been the one she would have turned to, talked to. He would have known what she should do and would have advised her, if only he were here…

Her mum was so different to how her dad had been – more insular, less open – guarded almost. Weird, Joanna could never understand why that should be but she supposed some people were just born that way. Although, thinking about it more, her grandparents had always seemed quite cold people, her mum had probably had a really strict upbringing with very little love in the house. She'd been their only child, too, so her childhood must actually have been quite sad and lonely.

In fact Joanna had never really considered all of this before but that was no doubt why her mum had become the person she was today. Even marriage hadn't changed the way she was, her mum and dad had never seemed that close – a bit like herself and David really, but without the temper. Her poor mum, she always looked so sad and lonely even now – and no wonder. Joanna felt bad – the close bond she and Hannah had had with their dad couldn't have helped; her mum must have felt pushed out, excluded a lot of the time. She really should make more of an effort, she'd give her a call tomorrow, too much else to think about today.

Joanna would have loved to have had a daughter herself, although that was an experience she'd never have now. Sadly, her thoughts took her back to the miscarriage she'd had after Jack – to her angel baby. In her head she'd thought it was a girl and called her Angel, although she'd never truly know. Angel would have been twenty-four now, it was hard to imagine. They could have been sitting here, together, gazing out to sea, talking, as only mothers and daughters do – they would have been close, she was sure of it.

Her eyes filled with tears at the thought of what could have been, at the pain of loss – it was something she didn't allow herself to visit often, the emotion it stirred inside her was so overwhelming. Nevertheless it was always there, festering inside her, and sometimes, just sometimes, she had no option but to let it out and release some of that pent-up grief that languished inside of her. She brushed away her tears, thankful at this moment to be alone, with no one here to witness them. No one else would understand. It had been twenty-four years ago, they would expect her to be over it, to have forgotten by now. But she would never forget Angel. Never.

Thankfully though, she'd had her amazing son to focus on – he truly had been her saviour. He had been such a huge blessing in her life, in fact she could hardly remember now a time pre-Jack. They were very close, sharing the same sense of humour as well as the same sense of fun. Many crazy memories had been made over the years. He had such a laid-back and easy-going personality and was kind and caring too but, at the same time, he would never shy away from hard work. She was so proud to be able to call herself his mum.

However, recently his whole personality seemed to be changing – he was losing his spark, which was why she was so worried about him now. He'd had girlfriends in the past and she'd always got on well with them, welcomed them into the house with open arms. But that little minx, Poxie – she was a different story altogether. The Poxie had a plan, and Joanna could see right through her. Jack was being reeled in like a slippery eel caught on a fishing hook and he hadn't even noticed.

Joanna wouldn't have been quite so concerned if Jack had at least looked happy – but he didn't. In fact he looked cowed and miserable most of the time, which was so unlike him. Even his sense of humour seemed to have practically disappeared; he was almost like a different person. She'd gone into his bedroom to get something the other day and had been shocked to see to see the transformation in there too. The film posters he'd had on the walls had all been taken down, ripped to shreds, a whole heap of them discarded in the bin. They'd been replaced by pictures of the Poxie in various provocative pouting poses, and by sheets of A4 paper with messages of her undying love for him, borders of lipstick kisses all around. His desk, awash with gifts from her, was almost groaning under the weight.

Joanna had mentioned it to him casually, not wishing to sound critical. He'd admitted that he actually hated what she'd done to his room, he'd liked it just the way it used to be but he'd not liked to tell her in case she'd got upset. The same with the gifts, they were getting to be an embarrassment, but again, he didn't want to upset her.

'I didn't realise she was such a sensitive little soul,' Joanna had said.

'It's not that, Mum – she's just really insecure. She doesn't have a great relationship with her family and she's back there living with them again now, hating every minute. She wants to get out and break free but that's not possible for her at the moment, she can't afford it.'

Alarm bells had started to ring in Joanna's head. 'You're not thinking of moving in with her are you – getting a place together?'

Jack had looked at her open eyed as well as open mouthed. 'Pfft! What? Do you think I'm crazy? She's okay, but I'd never want to live with her, not in a million years – she'd be a nightmare! You trying to get rid of me or something?'

'As if,' Joanna had smiled.

But later she'd remembered something else. 'So if they don't have a good relationship, how come Poxie's – sorry, Pixie's – mum had cooked you both a huge breakfast the other morning? That doesn't sound like an uncaring mum to me.'

'Oh Mum – trust you to pick up on that. You never forget anything, do you? I'll tell you why, Pixie's mum is a feeder. You know what I mean? She's just constantly making food for everyone and encouraging them to eat. I think it's just her way of trying to cover up all of the family problems that are going on underneath. You should see the size of them though, they're enormous – grotesque!'

'So what happened to Pixie? She's like a skeleton – I've never seen a living person who looked skinnier. It's painful to see her sitting at the table, she eats nothing.'

'I think she's borderline anorexic, in fact I'm sure she is. She has a really bad relationship with food – it's a control thing I think. Weirdly she'll suggest we go out for a meal sometimes and she'll just sit and watch me eat while she sits picking away at a bit of lettuce or something. She thinks she's fat as well, which is why she goes to the gym, but then when she gets there she doesn't have the energy to do anything. I really worry about her – but I do think she'd be so much better if she could move away from that house. It's killing her, it really is.'

'Anorexic? I hadn't realised. I know she looks it but...'

'Yeah – she has a lot of mental health issues all stemming from her background. That's why she dropped out of uni. I know I told you she got kicked out but I was just covering for her, she doesn't like people knowing about all the stuff she has going on. I feel really sorry for her.'

'Well don't feel too sorry,' Joanna had said. 'It's good that you're kind to people and always want to help but it's also all too easy to get dragged down by other people's problems. Be careful, Jack, you've got a lot going for you, don't throw it all away. I know it's not up to me to tell you how to run your life anymore but take care – that's all I'm saying.'

They'd hugged each other so tightly after that conversation it brought tears to her eyes just remembering. She only hoped he'd taken it all on board and that his kind heart didn't lead him onto a path down which he was reluctant to go. She loved her boy so much and just wanted him to be happy in his life, not led astray and making choices that could possibly destroy him.

Joanna was brought back to the here and now, feeling eyes upon her. 'Hello! Where did you come from?' A dog. Sat before her. Gazing longingly at the last piece of doughnut still cradled in her hand.

'Sorry,' shouted the out-of-breath voice of a figure who came racing up the beach to rescue her from the perils of his dog. 'Jasper – you're meant to come when I call you. Leave the lady alone.'

But Jasper wasn't going anywhere, not while there was food in the offing. 'Just one tiny bit?' his eyes pleaded.

'Can he?' asked Joanna.

'Oh go on then, I'm so sorry,' said the man, 'he knows he shouldn't be doing that. Are you okay, by the way?'

Feeding her last morsel to the dog, Joanna felt suddenly embarrassed and scrubbed the tears from her face with the corner of the blanket she had wrapped around herself. She huddled into it tightly, feeling the cold sea breeze whipping in around her shoulders through the gap she had created.

'I'm fine, honestly – but thank you, it's just been one of those days. Well, a few of those weeks actually.'

'We all have them,' he smiled. 'Thank you for being kind to my dog. See you around maybe?'

'Maybe.'

And with that he was gone. Some men were nice, what a pity she wasn't married to one of them.

*

So, what was she going to do with her life? She hadn't just come here today to think about her mum and her son, that was the easy bit. The biggest decisions she had to make were about David and about Gavin. After all these years of marriage, should she leave him? Is that what she wanted? Would that make her happy? But could she really visualise herself still being with David in a loveless marriage for another thirty years? Actually no, the very thought of that just wanted to make her curl up in a corner and die. Decision made then, maybe? Stop dithering, Joanna!

As for Gavin – it was hard to explain how she was attracted to him. Well, there was the obvious one of course – his body. And there couldn't be any more perfection than that! But he was younger, a friend of Jack's, which made her feel more like a cradle-snatcher than a ravishing cougar with a toy boy. She still didn't know his full story yet either. There must be at least one ex hovering in the background somewhere, possibly children too. Not many people get to that age without baggage of some description – especially people who look as good as Gavin. She needed to know more.

It was weird the connection she felt with him, especially having known him for such a short time. And it wasn't just about sexual attraction, or about the fact that he seemed like a genuinely nice guy, it went so much deeper than that – a spiritual connection almost. What worried her though was the thought of this relationship progressing. For a start, unless she left David, she really couldn't let this 'thing' she had with Gavin continue, a life filled with secrets and lies was just not in her nature – especially with Jack being involved too. And yet the thought of it, the thought of ending it all and going back to a life without sparkle again, would surely drain her soul.

The waves lapped softly across the sand, not far away from her now. The tide was coming in, she should think about moving soon. She stood, holding the blanket firmly around herself to keep out the cold as she made her way back towards the steps, pausing momentarily to pick up a flat stone from the sand and skim it purposefully over the waves. 'Tell me what to do!' she shouted – to her dad, to the sea, to the seagulls circling above, to anyone who could help her – as the skimming stone bounced across the water. There is no easy answer, Joanna, the decision can only be yours.

Chapter Seven

It was starting to get dark by the time she got home. As she turned her key in the front door to let herself into the house she was suddenly filled with guilt. She really should have rung and told him where she was, she'd been so wrapped up in her own problems that the thought had never even entered her head.

'Where the hell have you been? I was worried. I tried ringing your mobile but you didn't answer,' greeted David, a worried frown upon his face.

'Sorry – I should have phoned. I just didn't think, I'm so sorry. I heard my phone ringing when I was in the car but I was driving so I couldn't take the call.'

'Where've you been anyway?'

'Seaside.'

'What?!'

Even she realised it must sound a bit weird. 'It was just one of those spur of the moment things, you know? I was just having a bit of a drive around and before I knew it I was halfway there! So I thought "Why not?" Do you never get the urge to do stuff like that? Breakaway from the norm and do something a bit mental? It's really good for the soul, I reckon – gives you a whole new lease of life.'

'Can't say that I do – no. I like my routine – I like things to be planned out so I know what I'm doing. Anyway could you call me please next time you decide to do something "mental" like that, just so I know where you are.'

'Sorry. I will,' she said, walking through to the kitchen, David following. 'What's all this?' she asked suddenly, eyes focusing upon the table, which was set for two. Candles, champagne on ice, linen napkins – the lot.

'You said we should make more of an effort if we want to save our marriage, so that's what I'm trying to do. I followed one of your recipes – there's a casserole in the oven. I just hope it hasn't burnt now, it was ready about an hour ago – that's one of the reasons I was phoning, I didn't know how long you were going to be. There are some flowers for you over there as well. Would you like me to put them in water while you go up and get changed?'

'How amazing – I'm in shock!' she grinned. 'What a lovely surprise, thank you. I'm so sorry for keeping you waiting, I had no idea. I'll just nip upstairs quickly – back in a minute.'

Oh David, David, David. Too little, too late?

*

The meal was actually rather nice, even if the conversation was a little stilted. He asked about her day at the seaside but there was nothing much to say about it really – that she'd sat wrapped in a tartan blanket gazing out to sea all afternoon didn't exactly cut it – it didn't even sound very believable. Buying a doughnut and then sharing a piece of it with some random dog was all she could tell him. He looked bemused.

'And so the trip was worth it, was it?'

'I think so. I feel better for it anyway.'

He stared at her like she was some kind of weirdo. Perhaps she was. As though scrambling around for topics of conversation to fill in the awkward silences, his next question took her by surprise.

'Were you thinking of getting some jobs done around the house? Updating and stuff. I know, I agree, we've been a bit lax in that department. I'm not very good at DIY, as you know, and it kind of puts me off from even thinking about it. The kitchen and bathroom are starting to look a bit shabby though, I suppose. Why don't you get some quotes and then we can decide?'

'Uh? Where did that come from? We've never talked about this before.'

'I know we haven't, but I saw you'd picked up a business card for a plumber, so I thought you must have been thinking about getting something done, I thought maybe this was all part of changing things – working at trying to save our marriage.'

Joanna's stomach did a double backwards flip as her heart began to race. 'Business card?' she asked, giving a rather sterling performance considering drama had always been her weakest subject at school.

'Yes, it was in your phone case, I saw it the other day.'

'What were you doing looking in my phone?' she asked, guardedly – forgetting for the moment that she was meant to be playing it cool.

'I wasn't. It was the day you'd gone jogging and fallen over. You'd left your phone behind if you remember. Hannah rang it expecting you to answer but she got me instead. I answered it because, well, it could have been important... and it was sitting on the kitchen table right next to me. The card fell out as I picked up the phone and opened it and when I saw it was for a plumber, that's what made me think. Anyway, it's not important. Dessert? I got your favourite – chocolate brownies.'

Joanna acknowledged his question with a nod, her head awash with guilt. She'd done nothing wrong – not yet, not really. And yet, had she been on trial for murder she could not have felt any worse.

*

There is nothing quite like a warm chocolate brownie to soothe your furrowed brow and make your problems ooze away, even if it is only temporarily.

'Mmmm. This is gorgeous,' she said, her eyes closed in ecstasy.

'There's another if you'd like it?'

'You're spoiling me.'

'I aim to please.'

Amid chocolate heaven they heard the front door open.

'Hello – anyone home?'

'In here, Jack – chocolate brownies if you'd like one.'

'Ah no – I've just eaten thanks.'

'Have you managed to escape the Poxie tonight? She's usually attached to you like a limpet.'

'Erm...' started Jack, embarrassed.

'Hi,' said a voice from the doorway.

'Oh sorry, Pixie, I didn't realise you were here.'

'Come in,' said David, lecherous old man voice to the fore. 'Come and sit next to me. Would you like a glass of champagne, there's still some left in the bottle?'

Pixie shook her head. A 'no' on both counts.

'We do have some news to tell you though,' said Jack, looking somewhat underwhelmed by it all. 'We've found a flat, or rather Pixie has. We're going to be moving in together – get the keys next week. Sorry, Mum,' he said, looking anxiously at Joanna's crestfallen face.

'Hey – you don't have to apologise to your mother, you're twenty-nine years old, for God's sake. It's time you found a place of your own – you don't want to be tied to your mother's apron strings for the rest of your life do you? Good luck to you – let's have a drink to it.'

But Joanna found it hard to muster any enthusiasm whatsoever. It was only a few days ago that Jack had said there was no way he'd ever want to live with Pixie. She was Trouble, that one, and with a capital 'T'. He was committing himself to a miserable future filled with problems; this was the first step on a long, slippery slope. She knew it, and so did he, but he seemed almost powerless to make it stop.

The problem was that, like so many young people, he thought he was invincible. He wrongly assumed he'd be able to escape whenever he wanted to, simply walk away. He thought, this was 'just for now' to help her out. But there was no way, she'd seen it all too often. Women like Pixie, they grab you by the throat and sink their claws in. Sometimes they may move on if they find something better, but they won't ever let go. They just leave you with the thumbscrews on until they bleed you dry – every aspect of your life. Oh Jack – how she wished he would open his eyes before it was too late, she wanted to shake him, knock some sense into him – he was going to ruin his whole life.

'Look, I insist,' said David, who was gradually getting more and more intoxicated. 'I'm going to open another bottle. It's not every day your son and heir announces he's going to move out of the happy homestead – we need to celebrate. And get a smile on your face for God's sake, Joanna – I thought you'd be feeling happy after your day out at the seaside.'

'Seaside?' Jack turned to look at her. 'On your own?' he questioned, pointedly, staring into her eyes as though he'd suddenly added two and two together and made fifteen.

'Well of course she went on her own. Not going to drag me there was she? I hate going on pointless trips like that – an absolute waste of time.'

Jack continued to stare at her, not wanting to believe the thought that had entered his head. He knew his mum and dad weren't happy together but...

'On my own – yes. I like my own company sometimes and it was a pleasant enough day.'

Curious as he was, Jack let it pass. He'd come back to it later.

'Well cheers!' said David, having handed around champagne-filled glasses to everyone. 'Here's to the happy couple and their future life together.'

'Dad – we're not getting married! Just moving in together, that's all.'

'That's the first step though, son, the first step. Wait till you're an old married couple like me and your mother, eh? Not been so bad has it, darling?'

Oh… my… God. She wanted to kill someone. Any one of them at that moment. Jesus!

*

Jack was in the kitchen when she came downstairs the next morning. He was making a cup of tea for the Poxie, who was still in bed.

'Are you sure you know what you're doing?' she asked.

'Mother, I think I know how to make a cup of tea,' he quipped.

'You know what I mean. I'm worried about you – I just hope you realise what you're taking on.'

'I'm sorry, I hate upsetting you. You really don't have to worry though – it's fine, I know what I'm doing.'

'Do you though? Do you really? This is a massive commitment and it could wreck your entire life – and for what? It's not even as though you love her or anything – is it? You're just doing it because you feel sorry for her…'

'*Love* her? No – no way. I don't love her. It's just that she has so many problems and anxieties and the majority of them stem from living at home with her family. She's really got to move out and get away from them, she's so fragile. Sadly she doesn't earn enough money to pay rent on a place of her own and that's why I offered to help her out. I couldn't just leave her in the situation she's in, I honestly don't know how much longer she would survive. I couldn't live with myself if she decided to end it all, knowing that she'd reached out to me and I'd done nothing to help.'

Joanna gave him a hug. 'You really are a lovely guy, Jack – I'm so proud of you. Too kind for your own good sometimes but that's not always a bad quality to have. I just hope it doesn't all backfire on you, that's all I'm saying. Take care, won't you – and I'm always here for you, you know that.'

'Thanks, Mum, you don't know how much that means to me to hear you say that. I don't want to upset you, in fact that's the last thing I'd ever want to do,' he said, hugging her fiercely.

Eventually, breaking away, he leant back against the kitchen worktop, arms folded. 'By the way, enough of my problems, how about you? How well do you know Gavin? What's all this about the seaside? Come on – dish the dirt!'

'Jack! There isn't any "dirt", as you put it. He was the one who helped me the day I fell, when I was out jogging – he was really kind. And then funnily enough, by sheer coincidence, I bumped into him on the one and only day I've ever been to the gym. That's all there is to it, don't try to make it into more than it is.'

'But then he took you to the seaside.'

'He did not! Honestly he didn't. I went there on my own, like I said.'

'Hmm,' said Jack, stroking his chin. 'The lady doth protest too much, methinks.'

'Jack! Stop it – I'm telling you the truth, I've done nothing wrong.'

'Well I wouldn't blame you if you did, is all I'm saying. Gavin's a lovely bloke and my dad, well, he treats you like shit. You only have one life, Mum – don't ever forget that.'

'Pot kettle black, son, pot kettle black.'

*

It seemed like a very depressing week in many ways. Jack and the Poxie were backwards and forwards sorting out everything for their forthcoming move. Despite feeling less than enthusiastic at the prospect of it, Joanna did her best to help, sorting out saucepans, crockery, bedding, etc., things she no longer needed that would come in useful for them. Although when she overheard the Poxie saying to Jack, 'Huh – as if we'd want that old thing!' she became loath to sort out any more.

She felt particularly hurt when she saw her going through all of Jack's things, items he'd treasured, putting them into a bag to go to the council tip. Even worse was when she went through his wardrobe, sorting out his clothes, holding up things Joanna had recently bought for him which he'd chosen himself. 'Yuck,' the Poxie said, 'definitely the charity shop. Who on earth would ever buy stuff like that?' They were the most words Joanna had ever heard her say and they were said with such an evil, twisted smile – this girl definitely knew what she was doing.

David, on the other hand, was being smarmily nice – 'darling' seeming to be his every other word. She really couldn't cope. He seemed to think that the meal he'd cooked for her had resolved every problem in their marriage and couldn't understand why she wasn't welcoming him with open arms – he'd done his bit, now it was down to her. Fair enough, he hadn't lost his temper for a few days but she found it hard to believe that would last. It would take a course in anger management, at least, for him to rectify that trait and when she'd tentatively made that suggestion very recently, it had been greeted with such an explosive outburst of temper, she was reluctant to witness a repeat.

So, she was quite happy to receive the text:

'*Hey. Do you fancy meeting up?*'

'*Not sure. Bit busy.*'

Who was she kidding? The only thing she was busy doing was trying to resist the gin bottle which was calling her from the worktop. She had a glass in her hand in readiness, just in case, and there was still some cucumber left in the fridge, she'd noted that earlier.

'*Spare an hour?... Please?*'

Only an hour? She was hoping for much more than that.

'*Okay.*'

Hah – she took such a lot of persuading.

Chapter Eight

They met in the supermarket car park – romantic, hey? She – in all her finery, looking as though she was about to appear on *First Dates*, and he – in T-shirt and jeans, looking somewhat scruffy, as though fresh from a building site, which he probably was. Oh.

'Sorry, I feel a tad underdressed,' he smiled, as he greeted her warmly with a kiss on the cheek. 'I'm in the middle of a house renovation but needed a break – so much work on at the moment.'

'No worries, I always go to the supermarket dressed like this,' she grinned, feeling decidedly overdressed now – in fact, feeling like a harlot on the game.

'Shall we leave your car here and I'll drive you back to my place?'

She looked startled. Perhaps he thought she was up for it, the signals were all there. And to be honest, that had been kind of what she was hoping for, even though the thought of it did worry her somewhat. Were women like men in that respect – 'Use it or lose it'? Would everything still be in full working order? Thankfully she'd remembered to pop the K-Y into her handbag just in case. It was reassuring to know it was there.

Maybe he could read her mind. 'Remember the day we met in this very same supermarket, and I had to shout after you because you'd forgotten your tube of…'

'Yes,' she interrupted, 'don't remind me! How embarrassing.'

'And you blushed – just like you're doing now.'

'Shut up,' she said, punching him playfully on the arm, laughing as she did so. They were so comfortable together now, she felt as though she had known him all her life rather than for just a couple of weeks.

'So shall we then?' he continued.

Her eyes widened as she looked at him. 'What? Here?'

'What are you on about now?' he grinned, knowing full well what she meant. 'Shall we go back to my place and you leave your car here? We can hardly go into Morrison's for a coffee – can we? We don't want to run the risk of bumping into Jack again.'

She really didn't like all of this 'having to be secretive', it was just not her style and in any case they'd done nothing wrong. Yet.

'Okay, let's go to yours.'

*

'Coffee?' he asked.

She perched on the edge of the sofa, clutching her handbag with its hidden delights as though her life depended on it. Maybe it did. 'Please. No sugar.'

'Don't tell me – you're sweet enough,' he said, heading back into the room with it and putting the mugs down on the coffee table.

He didn't sit next to her, as she'd expected him to, but walked across the room to sit in the chair opposite.

'Sit back and relax,' he said, 'you look as though you're about to face a firing squad.'

'Sorry,' she said, shuffling back on her seat to make herself more comfortable.

'Well, I might as well come straight out with it,' he said, looking a little uncomfortable also, 'the reason I wanted to see you…'

Joanna shuffled a little more, gripping on to her handbag tightly, never more glad to have it with her; it felt like a comfort blanket almost.

'The reason is that I want to propose…'

What? He was going to ask her to marry him? But they barely knew each other. And anyway, she already had a husband – had he forgotten that?

'But Gavin, I can't. I would have loved to be able to say "yes" but I…'

'Hear me out, woman – I haven't even said anything yet! What did you think I was going to say?'

Poor Joanna – she blushed to the very roots of her highlights. OMG – why was she such a klutz? And the worst of it was, he knew exactly what she was thinking… and she knew that he knew. They rolled about with laughter. If there had been any ice, it was now well and truly broken. Contain yourself, woman! Her thoughts were getting out of hand and his didn't seem to be following along the same track at all. She took a sip of her coffee to calm herself down. Life wasn't all about K-Y Jelly, or certainly hers didn't seem to be.

For some reason Gavin suddenly started to look a bit uncomfortable – nervous almost.

'Sorry, you were just going to say something before, and then me and my big mouth shot you down. I didn't mean to interrupt – what were you going to say?' asked Joanna, still somewhat mortified by her klutz moment.

'Well,' he said, clearing his throat, 'this is going to sound even more random now and you may think I am completely crazy, but actually I want to offer you a job.'

'What?!' That was the last thing she'd been expecting. 'A job? What kind of a job?' Her mind suddenly sped into overdrive, returning down the route of her previous thoughts and the K-Y yet again. Mistress? Paramour? Bit on the side? Whatever you liked to call it really.

'PA – Personal Assistant.'

Oh. Well she'd not heard it called that before. She looked kind of stunned, as he'd known she would. She seemed lost for words, so he continued.

'I know this is all a bit weird but hear me out. I have to admit, I was physically attracted to you when we first met, still am, but I've… well, I've tried to push that to the back of my mind, at least for the time being. Like you said yourself, you have a husband and, choose what happens with your marriage, whether you decide to leave him or whether you decide to stay, you're definitely not on the lookout for another man. And like I told you, although I haven't gone into the full story, I've been screwed up by a past relationship too and am in no hurry to hurl myself head-first into another one, certainly not for now anyway. But, considering we've not known each other for very long, we definitely have a very special connection between us and I'm sure you must feel it too. It feels like more than just a friendship, it goes much deeper than that. I honestly don't know how to describe it – do you?'

In a weird kind of way, Joanna felt nothing but relief to hear what he had to say. Because, much as sex had seemingly been in the forefront of her mind, the thought of actually 'doing it' with someone so much younger and fitter than she, someone who was a friend of her son, combined with she, herself, not having had sex for years and still being married to David, had actually been stressing her out. Quite considerably. And, apart from anything else, if she left David, would she really want to jump straight into a relationship with another man? The answer was most decidedly 'no'. She'd want freedom, some time to live her own life, not to be tied to a man again – even one as fit as Gavin.

'Phew,' Joanna exhaled deeply, as though ridding herself of stress. 'You have no idea how pleased I am to hear you say all of this. I feel exactly the same. We do have some very weird kind of deep connection, I've never actually known anything quite like it before. I am attracted to you physically, there's no way I can deny that. But actually, at the same time, I'm scared. I think I've been so caught up in the idea of someone finding me attractive, it's lured me away from reality. Little niggles have been nibbling away at me trying to give me some kind of reality check, though. Like – I'm still living with my husband, and like – you're a friend of my son! And, not only that, but you're younger, fitter, and heaps more attractive than me, you could have anyone you wanted, why would you ever want me?'

Unexpectedly, she suddenly found herself feeling quite emotional.

'Hey, hey, hey,' he said, moving across to sit next to her, not liking to see her getting upset. 'Don't put yourself down.' He put his arm around her but her rant continued without her even realising it was there.

'It's true though. I'm almost forty-nine years old and I feel my life is over. What have I done? What have I actually achieved? I've been tied to the same man for more than half of my entire life and I don't even like him, never mind love him. Why don't I just leave him? Why don't I go?' Tears were sliding unchecked down her cheeks now.

'So why don't you?'

'I don't know, and that's the truth. But it's hard, it would change everything. And then there's Jack…'

'I'm sure Jack is perfectly capable.'

'He is, but then there's the Poxie, and that's a whole other story. And my mother – I feel permanently guilty about her. And Hannah – she's spent years having IVF, trying for a baby, and now she's had Lottie she's suddenly found herself facing a major crisis and she needs my support.'

'Joanna, I'm not suggesting you should move a million miles away, but I really do think you should leave David. Sounds to me like your marriage has definitely run its course. And I'm not saying that with any kind of ulterior motive, truly I'm not, my situation stands as I explained to you before. But I just feel it's time you got your life back before it's too late. The problem with you is that you put everyone else before yourself – it's wrong, you need time to yourself, time just to be you.'

She brushed away her tears with the back of her hand. He passed her a tissue from the box on the coffee table in front of them.

'Here, dry your eyes. There's a whole new world out there just waiting for you to conquer it, and the exciting thing is that you don't know what could happen. Anything is possible – absolutely anything. But from what I know of you it seems your life doesn't have much fun, just routine – the same things happening day after day. Predictable, dull and boring. Take this step forward and change things while you can. Be curious about what could be possible in your life, enjoy the mystery of not knowing what's going to happen next. It's exciting! You could have all kinds of adventures – things happening – your whole life changing for the better. Isn't that what you want, what you'd like to happen?'

He gazed into her eyes, his own bursting with enthusiasm. She so wanted to feel this hunger for life that he was trying his utmost to impart. His enthusiasm was infectious, she knew it made sense, it would empower her. She could be more than just somebody's wife and mother, somebody's daughter and sister… she could actually just BE. But it was scary. She was silent for a moment. And amazingly, a moment was all it took. She took his hands within her own, squeezing them tightly as she turned to face him, looking him straight in the eye. Determination lit up her face.

'You know what? I'm going to do it!'

And with that bold statement, and completely unexpectedly, her body shot forward as though suddenly filled with some kind of magnetic force, her lips locking firmly onto his. The action was fleeting and only lasted for a second. She sprang back, the shock electric. 'Oh!'

He looked equally startled. He wanted nothing more than for the kiss to last forever but… this wasn't the time. Right? No. They both knew, they'd both said. No. It wasn't.

'I'm so, so sorry, I didn't mean to do that, I don't know what came over me,' she gasped, feeling totally embarrassed. It was the first time her lips had touched another person's in a very long time – Joanna couldn't even remember the last time she and David had kissed.

'Do you hear me complaining?' smiled Gavin. 'Please don't feel embarrassed, it seemed like a perfectly natural thing to do. I'm just glad you've decided to take the world by storm. Maybe that kiss was symbolic – to celebrate the launch of the whole new you.'

'Perhaps it was,' said Joanna, still jittery from her actions but her eyes still alight with a new-found passion for life. Or maybe simply with a new-found passion, full stop. Because just seconds later, and with an urgency the likes of which she didn't know she even possessed, she suddenly launched herself with an overwhelming intensity upon his unsuspecting form. No way could he resist. He tried but his attempt was futile.

This time their kiss was long and lingering. It arose, on Joanna's part, from a sense of desperation, long time unfulfilled. But, despite the passion of the kiss and the stirrings it aroused in him, he knew this wasn't the right time. He knew if it continued she would regret what they had done, and there would be no going back – their friendship would suffer because of it. Loving her for who and what she was and wanting to protect her, and drawing on every last ounce of willpower he had remaining, Gavin drew back.

'Erm, sorry but… but I thought we just agreed we weren't going to do this,' he gasped, coming up for air.

Hot and flustered, breathing heavily with passion unspent, Joanna sat back upright – feeling a tad silly if she was honest. What was wrong with her, for goodness' sake? She was acting like a teenager – a schoolgirl with a crush. Grow up, Joanna, why *would* he fancy you? A cloud of embarrassment hung over her, she couldn't even look him in the eye.

'I'm sorry,' he said. 'Maybe I shouldn't have stopped – and believe me, it wasn't an easy thing to do. There's absolutely nothing I would have liked to do more than to continue. But the timing just isn't right. Because, like you said earlier, you've reached a bit of a crisis point in your life and, whether you decide to leave him or not, you're still living with your husband. I don't want to be the deciding factor in your marriage crisis and I don't want you to do anything in the heat of the moment that you might come to regret later.'

'I know. I am so embarrassed,' she said, shielding her face with her hands, still unable to look him in the eye.

'Please don't be. I'm not. Look at me, Joanna,' he said, his voice calm and soothing to her flustered state.

She lowered her hands to glance at him.

'I just feel that now would have been the wrong time,' he said. 'Who knows what will happen in the future but right now I don't want to be the cause of any complications… and I don't want us to do anything we might later regret, especially not anything that could potentially affect our friendship.'

'You're right. I'm actually glad we didn't take it any further,' she said, feeling awkward still, but just a shade more comfortable.

'I'm always right,' he grinned, winking cheekily in an attempt to lighten the atmosphere.

'Oh shut up,' she said with a little smile, punching him playfully in true Joanna style and feeling a lot more relaxed now. Why were other people so much more sensible than she was?

*

He made another coffee, unsurprisingly the first one had gone cold. 'Sooo…' he said, placing it down in front of her. 'We got a bit side-tracked, didn't we?' he said, still a little sheepishly. 'But at least now I've managed to convince you to sort your life out. God, that sounds so bad! So manipulative and controlling! And I'm really not like that – I'm really not. Sorry, just tell me to butt out and mind my own business if you like.'

'Don't be silly – I know you're not. Changing my life is something I've wanted to do for a very long time, you've given me exactly the push I needed.'

Gavin took a sip of his coffee, looking towards her, thoughtfully, as he swallowed.

'So, to get back to what I mentioned earlier… is it all right to still talk about this?'

'Of course it is. Go for it – I'm intrigued!'

'Okay I will, if you're sure. Basically, it all stems from the fact that I've been totally swamped with work just lately. My own fault, I know, I keep buying up properties at auction but then, obviously, they all need my attention.

'The idea, always, is to get a quick turnaround – buy them cheaply, do them up and then either sell on or rent them out depending on the market. It's my passion, I love it – but, at the same time, I take on so much that it's hard to keep on top of things. So, the only solution I can come to is that I'm going to have to take somebody on. And, the thing is, it's going to have to be someone I get on with, someone I know I can trust. Which… is where you come in.'

'What? Me? I know I can do many things but bricklaying was never one of my strongest skills – not last time I looked anyway,' she quipped, almost laughing out loud, any embarrassment left between them now virtually gone.

'A brickie, yeah – I can just see you as a brickie,' he teased. 'No, I mean more on the project management kind of things, admin – making sure everything gets done on time, chasing people up. But then the interior design kind of stuff as well, the styling, knowing what looks good – it needs a woman's touch sometimes. Hopefully you wouldn't be averse to doing some painting too, as well as some gardening – and I'd hope you might come to the auctions with me occasionally to help me keep my sensible head on. So basically, it's not just a PA I'm looking for, more a Jack-of-all-trades – just not a builder, I've got enough of those.'

Speechless was an understatement.

'Hello-o-o. Anybody there?' Gavin waved his hand in front of her face, teasingly.

'But – but, why would you offer a job like that to me, you hardly know me. You've no idea what my skillsets are, whether I could do any of those things. This is crazy.'

'Not crazy at all. How do you know what anyone is capable of doing? The job is so random and varied – it's not like it's anything you could have a qualification in, so how would I know, even if I interviewed a pile of people, that anyone would be capable of doing everything I needed. For a start, people in interviews always tend to lie and make out they can do everything even though the likelihood is they've never even tried it before. Then when it comes to doing the actual job they just botch it up. Weird as it seems, I trust you and I know we could work together. You're a smart, capable woman with office experience and, I'm sure, a multitude of home-making skills. Definitely the woman for the job then, I'd say.'

'Hah – got it all worked out, haven't you?'

'Yup.'

'Cheeky,' she said, slapping him playfully on the arm. 'To be fair, though, it does sound like my absolute dream job. I'm good at organising, love interior design and decorating – and even my gardening skills aren't too shabby. As for the auction, that really does appeal to me. How much would you be able to pay me though? Not that I'm earning a fortune where I am now.'

'I'm sure I'd be able to match what you're currently earning, maybe even a bit more, we'd have to discuss that. And do you know what? Oh, I've got all sorts running through my head now! But if you did decide to leave David we could maybe pick up a little property for you cheap at auction – something you could rent from me that you could do up yourself, something to practise your skills on. Oh, don't worry, no strings attached, nothing like that, it would be a proper business arrangement, a contract and everything.'

'I'm kinda speechless – you realise that. Lost for words. I'm going to have to think about it, obviously, and get back to you. Whatever made you think of this crazy idea?'

'Dunno. But once I did, it actually didn't seem so crazy. Everything just seemed to fall into place. Like it was meant to be. Fate.'

'I'm a great believer in fate.'

Chapter Nine

The house was empty when Joanna got home... or at least she'd thought it was. On closer inspection, though, she discovered Sleeping Beauty asleep on the living room sofa – David, of course. Amazingly, he wasn't even snoring, which was why she'd thought no one was at home. The open newspaper lay across his chest, he must have fallen asleep mid-read – the news from around the world was obviously extremely riveting today. As for any local news or personal stories, that was usually of much lesser importance to David. But the news she had bubbling up inside her would certainly wake him from his slumbers. Nervous as she was at the prospect of telling him, she couldn't help but feel a little fountain of joy inside, which made her want to smile.

Should she wake him, tell him all of her news in its entirety? Or leave him to sleep, so that he didn't wake up in a grumpy mood – tell him a bit at a time. Deciding on the latter, Joanna made to leave the room. A long peaceful soak in the bath was just what she needed, a nice hot bath was where she did her thinking, it always helped to put everything into perspective. She was just stepping out of the door to head towards the bathroom when she heard, 'Joanna!' He was awake.

'I thought I heard you – where've you been? Blimey,' he

exclaimed, 'you're all tarted up. Not got another man have you?'
he guffawed, as though the thought of another man ever taking a
second glance at Joanna was hilarious.

Huh – what a prat. How had she put up with him for so long?
Okay, split-second decision, she'd mention the job. That would
explain why she was 'all tarted up', as he had so succinctly put it.

'I've been for a job interview actually,' she said, almost puffing
out her chest with pride.

'What's wrong with the job you've got? You've been there for
years.'

'Precisely. Time for a change.'

'Is this all to do with the marriage thing – making a new start
and all that?'

'Kind of, yes.'

'What time's dinner?'

Great. So he couldn't even be bothered to ask about the job
– no interest whatsoever. The only thing he was bothered about
was his dinner and how much longer it would be until she would
be serving it. That really was all she meant to him, a meal on
the table. A servant in every aspect but name. She was definitely
making the right decision. If she'd had any doubts before, they
were now gone.

*

The day Jack moved out was an emotional one for Joanna. It
felt like the end of an era, which it was in so many ways. She, of
course, was the only one who knew that this moment was the last
time their little family unit would ever be intact. They thought she
was upset because she'd had Jack 'tied to her apron strings', as
David was often heard to remark – they thought she was simply
overplaying the mother/son thing, possessive to the core. But it
was so much more. Jack had left home before – he'd been away to

drama school, and he'd lived in London for a while too – but on neither of those occasions had she felt like this.

Had Jack been moving into a place of his own, or with someone who would make him happy and with whom she got along too, then she would have been pleased for him, overjoyed in fact. But the Poxie – she was evil with her warped and twisted little mind. She was like a thorn that gets under your skin and causes more and more pain – and no matter how hard you try to get it out, it just sinks further in, deeper and deeper until it's out of your grasp. And you know that even though it hurts now it will probably only get worse, become infected, start to fester and there isn't a pill in the world, antibiotic or otherwise, that can cure the damage done.

She waved them off that morning with a heavy heart and insincere good wishes. It pained her to do so but it was hard to feel joyful about something that you knew was so wrong. Her mother would have told her to 'stop being maudlin' if she could have seen her face right now as she cleared up the mess they'd left behind. That very thought actually added to the weight of her burden. Was this how her mother had felt when she and Hannah had left home? And yet they had both done so without a backward glance, just as Jack had done now.

Thinking back, her poor mother hadn't had much happiness in her life – strict parents followed by a loveless marriage. In fact in many ways, her mother's adult life had mirrored her own. At least now she was lucky to have met Gavin – he had brought some light into her world, given her joy and happiness again, given her the prospect of some excitement to look forward to. Had her mother ever experienced real happiness? Had she ever truly known love? It wasn't the sort of topic they'd ever discussed – she wasn't the kind of person who could bring herself to talk about such things. But to think of her mother going through her whole life without love seemed… oh so sad. Looking back, Joanna realised she and Hannah hadn't helped the situation, in fact they'd probably made it worse. As 'daddy's girls' they'd always run to their dad for cuddles when they were small. He'd joined in their fun, played games with them, whilst their poor mother had always seemed to be busy in the kitchen. Cooking, baking, washing, cleaning – where had been the joy for her in that?

Guilt started to weigh heavily upon Joanna's shoulders now. The more she thought about it, the worse she felt. Is that why her mother seemed to have such a sad aura about her? Is that why she had always seemed to be so 'closed' and would never open up to anyone?

Her own adult life did mirror her mother's in some respects, but thankfully not in every single one. Her mother was seventy-four now – she was of a different generation. She'd been a stay-at-home mum as many had been back then – a slave to her home, to her kids and to her man, stoic in her sense of responsibility.

So, much as Joanna complained about her job on a regular basis, and about having to get up early to go to work, at least she went to work. She wasn't stuck at home all day with a humdrum routine and screaming children, she was able to escape into another world, think of things other than nursery rhymes, meet different people, broaden her horizons – it was probably what had kept her sane over the years. Or sane-ish, some may say!

And she'd had Jack, too, not two little girls who would run to cuddle their daddy at every given opportunity, Jack and his daddy had rarely spent any time together at all as he'd been growing up. In fact Jack had always tried to keep out of his way, wary of crossing the line and coming face to face with that explosive temper. Like his mum, Jack did not like confrontation and always tried to avoid it if at all possible. So yes, she'd spent a lot of time with Jack – and it had been fun. Lego and dinosaurs, Scalextric and football, not forgetting the incessant laughter. There had definitely been happiness in her life. But mostly it had been thanks to Jack. Her face clouded over...

Right, enough of this maudlin, she needed something to take her out of herself. Perhaps this was the time to do something she'd been intending to do for the past couple of weeks – go and visit her mother. On this occasion the idea didn't stem from a sense of duty either, as it usually tended to do. Right now she needed to see her mum. She needed to feel that reassurance of still having family who loved her – not just Hannah, that wouldn't suffice. She needed mother-love to fill the void and she knew that, deep down, her mother did love her, even if she wasn't often able to show it. Her dad had always been the demonstrative one, her mother had shown her love simply by caring for them and by always being there.

*

Her mum lived about a forty-minute drive away. She still lived in the family home, the house in which she'd raised her girls. It really was far too big for her now, but much as both Hannah and Joanna had tried to convince her to move to somewhere smaller, somewhere less isolated and easier to maintain, she was adamant – she was staying put. It was understandable in a way. She'd lived in the same house for fifty years and knew every nook and cranny, every creaking floorboard, every clunk the boiler made. It was all so familiar to her – all of these little quirks made it not just a house but a home.

There were two more houses in the lane also, so she wasn't completely isolated. In fact she knew both lots of neighbours really well, they'd lived there for almost as long as she had. And although they didn't go in and out of each other's houses often, they were always there for each other in times of crisis or for the occasional chat over the garden gate.

For the girls it had been a great place to grow up, the neighbours' children had been of a similar age to them. Along the lane and in the open countryside surrounding it, they had been free to roam

– build dens, collect caterpillars in jam jars, make daisy chains to decorate themselves and their hair, pick the blackberries growing wild in the hedgerow and take them back to Mum to help make jam. Even on their bikes they'd been free to whizz up and down the lane from a very early age – it was a safe place, a 'dead-end', a lane for residents' use only. It really had been the perfect place in which to raise a family and was in such a beautiful location – idyllic. Joanna could understand why she would be reluctant to leave it – she lived there in her own little bubble of tranquillity, disturbed by no one, troubled by none.

To Joanna, it almost seemed like she was stepping back in time when she came to visit. Weirdly, she felt seven years old and four feet tall, her hair in pigtails. When she caught sight of her reflection in the glass of the front door as she rang the bell, she was surprised to see herself looking as she did – an adult. An adult Joanna. She just didn't feel very much like a grown-up at the moment. Being a child without responsibilities and without decisions to make had been good; she wished she'd appreciated it more at the time.

'Well hello – what a lovely surprise! I didn't know you were coming today, you never said.'

Her mother seemed genuinely overjoyed to see her. She welcomed her with open arms – well, almost, she really wasn't a huggy person although she did give her a kiss on the cheek, two actually.

'Hey, what's with the continental kissing – not taken an Italian lover since I saw you last, have you?' quipped Joanna, attempting to cover her own ineptitude with humour, as she always did. Right now she really wanted nothing more than to feel able to throw her arms around her mother and hold her close, and for her mother to hug her tightly too but, as always, something held her back. She knew how much her mother hated hugs and, desperate though she was, her fear of rebuff was far, far worse.

'I'm just pleased to see you, that's all – it's been a while.'

'I know, I'm sorry – I've just been so busy,' said Joanna, guilt invading every pore and marching around in hobnail boots.

'Well never mind, you're here now. Let's get you inside and I'll put the kettle on. Actually no, come straight through and we can sit outside in the garden, it's beautiful out there today.'

Hah – nothing had changed. Joanna followed her thinking how funny it was that her mother was so transparent. What she'd really meant was that she'd just finished giving the lounge a thorough clean and as it was now so immaculate, she really didn't want anyone going in there today. Yep, her mother had OCD overload.

'Tea or coffee?'

'Tea please.'

'Earl Grey? Chamomile? Peppermint?'

'What is this – tea at the Ritz or something? Do you have plain?'

'Oh, you're so common,' smiled her mum.

'I know, it's the way I was brought up.'

It was nice to see her mum smiling, she seemed happier today somehow, more content. They chatted about Hannah and baby Lottie, although Joanna didn't mention the problem with Marcus, that was up to Hannah if and when she needed to tell their mum. Helping out with Lottie was something her mum said she would love to do if only she lived a little closer to them. Although in reality she wouldn't want to leave her lovely house, she was comfortable here – and would she really want to have to be dealing with a crying baby or a screaming toddler now, at her age? No, maybe not. There was a lot to be said for solitude.

Joanna made her laugh when she told her about the Poxie, in fact she laughed herself too. It would have been even funnier if it hadn't been so tragic.

'Is that how it made you feel, Mum, when Hannah and I left home? Really sad – like it was the end of an era, like your role in life was over?'

'The empty-nest syndrome, that's what they call it. It was all so long ago now but yes, I can still remember feeling that way. Life changes so much when your children move out. But I knew it was what you both wanted. You were both getting married and building lives of your own. That's a mother's job, to raise her children to be confident and well and happy and then to let them fly free when the time is right for them to go.'

'But what about when you know it isn't the right time for them to go? Like Jack… like I know it's definitely *not* the right time for him to go. Well actually no, that's wrong, it could be the right time, it's just the route he's taken that's all so wrong. How can he ever be happy now? He's going to ruin his entire future. It's just like a disaster waiting to happen and there's absolutely nothing I can do about it.'

'Other than wait, be there to help him pick up the pieces when it all falls apart like I did,' said her mother. Pointedly.

Joanna looked up at her, startled. Had her mother known all along? Had she known that she'd never truly been in love with David right from the beginning?

'What d'you mean?'

'I mean that sometimes you have to stand back and let your children make their own decisions, it's not easy but you have to do it, they have to learn by their own mistakes.'

'So?'

'So when Hannah left home to get married I really didn't have any concerns. Marcus was a lovely guy and I got on well with him, he made a real effort to fit in with us all and soon became a big part of the family, as I'm sure you must remember. They were very much in love, had bought their own house and everything just seemed to be falling into place for them. It was plain to see how happy they were, they were besotted with each other, and that made me happy too. So even though Hannah was my baby, the last one to leave home, it didn't make me feel sad, not really, because I felt as though my family was getting bigger, not smaller – I felt as though I was gaining a son.

'With you though it was different. To be perfectly honest, I never really liked David, there was just something about him. He always seemed so self-obsessed and never made any effort whatsoever to fit in with our family. I didn't like the way he tried to control you all the time either. But most of all you never seemed to look happy when you were with him, that was my main concern. You certainly didn't strike me as being someone who was head over heels in love – I never witnessed any spark between you at all. It seemed to me that David was the one who made all of the decisions and you just fitted in for the sake of a peaceful life.'

'So why did you never say anything? Give me some advice, tell me not to marry him? I thought you got on okay with David, you were always pleasant and friendly, chatting to him whenever he came to the house.'

'That – it was all just an act. It wasn't in my nature to be hostile towards the man you were intent on marrying – I didn't want it to drive a wedge between us, that was my fear. But why did you stay with him and agree to marry him if you weren't happy?'

'Because when I was with him it raised my status amongst our friends, you seem to "fit in" more when you're in a couple rather than when you're a singleton. Then when he asked me to marry him it was in front of everyone and they were all so excited for me – how could I possibly say no? After that it just seemed to snowball – everybody talking about wedding plans, looking forward to the big day. It felt as though I was on a roller coaster and it was impossible to get off. Even you seemed happy.'

'Because I thought that's what you wanted. Imagine if I'd thrown him out, banned him from the house and told you that you couldn't get married to him or even see him. How would you have reacted do you think? Knowing what you're like, you would probably still have gone ahead with the wedding just to spite me!'

Even Joanna raised a glimmer of a smile at that thought. 'You're probably right,' she said. 'I was a stroppy little bugger at times, wasn't I?'

'You're telling me! In fact I can clearly remember asking you, on the morning of the wedding, if you were quite sure you were doing the right thing. You looked what I could only describe as resigned, rather than excited, and I wanted you to know that, even at that moment, it wasn't too late to change your mind. "Butt out, mother," you snarled at me, "mind your own business." What more could I do? It broke my heart to see you looking so sad just as you were about to enter into a lifelong commitment.'

'I remember that – I remember wanting to throw myself into your arms and ask you to save me, get you to tell them all to go home, there wasn't going to be a wedding. But I was scared of what everyone would think of me, I just couldn't do it, so I had a bit of a strop with you instead. Huh, lifelong commitment eh?'

'Indeed. Another cup?'

'Ta.' Joanna seemed lost in her own little world. Her mother did too, actually. The second cup of tea was of little importance – the time it took to refill the kettle and boil it, more so. It gave them each a few minutes to gather their thoughts.

'I wanted to talk to you about something…' they both said simultaneously as Barbara put down the tray onto the table. They giggled, immediately linking little fingers to break the jinx, just as they used to years ago. The moment came as somewhat of a relief, it lightened the nervous tension of the unspoken thoughts that had been hovering wordlessly in the air.

'After you,' said Barbara, cradling her mug between her hands as though drawing comfort from it.

'No. After you,' said Joanna, suddenly taking fright, not wanting to give voice to the plan that had imprinted itself in her head overriding all other thoughts. Once she'd said it out loud to her mother that would be it, the decision would have been made.

Telling Gavin had been the easy one, a different thing altogether. This was her mother. The matriarch.

'I insist,' said Barbara, having an anxious moment of her own. What if her children didn't like the idea? What if they were disgusted by her? What would she do then?

'I'm going to leave David.' Straight and to the point, there was no other way.

'Well hallelujah and praise be to that! How many years have I been waiting for you to say it? I don't know why you were looking so nervous, it's the best news I've had in weeks.'

'Sorry, it's just that when you put it into words it all seems so final.'

'Well it is I hope. Have you met someone else?'

'Kind of... yes. Well, no. Not like that. Not yet anyway. Well maybe.'

'Strewth, girl – what kind of an answer is that?'

'A confused one, I know. The fact of the matter is that, yes, I have met someone and we've become really good friends even though we've only known each other for a short while. He's even offered me a job, for goodness' sake! He runs his own business and is looking to take someone on to help him out – a project manager type of role, someone with office experience. Sounds really interesting. But what I don't want to do is to get into a relationship with him because, once I cross that line, I'd run the risk of losing our friendship, the job, everything. Things could change, who knows? But, for the moment, I'm happy to have found a really good friend.'

'It all sounds very perfect – is he happy with that too?'

'Yeah. We talked about it and we agreed, it's the sensible thing to do.'

'Sometimes sense can fly out of the window, you know. Anyway, so you're finally leaving David. Have you told him yet?'

'No. Building up to it. I reckon he'll go mental.'

'Well he's brought it all on himself. If he'd treated you better over the years you wouldn't have wanted to go. Because it is a big thing, you know, starting afresh. Making the decision to go is the easy bit by comparison. Where will you go for a start? Have you found somewhere? Because it's not going to be easy to find somewhere to rent on just the one wage – not to the standard you're used to anyway. And then there's the bills on top – have you thought about that?'

'Mother, you're not trying to put me off are you? I thought you were happy about it?'

'I'm delighted about it, of course I am. Just pointing out the grim facts of reality that's all. I still worry about you at whatever age and always will – it's programmed into my mother-brain, I can't help it.'

'I know. I'm the same with Jack...' and the whole Poxie story was repeated, in more detail this time.

Barbara listened in disbelief. That he could be so easily influenced by someone, especially someone like that, seemed insane – he'd always been so sensible.

'He's too kind for his own good sometimes, people take advantage.'

'That's exactly what I said to him. He thinks he'll just be able to walk away if it all goes wrong but he's never come across people like the Poxie before.'

'Like I said to you though,' said Barbara, 'there's absolutely nothing you can do about it. It's one of the hardest jobs a mother has to do – stepping back to watch as her adult son or daughter throws themselves into a situation you know will end in disaster. It's horrible, you feel torn, but all you can do is wait, and be there for them when they eventually realise their mistake.'

'Like you did for me, you mean.'

'Exactly that.'

Chapter Ten

Joanna drove home that afternoon, feeling closer to her mother than she had in a very long time. She felt warm and fuzzy inside knowing she was loved, and to feel loved, especially by a parent, is one of the most life-affirming things for anyone. It gave her the inner strength which she knew she was going to need in the days and weeks ahead.

Actually though, Joanna remembered, she'd been so busy talking about herself she'd forgotten to ask her mum what she'd been going to tell her. Could she have met another man? Surely not, that would seem really strange seeing her with someone else – like there was an imposter in the place where Dad should have been. Nevertheless, her mum deserved some happiness, she'd be pleased for her, truly she would.

Feeling empowered, she pulled into the drive. She expected David to be snoring on the sofa as she let herself into the house. But no. Fired up and obviously ready for an argument.

'Where the hell have you been?' he grumped, looking about as slobby as a man could get. How had she ever managed to stay with him for so long? It made her resolve to tell him even stronger – maybe even tonight. 'And what is the point of you having a phone if you don't ever answer it?'

'Sorry,' she said, taking her phone from her pocket to glance at it. Two missed calls. 'Sorry,' she repeated, 'it must have been on silent – didn't realise. I've just been over to see Mum, that's all. What did you want anyway?'

'Not me – your precious son. They want us to go over to their new place for a drink. Some sort of housewarming. Pixie's parents and her brother are going to be there. A kind of "meet the in-laws", I guess.'

Hmm. Great.

'David, we're not "in-laws", stop calling us that. Bad enough they're living together, we certainly don't want to see them getting married.'

'Speak for yourself, woman. I think she's a sexy little number that Pixie, I wouldn't mind having her as my daughter-in-law. In fact I wouldn't mind having her, full stop.'

'David!' Great. 'What time?'

'As soon as we can. Pixie's mum's bringing food, apparently. Better take some booze. Go and get ready, you know how long it takes you to make yourself look half decent. And judging by the state of you right now it'll be about midnight before we can get there.'

Even more great. How to fill a woman with confidence and make her feel good about herself. Got it in one. She climbed the stairs with a heavy heart and viewed the contents of her wardrobe with disdain. Sometimes David was right. She needed to lose weight. Half of her clothes didn't fit her, and the other half made her look like the Michelin Man – roly-poly spare tyres all the way. But hidden amongst all of the stunning creations, at which she gazed longingly and to which she whispered, 'One day', she managed to find a dress that resembled a tent. In fact maybe it was a tent, there was enough room for at least five people to sleep inside it. Black as well. A good colour. Not only was it a slimming colour but it was a sign of mourning. Appropriate in a way.

She put it on. Amazingly no squeezing in was required, even her boobs didn't cause trouble, thus proving that miracles do happen sometimes. A night out with the Poxies wearing a tent. Sounded almost like she was going camping – or glamping or something, although she didn't exactly feel very glam at this moment. Tentatively, she glanced into the mirror, hoping to see a vision of loveliness gazing back at her, hoping some miracle would have occurred. But no. In reality, the creature she saw before her looked more as though she was on her way to a Halloween party in a fancy-dress costume made from a bin liner – a wheelie bin liner at that. Jeez. But it would have to do. Nothing else would fit, especially if she was hoping to eat whilst she was there – plenty of room for expansion in a tent.

Sprucing it up with a string of chunky red beads, she felt a little better. A splash of red lipstick with red nails to match and she was done. Pity about the eyes. Despite the addition of two more coats of mascara, she was so tired that nothing could disguise the colour they were fast becoming. But at least they would match her lips. Colour co-ordination, that's what it was all about. Randomly that last thought made her giggle. The kind of tension-relieving giggle that almost has you out of control, gasping for breath, cheeks aching, tears streaming from your eyes. Laughing at nothing really, giddy as a schoolgirl. Did other people find themselves in fits of laughter when it all became too much, or was it just her? Better than the alternative she supposed.

She mopped up her eyes, adjusted her make-up and hunted in the bottom of the wardrobe for shoes. It would be a good evening, she was determined, she wasn't going to let anyone drag her down. She would see Jack and enjoy spending time with him, he would be excited to be showing her his new place, the Poxie and her Poxie family were just incidental. And who knew? She might even get along with them. Meanwhile, David and her big announcement, the thing that was really bothering her, would just have to wait.

*

The flat itself was in the centre of town. Really convenient for all the shops and bars and restaurants. It couldn't have been better situated actually. Joanna felt quite envious – a place like this would be perfect for her when she finally made the break with David. Hah – she could just imagine the Poxie's face if she announced she was moving in next door!

Jack welcomed them with a hug, looking so pleased to see them and proud at the prospect of showing them around his flat.

'Hey, steady on old chap – you only left us a couple of days ago.' A typical David remark in response to the effusive greeting.

To Joanna it seemed so much longer than just a couple of days. In fact she still struggled to grasp the fact that he'd left home and their family life would never be the same again. She hugged Jack with unexpected tears in her eyes. The tinkle of merry laughter from behind a closed door drew her back to the reality of the present moment. Obviously the other guests had already arrived. She suddenly felt quite nervous and wished she'd had a gin before she came.

Jack rolled his eyes towards the closed door. 'Pixie's mum,' he said, by way of explanation for the raucousness coming from within. 'There's one thing about her, she really does like a laugh. Come on through and let me introduce you.'

'Wow,' Joanna exclaimed, as he opened the door into the lounge, 'it's beautiful. How have you managed to get it looking so amazing in such a short time?' She moved towards Pixie's mum with hand outstretched to greet her but the lady was having none of it.

'Well how lovely to meet you, I've been so looking forward to it – haven't we Alan?' she said, giving her morose-looking, overly large husband a subtle kick on the shin to bring him back to life. 'I'm Cath, and not one for formalities. Let's have a hug, that's more my style,' she said, as she enfolded Joanna in her mounds of wobbly flesh for one of the most welcoming and comforting hugs the latter had ever known. 'I don't know what you must have thought when you saw me give Alan a kick,' she whispered, 'I have to do that occasionally to give him a kick-start, if you know what I mean.' Peals of laughter followed. In a weird kind of way Joanna found herself drawn to this woman, a reaction she hadn't expected at all.

'Hi, I'm Joanna,' she beamed, 'and the pleasure really is all mine, it's so lovely to meet you. D'you know, I felt really nervous about this moment but actually I needn't have worried at all, I think we're going to get along just fine.'

And indeed they did... at first. Cath seemed like a lovely woman. It appeared to Joanna that she had been misled by Jack's fleeting description of her. Admittedly, Cath and the rest of her family, with the exception of Pixie, were all grossly overweight and she was undoubtedly a feeder. Even this evening she had brought with her enough food to feed a small army and was constantly passing it round to everyone trying to guilt-trip them into eating it all because she'd 'spent two whole days preparing it'. In fact she was quite insistent that she wouldn't leave until it had all gone. But maybe that was just the mothering trait in her, trying to look after everyone, better too much food than too little. It didn't mean she was some kind of control freak necessarily.

The living space was open plan in design, which made it feel enormous. And it was so light – Joanna absolutely loved it, in fact she felt quite envious.

'It really is gorgeous, Jack, but how did you manage to get such beautiful things together to furnish it in such a short time – you didn't have any money for a start. It didn't come fully furnished, did it?'

Jack shook his head, somewhat embarrassed, and looked pointedly towards Cath.

'Ah – he has me to blame for that, I'm afraid,' she said. 'I was so pleased to hear they were moving in together that when they signed all the rental stuff for the flat I got the keys from them, came round to check it out and measure up and then went out and bought them everything I thought they should have. I think they were a bit overawed when it all arrived, weren't you guys? Got it looking just how I want it now though, I'm really pleased.'

Neither Pixie nor Jack responded to her question about being overawed. In fact they looked totally pissed off, to be honest. And who could blame them? Surely with a new place and a new partnership, you'd want to do all of that yourself. Even if you didn't have the money for the luxuries of life at first, you'd save up until you did. Meanwhile it's all about the planning and dreaming, not about your controlling mother going out and buying everything she thought you needed, all to her own taste. Unbelievable.

'Cath!' exclaimed a shocked Joanna, wishing she was able to say how she actually felt and not just half of it. 'It must have cost you an absolute fortune! How on earth did you afford to buy all of this? I feel really bad now, I only offered them second-hand bits and pieces, things I didn't want any more. Jack never said – no wonder he looked embarrassed.'

'Don't you worry about it, I've got plenty of money. We may not look rich but that useless layabout of a husband of mine is not so useless when it comes to raking in the money, he has all sorts of dodgy deals going on – keep us pretty much loaded, they do. So don't feel bad, you gave our Pix your son, he's far more valuable than any money or any pile of furniture. I know which I'd rather have, no contest – give me a young stud any day.' And the raucous laughter was back – she was definitely the queen of it.

Joanna was feeling just a little bit bewildered by this point. Much as there was a side to Cath that she genuinely liked, there was another side to her that seemed to trigger alarm bells with almost every sentence she uttered. As for "gave our Pix your son"

– much as he wasn't a commodity to give, the thought of her ever willingly giving him to Pixie was about as far removed from her to-do list as was flying to the moon.

Jack noticed her anxiety. 'Another gin, Mum?'

Joanna glanced around the room, her eyes spoke volumes. 'Make it a large one,' she said.

Cath leapt to her feet. Well, "leapt" was maybe an exaggeration. Battling her burdensome bulges of flesh as they rippled around her like waves at high tide, she struggled to her feet, was a much more accurate description. Yes, there was one good thing about this woman – she was making Joanna feel quite skinny.

'Have another big wedge of that chocolate cake to go with your gin,' said Cath, almost gasping for breath from the concerted effort she'd had to make to stand up.

'No thanks, honestly. I'm full, I think I'd actually burst if I ate another crumb.'

'I won't take no for an answer,' she huffed, ploughing in with the knife. 'You haven't got an ounce of flesh on you – need fattening up, you do.'

'Truly, I…'

Too late. Approximately one third of a huge chocolate gateau, smothered in gooey chocolate fondant and oozing with swirling coffee buttercream, landed on her empty plate with a thud. She could almost hear the calories struggling to escape from it, falling over each other in a desperate attempt to break free.

Nooo!!

'I'm sorry but I really can't eat that, I've eaten too much already. My poor stomach can't cope with any more.'

Cake knife in hand, Cath glared at her almost threateningly as she pointed it in her direction. 'I insist. I didn't spend all that time slaving away in my kitchen just to take it all back home with me again – what would be the point of that? Eat it up, it'll do you good,' she said, in the form of a command rather than a suggestion.

Jack noticed her discomfort but seemed powerless to do anything about it. 'You okay, Mum?' he asked, looking panicked at the thought that she might actually say 'No'.

What more could she do? 'I'm fine,' she said, taking a tentative bite whilst attempting to crush any urges from her brain to signal her gagging reflex to kick into action. Death by chocolate cake – we all have to die sometime and what a way this would be to go – she could have it written on her tombstone. Mind over matter, Joanna.

Things must have been pretty desperate, she was actually looking over towards David, not in the opposite direction as was the norm. Even he seemed abnormally quiet, not the usual loud-mouthed 'just call me Mr Wonderful' behaviour he usually displayed at social gatherings. Just for a second or two she managed to home in on their conversation, curious to know what was keeping David so silently attentive. She wished she hadn't bothered. Once you've heard something it cannot be unheard. But maybe, just maybe, she'd misheard.

Turning her attention away from the menfolk and attempting to refocus her mind, she looked towards Cath, before regretting that decision instantly. Babies, it is true, can get themselves into an incredible mess if presented with a plate containing a slice of gooey chocolate cake... but a woman of her age? Oh my God!

'Excuse me but I need to use the bathroom,' burst forth Joanna, in need of escape. 'Could you show me where it is please, Jack?'

'Sure, Mum – follow me,' he said, leading the way. 'Sorry,' he whispered, when they were out of earshot. 'Really sorry. Are you okay? I did warn you what they were like – nightmare aren't they? You see why I had to help Pixie get away from them? She's not like them at all, just lacking in confidence – and is there any wonder? I know you've not got the best impression of her so far but I think you'll like her when you get to know her a bit more, she's really sweet. What makes her so quiet whenever I bring her back home is Dad. She's quite shy anyway and you know what he's like with visitors, she feels quite intimidated by him.'

'Yep, I can understand that, I know exactly what he's like. But she won't have to put up with that for much longer.'

'What do you mean?'

'I'm leaving him.'

Jack's eyes widened in shock, his mouth fell agape. He paused momentarily as his thought processes whirled, spiralling him into action as he grabbed her into his arms and gave her one of the biggest, fiercest hugs ever.

'Oh, Mum, you don't know how happy that makes me feel. I know you've not been happy for years and I was really worried how life was going to be for you now I've moved out. Good for you! You're still young – time to do something for yourself now instead of worrying about everyone else. You can have a whole new life.' A sudden thought crossed his mind and he broke free from the hug to look her directly in the eye. 'This is not to do with Gavin, is it? You're not going to be moving in with him, are you? I mean he's a lovely guy and all that but ...'

'But he's young and he's your mate. You can stop right there, Jack. No, I'm not going to be moving in with Gavin. And before you ask – no, we're not having an affair. He's a good friend, that's all, and he's encouraged me to do something with my life instead of plodding along being unhappy like I have done for years.'

'Yeah, I told you he was a top bloke – good for him.'

'Just one thing, though, don't mention anything about this to your dad, I've not even told him yet. I'm waiting for the right moment, or plucking up courage, more like. Dreading it really, I just keep putting it off.'

'Understandably. I know what he's like, he's gonna go mental. Would you like me to come over and be there when you tell him? Would that make it any easier?'

'No, Jack, honestly. Thank you though, it was really kind of you to offer, but I'll be fine. I totally refuse to let that man intimidate me any longer.'

'Good on you, Mum – this inner strength of yours has been a long time coming.'

Eventually they went back in to join the others. Joanna cast her eyes around the room – did she really want to be here? She wouldn't be, of course, if it wasn't for Jack – how on earth had he managed to get himself involved with these people? Unbelievably, or maybe not, the entire remains of the chocolate cake had disappeared in that short time, the culprit easy to spot. How did she manage to consume so much food without physically exploding?

Joanna turned her attention to Pixie's brother, who had been sitting in a corner playing on his phone all evening, despite still managing to consume copious amounts of food. She felt a bit bad for not having paid him any attention. He was just a teenager, and that's what teenage boys do. However, despite several attempts to engage him in conversation, the inaudible grunts she received in reply didn't seem worth the effort.

She started to talk to Jack instead but, as they continued to chat, Joanna's attention was side-tracked by Pixie. Joanna watched her in amazement. What on earth was she doing? She appeared to be tearing narrow strips of paper from a magazine, curling them like curling ribbon around her finger, licking the ends and then proceeding to stick them all over Jack's face. Jack seemed oblivious, it was as though it wasn't happening. Joanna was completely fascinated.

'You okay, Mum?' he asked, before continuing the conversation he was having with her about his acting and about an audition he'd been on recently for which he'd had a call-back. He was very excited, it was for a lead in a soap and he was down to the last two – it would make a huge difference to him if he could get it. Joanna was so pleased for him but, as always, they both knew not to get their hopes up too much; acting was such a precarious career path to follow.

This was crazy. How could they possibly be having this

conversation with these curly things stuck all over his face? Jack must surely know how ridiculous she was making him look – why didn't he stop her and take them off? Every time he spoke they were bouncing up and down – she was finding it hard to think straight, let alone speak. Which was obviously why Pixie was doing it. Jealous of him speaking to his mother, wanting all the attention on herself. She really was the most insecure little person Joanna had ever met. But the latter had really had enough.

'May I ask a question – why are you doing that, Pixie? I'm just trying to…'

Resembling a startled rabbit, Pixie couldn't have looked more terrified if she'd threatened her with a gun. In fact Joanna was beginning to think maybe she had.

'Jack-yyyy…' came the wail, as she gazed at him with her 'poor me' woebegone eyes before dissolving into tears and rushing from the room.

Joanna was stunned. Jack looked bewildered, the paper curls quivering nervously on his face. Cath emitted a huge snore, having fallen asleep – the drama to her remained unnoticed.

'Sorry, Jack, I didn't mean any harm. All I said was …'

'I know. She's just very insecure that's all. I'd better go and deal with her.'

'Okay. We'll let ourselves out. Have fun,' she said, smiling, rolling her eyes towards the sleeping figure still snoring away. 'Just one thing though before we go.'

'What's that?' he asked, half-expecting some wise-words-of-wisdom kind of motherly advice, given the circumstances.

'Take those bloody curly things off your face!' she said, with a wink and a smile.

'Sure thing, Mama,' he grinned, giving her a big hug.

Jack. He was still her boy. They hadn't destroyed him yet. She just hoped he could stay strong in the face of such adversity. A lesser man would crumble with that lot.

Chapter Eleven

So okay, yes. Here she was a whole week later and… she still hadn't told David. Jack knew, her mother knew, Hannah knew, Gavin knew, everyone knew. Everyone except David.

Basically, this all boiled down to the fact that she was a wimp. In fact she was probably Queen of the Wimps. She'd been stuck in her own little rut for all of these years and had felt moderately safe in there. It hadn't been the all-singing, all-dancing kind of rut for the obvious reason that begins with the letter 'D', but nevertheless it had been warm and cosy most of the time, and stylish too because, after all, a rut is what you make it.

Consequently, for the Queen of the Wimps, to vacate the rut was a major challenge. Even attempting to scale the sides of the rut was probably, to Joanna, comparable to Chris Bonington climbing the North Wall of the Eiger. And he, of course, succeeded. All she had was a rickety old wooden ladder with crumbling rungs. She was doomed.

The problem Joanna had, well, just one of the very many, was that she had a big mouth. She was aware of having this particular problem just as much as she was aware of having big thighs and a big bottom, but at least she could do something about those. Exercise would not cure a big mouth; what she needed to do was learn to zip it occasionally. It was such a pity she hadn't thought about that earlier instead of telling everyone she was going to leave David because now they were all permanently on her case. 'Have you told him yet?' echoed permanently throughout her head in surround-sound, the question being fired at her from every direction. The pressure was on.

So today was all about making plans. For once in her life Joanna was thinking clearly and being sensible. Doing something as major and life-changing as this could not possibly be done on the spur of the moment, not that she would anyway, she was hardly a 'spur of the moment' type of girl. But she needed to have a plan in place. She couldn't just announce to David that she was leaving, pick up her suitcase and waltz out of the door with a toss of her hair and not a backward glance, could she? For a start – where would she go? Exactly. A cardboard box in a shop doorway wasn't exactly her style.

She thought about it for a little while, or maybe for a little bit longer, and finally reached a decision. Hannah, her beloved sister. She would go over there right now and ask if she could come and stay with them for a while. It wouldn't be forever, just a temporary thing until she found somewhere of her own.

'You mean you want to come here and stay with us?' Hannah's face registered shock. And horror actually. The hand that was patting baby Lottie on her back to rid her of post-feed wind stopped abruptly. This wasn't the reaction Joanna had been expecting. Silence. Followed by a loud burp from Lottie, echoing Joanna's feelings completely.

'Well yes, I was hoping that might be okay. It would only be for a while, just until I can get myself sorted out and find somewhere permanent. I wouldn't be any trouble.'

'Wouldn't it be better if you found somewhere permanent to move to first? I mean you've wasted all this time thinking about leaving, what's the sudden urgency?'

'Anybody would think you didn't want me here or something.' Joanna felt decidedly hurt. 'I thought you'd be pleased to have a bit of company and some help with Lottie – you said how exhausting you were finding it all. Don't worry though if you'd rather I didn't.'

'It's just that… well I told you about the problems Marcus and I are having. Just imagine his reaction if my sister suddenly lands on the doorstep, suitcase in hand. He'd go mad – it would finish him off completely.'

'Gee – thanks.'

'You know what I mean. He already begrudges me devoting so much of my time to Lottie, he thinks that when he's at home and not working, we should be spending all of our spare time together as a couple like we used to. I'm trying desperately hard to save our marriage here. Having a third adult living in the house with us would not help the situation at all – in fact it would only make it worse. I'm so sorry, Jo. I know you're my sister and I love you dearly, and under normal circumstances I'd do anything in my power to help you. But on this occasion, sadly, it has to be a "no".'

There was a similar reaction from her mother too when Joanna phoned her later that day.

'Stay here? With me?'

'Yes, I thought you might be glad of the company. It wouldn't be for very long, just until I get myself sorted out.'

'What – a couple of days?'

'Well no, I was thinking a bit longer than that. More like a couple of months, maybe?'

'*A couple of months?*' Shock-horror reaction. 'But… but the house. I can't cope with mess anymore, I like everywhere looking neat and tidy. Just imagine what a state everywhere would get in to if we were both here all the time. I remember how untidy you are, I couldn't cope, not now. And besides, I may have someone coming – what would happen if he came and you were there? No, I'm sorry but I really need my privacy.'

Great. Just great. And there had been Joanna thinking she had family who cared about her. Oh well, nothing else for it, time to check out Rightmove. That might be a good thing actually, she'd be independent right from the start, there'd be no turning back once she'd taken on a six-month lease. A frightening thought but it was doable. Time to unlock the gates to freedom. Yikes – that sounded so scary!

Hang on a minute… someone coming? *He?* She knew it – her mother had a man friend! She couldn't wait to tell Hannah. Okay, okay, Joanna, don't get side-tracked.

*

Letting sense and better judgement prevail, she switched on her laptop, located Rightmove's Property to Rent with ease, and found herself drawn into the fascinating world of being able to have a nosey inside other people's homes without them even being aware you were there. What fascinating stuff, she couldn't believe she'd never done this before – some people's homes were amazing.

Bringing herself back down to earth, she decided it may be best to add some filters. Looking around the interiors of luxuriously grand properties aimed at the millionaire lifestyle bracket was going to spoil her when it came to looking at the type of place she could actually afford to rent by herself. And indeed, as soon as she added a maximum of £600 pcm, her options were drastically reduced. That was just for an unfurnished place as well, furniture was something she was going to have to acquire and meanwhile she'd simply have to manage. Life was certainly going to change but she'd convinced herself now. No looking back, she was definitely doing the right thing. And she couldn't afford to be fussy either. Although looking at some of these properties as she scrolled down the page… well, she did have her standards.

None of them leapt out and said, 'Come and live in me', but a couple of them appeared to be mediocrely passable. She rang to book viewings on them and was surprised to learn she could have appointments to see both that very afternoon.

But OMG. Nothing could have prepared her for this. She hadn't been expecting perfection, although secretly maybe she had. Neither of these properties were it. In fact the second one could seriously have been used as the set for an episode of *Hammer House of Horror*; she'd actually been relieved to get out of there unscathed.

Feeling somewhat despondent, she headed back towards home. Oh well, this had only been her first day of house-hunting she was sure something would turn up eventually. Patience wasn't one of her best qualities but it was only a matter of time. The perfect little house would be waiting for her just around the corner.

And unbelievably, that was exactly what happened. Weird, fate, whatever you'd like to call it, as she turned around the very next corner there was the cutest little cottage with a sign outside declaring 'To Let'. She was in love with it already! Joanna brought her car to a screeching halt. Thankfully the driver of the car behind her managed to slam on his brakes just in time. The blasphemy and gesticulations which sprang forth through his open window towards her could do nothing to dampen her excitement.

'Sorry,' she mouthed to him, presenting a prayer-like pose with her hands.

'Stupid, bloody woman – shouldn't be on the road. You could have done some serious damage then.'

'Sorry,' she repeated, although she was finding it hard to look sombre, her mind was elsewhere.

Fortunately, he drove on. A few rather unpleasant hand gestures as he left, but he drove on, nevertheless. Joanna could hardly contain herself. She gazed at the cottage with a sigh of adoration. She was in love. It was the kind of home she'd dreamed of living in ever since she was a young girl but had never been able to do so because David hated old properties. Yep, they hadn't even been able to agree on that. He'd insisted on living somewhere modern, wouldn't even listen to the pleas she'd put forward for living in a character property. But hey, things would be different now – no David. She could choose to live wherever she wanted to live – she would be totally in charge of her own destiny.

But hang on a minute. There was the not-so-small issue of money. Like how much would it cost to rent a place like that? And how come she hadn't seen it listed on Rightmove? Thinking about it, there could only be only one possible reason really – that it was way over her maximum budget of £600. Her heart sank. She just knew she had to have that cottage. It took her several minutes to summon up enough courage, but eventually she took out her phone, googled Rightmove and Properties to Rent and put in a higher maximum price filter – £800 this time, just to be on the safe side; surely it couldn't be more than that.

The more she scrolled down, the lower the prices went, she prayed she'd be scrolling for a while. 'Ohhh, please let it be there somewhere,' she whispered, fingers crossed, heart thudding in her chest. And, as if by some fate of miracles, suddenly there it was – £625. She took a deep breath and exhaled some of the tension from her body. Okay, she knew £600 had been her absolute maximum budget but another £25 per month was nothing really. She could cut down on gin to make up for it – she wouldn't need to drink as much anyway with David no longer being there to rile her.

From the photographs it looked absolutely gorgeous, cosy and snug, just as she'd imagined it. And beams – it had beams, she'd always wanted a house with beams, she was almost drooling. She wanted this house so badly, more than she'd ever wanted anything, and knew she needed to move fast before someone else beat her to it.

Completely ignoring the sign that said 'Viewing by Appointment Only', Joanna sprang into action and boldly marched up to the front door. Even that was cute, as was the doorbell which had a chain to pull, reminiscent of an old-fashioned toilet. She pulled it warily, half expecting a flush of water to cascade down upon her head. But thankfully no, instead it pealed out with the sound of an old shop doorbell from times gone by.

Her eyes were so busy drinking in the ambience of the place, the wisteria around the door laden with its beautiful heavy purple blooms and the scent from the lavender in the terracotta pot next to the door, that she didn't notice time pass. But then she heard a frail voice from inside the house.

'Sorry to keep you waiting, I'll be there in a minute.'

'Not a problem. No need to hurry.'

Eventually the door creaked open – well, ajar at least, and the face of an elderly lady appeared, looking somewhat flummoxed.

'Oh – I thought you were the Tesco man with my shopping but you're not are you?'

'No, I'm definitely not him,' smiled Joanna.

'Who are you then? I'm not meant to answer the door to strangers. My son tells me that. He thinks I'm going a bit doolally you know, just because I'm eighty-nine. But I'm not, my mind's as sharp as it ever was, it's all my other bits that keep dropping off. Old age is no fun, I'm telling you, make the most of your life while you're still young enough to enjoy it. Anyway, listen to me rambling on – what can I do for you?'

'Oh, sorry, yes – my name's Joanna Donohue and I was just driving past when I saw the "To Let" sign outside your cottage. It looks so beautiful and just exactly what I'm looking for. I'm just about to split up with my husband you see and...' And, without a word of warning, Joanna suddenly burst into tears. God, how embarrassing – what was wrong with her? This was a good thing, something she wanted to happen, what was she getting emotional about? 'Sorry, I'm so sorry,' she snuffled, rubbing her eyes with her sleeve, a tissue nowhere to be found, 'I don't know where that came from.'

'Well I do, my love, I've had a husband too. Not now though, he's long gone – thank goodness. Come on in and let me make you a nice cup of tea, then you can tell me all your problems – and I'll find you a tissue too, you look as though you could use one.'

'But, but… what about your son? Won't he be cross if he knows I've been in? I don't want to upset him. Perhaps I can come round another time when he's here too.'

'Nonsense – he's not the boss! I could do with a bit of company if the truth be known and you seem like a really nice young lady to me. Come on in and let's have a chat. Tell you what, I'll give him a ring and tell him what's happening if that makes you feel any better. He only lives a couple of streets away and he's at home today so he'll probably be able to pop round and give you a guided tour – I take it that's what you knocked on the door for in the first place, wasn't it?'

'It was, yes, thank you.'

'Hang on a minute I've got my mobile here somewhere in my pocket,' she said, rooting around amongst all of the debris it contained. 'Dratted thing, where's it gone? My name's Nelly by the way. Ah, here we go – found it,' she said, triumphantly, as she proceeded to ring her son. 'Martin? It's me. No of course there's nothing wrong, I'm quite capable of looking after myself you know. Just wanted to let you know I've got a young lady here who's interested in renting the cottage, do you want to pop over and show her round? Yes, I know it's meant to go through the letting agent but she was just driving past and saw it so she knocked on the door to see if she could view it now… Yes I know you're busy but I've invited her in for a cup of tea anyway so there's no hurry… Martin if you're coming round in half an hour she's hardly going to mug me in that bit of time is she? Don't be so ridiculous… okay, we'll see you shortly then. Bye.' Nelly hit the red button on her mobile with a vengeance. 'Sons! He's enough to make me say a naughty word at times – in fact I do when I'm in on my own. Never in front of anyone else, though, I just have to bite my tongue – that's when my dentures will let me,' she chuckled. 'Anyway, come on in and make yourself comfortable. Martin will be here in about half an hour so we've just got time to have a nice cup of tea while you tell me all about yourself and what's making you so sad. I'm a good listener you know.'

'Well if you're sure, and if Martin's okay with that.' This lady was kindness personified. 'Thank you so much.'

'No need to thank me, my love, it should be me doing the thanking – you have no idea how lonely it gets sitting here day after day on my own, it's such a relief to get a bit of company. You make yourself comfortable in that chair while I make us a drink. Tea okay for you? Milk? Sugar?'

'Tea's just perfect, thank you. Just milk, please.'

Joanna perched herself on the edge of the seat, pleased to have this moment to herself to let her eyes wander and drink in every detail. OMG this was so perfect, it really did feel like home. The whole place was oozing with charm and character and not just because of the beams and the inglenook fireplace, beautiful though they were. Held within its walls were memories of lives – people who had lived here through the decades of times gone by. Forgotten by many, maybe, but not forgotten by this beautiful cottage whose character had been formed by them alone.

By the time Nelly shuffled back into the room bearing tea, Joanna's eyes were brimming with tears once again.

'Oh I'm sorry,' she said, leaping to her feet feeling guilty but just in time to rescue the tea. 'I should have come and carried them in for you instead of sitting here being maudlin, I never thought.'

'Thanks, love,' said Nelly, relinquishing her grasp on the cups with gratitude. 'They were nearly goners then. I'm not as capable as I used to be, although I don't like to admit it. And don't ever tell Martin I said that, will you? He already thinks I'm over the hill – don't want him giving me the final push, do we? Anyway sit back down and make yourself comfortable, I want to hear all about this husband of yours and what's happening. If you want to tell me that is – I'm being a bit presumptuous here, aren't I? Actually though, bring that box of tissues over from the window ledge, I've got a feeling you might need them.'

Chapter Twelve

Joanna settled down in the comfortable fireside chair. To her this felt like bliss, sitting here beside the fire in this cosy cottage that she'd taken to her heart and having the chance to unburden herself to this kind motherly soul who she just knew would be totally non-judgemental. Even that made her want to cry – what was wrong with her?

'Take your time, love, there's no hurry. I know Martin's coming later but I can always get him to have a drink in the kitchen while we're talking – and there's cake, he'll do anything for cake,' she chuckled. 'He's good like that though, despite all the moaning I do about him. For a man he's so calm and patient and kind-hearted – he's had to learn to be, I suppose, he's had a lot to deal with.'

Suddenly an awkward silence descended on the room, with Joanna feeling uncharacteristically shy. She sipped at her tea, nervously, to fill the gap, unsure of what to say or where to begin. Sensitive to her reticence to open up the conversation, Nelly butted in.

'So, you're just about to leave your husband – does he know yet? You don't have to tell me anything if you don't want to, you know. I just thought it might help you to talk about it – clear your head a bit. I suppose you've got lots of friends and family you can talk to, of course, but sometimes it helps to talk to a complete stranger, someone who's not directly involved. As I say, though, no need to talk about it at all if you'd rather not, we could just sit here and chat about the cottage and my life instead. Oh, love – the tales I could tell you!' she chortled, her eyes twinkling with glee.

Joanna smiled. For who could not smile when faced with such exuberance from one such as Nelly? 'I'd love to talk to you about it – if you sure I'm not taking up too much of your time.'

'Time, my love, is one thing I have plenty of. So, this husband of yours – does he have a name?'

'His name is David…'

And so the story began. From how they'd met and how she'd fallen into marriage because it was 'expected' of her, to having Jack and how he'd now left home to live with the Poxie. She told of David's outbursts and how he made her feel, and of Gavin and how she'd felt attracted to him but knew it could go no further. It was all there, warts and all, the life of Joanna Donohue in a nutshell.

'Eeeh love, that K-Y Jelly story – I've not heard of that stuff for years,' chuckled Nelly. 'I'd need to use a whole tube every time these days if I could meet a nice young man. Ooh the thought of it,' she sighed, eyes a-twinkle. 'Does he have a brother? Send him this way if so, I could do with a bit of excitement – you have to keep the boiler stoked, if you know what I mean, even at my age.'

Despite the way she was feeling right now, Joanna couldn't help but join in the raucous laughter that came from Nelly, who was laughing so hard she was in danger of losing her dentures.

'Mother?' came a voice from the kitchen. The person from whence it came walked through to join them in disbelief. 'I haven't heard so much frivolity going on in this house for years.'

'Martin! This lovely lady is Joanna, the one I was telling you about, the one who's interested in renting the cottage.'

'Ah, hello,' he said, stepping forward politely to shake her hand. 'I'm pleased to meet you.'

'Likewise,' said Joanna. 'I hope you didn't mind me just calling on the off chance like that, I know I should have rung the letting agent and made an appointment but when I was driving past and saw this beautiful cottage... well, it was love at first sight and I just didn't want to miss it.'

'Not a problem,' smiled Martin. 'In fact I'm glad you came, you seem to have given my mum a new lease of life. I can't remember the last time I heard her laugh like that.'

'You see, Martin, I told you – I'm not over the hill yet and I'm certainly not doolally. Just short of company, that's all. There's not much to laugh about these days when you're stuck in here on your own, twenty-four hours a day.

'This young lady's been a real tonic – I told you she wasn't the type to mug me, didn't I? Now, go and show her round while I finish my tea, we can finish our conversation later.'

*

The guided tour certainly did not disappoint. Joanna constantly had to restrain herself from squealing with delight – it was all so perfect. Surprisingly, Martin was quite apologetic. 'I'm so sorry, it really could do with a coat of paint everywhere to freshen it up a bit but I just haven't got the time to do it. Mum is going to be moving out at the end of the month and there's so much to get organised before then. To be honest I hadn't realised quite how shabby-looking it had got, it's only now, looking at it...'

'Oh please don't worry about that, I'm so busy gazing around, thinking this is the cottage of my dreams, I hadn't even given the paintwork a second glance. I could soon slap a bit of paint on anyway, if I'm lucky enough to become the new tenant. Have you had many people looking round?'

'No, you're only the second actually, it only went on the market last week. I've been unsure what to do, you see. Mum's really not happy living here on her own, not seeing anyone, and actually I don't feel she's safe here either now. I've been trying to convince her to move to a retirement apartment for some time but it's only been these last couple of months that she's agreed it would be better for her. She couldn't bear the thought of selling this place, though, it holds too many memories – and I can understand that. So we came up with the solution that if we rented out the cottage, the income from it would help towards covering the rental on the retirement apartment. How do you feel about it? Interested?'

'I think you can tell by my reaction – yes, I am most definitely interested! What's happening with all of the furniture and stuff – will she be taking it with her?'

'Some of it, certainly. But there'll be quite a lot that just wouldn't be suitable. I'm renting the cottage out as "unfurnished" simply because the stuff in here has mostly seen better days, but you're welcome to have it if you like. It would probably end up in the charity shop otherwise.'

'Wow, thank you so much, this day just gets better and better.' Joanna glanced at her watch. 'Gosh – five o'clock already, how did that happen? They'll be closed now but I'll ring the letting agent first thing in the morning to tell them I definitely want it. Oh, this is so exciting, you have no idea!' In fact she felt like throwing her arms around him and giving him a great big kiss. Thankfully she managed to restrain herself.

They made their way back downstairs, Joanna beaming from ear to ear.

'Nelly – it's absolutely gorgeous, just as I imagined it would be. I've been dreaming of living in a place like this all of my life but never dreamt it could ever happen. Oh, I'm so excited!'

'Well don't go getting too excited – remember you haven't told your husband yet, he doesn't have a clue what's happening.'

'Husband?' queried Martin.

'Yeah. In a long marriage that lost its sparkle years ago – if it ever had any. And now I have an empty nest too – high time this little bird flew free I think. Life's too short, and I keep getting reminded of that fact.'

'That's so very true,' said Martin, the sadness in his eyes almost palpable. Nelly too became suddenly subdued.

'Sorry if I touched on something that…'

'It's okay, you weren't to know. My wife died three years ago. Cancer.' The emotion of telling someone new almost overcame him. Even now, after all of this time, it still felt so raw.

Nelly butted in to rescue him. 'It's been tough. She was so ill. They were devoted and Martin nursed her all the way through. He was amazing.'

'Oh Ma, don't – she was the amazing one.'

Tears had welled in Joanna's eyes, her problems were nothing in comparison to this. 'I'm so sorry,' she said, 'life can be so cruel. I can only begin to imagine what it's been like for you.'

'Anyway, let's not all get maudlin. Who'd like a cup of tea – or even whisky if you fancy something a bit stronger, I keep it in for medicinal purposes you know,' chuckled Nelly with a wink.

'Not for me, Mother, I have to go. I only popped round to check everything was okay, got a load of work to catch up on.'

'I'd better be going too, Nelly, thanks all the same. I hadn't realised quite how late it was. I'm going to contact the letting agent first thing in the morning though and hopefully we can get the ball rolling – I seriously can't wait!'

*

With her promise of going to visit Nelly again very soon still ringing in her ears, Joanna drove home. Excitement at the prospect of her new home and the new life that lay ahead of her was almost overwhelming. That beautiful cottage! The flipside, of course, was tinged with sadness as she thought of the two people whose lives had touched her so deeply even though she'd only met them that afternoon.

Nelly, such a character, so full of fun. And she was right – old age was certainly not something to look forward to. Not only do your health and your faculties start to deteriorate but, as in Nelly's case, so many friends and family have died or have simply moved away over the years. The sense of loss must be overwhelming, particularly when you're not as mobile as you used to be and can't get out and about to see people, how depressing that must be. Loneliness is a terrible thing and must affect so many elderly people. She vowed that she would keep her promise to visit Nelly, it felt like the least that she could do, especially if she was going to get the chance to make that beautiful cottage her home. The cottage! A little frisson of excitement whooshed through her veins every time she thought about it. As Martin had showed her around it had felt like walking through paradise. Her dream home.

But Martin. Her thoughts drifted back to the sad aura that surrounded him. He seemed like such a nice man – so gentle and kind. Joanna could only begin to imagine the torture he must have had to endure as he'd watched his poor wife suffer and how broken it must have left him after losing her at such a young age. Life can be so cruel. How do people cope? It certainly put her own problems into perspective. Her mother had been right – there was always someone worse off than yourself.

*

So lost in her thoughts was she, Joanna must have been on autopilot. She was actually surprised to suddenly find herself parking on the driveway of her house without even remembering how she got there – scary indeed! She took a deep breath and attempted to compose herself. There was no putting it off any longer. She was going to leave David. She was putting things in motion and tonight was the night she was going to have to tell him. Good luck with that one, Joanna.

Grabbing firmly onto her handbag like it was some kind of ally, she got out of the car and pressed the key to lock it. Glancing to her left as she did so, she noticed a car parked by the edge of the kerb in front of their house. It looked vaguely familiar but she dismissed any further thoughts – they never had visitors, not unless she'd invited them. Anyway, she had bigger things on her mind right now.

Nevertheless, someone was definitely here. As she let herself in through the front door she heard voices coming from the kitchen. David's, loud and overbearing as usual, but then another quieter... Jesus, Mary and Joseph! She wasn't given to blasphemy under normal circumstances but this was way beyond her wildest nightmare.

'Darling,' called David. 'Come through to the kitchen, there's someone I'd like you to meet.'

Her legs would hardly carry her there but unfortunately they had no option.

'This is Gavin,' David continued. 'Remember that card you picked up from the gym, the one about a plumber? Well, I know we've spoken about having some work done before but we never actually did anything about it, did we? So I thought I'd take matters into my own hands today. I rang Gavin and asked him to come over and give us an estimate for doing the bathroom. There – you're shocked, aren't you? I knew you would be.'

'But... but...' the words just tied themselves in knots and abjectly refused to exit her mouth.

Gavin gazed at her in total confusion, wishing the ground would open up and swallow them both in one mouthful that very instant.

'Come on, Joanna – what do you think? You're not usually stuck for words.'

'I... I think we should leave it for now. We hadn't made any definite plans.'

'No, Gavin's come over here specially to give us an estimate. He's a busy man, I'm sure, but he fitted us in. Let's not mess him about now he's taken the trouble.'

'It's fine, honestly. I had to come over this way anyway to do a quote for someone else, so it wasn't any trouble. I can come back another day when you've decided what it is you want to have done – not a problem.' He couldn't get out of the door fast enough but...

'No, no, no – I insist. Let Joanna take you to have a look at the bathroom now, while you're here. She can discuss it with you then – you might be able to come up with a few ideas. No good asking me, I'm rubbish at stuff like that – I'd still be performing my ablutions in my grandmother's old tin bath in front of the fire if it was left up to me. Hahaha,' he guffawed, getting louder by the minute. 'God, that actually sounds quite disgusting. Go on, darling, take this young man upstairs and talk about what you'd like him to do for you. I'll wait down here and open the wine – you will stay and have a drink with us, won't you? Yes, of course you will.'

Gavin was dying on the spot. 'Oh no, thanks all the same but I'm driving.'

'Nonsense. One glass won't do any harm. In fact you'll still be a better driver after one glass than this wife of mine is after none – isn't that right, darling? Hahaha.'

What an objectionable specimen of a man. Gavin could see exactly why Joanna wanted to leave him. In fact he was surprised she had stuck it for so long. He looked towards her, questioningly. There was nothing he wanted to do more than to get out of this house right now, preferably taking her with him, but he didn't want to leave her in the lurch; he wasn't sure what this monster could be capable of. Probably best to play along with him, for the moment at least.

'Come on, let me show you the bathroom,' said Joanna, in a voice weighed down with resignation. Short of squaring up to David, abjectly refusing to do as he instructed and thus igniting the spark of a full-blown temper tantrum in front of Gavin, which she was totally reluctant to do, there really was no other option.

Somewhat hesitantly, Gavin followed her up the stairs. He felt doomed. He could have walked away, insisted, left the house – but he couldn't have just abandoned her. Desperate measures. This must be how a starving mouse feels when it's tempted to run headlong into a trap simply for a piece of cheese. No cheese here, but it made Gavin realise he would do anything for this woman despite the overwhelming fear that her husband had, indeed, set them a trap.

Joanna almost dragged him into the bathroom in a state of panic. She'd already been dreading facing David this evening to break the news of her impending move to him, this additional crisis was not what she'd envisaged at all.

'He knows, doesn't he?' she whispered agitatedly. 'He thinks there's something going on.'

'But we haven't actually done anything.'

'I know, but why else would he have done this? He's so predictable and this is just the way he would react – he likes nothing better than to see me squirm, he'll be taking great delight from it.'

'And actually I think I might have made it worse,' said Gavin, hanging his head in shame. 'I'm so sorry but I had no idea this was your house until I came inside and we got talking. He told me about the jobs his wife, Joanna, wanted to be done and about how his son, Jack, had left home recently. I don't know how it happened, but when I put two and two together I think I was so shocked to realise whose house I was in, that the words just fell out of my mouth. "Oh, I know them," – what a stupid thing to say.'

'Gavin!'

'I know – I'm such an idiot. I was hoping he might not have picked up on the word "them" and thought I'd just said "him" meaning Jack. In fact I kept going on and on about Jack and what good mates we were, hoping to cover up what I'd said – but no chance. He was on it straightaway – interrupted me, wanting to know how I knew you. Hopefully I covered it pretty well though – said we knew each other from the gym and that'd be where you'd picked up my business card as I always leave a pile of them on display in there. I was quite surprised when he said that would be impossible as you don't go to the gym but I thought that must be just him being a bit weird. Of course you go to the gym, I've seen you there. He didn't seem to believe me though.'

Oh God, cringe overload. Never tell a lie, it will always come back to haunt you. No matter if it's a big lie or merely a mini deviation from the truth – it's still a lie.

Moving swiftly on. 'He thinks we're having a full-blown affair, doesn't he? He's gathering evidence to confront us. What's he going to be like when we go back downstairs? I'm scared now – he's got a temper like a raging bull when he's roused.'

'Jeez – thanks, you're freaking me out a bit as well now.'

'Gavin, have you seen the muscles on you as opposed to the flab on him? I don't think you have anything to fear,' she even managed a little smile momentarily.

'I wouldn't want it to come to that,' stated Gavin.

'No, neither would I. Do you know, I was going to tell him tonight that I'm leaving him? I had it all planned.'

'Yeah right – you've been saying that for ages.'

'No, truly. I've found somewhere to rent – I've been for a viewing this afternoon and I'm going to ring the letting agent in the morning for an appointment to go in and sort it all out. Gavin, you should see it – it's absolutely gorgeous, I'm so excited!'

'That's amazing – well done! Like I said, we could find you a little property to buy and do up eventually if you like, but this will be a great starting point for you.'

'Starting point?!' her mouth fell open in amazement. 'Gavin, I don't think you realise, this cottage is my dream home, the only way you'll ever get me out of there is to prise me out with a crowbar.'

He smiled at her reaction. 'Unless the owner wants his cottage back at some point though, that's always the downside of living in rented property, it's never truly yours.'

'I know but ohhhh, just wait until you see it, Gavin...'

'Oh, so I will be getting an invite then, will I?'

'Of course you will, in fact you can be my first guest – although you'll have to be quick off the mark if you want to beat Hannah.'

All this talk about the cottage soon brought the sparkle back to Joanna's eyes, she looked like a young girl about to embark on an exciting adventure, which was exactly how she felt.

'Well done, you.' Gavin was so pleased for her. For that brief moment, lost in the joy of her breaking news, they forgot all about where they were and what it was they were meant to be doing. He hugged her tightly and kissed her excitedly on the lips, so happy that she really had taken the first step towards changing her life for the better.

'I don't know what you two are doing up there,' came a voice from below. 'There seems to be a lot of talking going on, I don't know about action. Have you finished measuring up the bathroom yet?'

OMG – did he have a spy camera rigged up somewhere or what? She wouldn't have put it past him. She looked at Gavin wild-eyed, gasping, shaking with fear.

'Nearly finished. Down in a minute,' she shouted in reply.

'Don't worry, he couldn't have seen anything,' said Gavin, looking like a man condemned and about to be hanged. 'He's playing games with his suspicions, that's all. Let's take some measurements quickly, just in case, then we'll go back downstairs and brave it out.'

Chapter Thirteen

Like lambs to the slaughter. Despite being two fully grown, perfectly capable adults whose indiscretions had been practically non-existent, and certainly only mild, they came back down the stairs feeling like two guilty teenagers whose parents had just discovered their misdemeanours. Nevertheless, they weren't about to let that show. Because they'd done nothing wrong, nothing major anyway, and they had to keep reminding themselves of that fact. They walked into the kitchen, heads held high, ready to brazen it out.

'Ah – so here you are. Had fun did you?'

'What?' Joanna furrowed her brow and glared at him defiantly. After all, she had nothing to fear. Gavin was here and she knew he would protect her. She felt empowered. She had the upper hand now, little did David know she would soon be gone.

'Had fun redesigning the bathroom – what did you think I meant?'

'Yeah, Joanna came up with some good stuff and we had a play around with it.'

A sleazy smile crept across David's face, although his dark brooding eyes told a different story. 'I bet you did.'

Joanna really wanted to slap that sleazy smile right off his face but somehow managed to restrain herself, as she had done for the past thirty years. It was becoming increasingly difficult though. However, one act of violence leads to another – she did not want to incite him and make things any worse than they already were.

'I'll take all the measurements home with me and see what I can come up with. Hopefully I'll have an estimate to you by the end of the week, if that's okay? Anyway, I must be off.' He was trying to ignore the look of desperation he could see on Joanna's face as he glanced towards her, convinced that if he stayed it would only make matters worse. 'Thank you for the offer of the drink but I really must be going, I've got…'

'No. I insist,' David commanded, slamming the side of his fist down onto the table as if to emphasise the point.

'But David you can't make him stay – not if he's got things to do,' pleaded Joanna, her voice tailing off towards the end of the sentence.

'Don't you dare to tell me what I can and cannot do, woman,' he stormed. 'Now get two more glasses and another bottle of red then you can both sit down to join me. I think it's time we had a little chat, don't you?'

His lip curled with anger as he spoke. Joanna did as she was told; there seemed little point in doing anything else, it would only antagonise him further. As she returned to the table, she shot a quick glance towards Gavin, concerned about how he must be feeling. He'd done nothing to deserve any of this. He caught her eye, his expression blank.

'You think I'm stupid, don't you?' growled David, his face bitter with contempt as he slowly poured the wine before slamming the bottle back down onto the table to face them. His eyes narrowed as they flittered from one to the other. 'So how long has it been going on, this "affair" of yours? Although I must say, young man, I don't know what you see in her, she looks old enough to be your mother.'

'David, can we just get this straight? Read my lips… "Gavin and I are NOT having an affair!"'

'Hahaha – pigs might fly. No point trying to deny it, Joanna, it's obvious you are. And who could blame you? He must seem like quite a catch. You must feel flattered at your age that you can manage to attract someone so young and fit. But as for you, young man, with looks like yours, you could have any woman you wanted, what's the appeal of getting with an old hag like this one? She was a bit of a goer thirty years ago but now – well, look at the state of her.'

Gavin could stay silent no longer. He refused to sit back and listen to any woman being spoken about like that, particularly this woman.

'Do NOT put Joanna down like that, she's beautiful and certainly far, far better than you deserve.'

'Oh, so lover boy speaks then, does he? He has a tongue in his head after all – and a barbed one at that. Joanna is my wife, young man, you'd do well to remember that – and I'll speak about her any way I like, thank you very much.'

'Not in my presence you won't. Oh, and just for the record, I am not "lover boy". We are friends, yes, but certainly not lovers.'

'And you expect me to believe that?'

'Well yes, I do actually – because it's the truth. Joanna and I met at the gym and have become good friends – nothing more. Although in fact there is something more. For your information I've offered her a job – I'm a property developer and she's coming to work for me on the admin side.'

'Over my dead body!'

'If that's what it takes – yes.'

'Look, could we all calm down a bit, please? This is getting completely out of hand. Can we just talk like sensible human beings? There's nothing going on between Gavin and me, we're good friends and that's all. As for the job – I told you I'd been for a job interview the other day and your only response was to ask me what time dinner would be ready. You weren't in the least bit interested and simply didn't want to know so I really didn't think it was worth pursuing the subject. After all, I'd still be bringing in the same money and I knew that would be all you'd be concerned about, so what was the point? Because, as you know, we never talk about anything anymore, you'd rather sit and watch your beloved TV or read your bloody newspaper.'

With a deep-throated growl, David knocked back the remains of the wine down his throat in one gulp before slamming the empty glass down onto the table. He leant forward in his seat breathing heavily, lips pursed in anger, jowls bursting with venom as he spat the words towards her, saliva spraying forth.

'You are my wife, Joanna, and I absolutely forbid you to go and work for this man or to see him ever again. Do I make myself clear? As for you, you no-good moron,' he growled, drunkenly scrambling to his feet, turning his full attention towards Gavin, leaning over and grabbing him by the front of his sweater, pulling him towards himself, 'Get out of my house NOW! And keep away from my wife. Do you hear me?'

Knocking the hands away with a sideward swipe, Gavin got up from the table, his height towering above David, muscles twitching, ready for a fight. But he knew violence would only escalate the situation and make things worse for Joanna. He took a deep breath and tried to cool things down.

'Could you keep your hands off me, please? This isn't helping anyone,' he said, in a voice much calmer than he felt. He glanced at Joanna; she was close to tears.

'"This isn't helping anyone"?' spat David. 'Why the hell should I want to help anyone? You've done nothing but try to screw me over, the pair of you…'

A sudden noise from the hallway interrupted his words. The front door opened, a waft of cold air blew in, heralding the arrival of someone. It could only be one person. Only one person had a key. The door slammed shut. Jack. Never had Joanna been so glad to see him.

'Hi… oh! What have we here? I take it your secret's out then, Mother.'

Well, she'd thought she was glad to see him. Oh God…

*

Jack's eyes darted nervously around the room, suddenly sensing the tension. Wondering exactly what he'd walked in on, realising he'd jumped right into the middle of it with his size eleven foot. OMG this looked serious – even worse than his own problems.

'And what secret would that be then, Jack?' asked David. 'Why don't you pull up a chair and join us? It would appear everyone has secrets this evening. Everyone except for me, that is.'

Joanna closed her eyes and threw back her head with a deep intake of breath, the stress almost unbearable. At least there was Jack here as well as Gavin now should the violence escalate again; between them they would be able to restrain him. She sat forward in her chair, eyes still closed, elbows on the table, slowly rubbing her forehead back and forth with her fingertips.

'I'm waiting… Jack?'

Jack squirmed in his seat. This had already been one of the worst days of his life and it seemed it was about to get a whole lot worse. Joanna opened her eyes and looked at him, holding up her hand, palm forward, to silence him. It was up to her. She was the one who had got them all into this mess, she would be the one to sort it out.

'What's the matter – cat got your tongue?' sneered David.

'This really has nothing to do with Jack, or with Gavin either for that matter. It's about me and you. About our marriage…'

'Oh God, here we go. Not that again. I suppose this is all my fault then, is it? You're going to try and lay all the blame on me. Poor little hard-done-to Joanna. You make me sick – do you know that? And no, I don't want to hear from you, I want to hear from this precious son of yours, the one who knows a secret. So cut him loose from your apron strings for once and let him speak for a minute, will you?'

'No I won't, David, actually. Hear me out. I need to talk to you. I intended to do so tonight anyway because something happened today…'

'Yeah, right – you shagged the plumber.'

'Don't be so disgusting. Let me speak. Please. I never intended to have this conversation with you in front of other people but because of the way things have turned out this evening it's really left me with no option…'

'I can go if you'd prefer,' interrupted Gavin.

'No, stay – please stay. You too, Jack.' Unsure what David's reaction would be, she was actually grateful for their presence.

'You see, David, I'm simply not happy, I haven't been for a long time. But I plodded on because it's what you do, you get stuck in a rut and sometimes it's just easier to stay where you are than to do anything about it. Especially when there are children – we had Jack and I wouldn't have wanted him growing up in a life split into two halves with all the acrimony that goes with that. So I stayed, and you were always at work, and I just got on with it because I thought that was the best thing to do.'

She paused, momentarily, to risk a glance towards David to judge his reaction to what she was saying, but none was forthcoming. He remained broodily silent staring into his wine glass, lips pursed, face expressionless.

'But now Jack has left home, the place feels so empty. In fact people do call it "the empty-nest syndrome" and it's true – it does make you stop and evaluate your life. It doesn't help either that I'm going to be forty-nine this year – fifty next – half a century! All of that life gone and what have I achieved? It might help if we were happy, but we're not – even you must agree with that. We hardly speak to each other, never mind have a conversation and there's certainly no fun or laughter in this house anymore. We're just like two people sharing a house – no connection whatsoever.

'So I started to think that maybe now is the time to do something about it – for both of our sakes, not just mine. And I know you think I've been having an affair but I truly have not. I met Gavin, he's become a friend, nothing more – in fact he's a friend of Jack's, not just of mine. But what I did decide was that our marriage is definitely not working – not for me, not for either of us. I tried to bring a bit of a spark into it recently, as you know, but it simply wasn't happening, I think we left it too late for that. So no, whatever we had is definitely over, there's no turning back now.

'And so today I made the decision to start looking for somewhere else for me to live – somewhere on my own, not with Gavin, before you start jumping to any conclusions. And I found a place I can afford to rent. It's only small but it's big enough for me. I'm sorry. I was going to tell you about it tonight, before all of this happened. I'm going to see the letting agent in the morning – hopefully I should be able to move in at the beginning of next month. That'll just give me time to…'

'Get out,' snarled David, his eyes still focused on nothing but the wine glass in front of him.

'What?'

'You heard me. I said get the hell out of here – and that goes for all of you!'

'But David, I'm not ready, the house isn't ready, I have nowhere to go yet.'

'Is that my problem? You've chosen to go, so go. NOW! I won't be responsible for my actions otherwise…'

Jack was freaking out just a little bit. These were his parents – his whole world was falling apart. For his mum's sake he tried to pull himself together.

'Go upstairs and get a few bits you're going to need in a bag, Mum. I'll help you, we'll sort something out. Hurry.'

'What's this – the prodigal son comes good?' spat David. 'Just answer me one question, Jack. What was that "secret" – did you know all about this?'

Jack hung his head shamefacedly, hardly daring to speak, afraid of the reaction it may provoke. 'Okay. Mum told me she was going to leave you, yes. She told me when you both came round to see the flat. I didn't know when, or how soon though, and I didn't know she'd actually found somewhere to go,' he said, his voice barely audible.

David sighed with contempt, his eyes narrowed. He filled his glass again, the others watching somewhat nervously as he took a large swig.

'And you, Mr Plumber Man, did you know about all of this too?'

Gavin thought it best to be honest. 'I knew she was thinking of leaving you but I didn't know when and I didn't know she'd been looking for somewhere to go. She only told me about the place she'd found when we went upstairs to measure the bathroom earlier.'

'Great. Just fuckin' great.'

David was giving a false impression of someone appearing to be incredibly calm but tension was hovering over him like a black cloud. He resembled a time bomb ticking... loudly.

'Could you hurry, Mum, please – we need to go!' Jack was physically shaking with fear now.

'Coming. I'm coming,' she said rushing down the stairs, several large bags in tow. For who knew when she'd ever be able to get back into this house again to get the rest of her stuff and, indeed, whether it would still be there?

Standing in the hallway, bags in hand, she felt suddenly emotional – she was saying a final goodbye to everything that was familiar, everything that had been such a huge part of her life.

'I'm going now, David, I'm sorry it all had to end this way, it's not how I meant it to happen. But it's for the best, for both of us. There'll always be a little bit of me that loves you still. We've shared so much and spent so many years of our lives together that it would be impossible to just walk away and forget those memories – thirty years is a long time…'

'I said GET OUT!!!' screamed David, as he hurled his glass and its entire contents towards her head, just missing her by a mere sliver. The wine bottle followed, Gavin ducking thankfully in time to miss it.

'Come on, Mum – let's get out of here.'

*

Safely outside the door, Joanna was in floods of tears. She had known leaving him was not going to be easy but had never imagined it would end this way. Thirty years of her life – gone.

'Don't worry, Mum, we'll sort something out – you'll be okay,' said Jack, trying to comfort her but he, himself, was in a state of shock. This was his life too – his childhood home, his comfort blanket. It had always been there for him, as had his parents, when times had got tough and he'd needed support – as he did now.

Gavin put his arms around both of them and hugged them to him. He could only imagine what they were going through. His heart went out not only to Joanna but to Jack too. They looked totally bereft, both of them. He knew, though, that he would have to move them on; it wasn't safe for them to be standing here just outside the door, that lunatic could come out at any minute.

'Can I come and stay at yours for a bit, Jack?' Joanna asked, between her sobs. 'Would Pixie mind, do you think? I know she doesn't like me very much but even she wouldn't want to leave me sleeping out on the street, would she?'

The silence was deafening for a moment. Jack looked uncomfortable.

'Jack?'

'This is such bad timing and I feel so bad…'

'What? Jack – you're scaring me now. As if tonight hasn't been bad enough.'

'I know and I'm sorry. But that's why I came round tonight. Pixie and me… well… we split up. Today. It wasn't good. And that's why I came round. To see if I could move back home. She threw me out and I've got nowhere else to go – I've not even got any of my stuff.'

'Well at least I'm one up on you there then!' said Joanna, forcing half a smile. 'Oh Jack – what are we like? And the timing couldn't have been worse, could it? What are we going to do? Don't fancy sharing a cardboard box with your mum, do you?' she quipped, forgetting her own troubles for the moment and just trying to lighten his mood; she hated to see him looking so sad.

'Might be the best offer I get all night,' he said, his mood impenetrable.

'Come on, you two, cheer up. Things could be worse – nobody died. And I thought that could have been a distinct possibility at one point tonight. So cut all this talk about cardboard boxes – you've got my gaff, haven't you? Plenty of room in that place, I'm rattling around in it living on my own. So come, before we get any more flying missiles whizzing past our heads – let's go.'

'But Gavin…' they chorused in unison.

'I won't take no for an answer. Now come!'

Chapter Fourteen

Gavin's apartment had seemed huge on her previous visits but with the three of them plus all of her stuff inside the place, it seemed to have shrunk to half the size. It had looked so immaculate as well, until they'd come in.

'Put your things in the bedroom,' instructed Gavin. 'You can have the bed – Jack and I can bunk down on one of the sofas each for now.'

'Gavin – I can't turf you out of your bed, don't be silly. I'll have the sofa. It won't be the first time I've slept in the same room as Jack – I'll be fine. It's good of you to have us here, we can't be turfing you out of your bed as well.'

'Nonsense, you're having the bed and that's final. Of course, if you really don't want to throw me out of it I could stay... with you,' he said with a cheeky wink. 'Other than that it's the sofa for me. Your choice.'

'Okay, you win. I'll take the bed, you take the sofa.'

'Thank God for that!' interrupted Jack. 'If you think I'm sleeping out here while my mate's in bed with my mum in the very next room... ugh, I can't even bear to think about it.'

Eventually, after much banter and a shared takeaway pizza, Gavin announced he had to go out. They were both reluctant to see him go, he'd certainly lifted their spirits after such a traumatic day.

'Do you have to go out?' asked Joanna, putting on her most appealing face. She'd not had so much fun in a long time. These two were just the tonic she needed, convincing her that she'd definitely done the right thing in leaving David, despite the circumstances in which it had all happened.

''Fraid so,' he said, sorry to be leaving them but at the same time there was no way he could not go. She would be waiting for him and he was desperate to see her.

'Sorry,' he said, feeling torn, and feeling really guilty at just abandoning them. 'I'll be in tomorrow, honestly I will, but there's somewhere I've simply got to go tonight. Had it been anything else I would have cancelled but this is really important – she'd be upset if I said I couldn't make it, I can't let her down.'

'Oooh – she! You kept that one quiet, didn't you? said Jack.

'Mate – it's not like that.'

'Yeah right – that's what they all say.'

'No. Truly. This is not.'

'Yeah, yeah, yeah, I believe yer – not.'

'Shut it, small fry. Look, I'll see you both later – I won't be late back.'

'*If* you come back tonight.'

'Shut it, Jack.'

Joanna stared after him in disbelief. He had another woman? How come she knew nothing about this? How come he'd never mentioned it to her before? She knew she had no claims over Gavin – she hadn't even known him for that long – but nevertheless. They'd kissed. They'd even been almost tempted to… thank goodness they hadn't! But, aside from that, she'd thought they had something special – how wrong could you be?

'Men. They're all rubbish.' Had she just said that out loud? Judging by the expression on Jack's face – yes, she had.

'Oy! Don't include me in that, Mother dear, I'm your ever-loving son.'

'Sorry, merely thinking out loud. Gavin. What was all that about?'

'God knows. But why should it matter? I thought there was nothing going on between the two of you. Hmm... or maybe there is?'

'Jack! No there isn't anything "going on" as you put it. But I feel a little bit hurt, that's all, that he's never mentioned her before – this other woman.'

'"This other woman" – eh? Just a tad of jealousy creeping in now, is there? The green-eyed monster?'

'Jack! Will you stop it? Gavin and I are good friends, that's all. But we discuss everything, like good friends do. So how come he's never mentioned this woman before?'

'Tah-dah – the mystery deepens.'

*

In some respects it was a good thing that Gavin had gone out for the evening, it gave mother and son time to talk. Jack was a bit reluctant to do so, as she knew he would be, hence a lot of clowning around to cover up his reticence; it was his forte.

'So, what are you going to be doing with all of this new-found freedom of yours now you've left Dad? And what about this cosy little love nest you're getting too, you've not told me anything about that yet. Whereabouts is it? Just think, you'll be able to go on Tinder and Match.com and all of those. It'll be a whole new world – bet you can't wait, eh, can you? Have you ever seen the sort of things they put on those dating sites though? I reckon you'll be grossed out when you see some of those pictures. They send photos of...'

'Their body parts. Bits of their anatomy I won't want to see. Yes, Jack, I know. I may be older than you but I'm not completely out of touch with life, you know. Anyway, stop messing about and be serious for a minute, if that's possible. Tell me what's happened with you and Pixie – why has she thrown you out?'

'Hmm… that.' His expression changed and he sank back into the sofa with a sigh. He remained silent for a moment or two, staring down at his hands, looking like he had the weight of the world on his shoulders, for indeed that was how he felt.

He couldn't even look at Joanna. 'She's pregnant,' he said in a low voice, sounding as though the stuffing had been completely knocked out of him.

'Jack! What have I always said to you?'

'I know, but we've been together a while. And she was on the pill, or at least she told me she was. But yes, I know, I'm stupid.'

'So,' said Joanna, still reeling from the shock even though she'd always had a hunch this would happen. 'Why would that be a reason to throw you out? I would have thought she'd have been delighted.'

'Yeah, she was.'

'I'm sure that was her intention all along – a good way to trap you,' said Joanna. 'God, she's so transparent that girl. So what happened?'

'Thing is, Mum, I know she's just not capable of having a child – she can't look after herself, never mind a baby. Can you imagine?'

'Yeah – it'd be you looking after the both of them.'

'Exactly. So I suggested she should have an abortion. I said I'd go with her to see her GP and we'd get something sorted out. Like I said to her, she's only young, there's plenty of time for her to think about having children when she's a bit older and more settled.'

'And her reaction was?'

'I think you can imagine. She went mental – throwing everything at me she could lay her hands on, screaming at me to get out. It was like a war zone when I left.'

'Oh Jack. What are you going to do?'

'I've got no idea. All I know is that I can't let her go ahead and have this baby – it would be a nightmare. Just think of it. She needs to sort her own head out first, she has so many problems and having a baby would only make things worse. And, as for me, my life would be over before it's even begun.'

'I did warn you, Jack…'

'I know you did. If only I'd listened.'

*

With Gavin now having gone out for the evening, it gave Joanna time to claim the sofa for herself. There was no way she could take his bed away from him – she would have felt even more guilty, they were already inconveniencing him far too much.

Neither of them managed to get much sleep that night, although neither knew the other lay awake. They were each lost in their own traumas of the previous day, ideas and worries churning around inside their heads. At least for Joanna she'd now done the bit she'd been dreading the most – telling David. Hopefully from here on in her life would get better. She'd be free to follow her dreams and do whatever she wanted to do – no one would be there to hold her back.

In a way it was quite scary, she had to admit. She'd never lived on her own before. Madness really – forty-nine years old and had never lived on her own! Definitely time to stand on her own two feet and explore what life had to offer, she'd been stuck in that stifling little rut for far too long. She did worry about David though and that surprised her really. He'd looked so… so… *abandoned* when they'd left… so alone. Would he be able to cope on his own? She'd done everything for him for the past thirty years and prior to that he'd been just a young lad, taken care of by his parents.

Would he know how to use a vacuum cleaner, a washing machine, an iron? Would he remember to sort out the bills, buy the groceries, cook himself something to eat? He'd never done any of those things, he'd just been waited on hand and foot. Suddenly she felt guilty for not being there, for not preparing him more for when she'd left. In fact she had to give herself a little shake – that was ridiculous. He was his own person.

It was his own fault that he was the way he was. If he'd involved himself more with the general day-to-day life around him instead of blocking it all out with the TV, then maybe none of this would have happened. They could have still been together; shared day-to-day experiences of family life would have brought them closer. She really had nothing to feel guilty about, he'd brought it all upon himself. Nevertheless…

Sprawled across the adjacent sofa, Jack was doing some soul-searching of his own. What *had* he done? The very reason he'd moved in with Pixie in the first place was because he was worried about the state of her mental health. Worried that she might do something to harm herself. Had he seen himself in the role of some kind of superhero, flying in like superman to rescue her? Well a great job he'd made of that, hadn't he? She was in a bigger mess now than she'd ever been.

The thing was – did he love her? He had feelings for her, sure. But love? Hmm… In actual fact she'd been an absolute nightmare to live with – like walking on eggshells twenty-four hours a day. The slightest thing that went wrong she'd be up like a rocket – he couldn't cope, he liked peace, he was a laid-back, easy-going kind of guy.

But a baby? That's the last thing he wanted – right now at any rate. And how underhand had that been? She'd told him she was on the pill and he'd believed her – why would he not? Maybe he was just naive – or stupid, or both.

Just imagine though, life with Pixie and a baby, not a lot of money and cooped up in that little flat. No outside space, baby screaming and Pixie throwing tantrums with accompanying flying missiles at regular intervals. Is that how he wanted his life to be? Because once a baby arrived that is exactly how it would be and, because of the baby, he would be committed to a certain extent to that relationship for the rest of that child's life. Committed to a mental institution, more like.

He felt bad. It wasn't the baby's fault. It had done nothing wrong, it hadn't asked to be conceived. And here he was, insisting that the baby should be murdered – his own child! How could he even think that way? But no, he must stop thinking like that. It wasn't like it was a real baby, not yet – just a collection of cells. It wasn't like it was a real person, with feelings and everything. But how did they know? How did they know it didn't have feelings – would it know it wasn't wanted and he'd arranged to have it killed?

OMG Jack, stop it – you're being ridiculous now. This is crazy. It really is just a few cells – nothing more. Imagine what it would be like if you just left it and she didn't have an abortion. If the cells were left to grow and develop into a baby because you'd done nothing about it. And this little person was brought into this world – Pixie's world, Pixie and all her family's world. What kind of a life would it have? Would it not be better to terminate it now before its life has even begun? Oh God – what a mess.

*

'Morning campers,' called Gavin, as he breezed through their room bright and early, wrapped in a towel, fresh from the shower. 'Bathroom's free if anybody wants it.'

'Man... what time is it?' yawned Jack, stretching, making some half-hearted attempt to open his eyes and face the new day ahead... with difficulty. 'Didn't hear you come in last night. In fact I didn't think you *had* come in. How was it?'

'Yeah, got back about eleven I think. Meant to leave earlier but we got chatting and... well, you know how it is.'

'Yeah mate – couldn't leave her in the lurch, so to speak, could you?'

'Jack – I told you! It's really not like that. We got chatting, that's all.'

Unable to feign invisibility any longer, Joanna opened her eyes and looked over towards him from the warmth and cosiness of her sleeping bag. For some inexplicable reason she was feeling ridiculously horny. Perhaps it was this sense of achievement, of actually being free again, about to step into a brave new world. Whatever it was, the sight of Gavin's half-naked torso, with the towel to protect his modesty leaving little to the imagination, did nothing to help.

Unintentionally, a groan escaped her lips as she shuffled to a more comfortable position.

'Sorry – did we wake you?'

'No – I was already awake. What time is it?' she asked, still in frustration overload. If only. She wouldn't even have needed the help of the K-Y this morning.

'Just gone half past seven. Can I get you anything? A cup of tea?'

'No ta. Just go and put some clothes on, I'm not used to seeing fit young men strutting their stuff in front of me – especially at this time of day.'

'Mother! Stop lusting after my mate, could you? Especially not in front of me – that's disgusting.'

'Okay, sorry – I'll go,' grinned Gavin. 'Shower's free though if you want it.'

'Yeah, she does. A cold one. Now.'

*

It was with some relief that Joanna waved Gavin and Jack off to work. Well, to work in Gavin's case, to the gym in Jack's – he needed a workout to burn off a bit of that tension. As for Joanna, she needed a bit of space, a few moments to herself. The past twenty-four hours had been completely insane. So much had happened, her world had turned completely upside down, back to front and knocked her sideways – what did she expect? Her life had been in need of a shake-up for years and here it was, actually happening. She just needed some time to get her head round it all. Remember that oyster-popping moment she'd craved? This was it!

So today was the first day of the rest of her life. Of course it was, it's the same for everyone. But for Joanna, this day was special. This was the first day of a whole new life – an independent life where she would be totally in control of everything. Every path she took from this day forward would be one she took from choice. No more having to take others into consideration, no more doing things just to 'fit in'. She was a free woman and she could do exactly as she wished. And if that sounded selfish – then tough!

Glancing at the clock though suddenly gave her a bit of a reality check. Independent woman she may be, but there was one area of her life that she hadn't changed yet and that was her job. Ten minutes to nine and she was still in her dressing gown. And apart from anything else, primarily like lack of motivation, she just didn't have time to go to work today. She had her life to sort out and, superwoman or not, you can't do that in your lunch break.

Lying was not exactly something she was comfortable with. In fact it was a well-known fact amongst those who knew her well that liars were at the top of her pet hate list. So she dithered about a bit but then remembered – she was a strong woman. Grabbing the phone in her new-found determination, she pressed the number for the office, spoke to the snooty Cat and asked her to relay the message that she was ill and wouldn't be in today.

Thankfully, being the solid and reliable Joanna they knew her as, no one suspected a thing. It wasn't as though she did this sort of thing regularly, in fact it was a one-off. The pre-yesterday Joanna would have felt consumed by guilt but today's Joanna felt remarkably proud of herself. She was a strong woman, she was capable of anything. And in fact she'd be giving her notice next week... because she was going to work for Gavin!

In this burst of positivity and enthusiasm she decided that instead of just ringing the letting agent, she would go and speak to them face to face – for who could resist her when they saw how keen she was to rent Bluebell Cottage? Amazing how quickly a splash of make-up, a brush of the hair and some reasonably smart clothes could transform her from a slobby dressing-gowned layabout to a highly respectable and desirable tenant when she put her mind to it. A quick slurp of her tea... eww, that was cold... and she was gone.

However, things were not that straightforward – are they ever? The letting agent could not have been nicer. He welcomed her in, gave her a seat and even offered her a cup of tea. But then, in complete contrast, the news he had to tell her was not nice. For when they finally stopped the general chit-chat and got down to business, the latest updated information he had about Bluebell Cottage was... that it had been withdrawn from the market.

Okay, so it wasn't the done thing to burst into tears in a letting agent's office. The poor man looked petrified to be honest. His eyes darted about not knowing which way to look as she continued to sob like a baby. Embarrassment flooded his office. He passed her a tissue.

'Another cup of tea?' he asked, anything to get out of the room.

She nodded her head vigorously, anxious to be left alone for a minute too. Withdrawn from the market – how could that be?

'I'm sorry I can't give you any further information,' the letting agent said, returning several minutes later with the tea, looking towards her somewhat nervously as he entered the room. 'All I know is that we received a phone call early this morning from the gentleman who is dealing with the letting of Bluebell Cottage on behalf of his mother. He apologised and said that she'd changed her mind and she no longer wished to rent out the property. Sad, I know, but it's the way these things go sometimes.

'However, all is not lost. I've just been checking through our files and we have several other properties I think you may be interested in. This one in particular,' he said. 'It's another character property, slightly bigger if anything and yet still at the same rental price. Would you like me to try and arrange a viewing for you for later today?'

Did this man not have feelings? Did he not realise what she was going through here? 'No, I certainly do not! I had my heart set on Bluebell Cottage and if I can't have that then I don't want any other,' she said, rising to her feet in a swirl of indignation.

'Sorry, my mistake. When we spoke earlier I was under the impression you needed somewhere to move into pretty quickly – hence the other suggestions. I didn't mean to upset you, just didn't want to see you ending up homeless, that's all.' He even gave a little snigger at his last sentence, as if he'd told some kind of joke. Idiot.

Head held high, she flounced out of his office with a throwaway 'Goodbye' over her shoulder. She felt at the lowest point she'd ever been in a very long time because what he'd said was true. That's exactly what she was. Homeless. And she'd brought it all upon herself.

Back in the car she took a few minutes for herself, unable to face driving anywhere at that moment. She clutched the top of the steering wheel as she slouched forward, resting her forehead on her hands. 'Stupid, stupid, stupid,' she admonished herself. Why had she reacted that way? The poor man had only been trying to help. And he had been right, she needed somewhere to live urgently, right now – she didn't have the time to waste hankering after Bluebell Cottage. It had gone – face it. And now, thanks to her own stupidity, she was probably banned from dealing with that letting agent ever again. Oh God, she really was such a klutz at times.

Reluctantly, but realising she couldn't sit there forever, she started the engine. As though on some kind of autopilot, she set off towards home but then the sudden realisation slapped her across the head like a wet fish – splat. No, she was not driving home. She would never be driving home again – not to that home anyway. Tears welled in her eyes once more. Time to face it, that idiot of a man had been right – she was homeless. And if it wasn't for having such a good friend in Gavin, she could actually have found herself sleeping on the streets tonight – certainly neither her mum nor her sister had wanted her staying with them.

How had it come to this? Yesterday she had been so full of positivity, excited at the prospect of having a whole new life stretching out before her, a beautiful cottage, a new job, freedom, independence. And now, just twenty-four hours later and through no real fault of her own, she'd been dragged onto the helter-skelter of life, everything spiralling out of control until she'd landed at the bottom in the mud with a splat. Thank goodness she'd had a safety mat.

And that safety mat was, of course, Gavin. She really would have been in dire straits without him right now. She turned at the next junction, driving towards his flat. It may not be home but, as a temporary solution, she'd be hard pressed to find anywhere better.

She turned up the radio in an attempt to drown out her sorrows with music. The Golden Hour – songs from the eighties and nineties, proclaimed the jingle. That actually did cheer her up just a little bit, that was her favourite time ever music-wise. 'Under Pressure', 'Purple Rain', she belted them all out at full blast, 'Young at Heart'… *Yeah that's me, young at heart*, she smiled to herself – *who sang that?* She'd thought it was Bananarama's song but that was blokes singing, surely. She turned up the volume as the radio presenter started to speak. 'And that last song you heard, "Young at Heart", was from Scottish band the Bluebells who had a hit with it in 1993.'

The Bluebells. Bluebell Cottage. Yes. For as much as she'd been trying to blast it out of her head by drowning herself in music, Bluebell Cottage was still very much there, prominently so, in the forefront of her mind. She had fallen in love with that cottage and the way she was feeling right now, nothing else could ever measure up to it.

What she didn't understand was how enthusiastic both Nelly and Martin had seemed yesterday. They'd seemed to like her; in fact Joanna had been under the impression that their friendship would continue even though she was to be their tenant. But obviously not. How could she have got it so wrong? She'd always considered herself to be a good judge of character but now she was beginning to doubt herself.

There was only one answer to this. Otherwise she was going to be tying herself in knots, going round and round in circles trying to work out where it had all gone wrong. She stopped the car, reversed into someone's driveway (sorry, people!) and drove on – but this time in the direction of Bluebell Cottage.

*

She stood on the doorstep filled with even more trepidation than she had been the first time around. Had that really only been yesterday? So much had happened since then – and not much of it good. She stood… and she stood… and she stood. And waited. Was Nelly not even going to answer the door to her now? Had she done something to upset her? Trepidation overload.

But wait. Had she even rung the doorbell? OMG, Joanna, you get worse! She pulled the doorbell chain and gave a half-hearted smile as it rang out its welcome. Even the doorbell had character.

'Coming,' called out the familiar voice. 'Takes me a while but I'm on my way.'

'That's okay, Nelly – no need to hurry, it's only me.'

'Joanna!' exclaimed Nelly as she opened the front door, a huge smile on her face. 'I'm so pleased to see you – I bet you must have been wondering what had happened. Come in, come in, have a seat by the fire while I go and put the kettle on,' she said, bustling about like a fussy old mother hen.

'I hope you didn't mind me calling round,' said Joanna.

'Of course not, I wanted you to come, otherwise I wasn't sure how I was going to be able to contact you. But I knew you'd come. Martin wasn't sure we were doing the right thing but I insisted. Like I said to him, it's my house and I'll do what I want, thank you very much. He's not the boss of me, you know – thinks he is but he's not. Milk and no sugar is it, love?'

'Sorry? Oh, in the tea. Yes please – thank you. That was well remembered.'

'Yes, I'm not as daft as our Martin thinks I am sometimes, it's just my other bits that are dropping off,' she chuckled, her blue eyes twinkling mischievously. 'Would you mind helping me carry these through, love, please? See what I mean? My brain's as sharp as a needle but my hands struggle to carry two cups of tea… and don't even get me started on my legs. Crazy isn't it? Not much fun getting old, love, I can tell you. Better than the alternative though I suppose. Gah!'

*

They made themselves comfortable by the fire but Joanna couldn't wait another minute, the question was just burning to be asked.

'So what's happening about the cottage? I went into town to see the letting agent this morning and he told me you'd taken it off the market.'

'It's true, we have,' said Nelly, looking strangely sad.

Joanna's heart sank. 'But I don't understand. It all sounded so definite yesterday…'

'And it is,' said Nelly, with a grin,

Joanna looked puzzled. 'But…'

Nelly chuckled, her whole body shaking up and down with laughter. 'Eeeh love, I'm so sorry – I can be such a torment at times,' she said, wiping the tears from her eyes. 'You should have seen your face though. Our Martin always goes mad at me when I torment him like that.'

'So… you still haven't told me yet.' Dare she even have a glimmer of hope? 'What's happening with the cottage?'

'It's yours, love. All ready for you to move in to as soon as I move out at the end of the month.'

'Oh Nelly,' cried Joanna, almost leaping from her seat to rush across and give the old lady a big hug. 'I can't tell you what that means to me. I've been in absolute bits this morning thinking I was going to have to look for somewhere else to live and knowing I was never going to find anywhere I loved as much as this cottage. Thank you, thank you sooo much.'

'Blimey, it's been a long time since anyone gave me a hug like that – it was almost worth giving up my house for,' she joked. 'We just decided to cut out the letting agent, that was all. There didn't seem much point. I know I haven't known you for long but I know I can trust you. And when Martin met you he felt exactly the same way too. It may sound a bit crazy but in my opinion crazy is often good.

'I mean what is the point of paying all that money to a letting agent when we can sort it all out ourselves? I trust my instincts, they are always right – they've never let me down yet, they're not going to let me down now, and I just know you will never let me down either. We'll make it all official, like, draw up a contract and everything, so you won't have anything to worry about. Are you happy with that?'

'Happy? I feel as though I could explode with happiness right now,' beamed Joanna, absolutely glowing with joy. What a difference an hour can make. In fact what a difference twenty-four hours can make. She'd never been on such a roller-coaster ride in her life!

Chapter Fifteen

Joanna was on a total high. Bluebell Cottage was to be hers! She would be free, single, new home, new job, not a care in the world. Really? Hmm, unlikely – life doesn't happen like that. Particularly not to Joanna.

Nevertheless, she felt so excited she could burst and needed to share all her happenings with someone. What better person than her sister? Hannah didn't even know she'd left David yet, never mind that she'd found herself the perfect place to live – she couldn't wait to tell her. Grabbing her mobile from her handbag, she pressed Hannah's number, her fingers almost tripping over each other with excitement.

'Hey you, I have news and you're gonna like it. Can I come round – are you at home?'

'Mm.'

'Hannah? Are you okay?'

'No.'

'Are you crying? What's wrong?'

Silence.

'Look, don't worry – whatever it is, we'll sort it. I'll be there in about twenty minutes – okay?'

Joanna started the engine and pulled away from the kerb.

A quick wave to Nelly who was still standing watching from the window, and then she was on her way. Oh Hannah. Much as she loved her sister, she really didn't feel in the mood for helping her out today. She'd had enough stress of her own in the past twenty-four hours, to say nothing of the past thirty years. Having just managed to lift herself up onto a high today against all odds, she really didn't want dragging back down into another bad place. But hey, she was her sister, what more could she do?

*

Upon reaching the house, the front door opened before she'd even had time to walk up the path towards it. Hannah stood there puffy-eyed, arms outstretched, playing the queen of tragedy to perfection. Drama had always been her strongest subject at school, must be where Jack got his thespian tendencies from – it certainly wasn't from her.

'Joanna,' she wailed. 'Thank God you came. I don't know what to do.'

Well I'm not thanking anybody, especially God, Joanna thought to herself, feeling her elation of just an hour ago curl up into a ball and start to wither and die. She really did not want to have to deal with this, not today. And if that made her a horrible person then, okay, she was a horrible person – but at least she was a free one, she reminded herself.

'Okay – what's happened? Let's get inside and then you can tell me all about it.' She couldn't wait, she thought, sarcasm to the fore. 'Come on, we're giving the neighbours a free floorshow here.' They truly were, curtains were twitching left, right and centre.

'I have some news to tell you too as it happens – quite a lot of news actually, you'll be shocked. Who's going first?' said Joanna, knowing full well what would happen. Whatever was happening in Hannah's life was always deemed to be more important.

'He's left me,' wailed Hannah.

'And I've left him,' said Joanna.

'Did you even hear me?' said Hannah, quite crossly. This momentous thing had happened to her and her sister didn't even seem to care. 'He's left me – gone. He says it's only for a few days while he gets his head together but I don't believe him, I don't think he's ever coming back. What am I going to do, Jo – what am I going to do without him?'

'Well if it's just for a few days…'

'Just for a few days? You surely can't believe that. This is a disaster, I have to face it – he's gone, never coming back. What am I going to do? I can't stay here on my own, I just can't.'

'You're not on your own – you have Lottie.'

'Joanna – don't be so flippant!' she snapped, teary eyes blazing. 'You know what I mean. I can't cope on my own, not with a baby and everything. No, there's only one thing for it, you're going to have to leave David and come and live here with me then you can help me out with Lottie. It's the only solution. You've been wanting to leave him for ages – this is your perfect opportunity.'

Joanna sighed. She really wanted to say to Hannah, 'For goodness' sake, woman up,' but she knew she was going to have to pick her words carefully here if she didn't want an all-out war to develop. Nevertheless, there was no way she was going to put her own life on hold yet again, not even to help her sister.

'That's one of the things I was going to tell you. I've already left David. It all kicked off last night. He…'

'Brilliant – that's perfect timing then.'

Joanna was starting to feel real anger towards Hannah and this confused her. They'd always been so close, really never a cross word ever since they'd left their teenage-angst years behind, supported each other through everything. But now…

Maybe it was this recently discovered inner strength she'd found that made her view things differently. This time last week she would have been full of sympathy for Hannah, keen to come and stay with her for a while to help and support her. She would have listened to her tales of woe without wanting to scream at her to shut up. Now she just wanted to tell her she was selfish and give her a slap. Was that really mean? What had happened to her? Had she turned into some kind of evil monster instead of the caring sister she used to be?

The thing was, and the thing which riled her the most, was that up until this point Hannah's life had been textbook perfect, the complete antithesis of her own. For instance, whilst Joanna had always been small and dumpy and last in the queue for the good looks department, Hannah had wallowed in the fact that she'd been tall and slim and elegant and her beauty had known no bounds. And whilst Joanna had fallen into a marriage with David because that's what had seemed to be expected of her and had continued to 'stick it out' for thirty years for more or less the exact same reason, Hannah had fallen deeply in love with Marcus and he with her likewise and the two had enjoyed a blissful marriage with not a cloud on the horizon.

Even down to their children. Joanna loved Jack with all of her heart, undeniably so, but she would have given anything to have had a little girl too. The pink and the frills – a little mini-me, someone to hang out with as she'd got older. That, of course, had been Hannah's only problem in life up to that point, she'd been unable to get pregnant. But then, married to a man like Marcus who'd been loaded, money can overcome most things and indeed it had – it paid for several rounds of IVF and eventually she'd got pregnant. And hadn't it been so typical that Hannah had given birth to such an absolutely adorable baby girl – a beautiful bundle of pink perfection.

So yes, now it would appear the tide was turning. Hannah wasn't even interested in hearing about what had happened to Joanna in the past twenty-four hours, which was equally traumatic as what had happened to her, if not more so. She was so self-centred and Joanna was really only beginning to realise that now. It was all about her, no one else's problems were important, she always had to come first.

Maybe it was because she'd been the youngest, the spoilt younger child. As the older sibling, Joanna had been expected to be able to cope, to take care of her little sister. And she always had. Until now. But now was *her* time. She'd waited long enough for it and nothing was going to stand in her way. Selfish though it may sound, she refused to allow herself to be dragged back down now, not even by her sister.

'Look I'm sorry, Hannah but it's just not going to happen. I'm not going to come here to live with you.' Clear and to the point.

Hannah looked stunned. 'But you have to – I need you. Surely it's the obvious solution. I need help and you need somewhere to live. There is no other option.'

'Hannah, I asked you last week if I could come and live here for a while until I sorted myself out and you said "no". What was I meant to do? So I did the obvious thing and looked for somewhere to rent. Found it now and it's perfect – sorry but no way am I going to give that up.'

Hannah's eyes narrowed, her lips pursed. 'D'you not think that's just being incredibly mean? I'm going through an absolute nightmare here and all you can think about is yourself.'

The gloves were off. 'Well that's rich coming from you, Mrs Perfect Life who always gets everything her own way. I'm sorry, Hannah, but just for once you're going to have to stand on your own two feet. You're not the only one who's in the middle of a crisis, you know, but you didn't even want to hear about what had happened to me. All you were interested in was how you could make use of my situation to your own advantage. Anyway – enough. I don't want to argue with you, I have to go, I have stuff to do.'

Even Wuffles the dog looked nervous at the sound of their heated voices. Baby Lottie too was disturbed and started to cry. Loudly.

Hannah looked as though she was about to have a breakdown. She threw back her head and held her hands over her ears. 'Aaaagh!' she screamed. 'Go and get her, do something with her – anything! I really can't cope with this.'

The sound of the baby's cries tugged at Joanna's heartstrings. She could not let herself be drawn in but how could she go and just leave Lottie to cry like that? Involuntarily, her legs carried her towards the cot.

'Oh Lottie, Lottie – poor baby, it's okay. Come and have a cuddle with your Auntie Jo. Look, here's Wuffles come to have a look what's happening too. It's okay, it's okay, darling. Mummy's just having a bit of a wobble, that's all, she'll be fine in a minute. I know… you're probably hungry aren't you, but there's not a lot I can do about it, my baby-feeding equipment dried up years ago, you'll have to wait for your mummy for that. How about if you try having a suck at your dummy for now instead? Not quite the same but…' With a silent prayer she popped it into the little rosebud lips, both overjoyed and relieved to hear the contented sound of sucking that ensued.

Thankfully it was the only sound she could hear; silence permeated from the lounge. Was Hannah okay? Against her better wishes she tiptoed back in, Lottie still in her arms and Wuffles at her heel.

'I'm sorry, Hannah,' she said, 'I don't want to walk away and leave you like this. We haven't fallen out since we were teenagers and I don't want us to do so now. I…'

'Get out!'

'What?'

'You heard me. Just give me my baby and get out of my house, I never want to see you again.'

'But Hannah…'
'GO!'

*

Oh my God, she could hardly believe what had just happened – thrown out of the house by her own sister? She felt completely and utterly traumatised. That, on top of yesterday. Thrown out of two houses in two days – what was happening here? It was obviously her fault. She knew she'd changed, become a stronger person – but had she changed into some kind of monster – a selfish evil bitch?

She could at least maybe understand why yesterday had happened, in fact it had been long overdue in a way – well, that she should leave David anyway. And his reaction had been pretty much predictable given the circumstances and combined with his temper. But Hannah…? Joanna stumbled back down the path and almost fell into her car. It was as though a combination of everything that had happened to her over the past two days suddenly hit her like a tsunami and almost took her breath away. She sobbed as if her heart would break, her tears draining away some of the tension that had been building up inside her.

*

She couldn't even remember driving back to the flat, so lost she'd been in her emotions, thinking of Hannah. In fact she was amazed when she pulled up outside, shocked to find herself here. Surprised that, on autopilot, she hadn't driven herself home – or to what used to be her home. Oh my God. She prayed that both Gavin and Jack would be out, she needed some space, time to think. And gin. She needed gin for sure. And chocolate, that too. Amazingly there was an off-licence across the road from the flat, she remembered noting that earlier – feeling reassured that it would be there and helpful in times of need. Which this most certainly was.

Armed with her purchases, she let herself in, feeling relief to hear no answer when she called out 'hello'. She collapsed into a crumpled heap upon what she affectionately felt was her sofa, relief flooding over her that she was in a safe space, alone, and could give full vent to her emotion with no one to see or hear.

Through her gut-wrenching sobs, she failed to hear the bedroom door open or someone enter the room and stand over her, so lost was she in her own self-doubting misery. But she did hear a voice that said softly, 'Here, give me the gin, let me pour one for you – one for me too if you need a friend to talk to.'

Mortified that he'd seen her this way, she mopped herself up hastily and attempted to silence her sobs, although the hiccupping spasms of her breath seemed involuntary – completely beyond her control.

'S-sorry,' she gasped, in embarrassment overload, 'I didn't th-think you were h-here. I shouted b-but…'

'Hey, don't be sorry – nothing to be sorry about. We all have our bad days sometimes. And believe me gin does help, I've resorted to it myself on many an occasion. I take it this is about the cottage? You didn't get it after all?'

'No I did, I did,' she said, trying to pull herself together.

Gavin looked surprised. 'Then I thought you would have been over the moon. I thought we would have been drinking this gin to celebrate not to drown your sorrows. Although I have to say I think we needed Hendricks to celebrate rather than this stuff. This tastes more like paint stripper or some such – not that I've ever tasted paint stripper, obviously – but this is gross. Where the heck did you get it?' he said, wiping his mouth on the back of his hand with a grimace.

'From the off-licence across the road. It's not that bad. I've tasted worse many times – you're such a gin snob. Here have a slab of chocolate, it'll take the taste away.'

'Aha – I wondered why you bought the chocolate too,' he said, snapping a piece off and popping it into his mouth with a grin. 'Mmm, that's better.'

'See, a winning combination. You get the stress-busting relief from the gin and the orgasmic moment from the chocolate all happening at the same time.'

'Like the best orgasm you could ever wish for,' he said, his grin spreading wider, eyes ever hopeful.

'I wouldn't go that far,' she said, but even she was smiling now. Slightly anyway.

He took another swig of his gin with a shudder. 'Yuck... it really is, isn't it? He paused to look at her, his eyes so gentle and caring. 'So, tell me about the house first of all. You've definitely got it?'

'Yes, it was quite stressful though,' she said, regaling him with the whole saga. 'But it's definitely mine – I can move in at the end of the month. Bet you won't be sorry either. Can you cope with me until then?'

'No, I'll throw you out on the streets,' he joked, expecting her to laugh along with him. But what was meant as an innocent, harmless quip held a much deeper meaning for her. 'Hey, I'm not serious, I thought you knew that. What's wrong?'

The tears were back – in full force. 'Sorry. I've just had a weird couple of days, that's all. First there was David throwing us out of the house last night. And okay, I know I've been wanting to leave him for years but I just never expected it to end quite that way. Then on top of that today, Hannah threw me out of her house too – says she never wants to see me again.'

'Oh God! No wonder you were upset. You're usually so close, whatever triggered that?'

'Basically Marcus has left her and she can't cope. She wanted me to just ditch the cottage and go and live with her – then when I refused that's when it all kicked off and she threw me out. Does that make me a horrible person? It does, doesn't it? I feel like the worst sister in the world.'

'You're certainly not that. From what you tell me you've always been there for her and helped her out. But now you're trying to get your own life together and I can perfectly understand you saying "no" to her. It would be all too easy to get side-tracked and find yourself dragged down by other people's lives again. I really think you've just got to stay strong now. You've made the break, things are starting to come together for you, don't let anyone knock you off track – sister or no sister.'

'But doesn't that then make me incredibly selfish? I've always been the one for everyone to turn to whenever they've had a problem – I've never been used to putting myself first.'

'Well maybe that's where you've gone wrong. Maybe that's why you've been stuck in a rut and not been happy for the past thirty years. This is your time, Joanna – make the most of it. You only have one life, you know.'

She downed the remains of her glass, grimacing slightly at the flavour of the gin. 'You're right, I know you're right. But I still feel so guilty. What if she can't cope – what about Lottie? Even the dog – what about him? What about if I said I'd go and stay with her for a few days, just until the cottage is ready? She might have sorted herself out by then.'

'Do you really believe that? You know what'll happen, don't you? A few days in there and she'll come to depend on you completely. She'll be so reliant on you that you'll feel too guilty to leave. You'll end up having to give up the cottage and you'll be stuck in a rut once again – a different rut but nevertheless, and not even your own rut this time. Just think about it… I'm going for the Hendrick's, I think we need more gin if I'm ever going to convince you.'

She looked pensive when he returned with the bottle, and they sat in silence for a while.

'I know you're right…'

'Hallelujah!' he said, raising his glass to her.

'But…'

'Please. No "buts". She has friends, doesn't she? And a mother? Other people she can turn to – surely they'll help out.'

'I suppose so… it's just that it's always been me.'

'My point exactly.'

'And actually I don't think Marcus will be able to stay away – he loves her too much. He told her he was only going away for a few days to get his head around everything – life with a new baby can be tough – and I do think he'll be back.'

'There you go then. Problem solved. Just call me a genius.'

Once again they sat in silence. A companiable silence. This Hendrick's tasted so much better.

'Gavin?'

'Mm?'

'Will you take me to bed?'

??!!??!!

He hadn't been expecting that…

Chapter Sixteen

K-Y Jelly? Forget it. She need not have worried. Everything, most definitely, was still in full working order.

'Where did that come from?' he asked, his voice somewhat breathless.

'Well, if you need to ask… I thought you'd know all about these things at your age,' she quipped. At this moment she felt almost giddy with happiness – and that had nothing to do with the gin. It was as if she'd been reborn, years of pent-up frustration lifted from her.

'You truly are… amazing,' he said, turning his head lazily on the pillow to gaze at her.

'Well, no one ever said that to me before. Even though I'm older than you and I'm also your mate's mum?'

'Don't.'

'I know. Thank God he's at work.'

'I feel like I could lie here forever.'

'Me too,' she said, snuggling up to him closely. It felt so calm and relaxing and, just for the moment, she didn't have a care in the world. Cocooned in their own little bubble, they floated along in their state of bliss until, bodies entwined, they drifted slowly off to sleep.

*

More than an hour passed by until they awoke. Gavin was the first. He tried to lie still so as not to disturb her; he just wanted to savour the moment. But within minutes her eyes flickered and opened, looking surprised for a nanosecond before remembering.

'Hey,' he said softly.

Oh my God, it was true – she really had done it. She'd had sex with this beautiful man even though they'd sworn they wouldn't do it. But she'd instigated it, and they had, and she could, and it had been… bloody fabulous. And apologies, because under normal circumstances, she didn't even swear.

'Did we fall asleep? What time is it? I need to move…' she said, panicking just a little.

'Hey slow down – what's the hurry? You have all the time in the world now – remember? No more responsibilities, no one to consider but yourself. No meals to cook, we can ring for a takeaway. Jack's working so he won't be back until late.'

'Just as well really,' she grimaced, suddenly coming face to face with reality. In bed with her son's mate?! Really not good. But it was good – that was the problem.

'I hope you're not regretting what we just did, I know I'm not.'

'No, me neither. In fact, if you must know, it did me a world of good.'

'Glad to be of service,' he smirked.

'Sorry, I didn't mean it to sound like that. I mean…'

'Only teasing – I know what you mean. And it did me a world of good too as a matter of fact. And it doesn't have to mean we're in a relationship or anything, not unless you want us to be of course. It was just a one-off, for all kinds of reasons.'

'Exactly that.' How very grown up.

*

177

It was only later, as they sat at the table eating their meal, a Chinese from the local takeaway, that a remark Gavin had made earlier came back to her.

'I need to know more about you,' she said, assembling her crispy duck pancake and slathering it with even more hoisin sauce. Yum.

'What – now you've ravaged my body I'm not allowed any secrets from you?'

'Something like that – yes,' she joked.

'Okay – fire with the questions, what would you like to know?'

'Remember earlier, when I said that what we did had done me good – well, you said it had done you good too. And from the look that passed across your face as you said it, I don't think you meant the obvious – there was something much deeper than that.'

Upon hearing these words, tension slid silently into the room like an unwelcome guest; sadness flooded his face.

'Yeah,' he said with a sigh. 'Okay. I have an ex. We weren't married but we lived together for eight years. She just packed up and left one day without any explanation. She'd never said there was a problem, that she wasn't happy or anything. No hint of a clue at all. That was two years ago now and there's been nobody else since. The worst thing was we had a little girl and she took her too. Gone. Just like that… I have absolutely no idea where they are. No contact at all. I've searched and searched, done absolutely everything I can to find them. But nothing. Disappeared without a trace.'

'Oh my God! I am so sorry,' she said, her eyes welling, hardly able to grasp what he'd just told her. 'I've been going on and on about all of my problems to you ever since we first met and yet mine are nothing, absolutely nothing, in comparison to yours. I can't imagine what you must be going through – your child taken away from you like that and not being able to see her.'

'It's the not knowing that's the hardest part. Louisa, my ex, took the passports and everything, so they could be living absolutely anywhere. That's the thing, I like to think they're here in the UK somewhere, but who knows? They could be anywhere in the world and the likelihood is that I may never see my baby girl again... Sorry,' he said, brushing his tears away with the back of his hand, 'but that thought really cripples me. I try to keep it hidden away at the back of my mind. Like it's in a little box and I can lift the lid sometimes and take a look inside but only when no one else is watching. I find that's the only way I can cope with it. But sometimes, just sometimes, it catches me out... mostly when I'm in bed at night, trying to get to sleep, and I can't get her little face out of my mind...'

'Oh Gavin, I am so, so sorry. I can't imagine anything worse than being parted from your child and not knowing where she is or what's happening to her – it must haunt you constantly. Is there absolutely nothing more that can be done to help you find her?'

'Nothing. Absolutely nothing. I've tried everything. My only hope now is that maybe one day, when she turns eighteen, she'll come looking for me. That happens, you know. If you've been separated from your birth parents as a baby you go through your childhood feeling somehow as if you don't belong – like you've lost your identity, part of you is missing. And you do anything, just anything in your power to find that missing link. Whether it's a father or a mother you've grown up not knowing, you have this desperate urge to search for them, to make yourself whole again.'

The intensity in his eyes, of the way he spoke, made him look slightly unhinged. Joanna reached across the table to place her hand on his to bring him comfort. It worried her the effect this must be having on him and yet she'd never even realised, hadn't known about all of this until just a few minutes ago. Talking about it to her must obviously have brought it all to the surface and it was so raw for him. It was understandable that he tried to push it to the back of his mind most of the time; bringing it out and going through it – reliving it all again – must be so unbelievably painful.

'The joy of finding that missing parent though… the reunion…' his face was awash with tears as she squeezed his hand.

'You've been watching too many episodes of *Long Lost Family*, that Davina McCall's got a lot to answer for,' she joked, trying, in vain, to lighten his mood slightly; it worried her to see him suffering like this. It fell on stony ground.

'What's her name?'

He looked blank for a moment – confused. Like he was thinking of something else altogether.

'Who?'

'Your little girl – who else?'

'Oh, sorry. Yes. My baby girl is called Florence.'

'Florence. What a beautiful name. Unusual too – which might make it easier to trace her one day.'

'I can only hope…' he said.

*

They finished the remains of their meal mostly in silence, although Gavin left most of his. He couldn't eat; he just didn't have the appetite anymore. Momentarily, Joanna felt almost sorry she'd asked the question now – had she realised she was inviting such sadness to throw a shadow over their perfect moment she probably wouldn't have done so. A selfish thought, which lasted no more than a nanosecond because it was totally overshadowed by her compassion for Gavin, this beautiful, caring man. By her realising how much good it must have done him to talk about it instead of keeping it all bottled up. What a heavy burden that must be to carry around inside yourself day after day, having no one to share it with. She felt honoured that he felt he could trust her enough to open up to her.

He poured them another glass.

'This is where I drink far too much – when I think about Florence and what my life might have been. Louisa can go to hell as far as I'm concerned, but Florence, that's a different story. I never actually wanted children, it hadn't been my intention in life at all, but once she was here I absolutely doted on her. She was the light of my life. But now it's as though Louisa turned off the switch. The light went out.

'I feel like a shadow of the person I used to be now. And the sad thing is that the only hope I've got left is to pray that when she's older she *will* start asking questions and come looking for me. I just hope her mother doesn't try to fob her off with some made-up story about me being dead or something. And, if she does, then I hope Florence will realise what she's like and will carry on searching. I know she will find me one day, it's hard but it happens, I know it does. Sorry,' he said, 'I didn't mean to be pouring all this out on you – and I didn't mean to be blubbing all over the place either. Sometimes I think I need to man up.'

'Gavin, I've never met a better man than you – truly. And you need to do no such thing. I'm just so glad you felt able to share all this with me and I hope it helps you in some small way. You know you can talk to me about it at any time. Keeping it all locked away inside yourself won't do you any good at all – and we need you fit and well, ready for that day when Florence finally comes back home to look for her dad.'

Head still bowed, he turned slightly towards her with a watery smile, unable to speak for the moment. She took his hand in hers and squeezed it tightly.

'And can I just say, there is absolutely nothing wrong with a man shedding tears, that's the sign of a real man – it's when they don't that the problems arise.'

*

'Hello, hello, hello – what's going on here then?' asked Jack, making a sudden entrance. 'I always seem to catch you in compromising positions, Mother.'

'We weren't expecting you back until later.'

'Evidently! It's quarter past eleven – how much later did you expect me to be?'

'That time already? How did that happen?'

'Time flies when you're enjoying yourself obviously, Mother.'

'Cut the sarcasm – nothing's going on here. And even it was, what would it have to do with you?'

'Touché. Well, I would say I'd make myself scarce and go to bed but you seem to be sitting on it so that's that option out of the window.'

'It's probably time we all thought about turning in actually,' she said, her eyes still overflowing with sympathy for Gavin. She would have liked nothing more than to hug him right now, she could hardly bear to see the pain she'd unleashed in him, but she knew that probably wasn't a good idea.

'You use the bathroom first, Gavin, I'll stack the dishwasher so we don't have to face it all in the morning,' she said.

'Is that okay?' he asked. He looked drained.

'Of course it is. I'll see you tomorrow.'

'Goodnight then. And thank you.' Obviously not just for washing the dishes.

''Night, lover boy,' tittered Jack.

'Shut it, small fry – you know nothing,' said Joanna.

*

'So did you? Although I can hardly bear to hear the answer,' Jack grimaced, hands over his ears, as they settled down for the night on their respective sofas.

'That is actually none of your business, Jack.'

'Okay – so you did then, you would have been strongly denying it otherwise.'

'You can think whatever you like, Jack, but it's for me to know and for you to never find out, so keep that little nose of yours out of my affairs please.'

'Aha! So you *are* having an affair then?'

'Jack! Anyway, to change the subject, it's been quite an eventful day.'

'I bet it has.'

'Don't start that again, listen to what I'm saying. I've got the cottage – moving in at the end of the month.'

'We are?'

'No, just me.' A sudden pang of guilt – she'd never even considered Jack. What had she been thinking?

'What? You'd just leave me homeless? Your poor little boy – what kind of a mother are you?'

Okay, mother guilt to the fore now – even though he was almost thirty.

'I'm sorry, I just never thought. You'd left home, moved in with the Pox... er, Pixie and everything.'

'But I'm back now. I thought you'd be pleased to see me,' he said, pouting like a two-year-old.

'Well I suppose...'

'Hahaha – got you there, didn't I? No, I'm proud of you, Mum, the way you're changing your life. Leaving Dad after all this time, getting a new job and finding yourself somewhere to live. It's a big thing after being stuck in the one place for so long. I'm really pleased for you and I wouldn't dream of muscling in and invading your space – and besides, you never know what you might be getting up to.'

'Jack!' she scolded, but she felt such a warm glow of mother-love for him well up inside – never before had he said he was proud of her. 'Thank you for saying that though – it means a lot.'

'Don't say it enough, I suppose, but yeah I really am proud of you. And definitely, the cottage is yours to do what you please in. Me? I'm going to try and find myself a little flat, make a proper bachelor pad like I've always wanted... if I can get that Pixie off my back, that is.'

'Not heard anything from her?'

'Not today – no.'

Joanna so wanted to say, 'If only you'd listened to me you wouldn't have found yourself in this mess,' but she managed to hold her tongue. She didn't want to cause any bad feelings between them, he had problems enough.

'Perhaps just leave her to calm down for a couple of days, she might see it differently if she's on her own and has time to think.'

'Yeah that's what I'm hoping. Although I'm sure her mother will have waded in with advice by now – and God only knows what that will lead to.'

'A scary character, that one.'

'You're telling me.'

'By the way, I've fallen out with your Auntie Hannah – she threw me out of her house and she's not speaking to me now.'

'What?' said Jack, sitting bolt upright in his bed with the shock. His mum never fell out with Hannah, they were best friends. 'What was that about?'

'Not something I'm proud of really. Marcus has left her and she wanted me to move in.'

'And you said "no". I'm not surprised! Anyway Marcus will be back – he's never gonna stay away is he? I wouldn't worry about it, Mum, it'll all blow over before you know it.'

His words made her feel a whole lot better. In fact she was quite enjoying these late-night chats with her son. Time to settle down and get some sleep now, tomorrow was another day.

*

It had been an eventful week, to say the very least. Thankfully, the remainder of it had contained a lot less drama than the first half had done – in fact, in comparison, nothing much had happened at all.

Above everything, Joanna was pleased that her relationship with Gavin appeared to have remained virtually unchanged. She'd thought, having slept with him that one time, things could have been awkward between them, but it was as if by releasing all of the sexual tension that had hung in the air whenever they'd been around each other, they now felt more relaxed somehow.

Admittedly, Gavin had been a little bit quiet for a couple of days afterwards but, as she suspected when she asked him about it, that was because of all the painful memories of Florence that had been stirred up in his mind, not because of anything else. As he told her, he felt such relief to have found someone he could trust enough to share his feelings with. Trust was a real issue for him, he found it difficult to trust anyone. And he was grateful to her for not judging him when he'd ended up 'crying like a baby', as he put it. But once again Joanna reassured him that 'it takes a real man to show his true emotions'.

Joanna found it quite difficult to understand her true feelings towards Gavin in a way. She found him hugely attractive – what woman wouldn't? But at the same time he was younger, he was her son's mate – that latter thought somewhat off-putting in itself. But he'd helped her out in so many ways, she would never, ever have left her little rut – even though it had been squeezing the life out of her – if it hadn't been for Gavin. He'd saved her soul – saved her from drowning in a sea of despondency. He'd appeared before her like some kind of superhero, not bearing gifts but bearing K-Y Jelly in the middle of a supermarket.

That memory made her giggle every time she thought about it – what an introduction. And he'd looked like a sex god on legs – still did. Okay, so she did still fancy him, but she was trying not to. She'd been stuck in the same relationship for thirty years – stepping out of it and straight into another one was not what she had intended to do. Soulmates they were and soulmates they would stay. Bedmates – that was a different thing altogether and could not happen. Well, maybe one day... or maybe occasionally, who knew? This was her time now – time to spread her wings and live a little, 'play the field', as her friend Gemma would say. Hmm, well, tentatively at least.

So other than daydreaming about Gavin, which seemed to have occupied rather a lot of her time, not a lot had happened for the past two or three days. No more dramas at least, sadly no contact with Hannah. And no contact with her mother either, although that was entirely Joanna's fault, and the daughter-guilt crept in as if to prove it. She hadn't even told her she'd left David yet, or about the cottage or the fallout with Hannah. She'd do it later... or tomorrow, she just didn't have the heart for it today.

One thing that had happened though, which had happened yesterday in fact, was that she'd given in her notice at work. She'd checked with Gavin first, naturally, just to make doubly sure he still wanted her and he'd been amazed that she'd even felt it necessary to check. Of course he still wanted her, was desperate for her to start as soon as possible in fact. So with a smile that she found difficult to hide, she went in to see her boss, handed in her resignation, and proceeded to do a little happy dance around her office. She would have to work her notice but the end of an era was in sight. The sad thing was, though, that after all of those years of dedication, not one single person had said they would miss her. Heigh-ho.

Chapter Seventeen

She opened her eyes. It was Saturday. The weekend. Yesss!!!
No work today. But then the next thought hit her. She tried to
squash it down but there it was – up it popped again, there was
no escape. IT WAS HER BIRTHDAY! Okay, okay, don't shout.
And don't panic either. Forty-nine or 49… whichever way you
looked at it, nothing changed. She was forty-nine today, the last
year of her forties – next year she would be fifty. Half a century
of being Joanna.

A weird thought that, and one she'd never considered before.
In fact, she'd never heard anyone speak of it. You kind of think
you are who you are forever. And yet she herself thought, as did
many other people, that we'd all lived other lives on earth before
this one, that we came back again to start another life as someone
new – the same soul in a different body. And although she'd often
thought about that, about how her body would be different, about
how she would start off as a baby again and grow into a whole
new adult unlike the one she was now, she'd never thought about
her name before. Joanna was just a temporary name given to her
for the here and now. Gosh that was so weird. She'd only been a
Joanna for half a century, what had she been before… what would
she be next? She kinda liked the name Joanna, she'd better make

the most of it while it still belonged to her. Hang on a minute – is this what being forty-nine does to you, makes you sound deranged?

Thankfully, any further random thoughts from beneath the duvet were suddenly interrupted by not one but two melodious voices, although this did make her realise that Gavin had at least one fault after all. He wasn't Mr Perfect – his singing was abysmal. Nevertheless, it's the thought that counts.

'Happy birthday to you, Happy birthday to you…'

She opened one eye, the other scrunched up in disbelief. 'How did you…? I didn't think anyone would remember.'

'Of course I remembered – I'm your son, aren't I? And I told Gav, of course. So sit up woman, we have Prosecco here – and a croissant with a candle in it. Hurry, you have to blow it out.'

She battled the sleepy dust and forced herself to sit upright and blow out the candle, feeling quite touched by what they had done.

'Aww thanks, you two. I really wasn't expecting this. In fact it's probably the most excitement I've had on a birthday morning for thirty years. Cheers!' she said, chinking her glass with theirs.

'And there's more to come,' said Gavin. 'So posh yourself up a bit, 'cos we're taking you out to breakfast.'

'Breakfast? I've never been out to breakfast in my life – that's something other people do.'

'You forget, madame, your life has changed now, this is the start of a whole new you. Now drink up, eat your croissant and go and get changed, you can't go turning up at a posh restaurant for Eggs Benedict wearing your PJs now can you?'

*

She felt a million dollars. Killer heels, her best red dress and lips to match, swanning into the restaurant with a handsome young man on each arm really was the best ego boost ever. Not that she needed one at the moment, her self-esteem had shot up a trillionfold recently – life was good and getting better by the day. If this was what being forty-nine was like then she was happy with it – bring it on!

Heads turned to look at her as she floated elegantly across the room – well, as elegantly as she could in the killer heels. Ouch, her feet were in agony, chafed to shreds, they'd be recuperating in plasters and Germolene later but no one needed to know that, and it would all have been worth it. She was loving the attention she was getting. At one time she would have shied away from it but not now – how much she'd changed! It was simply fabulous having two young male escorts. She was convinced everyone in the restaurant thought she was a film star with her two male bodyguards, and who was she to disillusion them? She hammed up the role like a pro.

'You're loving this, aren't you?' said Gavin, beaming at her from across the table as they ate.

He called the waiter over and asked him to take a photo of them with the birthday girl, after briefly first of all glancing at Joanna and whispering to her to wipe the lipstick from her front teeth before she posed. She giggled – try as she might, sophistication was not a thing that came to her easily.

The whole experience was just magical, and became even more so as they suddenly found themselves surrounded by waiters singing 'Happy Birthday' as one of them placed a beautiful candlelit cake upon the table in front of her. Other diners joined in the singing and, as she blew out the candles, a huge cheer went up around the room.

'Who is she?' they heard people whisper.

Gavin turned around to the table behind them. 'Do you not recognise her? She's an upcoming star – her name is Joanna Donohue. Remember that name because one day you'll look back and think about this moment – the day you first saw her.'

He turned back and winked at Joanna.

'Ooh you are awful,' she whispered to him, wide-eyed. 'They'll all be googling now to try and find me.'

'Hahaha, you know you love it really. And it gives them something to talk about, they were sitting in silence before.'

She couldn't help but giggle – this was the best birthday ever.

'Excuse me,' piped up a voice from behind Gavin. 'Please could I have your autograph?' said a lady, holding a paper napkin towards her. 'I've never met anyone famous before.'

Several espresso martinis and a glass of champagne later, they somehow managed to walk out of the restaurant with aplomb, Joanna waving and blowing kisses to her audience. It was a different story once they were out of the door and round the corner though, where they stumbled over each other and almost landed in a heap, falling about with laughter.

*

Back at the flat they were still on a high. 'Drinks, anyone?' asked Gavin, waving yet another bottle of champagne in the air.

'Not for me, thanks,' said Joanna. 'Much as I don't like refusing, I think I've had quite enough for now. Wouldn't say no to a coffee though if you're offering.'

Jack's head was immersed in his phone. 'Sorry, what did you say?'

'Coffee?'

'Yeah, thanks. Better make it a strong one.'

'Same for us all, I think,' said Joanna, her ever-watchful mother-eye focused on her son. 'Something wrong, Jack? I noticed your phone kept beeping all the time we were out.'

'Yeah. Pixie. She won't leave me alone. She's wanting to meet up now to talk about it. But we've talked about it a zillion times and it always ends up the same way – her screaming abuse and hurling things at me. I've told her I'm not going to change my mind – she knows that already. She is totally not ready to be a mother – she can't look after herself never mind look after a baby as well, she needs to get her head sorted out first.'

'Oh Jack – what a mess. Maybe you should go round and try talking to her again. I know it's not easy but you got yourself into this and, much as I sympathise, it's not going to go away unless you do something about it.'

'I know, I know…'

'Sorry to sound like a nagging mother but there's the flat to sort out as well. You can't just keep paying rent on somewhere you're not going to be living and she won't be able to afford it by herself, will she?'

'Nope. But I reckon her mum will step in and help her with the rent, though, she won't want her to lose it. Not as though they're short of money, is it? You heard the story…'

'I did! Couldn't believe my ears when I overheard that conversation. Drug dealer. And there he was, boasting to your dad about all the money he makes. I was disgusted.'

Jack checked his phone again.

'So what are you going to do?'

'I suppose you're right. I'm going to have to go round and talk to her again. I'll text her now and tell her I'll go tomorrow.'

'Coffee is served,' said Gavin, breezing in bearing a tray. 'It all sounds very serious in here. Come on, open your cards – it's your birthday.'

'I've had such a good time this morning I forgot all about cards and messages and stuff – although I suppose my cards will mostly have gone to the house – no one knows where I am, apart from you two.' She tore open the envelopes eagerly, so touched that they had gone to so much trouble with everything. '"To My Best Friend" – aww, Gavin that's lovely, thank you so much. And "To The World's Best Mum" – wow, thank you, Jack – I really am getting spoilt today.'

"Cos you deserve it,' said Jack, giving her a hug. 'By the way, we didn't manage to get you a present so we're going to treat you to dinner. We're all booked up at the swishest place in Alderley Edge tonight, so don't go spilling anything on your posh frock before then, you'll need it for later.'

Her eyes sparkled with delight. This really was turning out to be the best birthday ever.

*

At Joanna's suggestion, they decided they'd spend a lazy afternoon in front of the TV, especially if they were going out again this evening. She hung up her best red dress to save it for the evening ahead and slipped into something a little more comfortable. She swore she'd gained another two inches around her waistline, and that was only with breakfast – goodness only knew what size she'd be when the day was over. But it was worth it. She could go back to the jogging tomorrow – or even to the gym. Well, maybe.

She settled back down on the sofa, scrolling on her phone. 'OMG – eighty-six people wishing me a happy birthday on Facebook,' she said, "hearting" them one at a time as she scrolled down. 'Isn't it lovely when people take the time to send messages? That's what I love about Facebook – it keeps you in touch with friends who live far away, people you'd probably lose touch with altogether if it wasn't for the power of social media. I know it has its faults, but it's great for keeping people connected – even for finding people you've lost sometimes.' She looked towards Gavin, suddenly realising what she'd said – just a throwaway comment not aimed at anyone in particular, hoping he hadn't heard.

'Yeah. Doesn't always work though – not many things are that straightforward.'

'Sorry – I didn't mean… '

'I know.'

'But maybe one day when she's older – who knows?'

'It would be good to think so,' he said, looking saddened.

'What? Who? Who's she?' asked Jack, suddenly aware there was a conversation going on around him.

'Nothing, Jack. Nothing for you to involve yourself in – get back to your phone.'

'Ohhh – do you know, sometimes you sound just like my mother.'

'That's because I am, Jack,' she smiled, 'that's because I am.'

Gavin's attention had returned to the TV – *Homes Under The Hammer.*

'Bit like a busman's holiday for you this, isn't it?' said Joanna.

He flashed her a smile but seemed engrossed. Just vaguely half watching, she turned back to her phone, only to discover four missed calls from earlier in the day: her mum, her friend Gemma, Hannah, and David. Her heart did a sudden little back flip. Hannah? *David?* Were they really just ringing to wish her a happy birthday? No – she thought not. And she really didn't want any trouble today – the day had been so perfect.

'Would it be okay if I use your bedroom for a little while to return a few calls please, Gavin? I won't be long.'

'Go for it,' he said, his head still occupied by Martin Roberts and Lucy Alexander, an old episode obviously.

Her mum was the first person she spoke to; she knew that would be an easy one and it was. There was so much to tell her though – about how she'd actually left David and found herself a place to live temporarily with a friend, about giving in her notice at work and starting a new job soon, and about Jack's situation with the Poxie. Oh my goodness, so much had happened in a week.

The second call, the one to her friend Gemma, was simple. Voicemail. 'Please leave a message after the tone', which she did.

The third one took a little more courage to make. Hannah picked up immediately, almost as if she'd been sitting with the phone in her hand, waiting for it to ring. 'Jo I am so, so, sorry – I was a complete bitch. I never meant to act like I did, I was just in such a panic.'

'Well I'm sorry too. Sorry I wasn't more sympathetic, I should have done more. How are you, and how's Lottie? I've been really worried but I was scared to call. Stupid isn't it? Scared to call my own sister – I do love you, you know.'

'I know you do, and I love you too... and happy birthday, by the way, I have a card and present here for you but just haven't got around to doing anything with them yet, sorry.'

'No worries – I know you've had a lot on your mind with Marcus and everything. Have you heard anything from him?'

'I've done more than that – he's here!'

'What?'

'He came home. Two days ago. Oh Jo, I can hardly believe the difference in him – it's amazing. He rang me and said he'd been going over and over everything in his head and realised he couldn't live without me and, even more than that, he actually said he'd been missing Lottie too and wanted to learn how to become a proper father to her. You can imagine my reaction – I was in bits. He came back home straight after the call and ohhh, it was just like I had the old Marcus back again. I love him so much, Joanna, and he loves me too, I know that now for sure. We've always been so devoted to each other and I have only just realised how jealous he was of Lottie taking up so much of my attention.

'The thing was that I was the one doing everything for Lottie and building up a strong bond with her, whereas Marcus wasn't getting involved at all and consequently he wasn't building any kind of a relationship with her. I couldn't understand this at the time and it used to cause all kinds of arguments, which we'd never been used to having. But I do understand now, he's told me – he was scared of her, she looked so tiny and vulnerable, he was frightened he'd do something to hurt her, he'd never been used to babies, had never even held one before.

'If only we'd talked it through properly at the time instead of arguing or stomping off in a sulk – or instead of the silent treatment with the slamming of the door and driving off out in frustration. But "if only" never got anyone anywhere so we have talked about it now – about everything, about how we feel and what makes us feel that way. And you know what? It's been so therapeutic – I feel our marriage is even stronger now because of it. But I know one thing for sure, we have the deepest love for each other that it is possible to have – nothing and no one will ever tear us apart again. And as for Lottie, we both absolutely dote on her and will do so for evermore. She binds us together and she'll be raised with such love and care from both of us, she is the luckiest little girl alive.'

'Wow – that's quite a speech, sis!'

'Sorry – yes, I know. But this is for real and it's important. And I just wanted you to know how happy we are – especially after the other day when I was such a pain.'

'You weren't being a pain, you were worried and upset. I was the one in the wrong – "selfish bitch" that's me.'

'Rubbish! You're the least selfish person I've ever met.'

'Until recently,' said Joanna. 'I think this new-found independence of mine comes with a price tag – I think it's changing me as a person.'

'Well that's good, isn't it? You've spent your life being at other people's beck and call – time for you to live a bit and do your own thing now. Sorry I never even asked anything about what was going on with you the other day, I was too steamed up with my own problems – see, that's me being selfish not you. I heard you say you'd left David but I never asked any more. What's happening? How's he taking it? Where are you living – or do I even need to ask?'

And so the whole saga had to be repeated once more. But Hannah sounded absolutely delighted for her, as had her mum in the conversation prior to this one. Joanna knew she was doing the right thing in changing her life, but it was good to have the reassurance of knowing that the other members of her family thought she was doing the right thing too. Forty-nine was looking pretty good so far.

Chapter Eighteen

There was only one blight on this day – the fact that she had a missed call on her phone from David. She kept trying to push it to the back of her mind – the day had been perfect in every way so far and she was reluctant to spoil it. But it wasn't just that – she was scared. And if that made her a wimp then so be it. He was obviously going to be livid with her and he'd had a few days to stew in his anger, most probably marinated in wine; the result would not be good.

She sat with the phone in her hand for several minutes, just staring at the screen. She even tried scrolling down her Facebook page as some form of distraction – like it was really important to check out what everyone was up to today. And anyway there were more 'Happy Birthday' messages to reply to, it would be rude not to answer them now – impolite. So she answered them all, thanked them profusely in fact. And she found out who was going where today and who was doing what, how sunny it was on the beach in Hastings – and, yum, as for that plate of food in Manchester, it looked totally delicious and definitely deserved a like.

Okay – enough. It had to be done. She wasn't going to be able to get on with the rest of her day otherwise. Just sitting here on the edge of the bed, scrolling through other people's lives like she was some kind of newsfeed junkie, was hardly going to make her birthday memorable, was it? Right. David. With determination she pressed the button – instantly regretting it, naturally. But too late.

'Sorry – I missed your call earlier.'

'Happy birthday.'

'Thanks.'

Silence.

'Is that all you rang me for?' she asked, shaking inside, thinking what his answer might be. It felt almost as if she was goading him – confident in the knowledge that she could just put down the phone; he had no idea where she was.

'Not exactly, no. You have birthday cards here that came in the post, you need to come and collect them. And... well, I want to see you to say sorry for the way I behaved the other night.'

Blimey. And he didn't even sound as though he'd been drinking.

'Me too, David. I never meant it all to end like that.'

'It doesn't have to. And it doesn't have to end. Come home, Joanna, I need you. I'll change, I promise I will. I'll stop drinking, I'll go to anger management classes, marriage guidance, whatever you want. Just say the word and I'll do it.'

Joanna could hardly believe what she was hearing, although she knew him of old. Empty words, that's all they were, promises he would never fulfil.

'Sorry, David, but it's too late now, we should have done all of that years ago.'

'You mean you're happy to throw all those years of marriage away, just on a whim?'

'It was more than that, David, and you know it. We haven't been happy together for years. Something had to change.'

'Well that's what I'm saying, we could go and see a marriage guidance counsellor. Like I've always said, they probably talk a load of garbage but if that's what you want then I'll do it.'

There was no getting through to him obviously. 'Look, I hear what you're saying but I'm telling you no, it's not happening.'

'Joanna, listen to me,' his tone was changing now. 'I've had enough of your silly games, this is getting ridiculous. I'm your husband, you're my wife, and I'm telling you to come home. Marriage is a legally binding commitment you know. And don't you *dare* to disobey me or I'll have you in court faster than your feet can touch the ground – drag you there myself if I have to. Oh and don't you worry, I've got money put aside that you know nothing about, I can hire top lawyers, barristers, whatever it takes, they'll drag up all the dirt they can find about your sordid little life and if there's nothing there then I'll make it up and they'll believe me. You're not going to get away with this lightly, you bitch – you'll have your name smeared all over the papers, in fact you'll wish you'd never been born. The only way you can stop this happening is to come back home today and we'll say nothing more about it. Your choice.'

Joanna was physically shaking, although her voice remained remarkably calm. 'But I haven't done anything wrong. All I've done is left you.'

'And you have the audacity to say that is doing nothing wrong? You're an evil, twisted bitch, Joanna, and the sooner the whole world knows that, the better.'

'David – marriages break up all the time, it's just amazing that ours has lasted for so long. But, believe me, nothing you say is going to make me change my mind. The decision has been made – I've left you, and you're just going to have to accept that.'

And on that note, before he could say another word, she pressed the red button… her biggest concern being that by doing so, she'd pressed *his* red button too.

*

She'd always known leaving him wouldn't be easy, which was part of the reason she'd stayed where she was for so long. Far too long. His mind was twisted, she knew that – a Jekyll and Hyde character for sure. She was only too well aware of the way he could slip into a different persona with ease, especially when meeting with people he wanted to impress. He possessed that chilling ability to be able to convince anyone of anything, should he so desire, with no actual thought for anyone or anything other than himself.

Sometimes, over the years, she'd felt bad for thinking of him in that way. No one else did, no one else seemed to see through him… other than Jack and Hannah and, as she had recently discovered, her mum. And that fact never ceased to amaze her. But then, the people they knew rarely saw that irascible side of him, the one that could be characterised by a raging bull. It came to the fore with abundance when anyone had the audacity to cross his path or upset him in any way, and often she'd feared where it may lead. But mostly it was saved for home, for herself and for Jack.

She'd internalised so much of this over the years, kept all the hurt and anxiety inside herself, almost afraid to let it out. Sometimes, though, she'd just had to speak about it or she'd feared she would go mad, so she'd talked to Hannah. But even that was difficult, she didn't want to be seen as a failure – the small dumpy sister with the bad marriage, whilst the tall, sylph-like Hannah was all loved-up with the hunky Marcus.

But maybe people didn't think too deeply about what went on in other people's lives because, well, why should they? Maybe it would feel too intrusive, maybe it was easier just to believe everything was fine. In fact if they were ever to be told it was not fine, would they even believe that to be true?

Her phone started to vibrate suddenly, intruding on her thoughts. For just a brief moment she couldn't place what it was, so lost had she been, dredging up fragile emotions she'd been trying to squash back down for years. She looked at the screen, a blank expression on her face. Gemma. It was the push she needed – somehow she brought herself back into focus.

The arousing solo performance of 'Happy birthday to you, Happy birthday to you…' went some way towards helping.

'Your singing voice hasn't improved much then,' said Joanna, laughing as she spoke. 'But thanks for the sentiment. Oh, and thanks for the effort too – although I don't think you'll be making it on to *The X Factor* any time soon.'

'Bloomin' cheek! I'll have you know I always came top in music when we were at school – don't you remember?'

'Nah – probably worked quite hard at erasing it from my mind, I would think.'

'Yep, I was Mrs Rogerson's pet. She used to say I had a lovely singing voice – the best one in the class.'

'Probably because you were the only one there – the rest of us always used to skive off music.'

'Hahaha – think you're funny, don't you?'

'I know I am. So anyway – how are you, what have you been up to?'

'I'm absolutely fine, my love. And hopefully so will you be when you hear what I've got to say.'

Joanna looked suspicious. She loved her friend to pieces but sometimes she came up with the craziest of ideas.

'Okay, hit me with it.'

'How do you fancy Paris?'

'I don't think I've ever met anyone called Paris.'

'Ha-ha, very funny – Paris the place not the person, you idiot. How do you fancy going there for the weekend, just me and you? Would David object, do you think?'

'Paris for a weekend away? Wow! Yes, David probably would have objected a couple of weeks ago, but not anymore – I've left him. So when were you thinking of going and how much is it going to cost? I'm just in the middle of moving house, so money's a bit tight at the moment. Love to go though, if I can scrape enough together. Starting a new job soon so that should help. What about in a couple of months to give me time to get settled in first?'

'Hang on, hang on… could you just stop and rewind for a minute? Am I hearing things or did you just say you've left David?'

'Yep – last week.'

'Oh my God – are you okay?'

'Never better. Will tell all later… but when did you want to go?'

Gemma was in shock. 'Can't believe you've actually left David. Amazing! Erm… it would have to be next weekend.'

'What?'

'Sorry. I know it's a bit sudden but I booked this hotel ages ago. I was meant to be going with Shelby, my sister, but now she can't go and I thought who better to ask than you – we'd have a great time!'

'I'm definitely up for it if I can afford – that's the only worrying bit.'

'Well the hotel's already been paid for by me so that won't cost you anything – you can call it a birthday present if you like. The flights are booked with EasyJet from Liverpool and I've already checked, they said they can transfer Shelby's flights into your name, you just have to pay a transfer fee, it won't be very much. The flights were pretty cheap too and Shelby said to tell you she's not in a hurry for the money, you can pay her when you can afford. So, all you'll need is your spending money – ration yourself with the alcohol, hahaha, and you'll be fine.'

'And you forget, I can always max out on my credit card now I haven't got David peering over my shoulder – happy days!'

'So you're up for it then?'

'Too right I am – I'm well excited!'

*

What a birthday this was turning out to be – and she still had the posh dinner with her two male escorts to get through yet. She just hoped she'd be able to stay awake. Falling asleep and taking a nose-dive into her dessert was really not the look she was going for. She was forty-nine and proud of it, she was free, a strong independent woman, a new career, mistress of her own destiny, about to go jet-setting around the world... well, for a weekend in Paris anyway. She slapped herself around the face, not only to drum it into herself that this was all true, but also to wake herself up – she had a feeling there would be a long night ahead.

And indeed there was – but what a fabulous night. The restaurant was unbelievable, the food top class, and amazingly she didn't manage to disgrace herself by falling asleep in her dessert or anywhere else for that matter. In fact the exhaustion she'd felt earlier completely disappeared. Jack and Gavin were such great company she was on an absolute high, running on adrenalin most probably – combined with the champagne, obviously. If this was what being forty-nine was like she need not have worried. As for being fifty next year – bring it on!

*

The next morning was a different story. Forty-nine? She felt more like ninety-four. And as usual after a heavy night, she asked herself that time-worn question – 'Why?' At least this time there'd been a reason behind it – what a birthday that had been! In the past, a heavy night of drinking had usually resulted from wanting to block something out. In fact she couldn't actually remember the last time she'd gone over the top with the alcohol for fun, there must have been one but she couldn't bring it to mind. Too much thinking hurt her head; even worse, it made David's face swim before her eyes – God, she prayed she wouldn't be sick. 'Heavenly

Father I have sinned…' What was going through her head now? It *was* Sunday, but even so.

Jack was still comatose on the other sofa – mind you, he often was at this time of day, even without the alcohol. Gavin, on the other hand, was up and dressed. He noticed her discomfort.

'What was that – rocket fuel?' she asked, clutching her head.

'Bloomin' cheek,' he said. 'It was actually Taittinger, if you must know. Only the best for you, darlin'.'

She winced as she spoke. 'I suppose we were drinking for most of the day – I dread to think what I must look like if the way I feel is anything to go by.'

'You look beautiful as always. Paracetamol?'

'Please,' she said. Just the sound of her own voice pounded like a hammer inside her head.

'And then I'm going to fry some bacon and make you a sandwich. You may not feel like it but, believe me, there's nothing better as a hangover cure – other than a McDonald's and, sorry, but I don't have time to go there this morning.'

She groaned her appreciation, swallowing down the tablets with some relief. Gavin. Was he for real, this man? He was certainly the best thing that had happened to her in a very long time. Thank God for K-Y Jelly – not in *that* way, just that without it they would never have met. Hmm. Even that sounded weird.

*

As the day wore on she felt so much better. The bacon sandwich tried-and-tested cure for hangovers had worked miracles. Whether it was a scientific fact that stodge soaked up excess alcohol, or whatever the reason was, she didn't actually care. She was no longer half dead but totally alive and that was all that mattered.

Neither Gavin nor Jack appeared to have been as badly affected as she had been. Whilst she had been wallowing in her cesspit of morning after the night before, they had both been up, breakfasted and off out to work – yes, even Jack, a fact from which she still hadn't recovered.

So she found herself alone in the apartment. But what to do? She didn't fancy slobbing around in front of the TV all day, that would only bring her headache back again. It was raining outside, otherwise she could have gone for a jog to burn off a few of yesterday's calories – ha-ha, who was she kidding? There was no way she would have gone even if the weather had been perfect for it. Jogging was for forty-eight-year-olds; she was forty-nine now – too old for such madcap frivolities. At her age it wouldn't be good for her boobs, they were already on track for a steady descent, too much jiggling about at this stage could prove fatal.

Perhaps she should visit Hannah and tell her all about her birthday and what a great day she'd had. But would she really be interested? Thinking about it, to visit Hannah was probably out of the question, she'd still be too loved up. The thought of listening to her gushing on about how amazing Marcus was – well, that was just too vomit-inducing to even contemplate.

She rang her mum, thinking it would be a good opportunity to drive over and see her. But no, her mum was expecting someone today so it wouldn't be convenient. She was being very cagey, actually. Joanna was intrigued. Who was this prospective new husband with whom her mother sounded so smitten? Despite all of her probing questions, no answers were forthcoming. 'You'll meet him all in good time,' was as much as she ever said. No name, no revelations, nothing. Fair enough, Joanna supposed. Just as long as he was kosher, not married to someone else and just leading her on… for sex. Oh my God, surely not – the very thought made her stomach lurch once more, the bacon sandwich almost coming up to greet her.

Bluebell Cottage, that's where she'd go, Nelly would surely be glad to see her. And, in any case, the thought of seeing the inside of the cottage again perked her up completely. She didn't have a phone number to check it was okay but she was sure it would be, Nelly was always glad of a visitor.

*

Walking up the garden path to the front door felt almost like coming home. In fact it was quite weird how comfortable it did feel. She pictured herself turning the key in the lock, letting herself in – a tingle of excitement flooded through her, she just couldn't wait. She rang the quirky old doorbell, smiling to herself as it jangled out its greeting, listening for that now-familiar voice shouting, 'Sorry to keep you waiting,' as Nelly struggled to the door. Funny how much her affection for this elderly lady had grown in such a short time.

But on this occasion, in fact, there wasn't a wait – or a voice. The door opened straightaway.

'Oh – I wasn't expecting to see you,' she said, taken by surprise.

'Likewise,' said Martin.

'Sorry. I was just at a bit of a loose end today, so thought what better idea than to drop by and see Nelly, have a cup of tea with her maybe, I know how lonely she gets when she's on her own. I didn't realise you'd be here though – I'll go, I can always come back another day.'

'What – not some kind of scary two-headed monster, am I?' he said, with a twinkle in his eye. 'Nonsense – come in,' he said, stepping aside. 'My mum will be really pleased to see you. So am I, to be honest.'

Giving him a quizzical look as she passed, Joanna went through to the lounge to give Nelly a hug.

'Well, we were just talking about you,' said the old lady, delighted to have a visitor.

'Nothing bad I hope.'

'Singing your praises, actually – saying how much we both liked you. And in fact, it's been a long time since I've known Martin to even look at another woman, let alone say that he likes her.'

If Joanna was the blushing type she would have been all shades of pink by now. As for poor Martin, he was undeniably crimson.

'Mother! Just stop before you say any more. So sorry, Joanna – it's my mum, she puts two and two together and makes fifteen sometimes.'

'Don't be ridiculous, Martin. I know two and two make four and I also know, when I see them, two people who are made for each other – don't try to deny it. Incidentally – are you suffering from high blood pressure like your father used to do? Your face is the colour of beetroot.'

With a sigh of exasperation, he turned and went into the kitchen, ostensibly to make the tea. Joanna could hear him fumbling around in the cupboards. She felt so sorry for him and didn't want things to be left to fester and become uncomfortable between them, which they obviously would if she didn't do something about it. Following him into the kitchen to speak to him out of Nelly's earshot seemed like the obvious solution, although the prospect of doing so wasn't one she relished, but nevertheless...

'Oh Nelly,' said Joanna, sensitive to how Martin must be feeling, she felt embarrassed enough herself. 'I'll go through and help him,' she said, not waiting for a response, although the thumbs-up sign and the delighted grin Nelly gave her said it all.

Martin had his back to her as she went in.

'That was awkward,' she said.

'Tell me about it,' he said.

'Don't worry, I know what mothers can be like – I am one.'

'Hahaha,' he laughed, nervously. 'Well hopefully you don't act like mine. She never thinks before she speaks, just comes straight out with it. I know she means well and she just wants to see me happy but because I said I liked you, that doesn't mean I want to rush off and marry you.'

'Well thank goodness for that, I only left my husband last week – hahaha. Seriously though, don't let what she said bother you, I don't want things to be awkward between us, I need all the friends I can get at the moment.'

'Then count me in,' he said, turning round to face her at last.

Something happened in that moment. Something totally unexpected. A sudden sensation that quivered through her, a feeling so strong it made the hairs stand up on the back of her neck. What was happening to her? She'd been with the same man for thirty years and had never allowed herself to be led astray. Now, suddenly, she seemed to be finding herself lusting after anything male that came her way. What kind of a woman was she in danger of becoming? Flustered, her eyes flicked away from him in a kind of panic – this could not be.

She was a strong woman looking forward to living a single, independent life. She didn't want or need a man cluttering up her life – except for sex. And Martin was clearly not a one-night stand kind of guy, she could see that. He was a solid, reliable, relationship type of guy – the kind of guy any girl would be proud to take home to meet mother. But not this girl – not at this point in her life at any rate. And in any case, he was to be her landlord, for goodness' sake.

Silence hung in the air like raindrops from a leaf – quivering, not knowing which way to fall until that gentle plop. His voice was equally gentle.

'You felt it too, huh?'

Tentatively she looked at him. She'd never studied his face so closely before because, well, why would she? But now... such a strong face, a masculine face, etched with the troubles of all he had been through. And yet, or maybe because of these troubles, a kind and gentle face, warm and sensitive, trustworthy and strong.

'Mm,' she said, flustered, her eyes swiftly darting away from his face as she inwardly battled with herself to resist the temptation of this beautiful man who stood before her.

'Bad timing though. I understand. You just split up with your husband, new job, new home – everything. Maybe one day – who knows? I'm not going anywhere. I hope we can still be friends though – I would like that.'

'Me too, Martin. Good friends, with no awkwardness or embarrassment between us.'

'Exactly that,' he said, with a lopsided grin she just knew she would find difficult to resist one day.

But that was one day. This was today. *Pull yourself together, Joanna.*

'Have you even filled that kettle yet?' she asked, waving a teaspoon towards him with a smile.

The tension lifted.

'Did anyone ever tell you how bossy you are?' he replied, his grin even wider now.

Chapter Nineteen

They were actually on the plane! Joanna could hardly believe things were going so smoothly. She'd managed to cram everything she'd thought she might possibly need into her specially purchased pink suitcase without a hitch. Obviously she'd had to sit on it and rock about a bit in order to do so, but it was in – squashed to smithereens, but it was in. If she bought any Parisian fashions whilst she was there they wouldn't stand a chance of squeezing into the case for the return journey, she'd just have to wear them all on the flight home – layer up, and look more like a little dumpling than ever.

Passport! Had she got it? Where the heck had she put it? She grabbed her handbag in a sudden fluster and proceeded to rummage.

'What's the matter now?' asked Gemma nonchalantly. She was used to her stress-headed friend who was the complete opposite of herself in that respect.

'Where's my passport? I had it when we were in the airport – have I dropped it? What have I done with it?'

'What's this?' asked Gemma, calmly reaching over to retrieve the missing item from amongst the pile of junk her friend was tipping out of her bag in a state of blind panic.

Joanna heaved a sigh of relief. 'Phew! Okay, smarty pants, why do you always know everything?'

'Because I'm perfect in every way, obviously,' she sighed – oozing with confidence as always, as she gave a casual flick of her long blonde hair. 'Seriously, you need to calm down, you'll be having a heart attack before we even get to Paris at this rate'.

Two gins later she was feeling so much better, relaxation was starting to creep in, tottering a little on its way, but nevertheless.

'Yay – we're on holiday!' she said, happily chinking glasses with her friend. 'I feel free as a bird flying in the sky…'

'That's 'cos you are a bird and you are flying in the sky, you dingbat!' laughed Gemma, as the two fell onto each other, laughing helplessly even though it really wasn't that funny.

The man on the end seat looked bemused, simultaneously thanking his lucky stars it was only a short flight.

In fact it seemed like no time at all until they were landing.

'Isn't it weird – John Lennon Airport, Charles de Gaulle Airport? Do you think there'll ever be a Joanna Donohue Airport? Can you imagine flying into your very own airport from some exotic location abroad somewhere? That would be so cool.'

'Just one problem – well no, two actually. Not only do you have to be dead, but you have to have achieved something really outstanding in your life before anybody would think of naming an airport after you. From what I can see you're certainly not dead, and as for the other thing…'

'Oy! I have achieved something outstanding actually. I left David, didn't I? Never in a million years did I think I'd have the guts to do that.'

'True. Nevertheless, I don't think you'll be qualifying for an airport naming ceremony anytime soon.'

Thankfully, it was a smooth landing. Joanna wiped her sweaty palms down her jeans – she always felt a huge sense of relief to find herself back on terra firma after a flight, short or not. They sailed their way through customs without a hitch, despite a little flirt with the guy, and waited patiently for their luggage to appear. Joanna stood transfixed, soaking up the sights and sounds. There was just something about the French language, French accents, French anything really, that always blew her away.

'It's not a good look, Jo.'

'What isn't?'

'You – standing there all open-mouthed and glassy-eyed, looking like you've landed on a different planet.'

'I feel as though I have…'

'There – bright pink.'

'What is?'

'Your suitcase. That's yours isn't it? Wake up! Grab it quick before it goes round again.'

'Sorry, yes,' she said, retrieving it just in time. 'It's just… well, this all seems so surreal somehow. I'm not used to jetting off for the weekend just on a whim. Whenever I've gone away anywhere with David it always had to be planned about a year ahead, with tick lists of things that had to be done before we left, itineraries of what we were going to do when we were there. So regimented it almost made me feel it wasn't worth going anywhere with all the effort it took. You can imagine as well, can't you, what a miserable time we'd have if anything veered away from the plan – and woe betide me if I ever forgot to pack anything.'

'Well forget about David, it's a good job you've come away with me – see how the other half live. I'm just a spur-of-the-moment person, planning's boring – there's nothing quite like a madcap idea when you need cheering up a bit. Oh – there's mine.'

'What?'

'Suitcase – you're still not quite with it are you?' Gemma grinned. 'Come on, let's go and find a taxi.'

'Taxi? David would have gone mad at the very thought.'

'For God's sake – David's not here! And if you think I'm

struggling on the Metro with this lot, well… no chance. Don't worry, my choice so I'm paying, no argument.'

*

The hotel was in Saint Germain. Joanna was really pleased they were going to be staying there. Although she'd only visited briefly once before it had seemed like exactly the kind of area she'd like to explore, a very artsy sort of place, one she'd love to have a mooch around in. The last occasion with David had been a nightmare. It had been a hot, sunny day and she'd forgotten to bring his sunglasses. He'd completely lost the plot with her in the middle of the street. It had been so embarrassing. Thinking back, that sounded absolutely ridiculous… *she* had forgotten to put *his* sunglasses in *her* handbag. So it had been her fault, as always – and enough to cause World War Fifty, obviously. Grrr. Why had she stayed with him for so long?

'Not moping about David again, are you?'

'Thinking. I would definitely call it thinking, not moping. Just remembering the last time I was in Saint Germain. How did you know, anyway?'

'Easy. Your face kinda scrunches up and steam comes out of your ears. Anyway, like I said – forget about him. We're here – let's just enjoy ourselves. Men? Who needs them!'

L'Hotel D'Or. It was in fact pretty fabulous. And although it was obviously not made of gold, the golden touches in the decor certainly made the place live up to its name. They gazed around in awe, resulting in a rare moment of speechlessness for both of them.

'Oh my gosh this is so beautiful. I know you said it was my birthday present but how on earth did you manage to afford this? I feel so guilty.'

'Don't. Truly. And, to be fair, it wasn't all that expensive, I got a cheap deal on the internet.'

'Still not cheap, I'm sure.'

'No, but it is your birthday present and I'm really looking forward to our girly weekend, it's been ages since we spent some time together. And anyway it was Shelby who let me down; you did me a favour. I'd have been here on my own if you'd said you couldn't come – that wouldn't have been much fun, would it?'

'Suppose. But I still feel guilty though.'

'Well don't.'

By the time they'd fought over wardrobe space in which to hang up their mountain of clothes, tossed a coin as to who was having which bed, and found enough space to lay out their collections of toiletries, make-up, perfumes, hair straighteners and associated paraphernalia, it was virtually time for dinner.

'Why did we bring so much stuff?' asked Gemma, wide-eyed, as they got ready to go downstairs.

'That's good, coming from you!' teased Joanna.

'I can never travel light. It's okay for men, they can just add a jumper or something if they're cold, everything matches anyway, and they only need one spare pair of shoes. It's totally different for women because you never know what you're going to need and then, whatever you decide to pack, you always have to remember the shoes and accessories to go with it.'

'And don't even get me started on toiletries and make-up and hair stuff – men don't have to worry about things like that – mostly, anyway.'

'If I'm ever reincarnated, I don't want to be a female anymore; man-life must be so much easier.'

They made their way downstairs in the lift, both peering into the mirror for a final check as they did so. The hotel restaurant seemed to be in full swing as they entered, smartly dressed cheerful waiters bobbing in and out between the tables, bearing trays of mouth-wateringly delicious-looking food. A live jazz band was playing, something they hadn't expected, adding to the Parisian atmosphere and jollity of the room. This was just perfect.

A smiling waiter came to greet them and showed them to

their table. He introduced himself as Olivier, his voice deep and husky as he attempted to converse with them, readily admitting his English wasn't good.

'*Mon Français est terrible!*' replied Joanna, almost drooling at the sound of his voice. As he passed the menu, her hand 'accidently' brushed against his. Oh my God, what was she turning into – some kind of cougar? She was old enough to be his mother... his grandmother almost.

'Joanna, I've never seen such outrageous flirting! Not from you – well, not for a while anyway.'

'I told you – it's the accent, well, the voice, it does it to me every time.'

'No hope for you this weekend then.'

'Let's hope not.'

Choosing from the menu took some time. A French dictionary would have been useful, or even Google if they hadn't left their phones upstairs, charging.

'What's *Palourdes au Gratin* do you think?'

'I've no idea. I'm tempted to try *Les Escargots au Beurre*, but something's holding me back.'

'The fact that they're snails maybe? I can understand why you'd be a bit reluctant.'

'Oh – is that what they are? Maybe not then.'

Sometime later, selections made, Joanna summoned Olivier back to the table with a smile as sexy as she could muster. He looked a bit nervous, to be fair.

'Joanna, you are awful,' said Gemma, cringing from the obvious, totally unsubtle performance she'd just witnessed. 'You've scared him off now, he thinks you would eat him alive.'

'Hmm – if he was on the menu I possibly would.'

'Joanna! How much have you had to drink today?'

'No more than you, actually, it's just that you seem better able to handle it than I do.'

'Tell you what, shall we stay here tonight instead of going out looking for another bar? With all this live music and everything, the atmosphere couldn't be better anywhere than it is here. I wasn't expecting it to be so good.'

'Sounds like a plan to me. That means we don't have far to stagger home at the end of the night as well, we can drink as much as we like.'

'Good point.'

It was good for them both to be able to spend time like this. Gemma was Joanna's oldest and closest friend. Their friendship had started in primary-school days and although geographically they now lived quite far away from each other, spiritually they were still as close as ever. Sadly, they were no longer able to spend time together as often as they would have liked but, when they did, it was as though they'd never been apart. It has been said that a woman doesn't need a therapist, all she needs to do is to sit down with a cup of tea and have a chat with her best friend. In Joanna's case this was true. Well maybe substitute the cup of tea for a G&T, but nevertheless.

So they chatted and chatted for hours – even Olivier was forgotten amid the soul-searching that was going on around this table that night. It was good for Joanna to be able to open up so freely. Although she talked about things with other people in her life, she never felt she could be quite so open and honest with anyone as she could with Gemma. There was nothing they didn't know about each other, absolutely nothing.

Like Gabriel, for example, and Joanna's never-forgotten night of passion after her hen party all those years ago. He remained in her thoughts even now, in fact fantasising about him on occasion during her marriage was what had helped to keep her sane – at least someone had wanted her, once.

'Did you ever do anything about trying to find him?'

'Yeah, I searched for him on Facebook a few years ago.'

'*Did* you?' said Gemma, eyes wide with surprise. 'You kept that quiet!'

'I know. I never got anywhere with it though or I would have told you. You'd think Gabriel would be an unusual name, wouldn't you? But no, there are loads of them. I could hardly pick the most likely one and contact him like some random madwoman stalker, saying we'd had a night of passion thirty years ago and I'd been lusting after him ever since, could I? Like that really would get him rushing towards me with open arms, overjoyed at the prospect of seeing me again, wouldn't it? More likely to take out a court order against me for stalking and have me locked up. He wouldn't even remember me anyway. Thirty years ago? He must have had thousands of women – well, hundreds at least. Probably married, fat, balding, and with a tribe of children by now too.'

'Well at least that would have killed off the fantasy.'

'True. I shall always remember Gabriel though because he was my first, and it was a special moment in my life. But that's all it was – a moment. For him I'm sure it was different. Don't suppose he's ever given me another thought.'

'Quite sad though really when you think about it,' said Gemma. 'You've only ever been with two men in your entire life – think of all the fun you've been missing.'

'Gemma! We're not all like you, you know.'

'Oy – what's that meant to mean?'

'Well, y'know…'

'So you think it's better just being stuck to the one man all your life even if you're not happy? You think that's better than doing something that *does* make you happy? Stop it! I can feel the guilt creeping into you now. You definitely did the right thing in leaving David, you know – don't ever doubt that. He led you a life of hell and it took a lot of courage for you to break away – so well done you for not putting up with that any longer. Get out and live your life now, play the field a bit and stop feeling guilty about David, I'm sure he'll cope.'

'You're right – I know you're right.'

'Blimey! Are you agreeing with me – that's a first'

'Yep. Must be the gin... or the smiles we keep getting from Olivier.'

'Yeah – I've noticed how he keeps glancing over,' said Joanna. 'So, how's your love life anyway? Anyone on the horizon – apart from Olivier obviously?'

'Hmm. There's been the odd one here and there – and some of them *have* been odd, believe me. I have a lot of male friends – some of them even with benefits,' grinned Gemma, 'but nobody special. Not that I'm looking for anybody, I'm quite happy on my own to be honest. Can do what I want when I want – suits me perfectly.' Gemma had never been married, had raised her son single-handedly and always been totally focused on her career.

'I've always admired you, the way you're so independent. You seem to know just what you want and go out and grab it with both hands, nothing ever seems to stand in your way,' said Joanna.

'That's because I won't let it,' smiled Gemma. 'Why do you think I never got married? That's where you went wrong. But all that's gonna change for you now. Single, after all these years.'

'I know. Quite scary really. Out of my comfort zone.'

'What's to be scary?' asked Gemma, topping up their glasses with Prosecco.

'Dunno.'

'There you go then. And you've got two men fighting over you already.'

'Hardly that! They're both so lovely though.'

'So who do you fancy the most?'

'Gemma! Hmm... well Gavin's definitely the hottest. He's younger and fitter and well, when Hannah saw him she was mesmerised and, as you know, it takes a lot to impress her – she was amazed I'd managed to keep my hands off him.'

'And had you?'

'As a matter of fact I had at that point – yes, you cheeky mare.'

Gemma giggled at her own directness, at how comfortable they always felt around each other. 'And since?'

'Huh, you don't give up do you?' replied Joanna with a grin. 'Okay, okay I give in. Yes, we have slept together – but only the once.'

'Yay! So that makes you a grand total of three now then – you'll be catching up to me shortly.'

'Ha-ha! Shut up. We've agreed that's the way it should stay though, for now at least. We have this amazing bond – he's like my alter ego, almost. But, and it's a big but, he's also going to be my boss, I'm due to start working for him shortly. So it was a mutual decision, we both agreed it would be a bad idea to start a full-blown relationship right now as it could lead to too many complications.'

'Sounds far too level-headed for me. Won't you be tempted? Won't you just want to rip his clothes off at every opportunity?'

'*Excusez-moi…*'

Olivier. What a moment to interrupt their conversation! He could not have failed to have overheard Gemma's last remark, which had certainly not been subtle.

'My shift… it is finished. We 'ave dancing 'ere soon. May I join you, *s'il vous plait?*'

A swift exchange of glances took place. He obviously thought his luck was in. Gemma smiled a gin-fuelled smile. '*Mai oui!*'

Joanna raised an eyebrow. But who was she to argue?

Chapter Twenty

It was 2am before they made it back up to their room – what a night! Who knew so much fun could be had without even leaving the hotel?

'He was quite the party animal, that one,' said Joanna, kicking off her shoes before collapsing onto her bed in an exhausted heap, relieved to be able to give her poor aching feet a rest at last. 'He seemed so quiet and reserved when he was waiting on tables, I didn't expect him to be such a livewire when he got on the dancefloor.'

'He certainly fancied his chances with you, that's for sure,' laughed Gemma, 'I never thought we'd manage to escape! He'll probably come knocking at the door in a minute.'

'Well if he does don't let him in. Weird, isn't it? I've never been with anybody in that way for all those years and now suddenly, since I've left David, they're almost queueing up. What does that say about me? What sort of message am I giving out?'

'Desperado maybe?'

'Oy! But I'm not, that's the whole point. I don't even want a man, I'm quite happy just being me.'

'As long as you don't start batting for the other side, Joanna. I love you dearly and I know we're sharing a room but…'

'Daft cow!'

*

From somewhere they managed to gather energy. The next day was spent in a whirl of activity doing the touristy thing to perfection. If Joanna had loved Paris and all things French before this day, she was even more in love with them now. They explored the picturesque alleyways, the galleries and the quirky little shops. The place was magical and everything Joanna had hoped it would be. They even splashed out on lunch at *Les Deux Magots*, a place she had been longing to visit. It was expensive but as she sat there soaking up the atmosphere in this little piece of Parisian history, it seemed it was undeniably worthwhile.

'I thought you said you were broke, Joanna.'

'I know. I am. And I shouldn't. But how could we have missed this? I've been wanting to come here for years but David...'

'Yeah, you don't need to tell me.'

'OMG... have you tasted this hot chocolate?'

'To die for... I know.'

'Let's hope we don't!'

*

Back at the hotel, exhausted from their day, they checked out the mini bar in their room.

'Perfect. Two G&Ts coming right up,' said Gemma, handing one to Joanna, who had already discarded her shoes and was sitting on the bed with her feet up, adding Party Feet patches to her rapidly rising blisters.

'What an amazing day – definitely worth getting sore feet for. Probably go down as being one of the best days of my life actually.'

'You saddo! Surely not.'

'No – I mean it. You know when there's somewhere you've

wanted to go to for ages and then, when you finally do, it's even better than you were hoping it would be? That.'

'Aww. That's so sweet. I'm really glad we came now.'

'Me too. Thank you so much for asking me to come with you – this day has been just epic. In fact everything has so far.'

'What – even Olivier and his crazy dancing?'

'Yep, even that – so shall we stay here again tonight then?'

'Are you sure you wouldn't like to go exploring again – find another bar somewhere?'

'Quite sure, as long as you're okay with that. Remember Olivier saying there's another jazz band on again tonight? We can do some more crazy dancing and he's great company – it would be a shame to miss it.'

'True,' said Gemma, sipping contentedly at her gin. 'The way I'm feeling right now I wouldn't have the energy to go out exploring anyway. This way, all we have to do is step into the lift – think I can just about manage that.'

'Gem, you've hardly talked about yourself this weekend. It's been all about me, me, me and I feel really bad now I've thought about it. Self-obsessed, that's what I am – thinking nobody else has problems only me. So, seriously, how are things with you?'

'I haven't talked about myself 'cos there's nothing to tell basically. I just plod along in my own little world, bothering no one and no one bothering me. And that's the way I like it, I suppose – most of the time anyway.'

'Too much of a workaholic, that's your problem.'

'I know, but I enjoy my job. It pays for my beautiful house, my car, exotic holidays all over the world…'

'"Erotic" did you say?'

'Ha-ha, very funny. Exotic, I said – I love to travel.'

'I know you do. Your holidays always sound like some wild kind of fantasy though to me. The furthest David ever wanted to go was Cornwall.'

'Nothing wrong with Cornwall.'

'I know but... anyway, we're meant to be talking about you, not me. Do you not get lonely on your travels, being on your own all the time? D'you not wish you had a man with you to share your experiences, somebody to snuggle up with at the end of the day?'

'What – like you did with David, do you mean?'

'Hah, yeah – point taken. But what about sex – do you not miss it?'

'I repeat. David.'

'Tell you what – I'll just shut up.'

'Good! Look, I was a single mum for all of those years, bringing up Joe. Didn't have any need of a man then and I don't now – nothing's changed. I do date sometimes and I'll have a one-night stand occasionally but, other than that, I'm happy as I am. My son, Joe, is the only man I need in my life. I miss him, obviously, now he's in Australia. But the flipside of that is cheap holidays when I fly out there. In fact now you're free and single you could come with me. Next year. Deal?'

'Wow! Australia?'

'Sure – why not?'

'You're on!'

*

Olivier's face lit up when they walked into the dining room that evening. Gemma noticed and smiled at him, whilst simultaneously giving Joanna a gentle nudge.

'Told you he liked you – look at his face!'

'Stop it, Gemma – I can't cope with another one.'

'What – not even one with a French accent?'

'Well... there is that I suppose,' Joanna giggled. God, they were acting like a couple of teenagers all over again. 'You're a bad influence, Gemma – stop it.'

'*Moi?*' she replied, the face of all innocence.

Olivier rushed over to show them to a table, effervescent in his broken English.

'You stay dancey, dancey later? I am so 'appy. We 'ave fun.'

'Yes, we look forward to it – Gemma can't wait, she likes to have fun,' grinned Joanna, receiving a not-so-subtle kick under the table from her mortified friend.

'Joanna! What did you say that for? He thinks I'm up for it now.'

'To get myself off the hook, of course,' she giggled. 'Anyway come on, you can't tell me you don't fancy him just a little bit – he is rather lush, don't you think?'

Actually that seemed to set the tone for the rest of the evening; they giggled their way through the entirety of it in pretty much the same vein. They ate and they drank and they drank and they drank, and they danced the night away. But sadly, as the clock struck midnight, poor Olivier's lustful thoughts were thwarted. He tried his best to persuade them, first one and then the other, and then even both, to accompany him to his room for '*un café*' but they assured him they could have one right there in the dining room if they so wished. He persisted by upping his offer to gin or even champagne – but no, he was rejected once more, well, several times actually.

With promises to return again one day, they left him standing, dejectedly, at the bottom of the stairs. They'd thought it best not to share the intimacy of a cosy lift with him to avoid the possibility of his lustful ardour being any further inflamed. Gemma blew kisses.

'Oy – stop it! You're only winding him up.'

'I know. Fun though, isn't it?'

*

The next morning they had planned to do all kinds of touristy things, but failed miserably. Well, not miserably exactly. They both had the hangovers from hell and to Joanna it seemed like the height of luxury not to have a regimented itinerary which had to be adhered to rigorously, no matter what. Nevertheless, they were determined to capture some of the beautiful early morning sunshine before having to leave for the airport and the flight back home again.

Dosed up with paracetamol and eyes shielded from the glare with dark glasses, they were really glad they had made the effort. They walked slowly along the banks of the Seine enjoying the peace and tranquillity that being beside water always brings – the sunlight dancing on the ripples, bordered by banks of dappled shade. They people-watched too, soaking up lasting Parisian memories to treasure as well as the sun's comforting golden rays. Lovers strolling hand in hand, joggers lost in musical worlds of headphones, friends, fashionistas, tourists just like them.

As they stopped for an energising shot of coffee at a pavement café, Joanna was almost surprised to find she had tears in her eyes – Gemma even more so as she caught her furtively dabbing her eyes with a tissue beneath the dark, concealing shades.

'What's up?' she asked, concerned.

'Nothing, honestly. Just felt a bit emotional suddenly, that's all. Thinking about what a fantastic weekend this has been. Thank you so much, Gem, I can't tell you how much I've enjoyed it.'

'No, thank you for coming with me. We don't seem to have done much but it's been such a lovely relaxing break, which was just what I needed. And getting to spend some quality time with my bestie too was the icing on the cake with a cherry on top,' smiled Gemma. 'So glad you came.'

'Me too. It's been epic. And it's reinforced everything for me really. Made me realise what I've been missing all these years, stuck in a marriage with a man I didn't love. I can't tell you how glad I am to have escaped the monotony and that feeling of being trapped, of not having a life, of being faceless – a nobody.'

'Well, you've got a life now, you can do exactly as you want – make the most of it.'

'Don't you worry, I fully intend to do so.'

They sat in silence for a while, each lost in their thoughts as they watched the world go by, thinking of the happy times they'd shared together over the years.

'Hey, do you remember those Happy Jars we used to keep, filling them with mementos and treasures and stuff, little notes about things we'd done and places we'd been to that had made us happy?'

'And then emptying them together at the end of each year, reading them out, reliving the memories,' interrupted Joanna. 'Are you psychic or what? I was just thinking about the exact same thing!'

'Spooky,' laughed Gemma. 'Seriously, though, we should start them again, it was fun.'

'And I've kept some souvenirs and receipts and things from this trip, they're in my suitcase,' said Joanna.

'Me too – let's do it!'

Chapter Twenty-one

Despite having had such an amazing weekend and a brilliant catch-up with Gemma, it felt good to be back home again. Well, not home exactly, she was still sofa-surfing at Gavin's although not for much longer. Just one more week and Bluebell Cottage would be hers – Joanna still couldn't quite get her head around it. Sometimes it all seemed too good to be true. In fact, she had to keep pinching herself just to make sure she wasn't dreaming. She wasn't, but after all she'd put up with for the past thirty years, she really felt like she was living the dream.

Jack was out when she arrived back, but Gavin was well and truly in and gave her the biggest bear hug of all time.

'I've missed you,' he said, sounding as though he truly meant it.

'I've only been gone for two days,' she giggled, happy at his welcome.

'I know but it's not the same when there are just two guys hanging around the place – it felt kinda empty.'

'So just any woman would have done,' she teased.

'Nah, you know what I'm sayin' – I really missed you, darlin'.'

'Aww, you big softie! Anyway, I hope you've got the champagne on ice ready to welcome me back. I've been staying in a luxury hotel you know, my standards have gone up – only the best for me now.'

'But of course – would you expect anything less of me?' he asked, suddenly producing two champagne flutes and an ice bucket with the dexterity of a magician. 'Oh, and before you ask, dinner is about to go into the oven – a little something French and garlicky to remind you of your weekend.'

Could this man get any better? The unpacking could wait.

*

Back to reality. Work. But it was her final week in this office – she would never have to put up with their miserable faces and their bitchiness again. And, after last night, nothing could wipe the smile from her face – not even the overbearing Cat, who always tried to put her down. 'But not anymore, you little feline fleabag,' muttered Joanna to herself in response to yet another bullying remark, the likes of which she'd become accustomed to. Others in the office, people she had never deemed as workmates, noticed her smile and were curious. In fact, one even ventured forth with an attempt at conversation.

'Bet you're really looking forward to getting out of this place, aren't you?'

'Yep.'

'No wonder you're smiling so much today.'

Joanna smiled and walked away. Okay, so maybe she was as much at fault as they were for the unfriendliness in that office. But she was hardly going to disclose the real reason for her smile today, was she? It wasn't as though they were bosom buddies or anything. Now if it had been Gemma, the truth would have been told – and dissected with glee.

Lunch break couldn't come soon enough today, there was shopping to be done. She'd been thinking about it all morning, between the smiles. She would be moving into Bluebell Cottage at the weekend and, despite the shiver of excitement the thought of that brought, there was also a second thought which screamed, 'Things!' Like bedding and towels, crockery and cutlery – so much! She was going to be renting the place unfurnished although, thankfully, they were going to be leaving the chair and sofa for her. Joanna had spoken to Martin about it all on the day she'd signed the contract and they'd agreed on what was to stay and what was to go.

Legally, she supposed she was entitled to have some of the stuff from the house she'd shared with David, but the more she'd thought about it, the more she'd thought it wasn't worth the hassle. And anyway, it would be nice to start afresh. She could buy things as she went along, as and when she could afford them. It was all so exciting! She couldn't wait to put her own stamp on the place, to have things she'd chosen herself without having to consult anyone else. She and David had never shared the same taste; she'd often had to have things around the home that she'd absolutely hated, had just given in for the sake of a quiet life. But no more. Bluebell Cottage would be a reflection of her, and her alone.

Joanna presumed she must have been working on autopilot for most of the morning. The work had been done but yet she had no recollection of actually doing it at all. It had definitely been less stressful that way – maybe she should try it more often. As long as she hadn't messed up, which was a worry, and which conceivably she could have done. Actually, though, what did it matter? She'd be leaving on Friday anyway, someone else could sort it all out.

At one o'clock precisely, Joanna left the building looking almost as though she'd been fired from a starting pistol. To be fair to her, though, it did feel a bit like that – she had just one hour to beat the clock. Luckily, the office block was reasonably central to the city. Even more luckily, there was a department store on the very same road.

As she entered the store the pressure was on. So much to find in such a short time. It reminded her of watching Dale Winton in *Supermarket Sweep* all those years ago and suddenly made her feel positively ancient. *Snap out of it, Joanna, you're in a hurry.*

It was such an amazing feeling to be choosing her own stuff – although she really wished she could spend all day in here instead of just the forty minutes she had left. The towels were an easy choice – plain white always looked good – but then when it came to the bedding there was so much to choose from, so many possibilities, making a choice was an almost impossible task.

The thing was, she'd been planning in her head to have an ultra-feminine bedroom – dusky pinks and creams, lacy drapes and furry cushions, pure girly boudoir style with matchy-matchy everything. After all, she'd never had a bedroom that was entirely her own before, she'd always had to share with someone else – firstly Hannah and then David. She gazed around the shop floor in wonderment, imagining, stroking the fabrics with her fingertips – it was important, they had to feel right. She floated around as though in a dream, drinking it in, holding items which interested her next to each other to check the shades, looking for contrasts, colours that would complement each other.

And she was loving every minute. This was the difference between men and women when they were shopping. Well, maybe not all men, but it certainly had been the case with David. Whilst she would be hovering about, checking, comparing everything, looking for the perfect item before even thinking about purchasing, David would just have looked at his watch, grabbed the first thing he saw, and bought it without thinking twice.

But at least he would have looked at his watch... oops! Five minutes to be back at her desk. No time to purchase anything, not even the towels. She returned them to the shelf and fled, quickly buying a chocolate bar from a kiosk on the way past – well two, actually. Chocolate, yes she felt guilty. But this was her lunch, she had to eat something, didn't she? The diet could start tomorrow.

*

Joanna was pleased to find she had the apartment to herself that evening. She knew Jack had a shift at Bojangles, and she'd received a call from Gavin to say he was going to be working until late on a house he'd purchased recently. He had a tenant lined up for it already so he needed to get on with it as quickly as possible.

'You could come over and give me a hand if you like,' he'd said, 'show me how good you are at wielding a paintbrush.'

She'd felt somewhat mean at turning him down, making the lame excuse of 'lots to do, I'm moving at the weekend.' Truthfully, that was not the real reason at all and she was sure he would know that and would understand. Last night had been a one-off – well okay, twice now – and she didn't want it to become a regular thing. Neither of them did. Supposedly. He was going to be her boss from next week and she really didn't want anything to jeopardise that. He was a friend of her son, for goodness' sake – a young stud. She'd only just got out of one relationship, no way did she want another. *Okay, keep telling yourself that, Joanna.*

Suddenly, she realised how hungry she was, starving actually because, thinking about it, she hadn't had anything for lunch. Well, chocolate, but that doesn't count does it? It's not like a proper meal. Disorganised as ever, she hadn't planned ahead and bought food on the way home from work, and she was reluctant to raid Gavin's fridge-freezer when he wasn't even at home. Only one option then. Fish and chips it was. As for the diet, it was on a slippery slope to nowhere.

She was there and back to the Jolly Fryer in an instant, before any fragment of diet willpower could sneak in unexpectedly and attempt to change her mind. She actually relished the fact that Jack was at work; had he been here his sarcasm at her weakness would have spoiled her enjoyment – he was always her voice of reason at times such as this. Salivating at the prospect of devouring her guilty purchases, she got herself a plate. At least she was satisfying her greed with a modicum of decorum. Being quite posh really.

Crazy phone – why did it always ring at the most inconvenient of times? Jack! Did he have a spy camera rigged up or something?

'Hello,' she barked into the phone. 'Yes, I know I'm eating fish and chips but…'

'What? What are you talking about? I'm ringing from the hospital…'

The guilt food was forgotten. 'The hospital? I thought you were at work. What's happened? Are you okay? I'm on my way – I'll be there in about half an hour.' Mother tiger protecting her cub alert to the fore, worry overdrive.

'No, stop! It's not me, it's Pixie. I was at work and she rang me in a big panic to say she was bleeding. We've been here for a while – they think she's lost the baby, Mum, she's just gone in for a scan now. I feel so guilty, like this is all my fault. She's devastated, she really is.'

'Oh Jack – please don't think that way. This is nobody's fault, these things happen.'

'I know. But I never wanted this baby – I told her she should have an abortion. How could I have said that about my own child?'

Was he crying? He was. Her heart was breaking for him. 'Oh Jack, please don't blame yourself, this…'

'Got to go, Mum, she's just coming out. Ring you later.'

As she hit the red button on her phone, Joanna was surprised by how emotional she felt. She was devastated for Jack, understandably so, realising just how much it was affecting him. But when it came to herself, she would have expected to feel relief. She knew how unstable Pixie was and knew the girl really wouldn't have been capable of being a fit mother to that poor little lost soul. She'd had worrying visions of what the future would hold for Jack, knowing what a devious and immature type of girl Pixie seemed to be.

But for all of that, Joanna had wished her no harm. She knew only too well the pain in every sense that miscarriage could bring; she'd experienced it for herself after several years of trying for a sibling for Jack – she'd never wanted him to be an only child. She'd called it Angel, her angel baby – only the size of a raspberry but yet, to her, it had been so real. Afterwards, she'd just felt so unbearably empty, inconsolable, devoid of purpose now this new life had inexplicably drained away from her. And furthermore, she'd felt worthless as a woman when she was told she'd never be able to conceive again. So yes, she did understand. And it went a long way towards explaining why Jack, her only son, was so very, very precious to her.

She shed tears of sadness as she sat there in the fading evening light, for the grandchild she would never know – hoping somewhere in the heavens above, her baby Angel would take care of him. And she cried for Jack, so desperately wanting to protect him from the pain he would be feeling – wishing, as his mother, she could take his hurt away, and feeling helpless in the face of such an impossible task.

And yet, above all at this moment, she felt a desperate sadness for Pixie – a feeling she would never have expected herself to have. But she knew the fragility of the girl and the weirdness of the family she came from – she knew how badly this would affect her and how much support she was going to need in the days and weeks ahead. And as the tears rolled down Joanna's face in the semi-darkness, she vowed that whatever had gone before, she would be the one to give her that support.

This heartfelt resolution seemed to provide her with some comfort. Drying her eyes, she turned on the light, which helped to lift her gloominess just a little further. The fish and chips. Things must have been bad, she'd forgotten all about them in the sadness of the past half hour. Cold fish and chips are never quite as appetising as hot ones fresh from the shop but, with extra vinegar added, they were still pretty good. In fact, they were more than pretty good, they were amazing. She shovelled them into her mouth like she didn't have another second to waste – the crispy brown batter and the soft white fish, the clumps of soggy chips dunked into the absolute highlight of all – the mushy peas. She ate them with her fingers, of course, couldn't do any other with fish and chips – God, she could be so common at times!

Typically, just as she was at her messiest and greasiest moment, her phone rang again. In the midst of her newly found euphoria, it gave her a heart-stopping moment. She didn't even glance at the screen, just pressed the green button in a panic, thinking it was Jack phoning from the hospital again. But no. Her mother. She wouldn't have bothered answering if she'd known. No, that was mean, she meant she would have called her back later. For goodness' sake. Would she ever get to eat these fish and chips? She was beginning to think there was some kind of conspiracy against her. The Fat Patrol.

'Hey Mum,' she said, almost choking on a chip in her haste to swallow it down in a hurry.

'Are you eating again? Every time I ring you seem to be chewing on something. What is it this time? Pizza again, I'll bet. You know you should eat more healthily, Joanna, start taking care of yourself, you're not getting any younger you know.'

'Thanks! None of us are, Mum.'

'So what are you having? I was right, wasn't I?'

'No – as if!' she said, quickly hiding her plate in the cupboard and replacing it with an empty one. 'I've just finished eating a salad, as a matter of fact. Look – here's my empty plate.'

'You never were a very good liar were you?' laughed Barbara, knowing her daughter all too well. 'Oh, and by the way, we're not on FaceTime or anything, just the normal phone so you don't need to hide whatever it was.'

Nothing ever got past Barbara.

'Anyway, what I rang for, apart from wanting to know how your weekend in Paris went, was to ask if you'd be free to come over here on Wednesday evening? There's something I need to talk to you and Hannah about, both at the same time.'

'Wow – this sounds serious. Should we be nervous? It's nothing horrible is it? You're not ill are you?' Joanna suddenly felt quite worried – maybe it wasn't just about their mum finding a new man, which is what they'd suspected.

'No – no need to worry. I'm definitely not ill, far from it in fact. I don't want to tell you now though, I want to do it when you're both together – and face to face, not over the phone. So, are you free to come on Wednesday? I've just spoken to Hannah and she said Wednesday would be best for her as Marcus will be at home to look after Lottie.'

'Yes, that's fine with me – I'm intrigued.'

And yes, Joanna really was intrigued. It had to be that their mum had found a new man. What else could it possibly be? Something so important that she had to speak to them both together. Face to face...

Chapter Twenty-two

Wednesday evening. Joanna wasn't quite sure how she felt at the prospect of hearing about, and maybe even meeting, the person who could possibly be their future step-father. It all felt a bit weird, to be honest.

On the one hand she felt as though by agreeing to meet him, and even more so if she actually found herself liking the guy, she would be letting down her dad. She had loved her dad so, so much, and in her head this seemed like the ultimate betrayal. If the relationship got serious and her mum ended up marrying this guy, then he would be moving into her dad's house, the house he had worked so hard to buy so that he could provide a beautiful home for them. Who was this guy, that he felt he could move in on her dad's wife, and on his home and his family?

But, on the other hand, there was her mum. Joanna didn't think her mum had ever been truly happy. She didn't think she'd ever been in love. The background from which she'd come had certainly been one that was strict and lacking in love and affection and that seemed to have shaped her into the closed-off person she had become. She'd been incapable of forming a close, loving relationship with her own daughters, and probably with her husband too, because she hadn't had that blueprint to work from –

she didn't know what love was. And so if this guy had come along now, and he'd been able to break down her barriers and show her how great life could be, did she not deserve a second chance at love? Begrudgingly, the answer had to be a 'yes'.

Joanna was glad she'd been home and got changed and done her hair and make-up before going. She'd originally planned to drive straight over there after work but decided she should smarten herself up a bit first – she didn't want any future step-dad of hers getting the wrong impression. Hannah had volunteered to drive them both over there and Joanna was pleased – at least she'd be able to have a drink and chill out a bit. As long as she didn't drink too much and open her mouth more than she intended – that was always a distinct possibility, and a prospect she didn't much relish.

Joanna had been so busy thinking about things that she didn't hear the beep of the car horn. Hannah came to the door and rang the bell – she was quite glad to be able to do so, actually, she'd heard so much about this amazing apartment from her sister and she was desperate to have a nosey inside.

'Wow!' she said, gazing around in awe as Joanna let her in. 'I see what you mean about this place now. It's stunning – like something off *Grand Designs!*'

'Well, I maybe wouldn't go quite that far but – it really is something else, isn't it? Come and have a quick look around before we go, Gavin's not back from work yet so there's nobody in but me.'

'And he lives here all on his own?'

'Yep.'

'Well, what a waste. If I wasn't so loved-up with Marcus, I'd be making a move on him myself. You must be mad.'

'What?'

'A hunk of a man like that who obviously has the hots for you, and you're moving out of this beautiful apartment to live in a ramshackle cottage all on your own? Stark staring bonkers, if you ask me.'

'Ha-ha. It's called "independence", Hannah, and I can't wait.'

They drove over to their mum's house in silence for a lot of the way. Trepidation hovered in the air. It was hard to put into words why they should be feeling so anxious. Their mother was a grown woman, she must know what she was doing and they should feel pleased for her that she'd found someone to share her life.

'I do feel pleased for her if the guy is genuine and he's making her happy – everyone deserves a slice of happiness and she's not had a lot of it in her life so far.'

'But what if he isn't genuine – how do we know? What if he's only after her for one thing?'

'Please don't say "sex", I just ate before I came out.'

'I meant "money", actually, but whatever, she's only seventy-four – still entitled to a love life.'

'P-lease! Seriously, though, I am a bit worried there might be something underhand going on – I feel a huge sense of responsibility for her.'

'Yes, me too – and it is a worry. But there are some genuine people out there, I just hope he is one of them. Listen to us! We haven't even met him yet – let's give the poor man a break.'

'Okay – no pre-judging allowed! We'll take him as we find him.'

Barbara greeted them at the door with a hug – a rather effusive hug actually. This man was obviously a having a good influence on her, whoever he was.

'Come through, I'll put the kettle on and make us a drink. Tea?'

'Got anything stronger, gin or something?' asked Joanna. 'I feel as though we might need it. What's all this about anyway?'

'Hang on, hang on – one job at a time. Let me get the drinks and then we can sit down and talk about it properly,' said Barbara, pouring a gin for herself as well. It seemed like a good idea; she was feeling nervous now the moment was actually here.

Hannah was suddenly feeling apprehensive too. 'Better make that three, Mum. I know I'm driving but one won't hurt. Whatever it is you're going to say sounds pretty major.'

'Shall we move into the lounge – have a comfortable seat? said Barbara, her face totally non-committal.

Joanna was feeling just a little bit freaked out by now. Her mum never willingly invited them into the lounge to sit on her best sofas – particularly with drinks. Under normal circumstances they would simply have sat around the kitchen table.

'Mum, please could you tell us what this is all about? I'm seriously starting to worry now.'

Barbara's eyes registered panic, but she knew it had to be done. She'd been building up to this moment for so long and in a way it would be relief to get it out – to let the truth be known at last. She took a large gulp of the gin and grimaced as it hit the back of her throat.

'Okay. I don't know where to start but, well, I suppose the beginning is as good a place as any.' She took a second drink. Joanna and Hannah glanced at each other – things really must be bad.

'Right, I'll stop delaying,' she said, swallowing nervously. 'Going back to the beginning means going back a long way, to a time when you were both young girls,' she cleared her throat, it was now or never. 'I was a stay-at-home mum,' she continued, 'as you know, and your dad was the one who went out to work. Now I know you both had a great relationship with your dad – he was a great dad, I couldn't ever fault him on that. But, when it came to him and me, our marriage was sadly lacking – in every department. I loved the two of you, please don't ever doubt that, but I was lonely – I was leading a humdrum existence and I felt desperate for some adult company. Oh – this is so embarrassing. Please don't hate me, will you?'

'Of course we won't hate you – you're our mum. Whatever you're going to tell us – we could never hate you,' said Joanna, looking towards a nervous-looking Hannah, who nodded her support.

'Well, one day we had a flood. The toilet cistern was overflowing and I couldn't stop it. I tried turning the stop tap but it was so stiff I just couldn't budge it at all. I tried ringing your dad's work to get him to come home but the number was constantly engaged and I was left in a total stress, permanently flushing the handle and scooping out water to keep the level in the cistern down. I was panicking, afraid of it all overflowing onto the carpet and flooding everywhere. And the two of you were crying, getting really upset at seeing what was happening – you can probably even remember.'

'I can actually, Mum – I can remember being really scared.'

'Me too. I didn't understand what was happening,' said Hannah.

'We didn't even have mobile phones then, so I was running backwards and forwards between the landline and phone directory, and then back to flush the water level down, trying desperately to find a plumber who could come and help me urgently.

'And amazingly, I did. He turned up like my knight in shining armour and I'd never been so pleased to see anyone in my life! He fixed the problem in no time at all whilst I was just a quivering wreck. Oh my goodness – was I grateful to him!

'I gave you both a cuddle and you calmed down – in fact you even went to get some of your toys to show to him while I was making a drink. But then you got bored of adult talk and wandered off into the other room to watch the television for a while.

'So we sat at the kitchen table, this plumber and I, and we chatted. He was incredibly easy to talk to. He told me his wife had left him, taken their children – how quiet his house was, how lonely he was now they had gone. I made another drink, I wanted to delay him, I didn't want him to leave, it was just so amazing having someone else to talk to – another adult. So we sat and we sat, and I told him how lonely I was too, how my marriage to your father was not a happy one – sorry girls, but it's true, it was not.'

'It's okay, Mum, it's okay – we know you were never really happy together,' said Joanna, wanting her to carry on but yet, at the same time, feeling worried about where this was leading.

Barbara glanced towards her with gratitude, although her eyes seemed almost unseeing. She carried on.

'He was a real flatterer this man. Pete, his name was – Pete the plumber. He told me I was beautiful and, yes, I should have seen through him and been wise as to what he was after. But nobody had ever told me I was beautiful before, not even your dad, and I was sucked in by his charm completely. I'm sure that if the two of you had not been in the house, things would have progressed there and then – but there you were. So we arranged to meet for a drink the next evening, and I made an excuse to your dad that I was going to see my parents, while he stayed here with you.

'This is so embarrassing. And it must seem completely out of character for the mother you thought you knew. I'm so sorry, but I have to tell you, it's important that you know the truth… So yes, I met him for a drink the next evening, and he took me back to his house. I went willingly, you understand, I wasn't a victim in that respect. I was enjoying the attention, the flattery, being thought of as special for once in my life. And it really was "for once in my life". Because, a few days later, when I hadn't heard any more from him, I rang Pete the plumber again. Voicemail. And then some days later when I rang to leave yet another message, this number was "no longer recognised". I'd been had, undoubtedly, in more ways than one.'

'Oh, Mum – I'm so sorry…' started Hannah.

But Barbara held up a hand to silence her. Now she had started, she wanted to continue, had to continue – it was a story she should have told them long ago.

'So the weeks went by and I started to feel a bit weird. At first I put it down to the stress all of this had caused me – he'd seemed like such a lovely man, I'd trusted him. But then I realised, you've guessed it, I'd missed my period. Pregnant.'

'Oh my God! So what happened? Did you lose the baby?' Joanna was seriously shocked – her poor mum, what she'd been through.

'I lost the baby all right, but not in the way you're meaning. I didn't have a miscarriage – no.' Barbara paused for a moment, her eyes clouding over, remembering how it had felt, that very worst moment of her entire life.

'I didn't know which way to turn. I had to tell your dad. We both knew the baby couldn't possibly have been his – we hadn't been intimate in that way for years. So I had to admit the truth and tell him what had happened. It was actually the first time we had really sat down and talked properly together in a very long time. I had actually fully expected him to go mad and throw me out. I was scared he would get to keep the two of you and never let me see you again, and that's what terrified me the most. But amazingly, he kept unbelievably calm and factual, resolute in the fact that we had to keep our family together, no matter what.

'I knew neither of us were in favour of abortion and, for a moment, I thought he was going to suggest bringing up the baby as if it was his own. But no, and understandably, he had a different plan. He had a cousin who lived in Suffolk; I'd only met her a few times but he said he'd phone her and ask if I could come and stay until after the baby was born and then get it adopted. To him it seemed like the logical solution – in fact, the only solution. And, up to a point, I could kind of see where he was coming from.'

'Oh God – that's where you were when you went away that time,' said Joanna. 'When we could only speak to you on the phone but we weren't allowed to visit because he said the person you'd had to go down to look after was very ill and wouldn't be able to have children running around. I remember getting really upset, we both were, because we were missing you – and he'd take us out for special treats to cheer us up. You were gone for ages – we thought you were never coming back.'

'I'm so sorry. You have no idea how much I missed you both, I was gone for three months and it seemed like forever. But, at the time, it seemed like the only solution. In your dad's mind he thought it was a straightforward plan, causing the least disruption to everyone. He thought I would just be able to come back home and carry on with my life just as I had before, problem solved. But life isn't like that. How can it be? I was overjoyed to be back with the two of you again, of course I was. But, I'd also had a baby…'

'Oh Mum!' they cried, almost in unison, in total shock at what they'd just heard, tears running freely down both of their faces.

'How have you managed to keep this to yourself for all of these years? I just can't imagine what it must be like to have a secret like that bottled up inside you,' said Joanna, going across to sit next to her mum so she could hug her.

Hannah perched on the arm of the sofa on the other side of her mum to join in the hug too. 'No wonder you look so sad sometimes – losing a baby like that must leave you absolutely heartbroken. I don't think I'd ever get over it.'

'I haven't, I really haven't. But…'

'So I take it the baby was adopted then – what happened?'

Sadly, Barbara nodded her head. 'Yes, I had him with me for two days – a beautiful baby boy. I called him Mark because he'd made such a mark on my heart and on my life. I fed him, I bathed him and I totally bonded with him – I can't tell you how gorgeous he was. I cuddled him constantly – even through the night. For how could I even think about sleeping, knowing I would be wasting precious moments that I could be sharing with my baby boy? I had such a limited amount of time to be with him, I couldn't bear to waste one single second. But then it came to the final moments. I fed him for the very last time and held him in my arms, my tears cascading down onto him. I whispered to him, telling him how much I loved him, how sorry I was, and how I would never, ever forget him. And then they came, and they took him away – they almost had to drag him from my arms. I sobbed and sobbed, my heart was torn apart that day, my body felt empty and lost, a huge part of my life had been wrenched away. In fact, if it hadn't been for the two of you, I wouldn't have wanted to live. You saved me – and I thank you for that.'

They hugged each other tighter – feeling closer, possibly, than they'd ever done before. Hannah and Joanna were both equally amazed that she'd kept this secret to herself for all of these years and never shared it with them before. It really did explain a lot to them, made them understand why she'd seemed distant a lot of the time, why she'd always seemed to keep a barrier between herself and everyone else, why she'd kept herself busy looking after them but always looked so sad. They only wished she'd been brave enough to share it with them before. It hadn't needed to have been carried around like a guilty secret – they would have helped her, supported her.

'You're such good girls, I love you both so much – you do know that don't you?'

'We love you too, Mum – and I think we need to tell each other that more often,' said Joanna through her tears.

Chapter Twenty-three

'Anyone fancy another drink?' asked Barbara, feeling emotionally drained by the story she'd just told, and reaching for the gin bottle.

'Steady on, Mum, I've never seen you drink so much,' said Hannah. 'Not for me, thanks, I'm driving. I wouldn't mind a coffee though, if you're offering.'

'Sure. Help yourself.'

'You mean you actually trust me to use your kitchen without making a mess?'

'Yup.'

Blimey, this gin must be good stuff!

Joanna joined her mother with another drink, still reeling from all they'd been told, and she had a feeling there were still more revelations to come. She was right.

Hannah returned with her coffee. 'Don't worry I didn't make a mess – and I wiped the worktop down when I'd finished. I was just thinking about everything you've told us though – what a shock! I don't know what we were expecting to hear when you said you wanted to see us, but it certainly wasn't that. Actually, I do know what we thought you were going to tell us – we thought you'd found yourself a man. I don't know what gave us that idea – well, I think it was Joanna who came up with it first.'

'Hey, don't you go blaming me,' laughed Joanna, 'I just said...'

'No bickering, girls, it's starting to sound like the old days around here. Seriously, I can categorically state that I do not have a new man in my life and nor am I in any hurry to get one either – I'm quite happy living here on my own, thank you very much. Actually, though, that's not strictly true. I *do* have a new man in my life but just not in the way you were meaning. And that leads me nicely on to the rest of the story I brought you here to tell you.'

'You mean there's more? Have you found him? Mark?'

'Amazingly I have – or rather, he found me!'

'Oh my God – that is incredible!' Joanna clasped her hands to her mouth, her eyes brimming with tears.

Hannah was speechless, her eyes and mouth both open wide. 'We have a brother?' she whispered eventually.

'Indeed you do. And you're going to love him as much as I do – I just know it. I only met him for the first time two weeks ago and it was, weirdly, like there was an instant connection. He told me he'd always known he was adopted. His adoptive mum used to tell him he had been chosen and that made him very special – he was their only child. Sadly, though, his adoptive father left them when Mark was still quite young and his mum struggled financially to raise him on her own. But there was always a lot of love in the house and Mark remembers his childhood as being a happy one. Nevertheless, he said he always felt that a little piece of him was missing – funny, I've heard adoptees talk about that feeling before.

'He said he'd had this urge to try and find me for many years but had been afraid to do anything about it. Not only had he not wanted to upset his mum, but he'd also been scared I might reject him when he found me. I can't tell you how bad I felt when he said that. He's got a real "thing" about rejection – it must all stem from what I did to him, rejecting him, giving him away when he was a tiny baby.'

'Don't blame yourself, Mum – you had no choice.'

'I know, but the guilt is still there. It doesn't go away and probably never will. Anyway, he talked about it with his mum – she sounds so lovely – and she encouraged him to start searching for me. She sounds like such a wise woman. She knew that if he didn't even look he would never be able to rest, he'd always have these unanswered questions whirling around inside his head. And, as she said to him, what was the point of living his whole life in fear of being rejected when actually, he may not be? If he was, they would have to live with it, she would help him, and they would try to draw a line under it. But the likelihood was that he wouldn't be rejected, although the sooner he found out the better. Her big worry was that if he kept dithering and not doing anything about searching because of his fear, then it could be too late – the longer he left it and the more likely it was for that to be a reality.'

'Oh my goodness – she sounds like such a lovely lady, so selfless. She must love him very much.'

'As he does her – and I would never want to do anything that would get in the way of that.'

'So what happened? How did he find you – did he just turn up on the doorstep?' asked Joanna, almost overwhelmed by the story.

'He went through all kinds of channels to find me. To be honest it was all just a blur when he was telling me – I was crying so much I could hardly take in what he was saying. But in the end, once he got on the right track, he said I was apparently relatively easy to find. The confusing part was that I had given birth in Suffolk and both Mark's birth and the adoption were registered there; your dad had made sure that would happen. But amazingly, they managed to track down your dad's cousin. She's in her nineties now and in a residential home down there, but thankfully still totally compos mentis.

'Mark and his mum went to visit her, he said she was amazing and was more than happy to tell them the whole story. She said it did her good to be able to look back and talk about it. She had worried about what had happened to him for all those years and was so relieved to know he was safe and that his adoptive mum had been such a loving mum to him. She also told him how pleased she was to hear he was going to try to make contact with me. She said she'd never been happy about the arrangements your dad had made but, as his only living blood relative apart from the two of you, she'd felt she couldn't go against his wishes.

'I really should get in touch with her, you know, when the excitement of all this has died down. She was so good to me when I descended on her, six months pregnant – she really looked after me and yet I hardly even knew her. I must have put her through hell, I was in such a state, crying and weeping everywhere – poor woman. And yet she was kindness itself, never complained at all. And obviously it was thanks to her Mark was able to find me – she had both my address and phone number in her little book and thankfully neither had ever changed. See, that's another good reason for me never having moved house. What if I'd emigrated to Australia or something? He may never have found me then.'

'Mum, I hardly think there's ever been any chance of you emigrating to Australia, do you?' said Hannah, smiling, lessening the intensity of the conversation slightly.

'Oy, cheeky! I'm not past it yet, you know – you never know what I might get up to,' said Barbara, reaching for the gin again. She felt she could relax and enjoy herself a bit more now all of the secrets were out. And soon she'd have all of her children around her – how great would that be? She'd never have believed it could ever have been possible until that phone call came, out of the blue. This really was like a miracle, she'd never felt so happy in her entire life.

'So when do we get to meet our brother?' asked Joanna. 'I can't wait to see him. Does he look like either of us, or like you? Do you have a photograph? I need to see what he looks like.'

'I don't actually. I've only seen him twice myself so far and each time we've met we've been talking so much I've forgotten to take one. I suppose he's a bit of a mixture really, like all of us. He's tall and slim like Hannah but he's more like you around his mouth, I think.'

'A big mouth just like mine, you mean. Lucky guy! Ah well, at least he's not small and dumpy, that'd be even worse for a bloke than it is for me.'

'D'you know, I can't even remember what Plumber Pete looked like now and yet I was smitten with him at the time. Funny, isn't it?'

'Well, at least we have one thing to thank Plumber Pete for now, whoever he may be. We have a brother. We'd never have had one otherwise. I can't wait to meet him.'

'Well, you don't have to wait much longer, he'll be on his way.'

'What? He's coming here? Tonight?'

'Yes – isn't it amazing? I'm going to have all of my children in the same room – *together!* I can hardly believe it.'

'What time is he coming?'

'Nine o'clock and it's quarter to now so he won't be many minutes. Eek – I'm so excited! I just need to run to the bathroom quickly before he gets here – all that gin, it's going straight through me. Well, either that or the excitement, I can't decide which it is – but I must dash. Oh, and by the way,' she added, her head popping back round the doorway. 'His name's not Mark any more. His mum changed it when she adopted him. His name's Gavin – back in a minute.'

A stunned silence descended upon the room as she left. The two sisters gazed at each other, wide-eyed. The colour had drained from Joanna's face.

'No, don't be silly – it couldn't possibly be. There must be hundreds of men called Gavin – what are the chances of it being him? About zero, I would have thought,' said Hannah, trying to reassure her.

'Stranger things have happened,' said Joanna.

'Yeah but even if by the remotest chance it was him – so what? It's not as though you're actually with him or anything.'

'I know but…'

'He's here!' shouted an excited Barbara from the hallway. 'Mark!' they heard her cry. 'Oh sorry, Gavin – I need to get used to this. In my head you've been Mark for over forty years, it takes a bit of adjusting to. Anyway, come on through – come and meet your sisters.'

Now, coincidence is a rather long word and is capable of spreading far and wide in order to be all-inclusive and to cover a whole gamut of eventualities. In Joanna's eyes, though, this particular situation should have been far outside of its remit. It just didn't seem fair. The one man, *the one man*, that she'd slept with and felt anything for in almost thirty years turns out to be… *her brother??* This was just so typical of her luck.

'Gavin!' she said. 'Oh. My. God. It really *is* you – this is crazy.' She'd felt like a helium-filled balloon just half an hour ago, almost bursting with excitement. Now, suddenly, she felt deflated and flat.

'Joanna? I don't understand – what are you doing here?' Gavin looked totally confused – bewildered in fact.

'These are my daughters. Your two sisters – remember?' said Barbara. What was happening here? This wasn't how she'd been expecting it to be at all. 'Like I told you, they're both married with families of their own so I thought it would be better to let them tell you all about themselves when they met you this evening. So… here they are!'

'And you didn't even tell him our names?' said Joanna, incredulous at this whole situation.

'Well no, it didn't seem necessary. I thought we'd be able to catch up with all that tonight. I don't understand what the problem is – why is everyone looking so shocked?'

*

'Sorry,' said Gavin, not wanting to upset his mother, especially now, when he'd only just found her. 'Joanna and I have already met, that's why it came as such a shock.'

'Met? I think we've done a little more than that,' said Joanna.

'Okay, we've become really good friends.' He actually didn't want to upset anyone.

Barbara glanced from one to the other, fear prickling her spine. Was this the man Joanna had told her about, the man she'd said she liked?

'We're actually living together, Mum. I'm staying with Gavin at his flat until I can move into the cottage at the weekend.'

Barbara's face suddenly turned pale. 'Oh. My. God,' she said, slumping down onto the sofa, her legs no longer able to support her. This couldn't be happening – it was her worst nightmare. Buried deep down inside her, there'd always been this fear of what would happen if Mark, by some twist of fate, was to meet one of her daughters and fall in love. And now here it was, coming back to haunt her for the wrong she had done all those years ago.

Mark sat down next to her and put his arm around her. 'Mum, please don't worry, it truly isn't like it sounds. Joanna and I have become really good friends, that's all. So when she needed somewhere to stay until she could move into the cottage, I obviously offered her a bed at my place. I've got plenty of room so how could I not? Jack is staying there too, it's not just the two of us – is it, Jo?' he said, looking pointedly at Joanna, in need of backup, needing to reassure his newly found mum, hating to see her looking so worried and all because of him.

Having got over the initial shock, Joanna somehow managed to pull herself together and sat down next to them. 'He's right, Mum. Gavin really has become one of my best mates, Jack's too. We've often talked about why we feel so closely connected but never in a million years would we ever have guessed it's because we're brother and sister. That is mental – and yet it explains a lot.

I'm even going to be starting to work for him next week – I think I told you, although at that point none of us realised it was my brother I would be working for. God – this is crazy!'

'Hey, I'm feeling a bit left out over here,' said Hannah, moving closer towards them.

'That's 'cos you're not going to be the youngest anymore – no longer the spoilt brat,' quipped Joanna, still managing to hold onto her sense of humour at least – anything to lighten the implication of what she'd just learned.

'Shut it, small fry – that wasn't what I meant. All I was going to say was, could we all stand up please for a big family hug – and a family photo while we're at it too? Because I just wanted to say, "Welcome to the family," to our new baby brother. Isn't this just fantastic?'

In the midst of all the hugging and the excitement, they were suddenly aware Barbara had gone quiet. Drawing back to look at her they saw tears streaming down her face. They were tears of pure joy.

'I'm just so happy,' she sobbed. 'I have my children all around me and… and Mark… he called me Mum!'

*

Barbara's happiness was now complete. The emptiness and heartache she'd held inside herself for all of these years were now gone. She felt whole again, overflowing with joy at having her son back in her life – she felt free to smile at last, no more of those dark, heart-wrenching moments filled with tears. And even though there'd been the shock of Joanna already knowing him, it seemed her worries were unfounded – they were friends, nothing more. As she'd waved goodbye to her three amazing children as they'd driven away that night, she'd felt like the luckiest and proudest mother in the world – her heart was bursting with love for them all.

Hannah too was overjoyed to have discovered they had a baby brother, and especially so because that brother had turned out to be Gavin. He lived nearby, they would be able to see each other all the time. He seemed like such a lovely guy – she envisaged lots of family gatherings, happy days to come. Her only concern, obviously, was for her sister.

'You're being very quiet,' she said to her whilst driving them back home. 'You okay?'

'Yeah. Just thinking. Isn't it illegal to sleep with your brother?'

'Oh Jo, I'm so sorry. Try not to dwell on it, what's done is done, you can't change that. You didn't know – how could you? And it only happened once, it's not as though you're madly in love with him or anything. Is it?' she asked, glancing questioningly at Joanna as she did so.

'Twice actually. But no, we're very close but I'm not in love with him. He was just there for me at the right time, that's all it was. There was definitely an attraction between us, though, right from the moment we met. He's like my alter ego or something, we could never quite work it out.'

'It must be something in the genes, I don't know. The brother/sister thing.'

'I guess so. Weird, isn't it?'

Gavin had obviously driven much faster than Hannah, by the time Joanna arrived back he was already sitting at the table with snacks for them to nibble on and drinks already poured. The perfect man as ever – even tonight's bombshell didn't appear to have fazed him. She sat down next to him with a wry little smile and chinked her glass with his.

'Cheers, bro,' she said. 'Oh my God – I can hardly believe it! How crazy is this? It's like a story you'd read in a book, but it's not, it's real life – and it's *our* real lives. It's insane.'

'I know, it is pretty mental – kind of surreal. Seriously though, how freaked out are you on a scale of one to ten?'

'Weird question.'

'I know, but I just don't want you to be left feeling traumatised by it – you know, what we've done and everything.'

'Slept together, you mean. About a ten, to be honest. Or at least that's how I felt with the initial shock when we realised. But then I was talking to Hannah on the way home and, like she said, what's done is done and there's nothing that can be done about that now, we can't undo it. We weren't to know we were brother and sister – how could we? Yeah, so maybe I'd score about a two now, I've calmed down a lot after thinking about what she said. How about you?'

'Same probably. But so many good things have come from it all for me that it kind of overshadowed everything else. Sorry, I didn't mean that to be offensive in any way, it's just…'

'I know what you mean.'

'Tell you what, though, it certainly goes a long way towards explaining why we've felt such a close bond between us.'

'Doesn't it just? Amazing. But do you know, if I had the choice of choosing anyone in the world to be my brother, I'd pick you every time.'

'Aww, you're gonna make me cry in a minute. That reminds me of what my adoptive mum has always said to me – that she chose me to be her son and that's what made me so special to her.'

'I'd love to meet your adoptive mum one day, she sounds like such a lovely lady, so wise and selfless.'

'She really is, she means the world to me and yes, I need her to meet all of you,' he said. 'I need her to feel she's part of the family too, which she is. The last thing I'd ever want is for her to feel excluded.'

'And we'd never want that either, Gavin. We'll just be one big happy family – I can't wait to meet her. And you know what? I know I said it before but I'm going to love having you as my brother – and having your mum as my second mum too.'

Chapter Twenty-four

Moving day. She could hardly believe it was here. Today was the day she was actually going to be moving into Bluebell Cottage – she was beyond excited! Indeed, the fact that she was up, showered and halfway through her breakfast before Gavin had even put in an appearance this morning, proved exactly how excited she was.

'Morning,' he said, as he shuffled from his bedroom, still rubbing the sleep from his eyes. 'Blimey! What time is it?'

'Don't panic, it's only just turned half past seven. I need an early start though today. Moving day – or had you forgotten?'

'Forgotten? You've been reminding me constantly. Not a lot to take though, have you?'

'Not really, no – only the bags of stuff I managed to bring with me from home. Can't get into the cottage until after three o'clock though. Martin's in there this morning – cleaning. I told him to leave it and I'd do it myself but he insisted. Nelly only left yesterday and I think he feels embarrassed, he reckons it's a bit of a mess. Anyway, what I thought I'd do this morning was to have a quick trip to Ikea to get some of the bits I shall need. Aiming to get there for when they open – fancy coming, or are you working?'

'Yeah, why not? I could never turn down a trip to Ikea. I was meant to be working but hey, when you're your own boss you can do as you please – pretty much, anyway. And besides, I'll have my PA next week, she's starting on Monday, I'll have far less work to do then – hopefully,' he said, giving her a wink.

'Hahaha, but of course, she's a really hard worker this new PA of yours. And actually she was wondering, now she's virtually already a member of staff, whether her boss would like to take her to Ikea in the work van today? Just in case she ends up buying more than she intended,' she said, in a playful, almost flirty kind of way.

'Erm, remember I'm your brother now.'

'Oops, sorry!'

'Make me a cup of tea and you're forgiven. Yeah, I was going to take the van anyway. You never know what you might see.'

'Precisely. Just stop me going crazy though. Basic essentials – that's what we're going for.'

*

Gavin was in the shower and she was just finishing breakfast when her phone rang. Jack.

'Hey, stranger – how's it going?'

'Not great, that's for sure. Pixie's really down – we both are. But at least she's stopped blaming me for it all now and that's helping me to feel less guilty. I think we've both accepted the fact that this was going to have happened anyway, it was nothing to do with our argument. And actually, it's brought us a lot closer together, we're supporting each other instead of tearing each other apart and that can only be a good thing. I know it's only been a few days but Pixie's matured such a lot – she seems to have mellowed somehow.'

'Then I'm pleased for you, Jack. It's going to take some getting over for both of you but sometimes these things happen for a reason. So, I take it you'll be staying there with her for the unforeseeable if things have calmed down between the two of you?'

'Yeah, sorry Mum – she really needs me.'

'And you need each other, of course you do – no need to apologise to me, as long as I know you're doing what you want to do then I'm happy. Tell you what, though, if you feel up to it, why don't you and Pixie come over to see me tomorrow afternoon? It'll be my first day living on my own in Bluebell Cottage, so would love you to be my first visitors. Just for a cup of tea, nothing fancy. But it might do Pixie good to get out, and to talk to someone like me who's gone through the same experience in the past. And it would be good for us both to get to know each other properly without your dad being there and scaring her off.'

'Oh God – I forgot it was your moving day today. I'm so sorry, I feel really bad, I meant to come over to give you a hand.'

'Hey, don't apologise – there's nothing much to do anyway. I've hardly got anything yet, although Gavin's coming to Ikea with me this morning to pick up a few bits. I can't get into the cottage until after three, so that's good timing really. Oh, and by the way, I have major news – about Gavin. But I'll save that until I see you tomorrow.'

'Oh Mum – is that "like a sprat to catch a mackerel", or whatever that weird little phrase was that you always used to say? You can't leave it there, you've got to tell me now. You're not going to tell me you two are an item by any chance, are you?'

'Hahaha! No, I can categorically state that we are definitely not an item and never will be. You'll just have to wait until tomorrow though.'

'Okay, two can play at that game. I have major news too – and no, it's not about Pixie and me. Can't tell you now though. See you tomorrow.'

'You're such a tease, Jack.'

'And you're not? That's why you love me, Mama.'

*

Joanna was like a child in a sweetshop when they got to Ikea. Gavin was fascinated, he'd never seen this side of her before, she seemed to be grabbing everything in sight.

'I hate to say this, but I really don't think you need fancy candlesticks and pictures, not today anyway, and certainly not artificial houseplants that are going to fill up the van. I thought it was more about getting the basic essentials – like pots and pans, and duvet, pillows, towels, stuff like that, things you can't manage without,' said Gavin.

'You're right,' she said, reluctantly lugging the artificial tree back where to it belonged. 'See, this is why I needed you to come with me, to be my voice of reason, I get a bit carried away when I'm on my own.'

'So I see. Nothing to do with me having a large van then,' he teased.

'Well, yes, that too.' she admitted.

It was fun choosing everything with Gavin, and such a pleasure after having been used to shopping with David or on her own. In fact, she amazed herself by the speed at which she managed to choose all the kitchen stuff – and even the bedding. She decided just to get a rail to hang her clothes on for the moment – she could always get some kind of wardrobe at a later date. Oh, and a chest of drawers too – she'd need some storage space. This was turning out to be a much bigger task than she'd envisaged – more expensive too. And what a good job Gavin had come with the van, she'd never have fitted this lot into a mini.

Gavin went off in search of another trolley as the one they had was beginning to look seriously overloaded. Although they hadn't got much left to get now, had they? Still, if they were getting another trolley, she might as well fill it. Rushing back to the plant area, she was determined – she'd fallen in love with that tree, it would look spectacular standing in the corner of the living room covered in fairy lights. Ooh, fairy lights – that was something else she needed to get. The tree! Someone was just loading it onto their trolley – noooo. At full speed with her heavy load she almost careered into them.

'Sorry, but you can't have that – it's mine,' she blurted out in a panic, pillows cascading from her trolley as she brought it to a grinding halt.

'It so clearly isn't, love, it was sitting here on the shelf.'

'Well I got it first and I'm having it.'

'But then you must have put it back and I came along and found it. So, sorry love but it's mine now. Go and find yourself a different one.'

The steam spurting from Joanna's ears was almost visible to Gavin as he came up behind her. 'Hey, what's going on here – trolley rage, is it?'

'That woman stole my tree!'

'Joanna, it wasn't yours to steal – I thought we'd decided you should put it back, it would take up too much space in the van,' he said, calmly defusing the situation as he picked up the straying pillows from the floor.

'I suppose,' she said, somewhat shamefacedly – embarrassed to have been caught acting like a two-year-old in mid-tantrum. 'Sorry.'

Nevertheless, she couldn't resist looking back over her shoulder to comment, 'And don't call me love,' to the lady in question. Well, she had to save a bit of face, didn't she?

'So why did you go to get another trolley if it wasn't to surprise me by saying we'd have room for the tree after all?'

'Because – what are you going to sleep on tonight?'

'We got a duvet – there, look.'

'That's to go on top of you, Joanna – what about underneath?'

'Oh – the floor?'

'Precisely. Or rather, it will be if we don't get a bed.'

'Good thinking. What a good job you came with me.'

'Yeah – or you'd have been like a fairy sleeping on the top of the tree tonight.'

Aware that time was disappearing, they rushed along, amazingly choosing a bed at breakneck speed. The mattress took a little longer, but having tried them all, Joanna finally selected the cheapest – surprisingly. The assistant said she could get someone to get it for them but there would be a charge. 'That's fine,' said Gavin… but no, 'Not so fast,' said Joanna.

'I'm not going to pay extra just to have someone lift it down from the shelves for me – it'll be in sections, I'll get it myself.'

'Have you seen the size of a bed, Joanna?' said Gavin, thinking that any charge would be money well spent. 'And, I hate to say it but, have you seen the size of you?'

'Trust me. It's an advantage to be small when you get to the self-serve area. I've done it before. You may be tall but you would stand no chance.'

So, a chest of drawers and a bed and mattress it was then – all to be collected. It would appear that Joanna was seeing this as some sort of a challenge now – like she had been the one voted to do the task on *I'm A Celebrity*. Her competitive streak suddenly rose to the fore even though she didn't know she had one. Full speed ahead to the self-serve area it was then.

The chest of drawers was the easy bit. There it was, at the front of the shelf, waist height, simple. She lifted it onto the trolley, refusing all offers of help from Gavin, who stood back holding the trolley, looking bemused. The bed would be the tricky one – he was looking forward to this.

They checked the numbers, found the correct aisle and there it was – staring at her almost, daring her to attempt it. There were several parts to it, of course, all packaged separately, and each challenging in its own way. She took the easy pieces first, reaching in and passing them out to Gavin. 'Here, let me do it,' he said repeatedly. But no. The word 'stubborn' came into his mind but he thought it best not to use it.

The headboard and the footboard were difficult but not impossible. Not too heavy, just awkward. 'Let me help,' he said, knowing full well what the answer would be. Actually, he didn't even get an answer, just a disparaging look as she dragged and dragged until out they came. Spurred on by her success, she glared at the mattress, as though daring it to rise to the challenge. She knew this was going to be the difficult one but positivity was everything. It was vacuum packed which made it easier to manoeuvre but obviously wouldn't make it any less heavy. It seemed to glare at her, its eyes glinting through the plastic cover.

'Let me...'

'No!' And in she went. Gavin could now see what she had meant when she said it was an advantage to be small. Right in, to the very back of the shelf, where possibly no other customer had ever ventured; none would be able to. But she wiggled it, and she pushed and shoved with all of her Joanna Donohue might, until out it came. Thankfully, Gavin was there to guide it onto the trolley as it left the shelf. Job done.

'Well done, Ms Donohue, you're stronger than you look.'

'It's all of those gym workouts, obviously.'

They struggled along to the checkout point, their two overloaded trolleys precariously balanced.

'You know what? Even I can see this bed isn't going to fit into the van, not with everything else as well.'

'I was thinking that too but didn't like to mention it after all of your struggles.'

'Let's just book it in for a home delivery, save any problems. Otherwise we're going to be driving along with the back door tied open, losing all my other stuff as it flies out into the road. I can sleep on the sofa in the cottage for now, I'm used to sleeping on sofas, another couple of nights won't make much difference.'

*

It was just five minutes past three when they arrived at Bluebell Cottage. Joanna was bursting with excitement.

'I feel as though I should be carrying you over the threshold or something,' said Gavin.

'Nutter.'

They didn't have to ring the bell, Martin had seen them coming and was at the front door to welcome them in. It all seemed a bit surreal without Nelly, but he said she was loving life in her new place and was busily organising everyone already. She was a sociable creature and was really appreciating having company, lots of people to chat to.

Joanna introduced Gavin to Martin and gave him a guided tour, feeling every bit the very proud homeowner. Gavin was impressed. Martin had obviously been working hard – the whole place was virtually gleaming with cleanliness. He'd even found time to touch up some of the paintwork in places too. But the biggest surprise of all was the size of the rooms. With most of the furniture now gone, as well as all of the pictures and ornaments, everywhere looked so spacious.

'Yeah, I was surprised how much bigger it looked too,' said Martin, seeing the incredulous look on her face. 'She's a bit of a hoarder, my mum – everywhere always looked so cluttered. But I suppose you do accumulate a lot of stuff over the years and unless you're a serial de-clutterer, which I can categorically state that she isn't; it just sits there piling up over time and you don't even notice. I suppose it did me good to grow up with this lot in a way, it's made me a total minimalist. If something in my house doesn't get used, then out it goes.'

'How on earth did you manage to get rid of everything so quickly?' asked Joanna.

'House clearance. There was so much of it, there was no other way. For me to start selling all the individual bits and pieces… well, it would have taken forever. Anyway, enough of that – let's get your stuff in. Do you need a hand?'

Joanna hardly had enough for one person to carry, let alone three, so they were soon finished.

'I would have offered you a coffee, guys, except I don't have any,' she laughed. 'In fact that's one thing I do need to do when you've both gone – some grocery shopping.'

'Is that a hint, do you think?' said Gavin to Martin, with a smile.

'Could be. But just before we go I have a little something to welcome you to your new home,' he said, diving into a carrier bag he had standing in the corner. 'Champagne! And I even have glasses too.'

'A man after my own heart,' said Gavin.

Or a man after mine, thought Joanna, as she gazed at him through her rose-tinted glass. At both of them actually. How lucky she was to now have these two amazing men in her life. How fortunate she felt that her life had changed so much in such a short period of time. She wanted to cry with happiness but felt it would sound too silly and girly to explain. She would wait until they had gone. She could do whatever she liked then. She would be able to do whatever she liked from this day onwards for evermore.

'Are you crying?' asked Gavin. He knew her too well.

'Me? No…'

Chapter Twenty-five

After going back to the apartment in the van with Gavin so that she could collect her beloved Mini, Joanna had driven home via the supermarket, so at least she wouldn't starve in the foreseeable future – well, during the next week at least. It was amazing just how much food Joanna could consume in the course of a week. Most importantly though, she had chocolate and gin – she may be proud to be living in such a beautiful cottage, but it was good to see her priorities hadn't changed.

Feeling it was well deserved after such a hectic day, she poured herself a G&T, helped herself to a family-sized bar of chocolate from her newly purchased stash, and sank down into the all-enveloping comfort of the sofa that had been left for her by Nelly. Home. This was it. Hers alone. Everything here was hers and she could do with it whatever she wished. Which was exactly why her dinner tonight would consist of chocolate and gin. She was having a moment of rebellion – and it felt good!

Seriously, though, she felt so lucky. In two short months her life had changed beyond all recognition. It seemed like just yesterday since she was sitting back at home, or what used to be her home, bemoaning the fact that she was trapped in an unhappy marriage, plodding along in a humdrum existence in a life that was going nowhere – and look at her now.

Okay, so yes, some things hadn't changed. Like back then, on that particular day she was thinking of, she'd been contemplating the miserable state of her life whilst drinking gin and raiding the snack cupboard for a chocolate bar – a Bounty if her memory served her correctly. And here she was now in her happy new life. Still drinking gin – but of the cheaper variety and minus the slice of cucumber. Oh, and eating chocolate too – a much larger bar, granted, but this was a meal not just a snack – hey, she'd had a busy day, she'd been moving house for goodness' sake!

But basically so much *had* changed. And when all of those changes were added together, what it came down to was the fact that the thing which had changed most was herself. She'd felt downtrodden, unappreciated, unneeded – unloved a lot of the time. She'd felt fat, ugly and stupid, her self-esteem at an all-time low. Okay, so she'd laughed and joked about it, made fun of herself a lot of the time. But really, that had been just a cover-up for all of the insecurities that were happening beneath the facade. Because people love someone who can make them laugh. And they love someone who can make fun of themselves, joke about their own ineptitudes, ugliness, weight and lack of success – people can feed off this mask of jollity and it makes them feel superior, better about themselves. So, over time, Joanna had become the queen of self-deprecation because, basically, she had just wanted to be loved.

What she'd finally come to realise, though, during the past two months, was that it wasn't simply about making people laugh by making fun of yourself all the time. In fact, in some ways that only had a negative impact. Because while you were constantly making other people laugh at your shortcomings in order to make them love you for it, you were simultaneously reinforcing the idea in your own head that you actually did have all of these faults. And faults, shortcomings, whatever, were always a bad thing – right? Wrong. No wonder her feelings of self-worth had been so low. That, in addition to having David consistently telling her how useless she was.

Because everyone has faults; they would be robots not human beings if they didn't. Our faults are a part of who we are and, if they're not having a negative impact on anyone else, then you should accept them for what they are – change them if you wish, if you want to do so for yourself, but you shouldn't ever change for anyone else or just to 'fit in'. Nor should you put yourself down. Joanna realised that now. It had taken her almost fifty years to reach this point but finally... *finally*... she was happy in her own skin. There may be a lot of it but she was happy inside it. Oh, Joanna!

This was all getting very deep for a Saturday night – it must be the gin. She could have invited Gemma to come over, they could have been out on the town celebrating her house move. But actually no, she much preferred to be here, on her own in her lovely snug cottage, drinking gin, eating chocolate and thinking about life. In fact it was bliss. Was this a sign she was getting old? No, just a sign of contentment. She was happy within herself at last, and that was everything.

On a lighter note, though, maybe she *should* celebrate her new life. It would be good to have a get-together with all of the people that mattered to her, the ones who had helped her along the road towards this newly found happiness. People like Jack with his Poxie, her mum and Hannah, Marcus and Lottie. Her best friend Gemma, who had been in her life for so long, and Gavin, whom she'd known for such a short time and yet to whom she couldn't feel closer. Then there was Nelly, of course, for who could ever forget Nelly? And Martin, who was quickly becoming a big part of her life. And maybe even Gavin's birth mum too, she would love her to be part of this mix 'n' match family of hers.

Sorted! She would contact them all tomorrow and invite them to come over next Saturday. No need to consult David or anyone else now about whether that would be okay. She was in charge of her own life, mistress of her own destiny (ooh, she quite liked that phrase!), she could do exactly as she pleased. The celebration would mark the end of her first week in her new job as well. She was so excited. Was this what happiness was? She felt like she was flying. Maybe it was the gin...

*

She didn't sleep well that night. Too much excitement, combined with the fact that this sofa was far less comfortable for sleeping upon than Gavin's had been. It didn't bother her too much, though, her new bed would be arriving on Tuesday and meanwhile, she was so buzzing with happiness it was impossible for anything to drag her down. The sun was shining, both in reality and in her mind, sunlight beaming in through the windows of the cottage and in through the windows of her soul. She didn't think she had ever felt so happy in her entire life before.

Showered and dressed and with everything tidied away, she looked around the cottage, still luxuriating in the fact that this was actually her home. In fact, she had to keep pinching herself to realise it was true. She wandered around, dreaming, planning – so many things she still needed to get but she could just do it gradually, a bit at a time. In fact, that would probably make her appreciate everything more than if she'd had enough money to go out and buy it all at once. Amazing the things you could pick up from antiques centres and places like that, so cheap and yet so much better quality – much more in keeping with the cottage too. She was looking forward to mooching around these places, hunting for treasures, when she'd saved up some more money. One step at a time, she had all the time in the world now.

Even the little garden was gorgeous. She'd not paid much attention to it before, always too busy admiring the cottage itself, but it was great that she had an outside space – and a patio too. In fact, it might be nice to sit out in the sunshine with Jack and the Poxie when they arrived. Actually, she must stop that, stop calling her the Poxie – Pixie was her name and Joanna knew she would be even more fragile than ever now. She also knew that she was the one who needed to take this poor girl under her wing.

It was lunchtime when they arrived – typical Jack, he always needed feeding. She held her arms out to Pixie who, amazingly, let herself fall into them for a hug.

'I really am so sorry,' whispered Joanna to her, as she hugged her tightly, feeling almost afraid she would break. The girl's thin body felt so fragile, so delicate, as she held her in her arms.

'Thank you,' said Pixie, in a sad little voice.

Jack greeted his mum with a kiss then put his arm around Pixie, tears in his own eyes. 'It's been tough,' he said, 'but we're supporting each other, that's the main thing.'

'Jack's been great – I couldn't have coped without him this week,' she said.

'Likewise, Pix – you've been amazing, you really have.'

He looked at her with such love and adoration that it actually gave Joanna goosebumps. Although she'd only been in their company for a matter of minutes, it was easy to see there was a definite change in their relationship, something that went even deeper than their shared sense of loss.

'I'm really pleased that you're there for each other, you need all the support you can get at a time like this. I had a miscarriage myself many years ago and I know how heartbreaking it is, I really feel for you both. Come on through anyway – can I get you a drink? Something to eat? We could sit outside in the sunshine if you like. Nothing like a bit of sunshine for cheering you up. And I actually have a table and chairs out there – I'm not that organised in here yet, still need to buy a table.'

'I love your cottage,' said Pixie. 'It feels really cosy.'

'Thank you. I fell in love with it as soon as I saw it. Needs a few bits of furniture yet, as I say, but I'll get it all looking how I like it eventually.'

'Yeah, my mum did our place for us. I wish she'd just left us to sort it out ourselves, it's not how we'd like it at all.'

'Can't you change it?' asked Joanna.

'I don't know… she wouldn't be happy.'

'It's about what makes *you* happy that matters – it's your home, you're the one who's living there.'

'I know, but that's not the way her mind works.'

'Yes, I'm coming to realise that. Anyway, would you two like to go out and sit in the sunshine while I make us a drink and a sandwich?'

'I could help you if you like,' said Pixie.

'That's what I like to see, women in the kitchen,' said Jack, with a cheeky grin. 'I'll go outside and look at the garden.'

'Best place for you,' they both said simultaneously, Joanna slapping him as he passed.

'He's amazing your son, you know – apart from remarks like that, obviously!' giggled Pixie. 'I love him so much. You must have done such a brilliant job raising him for him to grow up to be the person he is today. I hope one day I can be as good a mum as you have been when we do eventually have a baby of our own.'

'What a lovely thing to say, Pixie – thank you so much. It wasn't always easy but I did my best, it's all any of us can do. But yes, I'm proud of Jack, he's a great guy. I know this has been a dreadful time for both of you; in fact, words can't express just how sad I feel for you. But, if it's possible to gain one grain of hope from such a bad experience, then I think you have done so – it really does seem to have brought you two close together. I've never seen you both look so in love – and I'm really pleased for you, truly I am.'

'Thank you,' said Pixie, as they hugged each other tearfully. 'You're so lovely, and I'm sorry I must always have seemed a bit weird whenever you've seen me before but I'm just not a very confident person. I get really anxious and shy in some situations and… well, to be honest, I was a bit scared of Jack's dad, he freaked me out a little bit.'

'No need to apologise, Pixie. I know, he can be a bit intimidating at times. But you don't have to worry, it's just me here now so no need to feel anxious anymore. You know what? I'm really glad we've had this conversation and I couldn't wish for anyone nicer to be with Jack. Just remember now, I'm here for you any time – treat this as your second home, if you like. In fact treat me as your second mum!'

'I would like that,' said Pixie, mopping up her tears. 'Thank you so much, you have absolutely made my day.'

'What's all this?' said Jack, coming in from the garden to see what had happened to the food. 'A man could waste away around here, I thought you were making sandwiches.'

'Oops – got a bit side-tracked didn't we, Pixie?'

Pixie gazed at him with adoration and kissed him on the cheek. 'I love your mum,' she said.

'Well that's good, 'cos I do too,' he said, with his cheeky smile. 'And I love you. Now – can we eat please, I'm starving!'

*

They sat out in the garden to eat. Unsurprisingly, it was Jack who did most of the eating – he wolfed down practically the entire plate of sandwiches himself. At first, Pixie had asked if it was okay if she just had an apple as she wasn't hungry but, when no one passed a comment about her not eating, it was good to see her change her mind and help herself to a sandwich. Joanna felt that maybe their earlier conversation might have done her some good. She really hoped so. She felt quite protective towards this girl now.

'You were going to tell me something,' said Jack to his mum. 'Breaking news, I reckon.'

'Less of the sarcasm, Jack, or I won't tell you at all. It's about Gavin.'

'Your errant lover.'

'Jack! How many times do I have to tell you? Stop it!'

'Jack – leave your mum alone, let her speak.'

'Oh God – this is what it's going to be like now, is it? Two of you on my case instead of one.'

Joanna winked at Pixie, conspiratorially – happy to see her joining in the family banter.

'You're really not going to believe this, Jack, but – it turns out that Gavin is actually my brother, your uncle.'

'Yeah, right. Pigs might fly too, Mother.'

'It's true, honestly. Your gran has told us about a baby she had years ago that she was forced to give up for adoption. That baby is now an adult, obviously, and has been trying to find her. It's a long story but it turns out that baby is none other than Gavin!'

'What?'

'Precisely! Pretty unbelievable, isn't it? But it really is true.'

'Wow – I'm in shock.'

'I know, we were like that. Getting a bit more used to it now but it's still all pretty hard to take in.'

'So…? Grandma…? So many questions, I don't even know where to start!'

'It's really hard to get your head around, isn't it? I was like that at first, still am in a way. And what a massive coincidence that it turned out to be someone we already knew.'

'Exactly, that's what makes it even worse – especially for you. How did you feel when you found out?'

'Traumatised, I think the word is,' said Joanna.

'I'm not surprised. So tell me more.'

'Another time, Jack. Like I say, it's a long story so I won't go into it all now, but suffice to say, Gavin is definitely my brother and therefore your uncle.'

'You know Gavin as well don't you, Pix? We talk to him at the gym sometimes,' said Jack.

'Yeah, Mr Body Beautiful – he's quite a hunk.'

'That's the one. My mum thought he was too. In fact she…'

'Jack! Stop it,' said Joanna.

'Good job you didn't eh, Mama? Wouldn't have been good would it – not with your own brother.'

A withering look from Joanna was all it took. Jack may be nearly thirty but his mum was still the boss – he knew when he'd overstepped the mark. In fact, he thought it best to change the subject – pronto. He could come back to that one another day.

'Actually, I have some news for you as well. Not sure how you're going to take it though,' said Jack.

'What kind of news? You've got me worried now.'

'It's about Dad.'

'Oh my God – what? What's happened?' she gasped, clasping her hand to her mouth, expecting something terrible. He would have been drinking, for sure. And without her being there to keep an eye on him, anything could have happened. Whatever it was, it would be her fault. She should never have left him in a state like that, he wouldn't be able to cope without her, she knew that. She felt so bad…

Jack's voice broke through her thoughts.

'He's got another woman.'

'What?' Was she hearing things? This couldn't be true. David? With another woman?

'Yep – you heard me right. I went round to see him last weekend – well, because I was worried about him, to be honest. I thought he might have got himself into a state, you know, with the drink and everything. So I didn't let him know I was coming, because I thought he would probably have said no, I just turned up and let myself in with my key like normal. I don't know who had the biggest shock.'

'Oh my God – don't tell me they were…'

'No – not that, thank goodness! That really would have turned my stomach. But no, they were sitting at the kitchen table having a curry – cooked by him for her, apparently. Sorry, Mum, I didn't know how to tell you – I didn't know quite how you'd take it, to be honest. It just all seems so soon.'

'It does seem a bit sudden, I agree. But if he's happy then I'm pleased for him, really I am. It'll actually save me having to worry about him if I know he has someone there to keep an eye on him.'

'Yeah, she seems really nice as well. I stayed and had a drink with them. They met on a dating site, apparently, and they've been inseparable ever since.'

'Woah – steady, you're gonna make me want to throw up in a minute.'

'Sorry.'

'No, don't be. I am a bit shocked, if I'm honest, but I'm just glad I don't have to feel guilty about him anymore. I really am free to get on with my own life now.'

*

When her guests had gone, Joanna settled herself down on the sofa with a good book and a cup of coffee. Ahh, this was the life – absolutely nothing to do for the rest of the evening now, if she didn't want to. Gone were the days when she had to start thinking about what to cook for dinner and what time she would need to start. She could just have chocolate and gin again if she so desired – no one to criticise, no one to stop her. But she wouldn't, even she wasn't that bad, in fact she may go crazy and have beans on toast. The joys of a single life.

The book was soon cast aside, though, with only the first page attempted. It was impossible to concentrate, her mind kept wandering back to David. It was so weird to imagine him being with someone else. And yet why should it be? She was making a new life for herself so why shouldn't he? No reason why not at all, obviously.

It was just that she couldn't imagine him making the effort. Like in all of those years he'd never put any effort into their marriage – but then, neither had she. And was he really having a full-blown relationship with this woman when they'd never slept together for all of those years? Amazing. Maybe that was it, familiarity had bred contempt – they'd both needed a kick-start to live their lives to the full again. She was happy for him, truly she was. She just hoped that in his new life he would seek some help to manage his anger issues; she would hate to see anyone else be repeatedly dragged down by him in the way she had been.

Her mind moved on to Jack and Pixie, and their baby that never was. Even though Joanna realised it would have been totally the wrong thing for them to have had a baby at this stage in their lives, a tiny little smidgeon of her had nevertheless felt a fleeting frisson of joy at the prospect of becoming a grandma. Yes, even she had to admit that, although she would never have mentioned it to Jack, obviously. However, thinking about it in the cold light of day, it would have been a disaster – and would she really have wanted to be classed as a 'grandmother' at the age of forty-nine?

She hated that, actually, the way people were labelled – particularly in newspapers. 'Grandmother, 50, involved in fatal car crash' gives the immediate impression that this person must be guilty of causing the crash, simply because she's a grandmother, and therefore obviously not capable of being alert enough to be a good driver. 'Barrister, 50, involved in fatal car crash' gives a completely different impression – in fact the person's age would not even, in all probability, be written in the headline. Oh, she could feel a bit of her fighting spirit coming out here. In fact, when she did eventually become a grandmother, she could start her own protest group – 'Justice for Grandmothers!' No hurry, though, Jack – take your time.

Right now, though, aside from the miscarriage, which would obviously take its toll on them both, she felt happy that they seemed to have grown so much closer. Sometimes, and much as you wouldn't wish it upon anyone, it takes a tragedy to make people realise what they have and what is important in their life. That was what seemed to have happened to them – well, to Jack in particular. As for Pixie, she had always seemed quite besotted with Jack. She was such an insecure person, in desperate need of being loved. Maybe now Jack was showing more signs of commitment towards her she would feel more secure within herself. It definitely seemed to be that way from what Joanna had seen today. She was like a different person, and a person Joanna could actually warm towards now. She really hoped that Jack was falling in love with her – it had certainly looked that way today.

Gosh, what a turnaround! Only a couple of weeks ago Joanna would have hated the idea of Pixie ever becoming her daughter-in-law – now, she would actually relish the prospect. Underneath all of that weirdness had been a timid little girl ruled with an iron fist by her overwhelming mother. Now, hopefully stepping aside from that a little bit and with Jack there to support her, she would be able to become her own person with her own strength of mind. Joanna was really looking forward to seeing more of Pixie from now on, being there for her when she needed her. In fact, Pixie could almost be the daughter she never had... not replacing Angel, though. Obviously, no one could ever do that.

Chapter Twenty-six

The first week in her new job was unbelievable. Was this work? It certainly didn't feel like it – more like going out and having fun with a friend. For a start, it felt so good not to be trapped in the same office day after day, the same boring old routine. Here, she never knew what she was going to be doing from one day to the next and she was just loving the variety.

Her first day had been a bit overwhelming as Gavin had spent the entire day going through all the files, accounts, budgets, plans, etc., with her. Office work was what she'd been used to but this just seemed more complex somehow. She was sure though that once she'd got her head around it, things would be fine – in fact, once she'd got into the swing of things she'd probably be able to reorganise it for him – make it more efficient. Oops, better be careful – control freak she may be but she didn't want him to sack her!

The next day had been totally different. She'd been to see Gavin's latest acquisition, the property he'd been working so hard on recently. 'Been to see' was maybe a bit of an understatement; 'painting the kitchen and starting to clear the garden' was a more accurate description. She'd wondered why he'd told her to bring some old clothes. If the first day had been mentally exhausting then the second day had been physically so – she'd definitely needed a hot bath to soak away all her aches and pains when she'd got home that night.

And so the week had continued; it was a whole new world, one that Joanna had never been a part of before but she was loving every minute – even the physically demanding minutes – consoling herself by thinking of all the calories she was burning. Gavin kept checking on her, making sure she was okay, particularly with the heavier tasks like the garden, but as she said to him, she was 'happy as a pig in muck'. She did realise that she may need to invest in a pair of overalls and some wellington boots, though, otherwise when a prospective new tenant knocks on the door unexpectedly, it's not easy to transform yourself from gardener to letting agent in about ten seconds in order to give them a guided tour.

But yes, she was absolutely loving it, in fact she couldn't have been happier in her work. Each day was a challenge, but a different challenge, and she found herself learning new skills along the way. Like, how to use a drill. Hard to believe she'd never used one before but she'd never had the need to do so. But her freshly painted kitchen had 'things' that needed hanging on the wall and she was the woman for the job. She was actually quite impressed with her handiwork when it was done, as was Gavin, who even offered to buy her lunch as a reward.

'Is this what's classed as a business lunch?' asked Joanna, as they ate hungrily.

'No, lunch with the boss is a more appropriate term, I think,' smiled Gavin.

'Well I hope this doesn't mean you want to have your wicked way with me,' she said, suddenly blushing at what she'd just said. 'Oops.'

'Yeah… I already did. It's not been awkward though between us, has it? Since we found out, I mean. Not since the initial shock anyway.'

'Amazingly, no, it's been okay – apart from me making stupid blunders like that of course. I have to admit, I thought we would find it a lot more difficult seeing each other, knowing what we know now – especially with us working together every day. But it's been good. I enjoy your company and… maybe it's because we weren't actually in a relationship, "in love" or anything, just very close, there to support each other.'

'Which is what brothers and sisters do anyway.'

'Exactly. As for the other stuff, well, I've managed without it for thirty years, what's another thirty?' she quipped, laughing at herself.

'Oh Joanna – you'll find that special someone one day.'

'Not sure that I'd want to.'

'What about Martin? He seems like a lovely guy.'

'Yeah, he is – but I'm really not looking at the moment, honestly. I'm happy being single, enjoying every day.'

'Me too. In fact, let's have a toast. To sisters and brothers, and to being there for each other always.'

'Cheers to that,' she said, as they chinked glasses.

'By the way,' she said, as they continued with their lunch, 'I don't think I've mentioned it to you yet, have I? How could I have forgotten? Please tell me you're going to be free on Saturday night.'

'Let me see… I'll have to consult my diary. Saturday? Oh no, I have a hot date on Saturday.'

'Gavin – are you serious? You can't have, I need you!' she said, in a state of panic – it wouldn't be the same without him.

'Joking! You should see your face,' he said, laughing. 'I'm coming to yours for the housewarming, Jack already told me. I thought I wasn't going to get an invitation for a minute – thought you must have gone off me now I'm just your brother.'

'As if. You are a torment! I really thought you weren't able to come when you said that. You're the most important guest, you've got to be there, I need to introduce you to everyone – especially Gemma, she's dying to meet you.'

'Should I be nervous?'

'Maybe. She *will* give you the third degree but you'll love her.'

'If she's anything like you, then I will.'

'Actually, do you think your mum would like to come? I know we haven't met yet and it might feel a little bit overwhelming for her, but I'd love her to be there. I'd hate her to feel excluded in any way and we're all like one big mix-matched family now.'

'How lovely – thank you so much for asking her, that means a lot. I'll speak to her tonight and see what she says, but I'm sure she'd love to come if she's free. Her name's Betty, by the way, to avoid any mum confusion.'

'Betty. I used to have an aunt called Betty.'

'Shut up – I couldn't cope with any more family connections.'

Joanna laughed. 'No, me neither. Nothing like that, thank goodness, just a close friend of the family, she died years ago so I know it's definitely not the same Betty. By the way, I keep meaning to ask, you were down south when you were adopted so I take it your mum and dad must have been living down there at the time – how come you ended up living up here?'

'Sounds like you wish I was still down there,' he teased.

'Don't be daft, you know that's not what I meant – just curious, that's all, it seems so random.'

'Does, doesn't it? But my dad – well, he was a hard worker no matter what else he did wrong in his life. According to my mum, I was only about two when he lost his job – there was mass unemployment everywhere, certainly no work in the area where we lived. So people were being encouraged to look outside of their local area, just to go anywhere they could – don't stop until they found a job, that kind of thing.

'In fact I read up about it years later. There was a speech made by one of Margaret Thatcher's cabinet ministers at the time, Norman Tebbit. The "on yer bike" campaign, people mockingly called it. He apparently received loads of backlash – but whatever, it certainly worked for my dad. Both he and my mum had lived in the same place forever so the thought of leaving was a bit of a wrench for them but he started to look further afield, all over the place – not actually on his bike, obviously! He applied for jobs anywhere and everywhere and eventually he managed to land himself some work up near Liverpool. They got themselves a council house there and that's where I spent all of my childhood.

'Sadly, though, when we'd been there a few years my dad went off with another woman, leaving my mum and me on our own – think I've told you that bit before. It was only much later, when I was looking for a place for myself and then for one for my mum, that I decided perhaps we should make the move to Cheshire. I really don't know what inspired me to do that – it must have been fate beckoning me or something. I'm so glad I did, though, I love it around here.'

'Some nice people in Cheshire.'

'Exactly.'

*

After lunch it seemed a bit of a comedown to have to go back and paint a bathroom, get changed back into her scruff again, especially as Gavin was going to be having the much more interesting task of going off to view a property. She didn't want to play on their relationship, it wouldn't be fair, after all he was the boss, she was merely his employee. Nevertheless, she couldn't help but produce just a little pout; it seemed to occur on its own, no help from her whatsoever.

'No, Joanna. I'm sorry but that bathroom really does need finishing today, paint doesn't just jump onto walls by itself you know.'

'What if I promise to work extra hard tomorrow?'

'You're meant to work extra hard every day.'

'I do! But extra, extra hard,' she said, gazing at him appealingly.

'Good grief, woman – you know just how to twist me round your little finger, don't you?'

*

If there was one thing Joanna loved, she'd discovered, it was looking around old properties. Even the tumbledown, falling-to-bits ones, such as the one they were going to view that day. It was due to be sold by auction and Gavin wanted to go and check it out to decide whether or not to bid on it if he could get it for a decent price.

As they stepped inside the door it felt a bit creepy; in fact, Joanna was pleased she was with Gavin and not just here on her own. It looked as though the occupant had suddenly had to leave in a great hurry – maybe they'd died here quite recently, which could explain this eeriness she was feeling. There was still a load of washing, left abandoned in the machine, probably mouldy by now, she really didn't want to examine it too closely. There was an abandoned coat hanging over the bannister at the bottom of the stairs too – an old person's coat, a man's coat, with a flat cap stuffed into the pocket but sticking out far enough to see. The furniture had all gone, leaving just a well-worn threadbare carpet on the living room floor – decorated with mouse droppings, she noted.

Gavin was poking around upstairs, checking out the damp patch in the bedroom where part of the ceiling had come down. She ventured with some trepidation into the bathroom, almost instantly regretting her decision. Had some people never heard of bleach? Obviously not. But then, a poor old man had been living here on his own, probably hardly able to look after himself, let alone a house too. The staircase felt decidedly creaky as she made her way back down. In fact, it seemed to creak even more than Nelly's knees on a bad day. She smiled to herself, wondering briefly how she was getting on in her new home.

She peered back into the living room again, checking first that there were no little four-legged, pink-tailed fluffballs scuttling across the floor. Looking at it more intently now, she could see this room did have possibilities. It had double-glazed windows and an open fire at least. Would probably need the chimney sweeping but even so, with a different fire surround, it could be quite a feature. She peered under the edge of the carpet where it had come loose. Wow – original wooden floorboards, this room could look amazing!

Having got over the original shock from when they'd first walked in, she was suddenly beginning to see this house had definite potential. The kitchen was quite small but there was plenty of room to extend if they wanted to. Even if they left it at the current size, it was workable – compact, but passable. It would need a total refit, of course. New units, white goods, tiling, the lot. She was really being able to visualise it all now, just as it would look if it was left up to her – and it would be, most probably, if Gavin decided to buy.

Stepping out into the garden felt a bit like stepping back in time, especially when she saw the outside loo and the crumbling coal shed. It actually looked as though no one had set foot out there for years – the poor man probably hadn't been able to do so. What a picture she was painting inside her head now of this former occupant – talk about imagination overload! He was probably nothing like that at all – it could even have been a woman or a young person, someone who had run out of money, who was at the end of their tether and had no other option but to leave in a hurry. Whatever the reason that had forced them to leave, she knew it hadn't been a happy one. And the fact that they'd had to live in this mess before reaching their crisis point just made her feel sad. She vowed that, if Gavin managed to buy this house, she would do everything in her power to make it a happy place again. This was a house that deserved a second chance on love.

'So, what are you thinking?' asked Gavin, as he came out into the garden to join her.

'I'm feeling sorry for this house,' she said, 'it all feels so sad.'

'First rule of property development – don't get emotionally involved. If we do manage to get it I'm thinking of putting you in charge of this one – the whole process, from the beginning to the end. You can ask me for help and I can advise you, but basically, you can make the decisions. I'll only step in to oversee stuff and to make sure there are no disasters. How do you feel about that? I think it's what is known as "throwing you in at the deep end".'

'Wow – I'm in shock! You trust me?'

'Of course I do – I wouldn't have suggested it otherwise.'

'I can't believe it!'

'Well, don't get too excited, we haven't got it yet. Come to the auction with me next week and we'll see how we get on. You need to help me keep my sensible head on, though. If you like a property as much as I like this one it's quite hard not to get carried away. When you think it's almost yours and then someone starts bidding against you and takes the price up above the amount that was your limit, it's hard just to drop out. It takes nerves of steel sometimes, believe me. But there's absolutely no point in paying over the odds for a property just because you really like it – you're never going to make a profit then, so what would be the point in that?

'Same with doing a place up too,' he said. 'You're in this game to improve properties and make them suitable for people to live in. It's all too easy though to slip into the mindset of thinking everything has to be done to your own taste. But it's not you who will be living in it, the aim is to find a tenant. Everything has to be neutral and be priced within the budget.'

'Ohhh – I hope I don't let you down,' she winced, suddenly a little fearful.

'Don't worry, I won't let you,' he said.

Chapter Twenty-seven

By the time the weekend came around, Joanna felt physically and mentally drained. What an amazing week it had been, though, well worth the aching bones and muscles she hadn't even known she possessed, and even worth the feeling that her brain had been stretched out on some kind of barbaric contraption. Six solid hours spent exercising in the gym could not have done her more good. Good? Well yes, 'no pain, no gain' don't they always say? And she could have sworn her waist measurement was a quarter of an inch smaller – bit difficult to tell precisely, as the markings on the tape measure had worn away just at that point, with overuse, she supposed. Better than a quarter of an inch bigger anyway.

No time to rest, though, today was Saturday, the big day – the housewarming party. She'd never thrown a party before and was a little bit nervous but, at the same time, she was so excited! Crazy, wasn't it? Almost fifty years old and she'd never had a party – not an adult party anyway, she'd had birthday parties as a child but as an adult it had never seemed the thing to do. David would have gone crazy if she'd even so much as suggested it.

So… what to do? She'd been to the supermarket the previous evening to stock up with food for everyone. Just lots of nibbles really, hopefully they wouldn't be too hungry. And alcohol, too, she hadn't forgotten that, obviously. What she'd failed to consider, though, in her whirlwind of madcap ideas, was where to lay everything out – she didn't have a table. Oh well, the kitchen worktop would have to suffice, it wasn't very big but she'd just have to keep putting the food out a bit at a time. Thankfully, she'd remembered to buy paper plates and plastic wine glasses at least, it would have been worse if she'd forgotten those.

People were due to start arriving at 2pm and, having just caught sight of herself in the mirror, she realised she'd better speed up a bit if she was going to give herself time to have a shower and get ready. To transform that bedraggled no-hope of a woman, of whom she'd just seen a reflection, into something drop-dead gorgeous and ready to wow the guests with her beauty, would take a miracle – and they were generally in short supply.

She wore her red dress. It gave her confidence and made her feel good about herself by concealing her fat rolls to perfection. She wasn't even having a 'bad hair day' today, which was a miracle in itself. And in fact, by the time she'd done her make-up and added a splash of red lipstick and donned her killer heels, even she had to admit – she looked quite passable. The heels made a big difference, quite literally – she may even be up to Hannah's shoulder today, height-wise. They would cripple her in the process but it would be worth it, and hopefully she still had a few Party Feet patches left over from the weekend in Paris.

Guests trickled in throughout the afternoon, all of them loving the cottage and showering her with compliments, and with gifts, and with love. Joanna had never felt so loved and was feeling quite emotional as she wandered around talking to everyone.

It was the first time Hannah and their mum had seen the cottage and it was important and reassuring to Joanna to hear they liked it so much. Almost like being a child again, doing something special, wanting to impress, needing their seal of approval.

'It really is gorgeous, so full of character,' said Barbara. 'I actually feel quite jealous.'

'Mum! You know you'd never move house.'

'True,' said Barbara, smiling, pleased to see her daughter looking so happy at last.

'You've done well,' said Hannah, with Marcus nodding his agreement. Even Lottie smiled – probably wind, but heigh-ho.

'Nelly!' said Joanna, breaking away from her family to greet her guest of honour – how she loved this lady. 'Come in, let me find you a seat – well it's your old seat actually. How are you? How are you finding your new life?'

'Eeh, love, I like the way you said "your new life" – sounds like I have another ninety years left now. And I hope I do! I'm having so much fun living in my new place seeing people every day and having things to do. I've even found myself a boyfriend, a bit of all right he is, too. I haven't got time for any of this dying malarkey,' she said, laughing so much her dentures were in serious danger of departing from her mouth. 'Oops, almost turned into a gummy mummy then... although I can't turn into a mummy, we've not even had sex yet. Need a whole tube of that K-Y Jelly when we do though eh, Joanna...'

'Mother!' said Martin, almost dying on the spot himself.

Joanna couldn't help but chuckle, 'Nelly – what are you like? Glad you've settled in and made some new friends anyway. Here, let me introduce you to my sister Hannah and baby Lottie,' she said, rescuing the situation. 'I just need Martin to fill up people's glasses for me, if you don't mind me stealing him for a minute.'

'Joanna, you can steal away with my son any time, I've told you that, nothing would make me happier. And I'd love to have a cuddle with this little baby, it'll be good practice for me if I'm going to become a gummy mummy one day.'

'Come with me,' said Joanna to Martin, acutely aware of his embarrassment.

'Now there's an offer you can't refuse, son.'

Oh Nelly.

*

Gavin arrived with Betty, his mum, shortly afterwards. Joanna welcomed her with open arms. Betty looked a bit nervous and, to be fair, who wouldn't be so in the situation she found herself in? For the past thirty years it had mostly been just the two of them, mother and son together. Now, Gavin had a whole 'other' family, people with whom she didn't really have any connection other than the fact that they had given her the chance to be a mum. She had a lot to be grateful to them for but it was scary too. She couldn't hope to compete with a whole family like this, there was only her – what if he preferred spending time with his newly found family? What if he broke away from her now and didn't want to see her anymore? This was his birth family – blood is thicker than water, so they say, and it's true. They all looked so close and so... full of fun. Why would they want to have any dealings with a little old insignificant frump like her?

Gavin, of course, was sensitive to her feelings. She had suffered from anxiety for many years and he knew this wouldn't be the easiest of occasions for her. He squeezed her hand as Joanna rushed towards her, arms outstretched.

'Don't worry, Mum,' he whispered in her ear, 'I love you, and I know everyone here will do too.'

'Gavin's mum!' exclaimed Joanna, as she enfolded Betty in her arms for the most welcoming of hugs imaginable. 'I can't tell you how excited I am to meet you, I'm so glad you came. We're like a complete family now we have you and Gavin, all united and whole again with no missing links. Mum! Hannah! Come and meet our other mum!'

Barbara's face was wreathed in smiles as she approached Betty, arms outstretched to greet her, so full of emotion. The two women hugged, united in a common bond, that of the love of their beautiful son. It really was quite a moment, one like no other.

'Oh Betty,' she said, her voice almost breaking with the gratitude she felt for this lady, 'I'm so happy to see you. I just can't thank you enough for everything – for all you've done for Gavin, the way you've raised him to be such a special person. I can't tell you what a relief it is to me to know he's okay – that he's been happy and loved and had a good life with you. I've been so worried for all of these years not knowing where he was or what his new adoptive parents would be like.'

'No, it's me who needs to thank you,' said Betty, tearfully, feeling herself warm to this lovely lady and beginning to hope now that any fears she'd had were completely unfounded. 'You gave me the chance to be a mum and that meant everything to me as I couldn't have children of my own. My life would have been so lonely and unfulfilled without Gavin, he means the world to me.'

'As do you to me, Mum,' said Gavin, hugging Betty tightly and smiling towards Barbara before giving her a hug too. 'I can't tell you how lucky I feel to know I now have not only one, but two gorgeous mums in my life.'

'You're gonna be spoiled rotten,' laughed Joanna.

'Trust me, I'm going to be the one doing the spoiling,' said Gavin, an arm around each of them. 'My two mums deserve the best of everything and I'm going to make sure they get it. D'you know, this has to be the happiest moment of my life and one I thought would never happen – I love you two so much,' he said, his voice breaking with emotion, as a solitary tear trickled down his face.

Such a special moment was inopportunely interrupted by Jack, whose arrival had gone unnoticed.

'Hello, hello, hello – what's going on here then? Not blubbing again are you, Gav? You need to man up. You're turning into a right wuss just lately.'

'Jack!' scolded Pixie. She, at least, was sensitive to the situation.

'Shut it, you,' said Gavin, 'you know nothing.'

'This is Jack, my errant son,' said Joanna, by way of introduction to Betty. 'His mouth is larger than his brain sometimes but he means no harm. And this lovely young lady is Pixie, Jack's partner... and hopefully my future daughter-in-law.'

Pixie blushed, simply glowing with happiness at the way she'd been introduced. She'd never felt 'accepted' anywhere before, just always on the edge, looking in at other people's supposedly happy lives, but never feeling a part of them. This was all so different, she felt loved, included, and that was all she had ever wanted. Her eyes brimmed with tears of emotion as she hugged everyone before turning back to Joanna to give her the biggest hug of all. 'Thank you,' she whispered in her ear. 'You don't know how much your words mean to me.'

'Don't think I didn't hear you, Mama, 'cos I did,' Jack whispered. 'But yeah, just watch this space... Oh, phew, saved by the bell,' he said, with an overdramatic mopping of his brow as the doorbell pealed out its greeting.

This could only be one person: Gemma. She swept in like the force of nature she was, despite being over an hour late and hardly knowing anyone else in the room. All eyes were upon her and that was just the way she liked it. If anyone could light up a room as they walked into it, that was Gemma. She had the looks, the confidence and the personality – just basically the *je ne sais quoi*. Gavin was transfixed, his attention drawn away from his two mums. He was completely captivated.

Joanna couldn't fail to notice. She nudged him as she passed. 'Rein it in, Gav, you don't need to make it look so obvious, you're almost drooling,' she giggled. 'Told you that you'd like her, didn't I?'

He appeared to have been struck dumb. Gazing in awe.

'Hi everyone,' gushed Gemma, her eyes skimming around the

room. 'Wow, this place is just gorgeous, Jo, I can see why you kept going on about it so much.'

Joanna threw her arms around her friend in a welcoming hug. 'Thanks, I'm pleased you like it, and I'm so glad you were able to come today.'

'Wouldn't have missed it for the world. I wanted to see the cottage, yes, but most of all I wanted to meet all these lovely people you've been telling me about – especially Nelly and the K-Y Man!'

'Eeeh, love,' cackled Nelly with delight, 'I can tell you and I are going to get on just fine. Keep your hands off my son, though, that's all I'm sayin'. Martin, that's him over there, I've got him lined up for your friend here, as soon as she's ready.'

'Nelly – you are a one!' admonished Joanna, as Gemma squealed with delight at this forthright old lady. She could well understand why Jo loved her so much, she was a real hoot. Fortunately, Martin remained oblivious.

Gavin, on the other hand, had eyes for no one but Gemma. As always, she shimmered and sparkled and lit up the room and he was drawn towards her like a moth to a lightbulb. Joanna just hoped he wouldn't end up getting burnt; he was far more sensitive than Gemma, still scarred from all that had gone before. And he was her brother – she felt very protective of him.

'Not jealous are you?' asked Martin, as he materialised from nowhere and put a drink into her hand.

'Why would I be? He's my brother, he's a free man. And anyway – what do you mean?'

'Well I know you had feelings for him at one time, before you knew…'

Joanna looked at him questioningly until the sudden realisation. 'Ah – Nelly!'

'Yeah, sorry – she has a lot to answer for, my mum.'

Joanna smiled. 'Gavin was just one of those people that came into my life at the right time, I think.'

'A bit like the way you came into mine?'

'Maybe,' she said, looking deep into his eyes, which read like an open book. He truly was a lovely man, one she was finding increasingly hard to resist.

A timely interruption came in the form of Gemma – who else? 'Sorry to intrude but do you have any champagne glasses?'

'You're joking aren't you? Plastic wine glasses are all I have.'

'God, you're so common! Okay, I suppose they'll just have to do. I brought champagne – quite a lot of champagne. Call it your house-warming present. It's in the car, could you come and help me bring it in please, Jo?'

'Course,' said Joanna, noting the look Gemma gave her and giving Martin a task to distract him from offering to come and help.

They made their way out to the car. 'So, what did you want to talk to me about – Gavin by any chance?' she asked, smiling knowingly.

'Is it that obvious? I just can't take my eyes off him. I don't know what's happening to me, I've never felt this way about any man before – not ever.'

'I think the feeling's mutual, by the look of him. He was kinda awestruck as soon as you walked in.'

'Really? I've noticed he keeps looking at me. Problem is, though – how do *you* feel? I know you had the hots for him yourself not so long ago.'

'Gemma, that was before I knew he was my brother. I could hardly go "having the hots" for him now, could I?'

'So you wouldn't mind if I made a move on him? You're sure? I wouldn't want to upset you…'

'Gem, you definitely wouldn't upset me – you go for it. He's a lovely man and I think you'd be good for each other. Just one thing, though, and I'm speaking as his big sister now – don't hurt him will you? He's been through a lot and he's not as tough as he seems – be gentle with him.'

'What are you saying about me?' laughed Gemma, tossing back her hair in pretence of being offended.

'You know what I mean – you eat men for breakfast.'

'Huh! No, this is different, I can feel it. I promise to be nice. It's time I settled down a bit, to be honest.'

'Just think. If you two were to get serious and get married we'd be kinda like sisters.'

'Wow – wouldn't that be amazing?' Gemma fell silent for a moment, as though lost in thought. 'You know, my life needs to change too. I've spent so much of it focused on my career, climbing the ladder of success without really thinking about myself as a person and what's important to me, what makes me happy. Money is important, sure it is, but it's not the be all and end all of everything. Life isn't a competition; it's about being happy within yourself, doing what's right for you.'

'And it's about finding your tribe and sticking with it – like the two of us. I think we've been our own little tribe, haven't we? Stuck together through thick and thin. I'm so grateful for our friendship, you know, truly – and I don't think I've ever said that before.'

'You soppy dingbat, you'll have me in tears in a minute and I've got my eye make-up on! I know what you mean, though, it's good we have such a shared history and know we're always there for each other no matter what. Love you,' said Gemma, hugging her tightly.

'Love you too,' said Joanna, so grateful for everything and everybody that was in her life right now. So pleased with herself for the way she'd gained the courage to climb out of her rut. She'd spread her wings and flown, left her old life behind and had finally found true happiness at last.

Acknowledgements

Huge thanks to my beta readers – Sophie, Bernice, Jackie and Viv. As always your comments are much appreciated – thank you.

For writing and publishing news, or
recommendations of new titles to read,
sign up to the Book Guild newsletter: